Stone, Jamila A.
Strange things await

SEP 1 7 2020

STRANGE THINGS AWAIT

Jamila A. Stone

BLACK GLORY
— PUBLISHING HOUSE —

Guernsey Memorial Library
3 Court Street
Norwich, NY 13815
www.guernseymemoriallibrary.org

Strange Things Await

Published by Black Glory Publishing House
Washington, DC

All rights reserved. No part of this book may be reproduced in any form or by any electronic or mechanical means including information storage and retrieval systems, without permission in writing from the author. The only exception is by a reviewer, who may quote short excerpts in a review.

All Rights Reserved
Copyright © 2019 by Jamila A. Stone
Cover designed by Michael Corvin

This book is a work of fiction. Names, characters, places, and incidents either are products of the author's imagination or are used fictitiously. Any resemblance to actual persons, living or dead, events, or locales is entirely coincidental.

Black Glory Publishing House
www.blackglorypublishinghouse.com

Printed in the United States of America

First Edition: April 2019
Second Edition: Sept 2019

ISBN-978-1-7339717-6-8

PROLOGUE

The blue rimmed moon shone brilliantly up above, neatly tucked in the heavens as a source of light within the millions of stars swarming around. The cold night was nothing short of beautiful and would have been even better if tomorrow was not Monday. It was the official start of school from summer break.

She avoided a large pothole by sidestepping it. She could hear herself breathe heavily while beads of sweat slowly formed atop her forehead. Natalie King mainly known as Nat looked down the road, filled with fallen leaves and littered with nothing but memories she wanted to forget. It was where "He" had been found and where she has made a habit of running through. She finds herself on this side of town very often. She had hoped to embrace the haunting memories that lurked by the sidewalk bearing the familiar brown bench.

"You can do this!" she mumbled to herself, before closing her eyes momentarily and sucking in ample amount of air into her lungs.

The plan was to be as daring as possible or at least sweat out her worries before returning home in time for her mother's return from work. One of the plus sides to having a mother who worked as the mayor was that she was sure she wouldn't return home until late at night when almost every other family were either crawled up in their beds or sharing some wonderful moments together.

Alone, and absolutely used to the feeling, Nat had found other ways to wear herself down on most nights. Especially ones like this where the following day might be a harrowing experience which she would rather skip and not even have to experience. Yet, as she approached the bench, she felt her heart leap dangerously in beats, and her throat slowly filled with lumps of paranoia from the images flashing through her mind.

    Allen Avenue wasn't the side of town she would normally visit. In fact, it wasn't the side of town "He" would venture into, but as fate would have it, it was where "He" had been found after three harrowing days of searching for him and filing countless police reports.

    "Keep your cool Nat," she tried to encourage herself, while her vision slowly fizzled out and her breathing threatened to betray her.

    The houses that lined the streets had begun to turn off their lights one after the other, while the streetlights only provided bits and patches of light. The darkness was a testament to poor maintenance and obvious neglect of the public properties. As much as she felt her heart threaten to give way, warning her to simply turn around and head back home, Nat wanted to be there. She felt she needed to be there.

    Slowly Nat halted her feet to a stop to gather up her courage. She walked over to the brown wooden bench which bore scratch marks and some graffiti affiliated to the south-side wolf pack she was familiar with. She paused momentarily with stiff nerves and looked around in hopes that everything that had happened around the bench just two weeks ago would make some sense to her.

    It had been precisely two weeks since that night, but it felt like it was just yesterday.

    "Why?" she asked out loud in a soft and puzzled tone to no one in particular.

    Staring at the worn down brick walls defaced by a mix of wonderful looking graffiti and horrendous name-signings, Nat wondered if there was even any sense to why "He" had been in that spot and why whoever did him in had chosen to drag him there leaving him to bleed to death without any medical assistance being rendered.

    Slowly turning to her left and relaxing on her left leg, she looked towards the next streetlight pole just a few feet from where she stood, dragging back the tormenting memories and the images which slowly began to flash in her mind in a disturbing pace and loop. Everything seemed vivid like it was happening all over again, and she could still see where she stood when her mother's car pulled to a halt and they both got out of it.

"I'm sorry Mrs. Mayor," the police officer who had called in the sight of a dead man lying in his own goo of blood on a city bench had said to Nat's mother immediately.

While they tried to prevent her mother from approaching the deceased man, Nat recalled how she stood by the car door for a moment, and then slowly, while nobody seemed to notice her existence yet, she walked towards the scene with her heart nearly in her own mouth. Within a few feet of where his body lay, she could tell the man was her father.

Mutilated in the most despicable of ways, and horrendous to stare at, considering his face had been slashed viciously, and his fingers all chopped off and left in the mix of his own blood on the ground, she could recognize the man anywhere. He donned the blue shirt with floral markings which Nat had picked out for him on the morning before he went missing.

The blaring sound from the ambulance still rang in her ears, and the endless chattering that came with such turmoil when bystanders mumbled about what could have been and why the man was killed still surfaced in her ears as well even while she tried to block them all out.

"This isn't a mugging," a police detective had said to his colleague while the paramedics wheeled away his chopped body. "This seems rather personal."

His colleague had simply replied, "Who would do this to Maxwell King? Everybody loves Max King."

The last sentence had been the reason Nat continued to visit the site and hoped to find something revealing.

Turning around and realizing Nat had been watching, the detective approached her with his hand coming to rest on her shoulder. "I am really sorry about your father Nat... he was a good man. Come, you shouldn't be here."

She could tell the pain from his eyes and she could sense the emotions in his voice as well, but Nat barely moved. Looking back now, she wondered if it was the grief that made her numb or if it simply was the sight of so much blood, more than anything she had seen in her life. Either way, it was right there before her and she had just witnessed her father's body being picked into a body bag.

The police and other authorities had done their parts, but nothing was forthcoming and even while she couldn't fair better, she hoped by some form of luck, that she would find something to simply tell a tale of what had happened to the one man she had ever loved so strongly in her life.

"What happened here dad?" Nat finally dragged herself back into consciousness.

She held out her cellphone and enhanced the scene with the camera in hopes of getting better lighting as she crouched closer to the edge of the bench. Asides from the wilted flowers which had been left there as a memorial to the man over the past weeks, there seemed to be nothing else of note or worthiness in sight, and it only sunk her heart and made her wail within.

"I will find the bastard who did this," she promised with teary eyes and sniffed. "I will find them no matter what it takes or however long it might be."

Thoughts of him slowly drained her eyes. The beads of tears now mixed with sweat from her forehead rolled down her face and landed gently on her lips. The night felt colder, and the air felt stranger while she sobbed endlessly and kicked hard against the bench in hopes it would all disappear from her memory, life or even from existence completely.

Nat closed her eyes firmly and felt the warm tears continue to pour down, before sniffing aloud and wiping her face dry with the back of her hand. Satisfied with having poured out some of the darkened emotions she had swelling within her, she slipped her hands into the pocket of her hoodie and managed to take one good look around one more time.

Her phone suddenly rang aloud which startled her to the point where she nearly screamed. Nat took the phone out from her pocket and looked at the name spread across the screen.

Initially hesitant, she succumbed and clamped her thumb on the green button before raising the cellphone to her ear, "Hey mom."

"Where are you Natalie?" the worried voice asked immediately. "You went back, there didn't you?"

Nat looked at the bench reeking of her personal misery and hoped to lie and possibly get her mother off her back as soon as possible.

"Err... no... I'm at..." she struggled to complete the sentence before getting interrupted.

"I'm already on the way to pick you up!" her mother yelled before ending the call.

Frustrated and disheartened, she flipped on the hood of her hoodie and searched her pocket for her earphones.

"Shit!" she mumbled, realizing they must have fallen out.

She turned around. She was feeling her heart weigh some more, indifferent towards finding some measure of peace which was why she had returned to the crime scene. Getting a few feet from the scene of her heartache, Nat paused and peeled her ears to the troubling sound of what she could only assume to be footsteps.

"Don't look back! Don't look back!" she warned herself while gulping down a full load of saliva and began intensifying her walk towards the brighter section of the street ahead.

The footsteps seemed to halt momentarily, before it quickened again and matched the quickness of hers. Nat could only hope it was some odd form of coincidence. She intensified her movements, quickened it into a jog and she felt her nerves free themselves as she got faster with each passing second. The night suddenly felt less comfortable to be out in, especially in the side of town she had found herself lurking around at such hours. It was eleven pm.

"Shit!" she mumbled, realizing what time of the month it was and how silly it was of her not to have noticed it earlier.

The full moon, and the absence of people on the streets was evidence enough and clear warning signs and reminders for her to be indoors already but she had completely forgotten.

Still racing as fast as her legs would carry her, she thought to herself, "That's why mom called me."

The footsteps behind her weren't disappearing into the darkness and even while she felt too petrified not knowing for sure what or whom was following her, she wasn't about to look back and give the pursuer the opportunity to gain on her. Nat hastened her steps and got into a full sprint. Being an athlete allowed her to maintain some good distance, but even that wouldn't matter if her pursuer was what she thought it might be.

Nights naturally crawled with vampires and werewolves, but the full moon granted the latter the advantage and made them even more terrifying to encounter. She could hear it growl now and it wasn't the growl of a vampire, which made her heart sink and her knees feel weak within seconds. It was fast and gaining on her as she made her way into another open street and looked around for any opened stores or buildings she could run into.

"Oh my God!" Nat yelled, as she felt her legs were about to fail her, while the supernatural strength from the growling and panting wolf behind her was about to catch up with her.

She held out both hands and stared at them, before closing her eyes momentarily. Nat swung her right hand backwards and towards the incoming beast she still could not see.

She yelled and tried pushing out her magic, hoping for the burst of flames that ought to conjure, but nothing came forth.

Not surprised but absolutely filled with fear, she looked back for the first time, and there it was. It seemed to be toying with her like it couldn't help itself. Nat was its meal for the night, whoever it was and however driven it might be by its bloodlust at the point in time. She could tell it wasn't a mature wolf either, which made it even more dangerous to deal with.

Nat tried to bring forth her magic again as she backed up, before falling over a large pile of trash she had not seen.

Landing painfully, she crawled backwards with her heart ramming hard against her ribcage, and her lips trembling as the large wolf halted and howled, before slowly closing in for what she knew was its kill. Nat jammed her hands in the air intermittently, hoping for something to come forth but she remained dry and empty, with her life now threatening to flash before her very eyes.

Sheltered partly by the darkness, while it walked through the sorted bouts of light, one thing remained visible and constant; its glowing yellow eyes. The eyes glowed with innocence on the verge of becoming contaminated with sin and violence. The werewolf was a newborn and whoever its host was, didn't appear able to control its insatiable hunger of its own accord just yet.

In one final attempt to save her own life, Nat tossed a glass bottle on the ground by her side at it but barely deterred the beast as it got within three feet of her.

An ear-piercing screech from a car speeding their way rang out, followed by a large burst of flame conjured from thin air sent the wolf scrambling towards the wall. The wolf angrily looked in the direction the burst of flame had come from. It didn't plan on going without a fight and it howled and growled terrifyingly.

"Get away from her!" the feminine voice of her mother yelled. Her mother thrust her hands out, crossed them then stepped forward with one foot which sent the wolf crashing hard into the wall behind it. Crumbling pieces of brick fell all around the werewolf.

The werewolf hurriedly got to its feet and whimpered away in pain. Nat felt her stomach sink but her heart race with joy upon seeing the familiar red luxury car belonging to her mother, while the worried looking elder had nothing but a frown. Her mom jumped back behind the driver's seat.

"Get in the car now!" she yelled.

Nat upped herself, managed to brush off the pain emanating from her knees and ran around the car before getting into the passenger seat.

An awkward silence soon broke through but not for long, as Samantha King tore into her daughter, "What on earth are you thinking sneaking out in the dead of the night and especially on a full moon!?"

Nat looked to her feet and remained as silent as possible.

"How many times do I have to tell you that this neighborhood is dangerous?" her mother said, putting the car into reverse and driving away immediately.

Nat bowed her head further, closed her eyes and wept profusely. "I just wanted to see things for myself... I needed to see it again."

"That didn't come off as a bright idea now did it? What if something had happened back there?" her mother asked. "You cannot control your abilities yet and it only makes you vulnerable until you learn to become the witch you have trapped inside of you."

Nat had heard the sermon a million times and could narrate the familiar lines without hassle.

"You should be in bed already, like the other kids who are already prepared to go back to school tomorrow," her mother continued.

Nat scoffed and shook her head. "I bet the other kids are sleeping in the same house with their father tonight and didn't have to see him get picked off in bits from a wooden bench in a park."

Samantha pulled the car into an abrupt halt just in front of a green lit traffic light without looking at her daughter. Her face bore emotions which Nat could see were eating at her, and her grip tightened around the steering wheel while she desperately tried to hold everything within herself.

"Natalie..." Samantha King turned to her daughter slowly. "Your father was... is my life and ever since he was murdered, I have not gone a day without wanting to find his killer and burn them to a crisp with my own hands."

Nat sighed softly and reached for her mother's hand. "I'm sorry I said what I said... it's just that..."

Her mother interjected and completed the line immediately. "... it has been tough on you and you wished he would be the one dropping you off for your first day as a sophomore in high school, as he dropped you off last year?"

She squeezed her hand tightly around Nat's and let out an exhausted smile.

"We will get through this." Her mother promised. "I will do everything within my powers to ensure we get through this."

Nat nodded her head and felt her mother lean closer towards her to plant a warm kiss atop her forehead.

"Let's get back home before we come across some really troubling creatures of the night," her mother floored the gas pedal and sped off immediately.

Nat stared out the window, before holding up her hands, "I tried to chase it away with fire, but I couldn't get anything bigger than a flame."

He mother smiled and gave no response before gracing the highway shrugging gently.

"You're fifteen darling and have been through a lot... I didn't really get a complete hold on my magic until I was seventeen and even pure-blood witches like us make many mistakes no matter their age." Samantha explained. "You don't need to rush yourself darling."

"Still, it would have been cool to save myself back there." Nat folded her arms across her chest and pouted as she leaned against the window and played with the curls of her hair.

Her mother chuckled aloud and burst into laughter.

"All in good time honey... all in good time." she whispered.

CHAPTER ONE

The morning felt like it held promise of fun and excitement, for everyone except Natalie King. Staring at the large sized print carrying the school name "Virtus Academy" boldly and impossible to miss, she made her way to the main hall entrance. Nat felt a breath of uncomfortable air caress the back of her neck as three girls giggled pass.

"We're finally seniors!" one giggled excitedly while her friends laughed.

Nat stood with envy, wondering what would come of her sophomore year and how she would successfully navigate the entire semester without any hassle or unwanted attention. Donning the same hoodie she had worn jogging the night before, in a bid to keep her face hidden, she looked to her chest to make certain the uniform crest was showing as she climbed the stairs and headed for the first floor.

"Excuse me miss!" someone called out from behind.

Nat, hoping she wasn't the one being called for whatever reason, ignored them and kept on walking briskly up the stairs before she heard the caller pursue her and then block her from making the last flight of stairs towards the corridor leading to her classroom. He stood right in her face, barely able to steady his breath, while he smiled and waved.

"I want to believe you are a student in this school correct?" he asked.

Nat took a moment to survey the casually dressed but attractive young man with a well-chiseled jaw and a rather slender frame which didn't do justice to his bold voice. Having never seen him through her freshman year classes and obviously having come in close contact with almost every teacher in the school, she chalked him off as someone whose importance wouldn't really matter.

"Yes, I am." she managed to reply with a raised brow and disinterested look.

He nodded, rubbed his palms together in a rather nervous manner and cleared his throat. "You shouldn't have a hoodie on or anything covering your uniform on the school premises."

Staring at him oddly and obviously without intent of listening to whatever he had to say, she nodded, sidestepped to get him out of her way, and silently walked up the remaining flight of stairs while she could feel his staunch and piercing gaze drilled into the back of her head. It was plain rude, but she wasn't in the mood for anyone telling her what to do.

The hallway lined with classrooms that roared with students who were waiting for the first bell to signal them to their classrooms and prepare for the day's lectures. She moved passed without being noticed, until she bumped into someone who equally wasn't paying attention to where they were going.

"Shit!" she heard a girl grumble, before looking into Nat's face with a scowl.

"I'm so sorry Saskia!" Nat apologized hurriedly, trying to help the junior pick up her purse that had fallen from her hand in the process of them colliding.

Going on a knee to pick up the brown leathered bag, Saskia halted Nat by her shoulder, dragged her by her hoodie and rammed her into the locker just to their left. With deeply burning eyes filled with rage, and her warm breath stinking of what Nat could only make to be weed, Saskia growled angrily.

"Fucking watch yourself and where the hell you're going!" Saskia threatened.

Nat tried to get the girl's grip off her hoodie but to no avail. The werecat hissed and threatened to ram her forehead into Nat but stopped just a few inches from her.

"Hey! You two! Break it up now!" the familiar voice of Mr. Sadon, their Demonology and Metamorphosis teacher roared from the end of the hall, causing the students around to scatter in different directions before making their way into their classrooms.

Nat felt relieved, but it wasn't a positive that it was Mr. Sadon, a man often times accused of being nothing but a dark witch who through a probation program was being made to teach for five years. This was going to be his last year of probation. Many twitched when he walked by in fear of what he could do, while others simply avoided him all together.

"Saskia!" he called out to the infuriated werecat. "A word in my office!"

Saskia stared at Nat and growled once again, before slowly crouching to pick up her pouch peeking with drugs of various kinds as she struggled to hide them underneath a stack of herbs.

"You had better watch your back Nat," she warned. "You wouldn't want to end up like your father."

She walked away, towards Mr. Sadon before disappearing out of sight and leaving Nat to battle with the emotions she had dearly tried to lock away.

"Saskia is always a bully. Don't allow her get to you," she mumbled to herself while trying to steady her breath. "Be positive… be positive… be…"

Nat paused at the entrance into her classroom as the teacher standing in the front of the class smiled at her and waved gently before placing his hands on his hips and raised his right brow. He looked more confident than the last time they had met, which was just on the stairwell. She figured he had walked past during her confrontation with Saskia.

"This is so not a good day," she thought to herself and slowly took off the hoodie as instructed by the teacher earlier before he could embarrass her in front of the class by asking again.

Young, dashingly handsome and with a magnetic smile the girls in the class obviously found themselves unable to resist, he had his fans drooling over him already by the looks on Tasha's face; the flirty witch whose reputation was well known in school.

"You can have your seat now miss." he ordered with an outstretched hand. "This class should begin shortly but first; I need to state some ground rules."

Nat barely heard anything he was saying while her gaze was locked to the ground. Her heart thumped nervously, and she wished she could continue to be homeschooled which was the norm for those with mystical abilities like herself and others in the classroom until they had attained a proper age to handle their uniqueness outside of their parents' watchful eyes.

Powers can showcase even when they're toddlers, which is why witches don't go to school with others until High School and more so why magical schools like Virtus were even in existence.

"You can sit with me," a dark-haired girl with freckles on her mahogany cheeks waved Nat over before pointing at the empty seat beside her.

Nat nodded gratefully, assumed her seat and did well enough to miss the lurking teacher's eyes as he continued to stare her way.

"Since when do teachers look this hot?" the girl to her right asked with a whisper.

Nat managed to nod her head and begin to unload her backpack before halting at the sight of her journal which was a gift from her father for her fourteenth birthday.

"I'm Sheila Grey." the girl reached over with an outstretched hand.

Nat took her time before receiving the hand warmly "Natalie."

She doesn't say her surname, considering almost the entire class knew who she was, being the mayor's kid and all. But this girl, she had never met, maybe she would get the wanted peace that would come with being an enigma. She simply wanted little to no drama as much as possible. The murder of the mayor's husband with him being famous in his own right as a doctor, was the talk of the town.

"Are you by any chance Samantha King's daughter?" Sheila asked with a raised brow.

Nat hoped to lie. Her instincts asked her to, and she parted her lips hoping to do just that but decided against it.

Nodding her head gently, she whispered her reply, "Yes."

Sheila gasped, clamped her hands over her mouth and suddenly bore an expression of pity on her face which Nat was very much familiar with. She didn't want it; she had no use for being pitied when it wouldn't undo things or bring back the important person in her world whom she had lost so unjustly. She looked away from Sheila and back at the journal in her hand.

Sheila fell silent momentarily before leaning closer to Nat and whispering. "I'm really sorry for your loss... your father was an important and well-respected man in the community, and he did a lot for my family after I was born more than I can recall."

The story was the same as everyone; her father was the emblem of perfection that only seemed to radiate even more after his demise. Yet, none of them had done anything purposeful to bring the killer to justice.

"I'm sorry you feel that way," Sheila apologized before looking away.

Perplexed and seeking meaning to her words, Nat looked back at the girl. "I'm sorry but I don't quite follow."

Sheila replied, "I can read your thoughts or at least some fragments of it since you don't seem to have the ability to block me out."

Nat's eyes glowed with interest and she wondered what else the girl was capable of. She figured she was a witch but having mastered her abilities to such extent would mean she wasn't just any witch from any meager coven.

"I'm a Salem witch," she replied, doing well to read Nat's thoughts again. "My ancestors migrated into Virtus Valley hundreds of years ago and haven't left since."

Nat had heard some bit about the mentioned coven. They weren't ones to be messed with but most of them always ended up getting entwined in a dark path in life, almost as though they are willed to find their own doom in the most disastrous manner any witch could leave the world.

"But..." Nat paused and looked towards the front of the class to ascertain she wasn't being watched. "You Salem witches hardly ever interact with others and don't see reasons to attend schools."

Sheila nodded graciously. "You're indeed correct but I have to be here... there is a prophesy about an impending darkness you see and..."

Sheila halted and looked towards the front of the class where the teacher had spotted them conversing. "Miss King and Miss Grey, would you like to share with the class just what tales you both find so fascinating that giving the class your attention isn't worth it?"

Half the class looked their way and the mumbles began to air. Nat bowed her head and closed her eyes without saying anything in response to the teacher.

Her first day at school was not going as she wanted it to.

"I can help you hear what many of them are thinking, if you are interested," Sheila offered.

Nat shook her head immediately before pausing and taking a brief look around. Some bore rather judgmental and disturbing looks on them, while others seemed genuinely concerned and hearty towards her.

"On second thought, please show me," Nat changed her mind.

Sheila held out her hand and instructed Nat to hold onto it. Watching Sheila roll back her eyes and spotting nothing but whiteness in her eye sockets, Nat felt her heart jump and her sweat pores open as she felt Sheila's hand tighten around hers firmly. The air grew thinner and her consciousness seemed to get sucked into it, as she drowned in a realm she couldn't quite make out.

"Whatever you do, don't let go of my hand," she heard Sheila's words ring aloud in her head loud and clear.

Through the darkness looming in her consciousness, came the sudden burst of light and the emergence of her classroom with the students casting stares her way without necessarily voicing out. Nat looked to her right, where Sheila stood, smiling and pointing to their seat so she could see for herself how things worked.

"Her father was Maxwell King... the man that owned the Oak clinic," a red-haired kid whispered to his friend.

Another, who's piercing gaze was solely on her thought to himself, "I wonder if the Oracles are going to get themselves involved in this."

"Will they get involved?" Nat asked.

Sheila shook her head disappointedly. "They only come out of wherever they are when the lives of supernatural creatures are at risk or when something really grave and threatening to the races happen."

It felt like a letdown and a disappointment that her father's death couldn't be treated like a matter of importance.

"Who cares if her father ran Oak Clinic and had every supernatural creature at peace in that bucket called a clinic," a girl bearing markings on her left arm in form of tribal tattoos hissed and looked away.

"That's Tania... a nosey and bitchy vampire," Sheila pointed out.

Nat nodded and hoped to steer clear of her every chance she got, before feeling something heavy come to rest on her shoulder, as did Sheila.

"Oh no!" Sheila sounded in fright before the entire realm began vanishing and blending back into darkness from whence it had come.

Nat parted her eyelids open to the sight of her class teacher staring down at them both with his hands on their shoulders independently. "No magic or use of special abilities is allowed in the classroom... you know the drill."

Sheila motioned to speak but found herself stuttering immediately, before hearing Nat cut in and explain, "It was all my fault... I conjured the mind spell."

Sheila held her face in her hand, obviously disappointed and wishing Nat had allowed her to speak.

"Mind spell?" the young teacher smiled and laughed. "Is that what a thought savoring spell is called these days?"

Sheila cast her partner a frown. "Thanks genius."

"You two should head over to the Headmaster's office immediately," he ordered with a calm tone and a smile on his lips. "Tell him Mr. Marshall sent you."

Grumbling and dissatisfied by the teacher's act, Sheila grinded her teeth and marched out of the class while her partner followed behind. Nat could hear some laughter while others continued their gossips which she could very well guess had something to do with her murdered father.

"Maybe being sent to the Headmaster's office is a blessing in disguise," Nat thought to herself.

Sheila didn't look as pleased as she turned back around and grabbed the girl by her shirt before shoving her. "Maybe it is good for you but not for me! I'm a freaking Salem witch, a member belonging to a blot of darkness in the community which they have tried to erase for years."

Sheila looked terrified and angry, without a doubt. Nat shoved her hands from her and sighed exhaustively before leading the way to their destination. Sheila followed her, mumbling angrily still as she was obviously displeased with the teacher's decision. The walk felt long, and the halls were all but empty except a few students most likely seniors and a passing staff member.

It's been no less than ten minutes since they arrived at the Headmaster's office. There they sat in front of his desk in silence while the burly looking man with a rather disturbing and more notable moustache, had not said a word to them. Sheila looked uneasy and as if she would make a run for it had the opportunity been provided to her.

The door behind them suddenly slammed shut and the man with the name "Alan Parker" glowing red in what appeared to be flowing liquid etched into the plaque on his desk suddenly moved, drew closer from his seat and stared some more at the girls.

"Sheila Grey," he whispered. "You're being sent to detention for a week for endangering another student by performing a mind spell which could have crippled her had it gone wrong."

Nat's lower jaw fell and felt like it had unhinged but she made no sound or motion to say a word.

Sheila looked livid and shook her head. "This is outrageous! I'm getting punished for such a simple spell! This school is nothing but a joke!"

"Silence, Miss Grey," the man roared, waving his hand in dismissal. She obeys his command.

Nat watched him turn his attention to her, lock his fingers into one another on both hands and smile with a rather mind rattling set of teeth coming into display.

"You should be careful who you open your mind to Natalie," he warned. "Not everyone can or should be trusted with the contents in one's head."

Sheila stared furiously at Nat who walked out the door immediately once they were granted the permission to leave.

"I told them it was a complete waste of time coming here!" Sheila yelled. "They always do this to us... they always find ways to blame us for things we haven't even done!"

Nat hoped to reach out to her but felt her hand get pushed away immediately.

"This doesn't end here... I promise you!" Sheila raged.

Watching her storm off in anger did well to indicate just how much of a short fuse she had and how bad Nat was at making friends. Nat turned around and found an audience staring at her as students had begun walking out of their classroom to witness the ruckus that was going on.

"Oh, great!" she sighed out in frustration.

She wished the day would come to an end already, but quite sadly for her, the hours were still long ahead.

CHAPTER TWO

The day soon felt better. It didn't really bring with it anything special other than having the chance to spend a little while on the track field. As she simply took in the sunlight, Nat felt some confidence slowly fill her up. Track was something she was good at. Sports in general. She had plans on trying out for the basketball team before her father died but she wasn't so sure anymore. Last semester it didn't matter how good she was, she was a freshman and couldn't even get a tryout. There was no freshman basketball team and the upperclassmen were all asses. She spent enough time getting benefits as the Mayor's kid at the start of the year which didn't make her many friends, so she didn't force herself onto the team.

Nat knuckled down, stretched in her track suit and prepared herself for some light running while they awaited track coach Vivian.

"This really blows," Saskia sounded uncomfortable while she hissed and kicked hard against the synthetic track surface.

So far so good, everything felt calm or at least normal. The silent whispers about her and her family had mellowed down, and everyone seemed interested in going about their own lives or at least it felt that way asides the fact that Saskia was making a mess of the peace Nat hoped would linger on into the closing of the day. A scrawny looking kid from a werecat clan who she couldn't recall emerged on the field, shaken and absolutely frightened for reasons best known to him.

"Go on Ramuel!" a dark-haired boy with reddish glowing eyes, a somewhat long face, abnormally smooth skin, and lengthy fingers cried from where he sat on a bench just a few feet from everyone. "Make my announcement or I will make you into a fur coat!"

Nat looked to the scrawny kid. He looked timid, shy and very much bullied by the dark-haired boy with chestnut skin. It was one of the problems with the organizational chain in the supernatural community. There were those who believed they were the apex predators and needn't bow or succumb to the tradition of having to work together.

It was one of the reasons why Nat's father had created the ultimate place called the "neutral zone" or at least, it was officially called "The Oak Clinic"; a place where all supernatural beings could get treated and cared for without any form of prejudice and with the strict rule that none could ever harm one another in there, even if they were enemies in the outside world. No fighting inside the zone.

Nat had never seen a werecat that timid, nor heard about one being so fragile in nature until she saw Ramuel.

"This… this… is an announcement for a party," he began, swallowing down hard after pronouncing a word.

He began handing out flyers, barely being able to look into the eyes of those he distributed the colored printed papers to. Nat motioned to step closer to him and speak with him, but the boy sitting atop the bench in the distance with a somewhat troubling expression spread across his face got to his feet and began walking towards her.

"Well… well… well," he purred and licked his lips.

Nat could sense trouble and she didn't want it.

He continued with an odd smile spread across his face, "If it isn't Natalie King."

He sounded like he knew her for sure. Nat had never met him before and knew little to anything about him. Nat did know he was known for being a bully and his family was full of killers. It made her stomach pit feel muddy with worries immediately. She stepped backwards but he only continued to draw closer. His confidence was without doubt high as a kite and the expression on his face meant he didn't really care for other people's emotions.

"You know what?" he rubbed his lip with his right thumb.

Nat shook her head and held up her right hand. "I don't want any trouble…"

He spread his arms far apart from his body and replied, "Oh no darling… I don't mean any trouble, or at least, I don't mean any provided you are my date to the rave tonight."

The others around slowly retreated while he came within inches of Nat. She could perceive him reeking of trouble while his wild grin bore his fangs.

As he reached for her hair, she could see his daylight ring on his index finger. She stepped back from him. He halted his hand in midair before dropping his arm. "You still haven't given me an answer."

Nat felt her fists clench tightly and her eyes filled with anger as she continued to share the limited air within the short breathing distance with him. He was a rich arrogant kid. Only the rich and powerful well-connected vampires have daylight jewelry. Every other vampire uses Soleil Silos lotion to walk in the daylight.

"I don't want anything to do with you," she declared out and rightfully.

He finally turned around, began to chuckle and slowly walk away from her.

"You see, there might be a teeny-weeny little problem with the answer you just gave me," he smiled cynically and bore out the claws on his right hand slowly.

Nat could feel him coming and armed with nothing but her wits and yet-to-mature magic, she hoped for something, a miracle or anything at all to help her against whatever he had planned. He swung around fast and swiftly, bearing his hand high before swinging for her face. His hand was halted. With his hand high in the air he wore a bewildered look on his face.

Nat felt her breath cease and her nostrils flare. She could have sworn he would have reached her already and the fact his hand had not connected was nothing short of a miracle.

"Are you crazy?" a male voice sounded from behind the vampire who was about to strike her.

Nat watched the tall kid, with deep green eyes and caramel colored skin emerge from behind her attacker.

"I was simply toying with her Russel, so let me go," he demanded.

Russel shook his head, turned around to look at Nat and asked in a concerned tone. "Are you okay?"

Nat managed to nod her head and sigh. A part of her wished he had not stepped in, while another part thanked the stars as she wondered what might have happened if his strike had connected.

"I cannot catch a break," Nat thought to herself before excusing herself from those around, walking away quickly.

It was just the middle of the day and she had managed to create two incidents where she was the center of attraction.

"Hamilton!" Russel yelled. "This madness has to stop damn it! You're going to get kicked out!"

Hamilton brushed past Russel and headed for the entrance into the main building, which was where Nat had gone through. Faster than anyone around him, he was out of sight in seconds and left Russel fearful of what the murderous and edgy vampire could do if he went unsupervised.

"Don't be stupid Hamilton," he closed his eyes with hopes that the vampire would pick up his words through his keen sense of hearing.

Hamilton replied with a chuckle and a soft purr, "I only want to play with her… you can stop me if you dare."

He wasn't goofing around and it worried Russel, who zoomed off immediately, just before their coach walked onto the field to begin their class.

Nat walked down the hall leading to the second floor before she cut through the rows of classes on her right to another hall as she headed for the nearest bathroom. It felt like it just might be the one peaceful place in school for her at the moment and finding it empty made her heart joyous. She approached the first stall, halted momentarily and looked ahead to the last one.

"That should do," she thought to herself before slowly walking over and slamming the door shut behind her.

Drowning in the silence and wondering why things seemed like they weren't going to fall in line, Nat took out her cellphone, flipped through the pages and began toggling through pictures she had taken with her father during the last fall. It was an awesome experience which had made him place the clinic with an understudy for a few days while they went hiking and camping.

"I miss you," she whispered with a finger on the screen while she relived what it felt like to have her father around and alive.

It felt more like a distant past now. One she would do anything to have again if granted the opportunity. Nat slipped the phone back into her bag and got back to her feet but stopped with her hands against the stall on both sides as her heart pounds upon hearing someone kick hard against the bathroom door.

"Come out… come out… let's have some fun!" Hamilton called out.

Nat struggled to breathe, trying hard not to alert his heightened sense of hearing of her presence just a few feet from him.

"I can smell your perfume Natalie," he sniffed aloud and let out a loud sigh. "There is no use trying to hide from me."

Nat's heart leapt towards her throat and her breathing simmered down dangerously. She could feel fear mixed with being helpless trickle down her spine amidst the inevitable fact that Hamilton would soon be unto her.

"You bastard!" she heard another boy's voice ring aloud, before a tussle broke through.

Hearing them hammer each other dangerously into the walls before heading out, Nat pinned her ears down with her fingers and prayed for it to end before hearing the chaos grow distant and eventually simmer into silence. She waited a few more minutes before peeking from her stall and notice in shock the level of destruction they had dealt the bathroom.

Without the need to wait any longer, she raced out, headed left, in the opposite direction to where the boys were fighting as evident by crashing lockers. Nat wanted out quick as possible. She couldn't figure out why her luck was rotten as she slipped into an empty classroom and slammed the door shut behind her. She looked around the classroom.

It was an astronomy class as evident by the charts on the walls and the jars containing what witches called space dust in them, lining almost every cabinet in the large classroom. She had never been in it before but was bound to have a few classes in there later.

"This is beautiful," she thought to herself, reaching for a jar containing golden glowing dust.

She reached towards the lower shelf, hoping to pick up what she assumed to be some kind of stick, but felt its coldness and softness before realizing she was pulling out a human's hand.

"Aaaaaggghhhh!" she screamed at the top of her lungs immediately.

It had been precisely twenty minutes since the incident and things had simmered down whilst some of the students cleaned up to prevent the school authorities from catching up to the acts of the two vampires. A couple of the witches in higher classes had partaken in the conjuring of reconstructive spells to help set things back as they ought to be.

They had mostly, if not all, done it for Russel and not because of Hamilton.

Yet, Nat had not been found since the fight broke through. She had done well to hide away but Russel and some of the witches were concerned. Whether Nat had been able to make friends or not was irrelevant, or her being just a sophomore. She was the mayor's daughter and more so part of an important witch family. Witches tend to stick together when necessary.

Locating Nat in a pile of her own fear, slumped to the ground and barely able to breathe wasn't hard once the senior class witches casted a location spell to find her. They had assumed the worst when Hamilton fled and wasn't seen on the school premise or even located because he managed to shield himself obviously with the help of another witch.

Nat watched Russel rush through the classroom door with a frightened look while two more students followed him closely.

"There... there... is a body there!" Nat pointed north of where she had tripped with widened eyes and a raging heartbeat.

Russel looked in the direction the young witch had pointed and felt his gut escape through his mouth as they stared at the badly mutilated body.

"Oh my God!" Russel exclaimed and managed to drag the shelf blocking the body out of the way.

He recognized the body to be one of the seniors.

"Amos Leon!" a girl standing just beside Russel mumbled.

They seemed to know him too well and felt stricken by his death. They turned around and cast Nat a bewildered look immediately.

"I had nothing to do with it!" Nat defended herself immediately. "I swear to you... I came in here to hide from that psycho and found him!"

The girls hovered around her suspiciously, but Russel went to examine the body. "She didn't do it."

The words gladdened Nat's heart, causing her to heave out a loud sigh.

"No offense meant," he turned to her and said. "Whoever did this would have to be powerful and skilled enough to overpower or handle Amos."

The girls nodded in agreement, clearing Nat from being their suspect.

"Does this happen often here?" Nat couldn't help but ask while one of the girls helped her up.

They shake their heads and sigh at once.

"We need to alert the teachers immediately," Russel insisted. "There are strange markings on his body, and it looks like his entire essence has been drained."

Nat understood what it meant to drain someone's essence and it made her insides crawl. It was a way to completely steal a witch's power from them and leave them dead without a single breath in their bodies.

"What about the markings on his neck and arms?" one of the girls asked Russel. "Those bites look awfully familiar like one you'd find when…"

Russel completed her sentence before turning around with a worried look on his face. "Like the ones you'd find on a vampire's victim."

Nat slowly approached the body while Russel called the school authorities immediately to brief them of the dead body found in one of the classrooms and who had found it. Nat felt sick to her gut while she stared at the body in pity and fright all mixed into one. She wondered if it was someone within the grounds that had done it.

"He just died," she whispered in a grief-stricken tone. "He looks freshly dead."

Russel stood between her and the dead body before placing his hands gently on her shoulders. "Look at me!"

Nat seemed cold in her gaze and absolutely stricken with grief while her mind lingered on the misery of being the one to find the body. It only ushered in memories of her father and the vile nature of the world they lived in.

"This wasn't your doing, okay?" Russel reminded her. "You cannot blame yourself for this, so snap out of it and let's get out of here."

He managed to get her to leave while her skin grew cold and her body shuddered.

"My name is Russel by the way," he formally introduced himself as teachers ran past them and towards the murder scene.

"Nice to meet you Russel," Nat replied with a weak handshake.

He hurried to a vending machine to collect some water for her. While they sat in the hallway news of Amos Leon's murder spread through the school like wildfire. Students continued to run past, each casting Nat a wary eye as they had learnt she was the finder of the body.

"You shouldn't worry about them," Russel assured her.

Nat took a long sip from her bottle and sighed out loud. "Here I was hoping for a fresh start only to become a dead body finder... my chances of being like every other normal kid in here just keeps plummeting."

Russel laughed, forcing her to pause and stare at him blankly.

"I'm sorry but you have to know it's hard for everyone here and especially when you're just a sophomore with a senior vampire down your neck," he replied. "You shouldn't let a few incidents get you down though... live life and enjoy it."

He patted her shoulder and got to his feet before humming to himself and walking away. Nat felt her cheeks get warm with copious amount of blood rushing into them.

Russel spoke over his shoulders without looking back, "See you at the rave tonight!"

She chuckled, took the final sip from her bottle and got up in hopes of returning to her dormitory, since the school seemed to be in chaos about the dead body found and they were talking about cancelling the remaining classes for the day.

"Who could have done it?" she asked herself,

Everything within her gut screamed about it being the mad vampire she had been hiding from earlier. He didn't seem to be the rational kind and had Russel not come to her rescue, she might have been his plaything without doubt.

"I really need to get my magic under wraps," she mumbled before walking down the staircase.

"Miss Natalie King!" a voice called to her, prompting her to halt and turn around.

It was Headmaster Alan Parker and he didn't seem entirely pleased.

"May I have a word with you and maybe even pick your brain on the unfortunate events that came to be in our school today?" he asked with an outstretched hand.

Nat felt scared to her bones immediately. He looked cold, sounded it, and felt it when he placed his hand on her shoulder as they headed back to his office.

CHAPTER THREE

Within the large abandoned building known to be the perfect hideout spot for students who were up to mischief ever since the old and largest dormitory had been abandoned for years, loud music could be heard blaring while bright and colorful lights shone from within it. Alexandra Aurelius also known mainly as Alex had arrived donning a seductively short black dress with her long hair down, so it danced to the tune in the air of its own accord as she swayed in steps.

"Hey girl!" Olivia Richards called to Alex, wrapping her arms around the ebony skinned and gorgeous looking girl. "You are definitely going to kill it in there."

Alex let off a wicked smile before looking around. "Where is Saskia?"

Olivia looked around immediately for the werecat who they planned on meeting up with. She spotted her selling drugs to students underneath a shade just by the building. She soon came rushing toward them bloodied around her knuckles smiling from ear to ear upon seeing Alex.

"Alexandra!" she cried in a cheerful and odd tone about to hug Alex who backed away. Saskia raised a brow before looking at the blood on her knuckles realizing Alex didn't want it on her dress.

"What is that?" Olivia inquired with a frown, even though she already knew.

Saskia replied bluntly, "Blood? This punk ass witch tried to shorten me and I decided he needed to learn a lesson."

Alex shook her head and sighed. She seemed disappointed as she walked away and heard the two girls follow her by the clacking of their heels.

"What?" Saskia whispered in a lost tone.

Olivia watched Alex get further ahead before whispering, "People are thinking we got something to do with the dead dude in school. Some even think you or Hamilton are responsible. We don't need our own shit exposed if you get caught around us doing stupid shit."

Saskia wore a slight impression faking how much she cared before bursting into a cynical and rather troubling laugh that only seemed to enrage Olivia who began to walk away.

Staring at the blood on her knuckles before licking them, Saskia yells out to them, "I don't give a fuck who killed who, as long as it doesn't mess with my very lucrative business."

Alex finally stopped before the entrance into the building, flanked by her girls and with one firm push, shoved the doors open to become the center of attraction for all that were dancing and partying within. Eyes rolled in their direction, while whistles aired louder and louder as the girls walked majestically to the makeshift bar in the top right-hand corner of the room.

"I'm definitely going to score a lot of cash in here tonight!" Saskia sounded in an elated tone, sighting some desperate and morally low young men who would need what she had to offer.

Alex knew better not to meddle in Saskia's affairs but nodded softly while pulling the girl closer. "Keep off the werewolves tonight… they are on edge and could bring more trouble than we might be able to handle."

Saskia shot her friend a rather bleak look before nudging the witch's hand off her and dancing along the floor and towards a group of six boys, all wearing the same facial expressions. Alex ordered for some drinks while Olivia was flirting with a werewolf by the name Adam whose pack didn't seem to be around the party.

"See you later Alex!" Olivia waved before disappearing towards the dance floor.

Alex waved her off, sprinkled some herbs into her alcohol and gulped it all down at once.

"Hey John!" she called out to the boy in charge of booze. "Hit me up with some more!"

There was no chance she was getting high. The root would grant her just about the same strength as a vampire downing countless bottles of alcohol without getting drunk. The party was just starting for Alex, but it was about to get steamier. A little ruckus had broken out outside the rave house, before two bodies came flying into the room accompanied by a tall, muscular vampire with his fangs all out and his eyes glowing dangerously.

He leaned closer to the two boys on the ground, yanked at their feet and pulled them closer, before holding them in both hands independently and waiting for the entire crowd to fixate their gaze on him.

"Let the party begin!" he cried, before looking to his right and tilting his captive's neck to the side just about enough to reveal his jugular vein.

Expanding his jaw and permitting his fangs to grow extensively from within his mouth, he wasted no time sinking them into the boy's neck, causing him to scream in agony and shudder aggressively while he struggled to break the powerful lock his attacker had on him. Few of the on-watchers on the party ground made an attempt to take action but knew better than to mess with a vampire who was deemed to be a direct bloodline descendant of a notorious and powerful vampire they all had read about in their folklores and tales.

"Hamilton, you will kill him!" Alex finally got up from her seat and approached her associate. He wasn't exactly a friend, but their worlds mixed frequently.

Hamilton looked up slowly, pulled out his extended canines while his long and sharp nails remained hooked into the boy's shoulder while he tried to prevent him from making a run.

"Hello, Alex" he chuckled madly and turned to the second captive he had in his left hand.

Alex could see the boys couldn't be any more than fourteen and he would have picked them somewhere along the road on his way over, judging by the dirt on their clothing.

She growled and fumed softly but with no harm meant. "They are minors Hamilton! They'll be easily missed!"

Hamilton retracted his fangs after having his fill of blood and replied, "They were breaking and entering someone's house when I caught them both... in fact, you should be thanking me for being an upstanding citizen."

Alex turned back around and brushed off his madness upon seeing there was no reasoning with the blood lust vampire.

Hamilton stared at the boys in his hands like they were his prey. Fueling off of their fear and misery, he held them both before him and sneered dangerously until one began to pee in his pants.

"What do we do with you two?" he licked his lips and smiled at them while he could hear their heart beats racing violently.

The pale faced one in his right hand stuttered, "Please let us go… we won't tell anyone!"

Hamilton shrugged, sighed and pulled them closer before staring right into their eyes and whispering, "You both will leave and forget anything about this place or that you met me and you will return to your homes to have a long night into the morning."

Their pupils dilated, and they slowly nodded their heads before he let them go and they began walking to the door like zombies lacking control of their own minds and focus.

"Now let's party!" he waved his arms in the air and approached a werecat who was dancing wildly on the dance floor.

Standing in the corner of the room as she eyed Hamilton and his dance partner, Nat clenched her fists and threatened to leap forward before feeling a firm grip around her wrist restrain her immediately.

Russel leaned closer until his head was close enough to her ear, "I know what you're thinking but don't do it."

She had not expected him to notice her, since she kept to herself and did well enough to remain hidden in the crowd with hopes that nobody would pay attention to her.

"What he did is against the law," she protested. "To have him do it in front of so many people is even more inhumane."

Russel burst into a stream of laughter which began to infuriate Nat and caused her to frown.

"What's so funny?" she asked with her arms folded across her chest and her raised brow growing higher with each passing second.

Russel could barely contain himself before simmering down and clearing his throat. "You said he was being inhumane while you clearly forget that he is a vampire… just like me… we feed on blood and are the ultimate predators of the night."

Finding him unbelievable and absolutely smug about the situation, she turned away hurriedly, hoping to head for the door but felt his grip get firmer around her hand as he turned her back around and slid his had around her waist. Feeling his heart pound against his ribcage and against her chest, Nat gulped down hard and tried not to look up at the darling young vampire.

Smiling tenderly as he leaned closer to her, he whispered, "I might just have to get you angry more often."

Perplexed and unsure about what he meant, she asked, "What?"

"You look absolutely stunning and even more beautiful when you're angry," he complemented her.

Nat looked to the ground immediately, clearing her throat. "Thanks."

Russel tightened his grip around her waist still running his slender fingers up and down her back. Her breathing slowed and her eyes slowly locked with his gaze, while he moved her to the rhythm of the music playing softly in the background and smiled the entire way through.

"I did not mean to sound insensitive earlier," he apologized. "We are vampires and often times many cannot really refrain from being the hideous beasts and creatures that many come to see us as."

Nat reached for his lips and placed a finger to it immediately, stopping him from talking as she leaned her head closer to his chest and continued to listen to the rhythm of his calm heartbeat.

"Should we move to the dance floor?" Russel asked.

She nodded, leaned away from his chest and walked with him towards the center of the room where the lights have now been darkened and couples paired themselves up to dance to the slow, melodious music on air. Nat momentarily sunk herself in the present, forgetting about her worries in school and those at home.

She realized that being with Russel brought a degree of relief which she sought for a while and above all, she loved his tender touch and the way he made her realize her thoughts were important. Her raging heart continued to betray her as Russel smiled at himself because he could hear it nervously beat underneath her chest.

"You move quite well for someone as nervous as you are right now," he whispered before planting a peck to her cheek.

Nat felt blood rush to the spot where his soft lips met with her skin, and her knees suddenly felt wobbly as though they were about to give in. Russel smiled to himself and held her by her hand, before leaning backwards and locking his gaze with hers. Time gave the illusion that it had stood still, and the air grew thinner by the passing second before Russel broke his focus from her oddly to look to his left.

"Hamilton!" he murmured, as he let go of Nat and stopped the fast and incoming attack with a single blow into the vampire's face.

Hamilton scrambled backwards as chaos immediately broke loose on the dance floor.

"Russel!" Nat called out to him, but he wasn't about to let the dangerous vampire anywhere near her.

The music stopped and those dancing soon began clearing away from the dance floor.

"Just leave him alone. Let's dance." Nat pleaded while she tugged at Russel's arm. He was too strong for her pull to have any effect.

Russel mumbled in an angry tone while not looking her way. "You couldn't hear him, but he has been goading us ever since we came to the dance floor… there is no way in hell I'm letting you get hurt."

Nat felt uncomfortable with the situation. Hamilton was no easy feat and if the stories which were peddled around were right, then his violent streak had no measure when he was in full vogue. Both vampires had the floor to themselves while they slowly began letting through their claws. Hamilton growled, licked his lips and let down his claws which grew dangerously long from his fingertips while they dripped of a slimy liquid that Russel knew too well to mean trouble.

"Stay right behind me Nat," he ordered. "Whatever you do, don't let his venom touch you."

Nat was well aware of how some vampire's venom could cause hallucination, paralysis or even death, depending on the potency of the vampire's strength and venom.

"I don't want to hurt her Russel," Hamilton slithered around the floor and smiled. "I just want to toy with her some."

Nat looked around and saw the frightened faces of the students around, with the exception of Alex and her crew, who watched on like they were enjoying the show.

"Call him off!" Nat screamed at Alex.

Olivia nudged at Alex and pointed in Nat's direction. "Someone is trying to tell you what to do."

Nat looked back at Hamilton who was fully ready to attack now and by the looks of it, willing to do anything to get to her, even if it meant harming Russel. Russel slowly bore his fangs immediately, showing off his glowing claws which obviously meant he wasn't just any vampire but one of a royal ancient bloodline.

"Come on!" Hamilton yelled, leaping forward at dangerous speed.

Russel did well enough to match him, jamming his claws into Hamilton's chest. Hamilton cried aloud but slowly began to chuckle sadistically.

"Is that all you got?" he asked the befuddled looking Russel. "I have felt much more pain than your little claws can deal me."

He tossed Russel away hard enough to have him crashing into a wall before falling to the ground in loud thud. Hamilton raced over with the intent to kick the fallen vampire, but Russel had increased his speed and gotten to his feet, before grabbing Hamilton by his leg.

"I wasn't joking when I said keep your filthy hands off of her!" Russel yelled.

Lifting Hamilton off the ground to the surprise of everyone in the room, Russel rammed his opponent into the wall, and he wasn't done yet. Russel made sure he got a better grip onto Hamilton's shirt and then hammered him face down into the floor. Hamilton coughed aloud and spat out some blood, but he obviously wasn't in the mood to back down.

Russel awaited the attack in good preparation, but it wasn't enough to handle what Hamilton had in store.

Olivia stared at Alex and asked, "Why is he fooling around?"

Alex took a sip from her beer bottle and replied, "Hamilton is no ordinary vampire. He is narcissistic to say the least and after toying with his prey for a while, well, Russel is about to find out."

Hamilton ran his claws along the wall, scratching through the brick like it was paper, before shooting Nat a wicked smile which made Russel shove her out of the way immediately. He had seen Hamilton coming but there was just no stopping the speed at which he moved. Seeing nothing but a blur of red from his shirt whizz by, before his clawed hand grabbed him in a choke hold and pinned him to the wall. Russel could have sworn he didn't see Hamilton move at all before getting to where he was.

Snarling and breathing close to Russel's face so the vampire could know very well just how weak and powerless he was against him, Hamilton whispered, "Your desire to protect the little witch just might get you killed."

Russel struggled but could barely move, as Hamilton's claw dug into his neck and sent his nerves numb within seconds, while his own claws slowly began to retract, and his fangs disappear within his mouth. Russel watched Hamilton bare his fangs and slowly begin to lean closer to Russel's neck before halting and holding out his left hand to prevent Nat from striking him with a piece of wood she had picked from the ground earlier.

"I will come for you soon little witch," he turned to her arrogantly and relieved her of the wooden chair leg before tossing it away.

Unknown to him, it wasn't her only play. Jamming a syringe, she had produced from her purse into his arm, Nat injected the heavy dose of green liquid into his body before hurrying backwards.

Hamilton watched the syringe fall to the ground with widened eyes and whispered, "Oh you little prick of a witch! What was that?"

Letting go of Russel who fell to the ground immediately, Hamilton clenched his hands around his throat and scratched against his skin violently as though he was on fire.

"Bitch! You injected me with werewolf venom!?" he yelled, groping his burning skin and swinging for her with his retracting claws before they finally disappeared.

Nat heard herself breathe aloud in fright, before hurrying over to assist Russel to his feet while Hamilton continued to battle with his transformation back into his human form. His bulk decreased, fangs retracted to normal, and his claws were gone. He staggered around the floor in pain while nobody seemed interested in helping him, before running out of the rave house as his breathing heightened and his vision became blurry.

Olivia looked pissed with rage and motioned to step forward but a blonde girl with sapphire colored eyes standing beside Alex managed to stop her. "I love it when a girl can hold her own."

Alex didn't seem to care. She slowly turned around and picked up her drink.

Russel coughed aloud while Nat helped him to his feet. "I never knew you had some fire in you."

Nat smiled and replied, "I never get caught off guard twice. He shouldn't be bothering anyone for the rest of the night."

Everyone soon seemed to forget about the vindictive and vile vampire who had almost ruined their fun for the night. Nat had done something right at least even while her heart felt heavy with guilt and worry as regards to what Hamilton would do next. He obviously wasn't one whose ego could handle being humiliated well.

"Can we finish our dance?" Nat whispered to Russel who had begun to heal from his battle wounds nicely.

He nodded, tucked his hand around her waist and replied, "Sure."

CHAPTER FOUR

The night had felt better and it came from that one kiss she had shared with the dashingly handsome vampire who fought hard for her. For Nat, it capped off the beautiful night even with Hamilton humiliated and leaving with promises of getting her, she couldn't help but feel somewhat proud of herself.

Doing her bid to avoid more drama from the other kids, she had chosen the alternate route leading to her dorm room, cutting through the almost worn off pathway just behind the rave house, heading north with the dorm house not yet in sight. It was going to be within her reach if she continued on her path for another ten minutes.

It was at that moment everything slowly began to feel odd. The air changed, followed by an uneasy feeling growing down her spine in form of tingling sensation which she had come to trust to mean that trouble was heading her way. It was something her mother had always asked her to watch out for; the sixth sense embedded into witches right from their time of birth.

"What now?" a rather embattled and worried Nat asked herself. She wished she had taken the normal quick route.

"Is anyone there?" Nat asked turning to her left, nothing. She held unto her purse tightly.

The air grew colder, and fog soon began to fill her surrounding oddly.

She began to quicken her steps and managed her breathing so her hearing could remain focused and sharp enough to pick up any odd sounds. The sounds came in plenty; from leaves being rustled aggressively, to twigs being stepped on and snapped. Yet, Nat choose not to look back; she couldn't deal with the thought of having a bunch of vampires hunting her down on Hamilton's behest.

"Russel!" she called out softly, wondering if she should have taken his advice and allowed him to walk her to her dorm before heading to his.

All she could do was to keep her unsteady breathing pattern steady as possible, while her feet walked as fast as they could carry her.

Yet, the dorm room seemed further away the more she attempted to get closer. In fact, for the past five minutes, she had managed to walk on the same spot without realizing it until she stepped on a large trunk of wood which had almost tripped her and then she first realized she was being tailed by someone.

"Witches!" Nat sounded in fear and mumbled underneath her warm breath.

Her lungs stung and her eyes burned as the fog slowly began to clear and grant her vision of her surroundings.

"One..." Nat counted the incoming figure from her left before looking around. "No... two... three... four!"

"I don't know what you want but I'm not going down easily!" she declared with her fists raised barely keeping them up. School grounds were supposed to be safe.

One to her left cackled in a dark laughter, while the others simply closed in without giving off any sound asides the crunching sound from the snapping twigs and dried grasses beneath their feet.

"This should be fun," one of them mumbled.

Another cut right in, "She seemed to have a lot of spark in her earlier."

Nat's mind raced wildly with thoughts and her entire body grew numb as the four finally came to full view. She stared at them one at a time and felt her inside walls collapse as she struggled to figure out what exactly it was that she was dealing with.

"What are... what are you?" she stuttered, noticing the same faces staring right back at her.

The four figures were impossible to tell apart and they donned nothing different as regards to their clothes nor their faces. She had never come across such an anomaly in her life and it threatened to topple her to the ground just by the eeriness of things.

Boxing her in, one stepped closer and smiled right into her face. "What's the matter little witch? You never seen perfect shape shifting before?"

Nat had never come across their kind before. She had indeed heard of them, but they never showed themselves out in the open a lot.

"But... but..." she stuttered.

"News flash!" another replied. "We aren't as hidden as many would believe."

Feeling the one to her left shove her hard to the ground, the four slowly transformed into girls of the same liking before turning into elderly men as they morphed their skin and facial features impressively, before finally settling to their initial look. It sickened her stomach and she was about to feel even more nauseated as they drew closer.

"We won't hurt you," one promised.

"We just want some sugar," another joked.

Nat struggled to fight them off with punches, but they succeeded in pinning her down regardless. With her hands pinned on either side by two of the shape shifters, one stood watch and the fourth slowly began slipping his pants down, Nat forced her hands free and ripped her nails into the fourth's face, causing him to shriek in pain as he struggled with his already fallen pants.

"You bitch!" he cried, yanked at his belt and began to wrap it around his knuckle.

Yet, she wasn't done and upon sighting a large branch in the nearby bush, she waved her hand at it and watched it levitate but not convincing enough in the air, while her captors laughed and made a mock of her. Feeling her anger fueled, she swung hard with every intent possible within her bones and the branch struck one of them in the face immediately.

It would be the act that got them even more enraged, and most notably, the one she had struck.

Nat watched his fast swinging hand reach her face, and suddenly knock her into a barely conscious state. He still wasn't done. He came swinging hard for the second time, but his fist didn't connect as something seemed to hold him back against his will. A glowing light, burning brightly in the distance approached and seemed to startle the shape shifters who turned their attention to the person.

"Leave the girl alone!" a feminine voice warned.

"This isn't any of your business bi..." one of the shape shifters had barely spoken when he started to clutch his throat with both hands.

Watching her assaulter choke and her savior approach in a steady walk, Nat managed to make out fuzzy images from her somewhat swollen eye from where she had been punched. They weren't having a good time with whoever had come to her rescue. The girl bore what appeared to be fire in both hands, before ramming it hard into one which caused the others to slowly crumble to the ground in agony.

"Show your real self you coward!" the girl demanded.

The four bodies slowly began to merge into one, while the single figure coughed and slowly got to his feet with a rather enraged look on his face.

"Who do you think you are?" he asked.

Lunging forward and hammering down Nat's savior, Nat could only attempt to crawl towards the fight to try and assist but it proved more difficult than she had imagined it would. Her spine felt stiff and her joints were unresponsive. Her rescuer seemed to be in trouble as the huge framed attacker now in his true form reached for a rock to his right and threatened to hammer it down on the girl he had pinned to the ground.

"Watch out!" Nat felt herself scream and try to warn the other girl.

Thankfully, the girl had managed to draw out a silver knife from within her boot, rammed it hard into the shape shifters' chest which sent it squabbling backwards in a painful roar. It struggled to hold the knife as he felt it burn his hands as he continued to growl then began to burn violently from the magical knife jammed into his heart.

Nat felt her heart threaten to give way. Sweat rolled down her face immediately as she came to the realization that someone had just killed for her. Her hands trembled while her weakened frame struggled to get back into a sitting position but found it to be almost impossible. The blow to her head not only left her with impaired vision but some way left her struggling for balance.

"You shouldn't try to overly exert yourself," the feminine voice said before laying her hand to rest on Nat's forehead. The voice is familiar.

Nat could hear the girl mumble words she recognized to be mild healing spells. Warmth quickly spread through her face and around the wound, causing it to close back up.

"You're good as new," she said, gently backing away while she held her hand out for Nat to grab hold of.

Nat opened her eyes and looked up at her savior, Alexandra, who slowly began stepping away.

"Alexandra!" another girl in a low-cut top came rushing through. "Oh my god, what happened?"

"Alexandra? Why the hell would she come to save me, she hates me," Nat thought with a soft gasp.

Alex motioned for her friend to remain where she was, before leading Nat out from the dark woods and turning around upon getting to a more lightened clearing leading towards the dorm. Nat motioned to speak with her, but Alex obviously wasn't interested in having a conversation. It was typical of Alex after all and after all those years, she still seemed to have a chip on her shoulder.

Nat felt rather happy to have been saved by her, though somewhat sad by the situation of things between her and the girl she used to call her best friend.

The following day Nat woke up late and had to rush to get ready for her classes. One downside to not having a roommate is not having someone to wake you up. Nat knew there were going to be too many questions and people pitying her on her return to school, so she let her mom use her connections to get Nat a private room. After first period, Nat found herself at her locker glancing over at Alex who was a few lockers down. Alex shut her locker and passed her without a glance in return. Watching Alex get further away, Nat whispered the words "Thank you," followed by a loud bang that startled her back into consciousness and faced to face with the frowning face of none other than Olivia, Alex's best friend.

Nat grit her teeth from the impact, "Olivia!"

"Hey loser!" she chuckled with her hand placed on Nat's locker to prevent her from being able to gain access to it.

Nat stared her in the face, wondering what she wanted and why she seemed interested in her.

"Last night never happened! Don't go around talking about it." Olivia whispered before leaning closer to Nat. "Got it?"

Nat felt herself choke on some air, clenched her fists into balls. Her face bore a frown as people walked past and continued to look in her direction.

"We wouldn't want anything else bad to happen to you," Olivia whispered in a threat.

Nat started to get pissed off but managed to keep her composure as Alex and two other girls walked back towards her and Olivia. "Seems you're the one talking about it, not me." She looked boldly into Olivia's eyes.

"Leave her alone Olivia!" Alex commanded which prompted Olivia to frown and shove Nat hard against the locker.

Falling to her knees and feeling her anger fueled, Nat wished they weren't in school at that moment so she could punch Olivia. She could not risk getting in trouble so soon. Her mother already called her frantic multiple times after hearing about the death of Amos.

"Let it go Nat," Russel came from her blind side and helped her up. "Those girls are no different from Hamilton, they mean trouble."

Nat wasn't entirely sure about the side to Alex which she had been allowed to see just last night. She wondered what the girl was doing with such a group of friends but brushed off her thoughts as the lecture bell went off to alert everyone to be in their respective classes.

"I'll see you at lunch in the cafeteria!" Russel kissed her cheek and waved her goodbye before hurrying away.

Nat waved back wondering what would come of them both. Her heart felt somewhat excited about meeting with him. They had a lot to talk about especially about the kiss which had happened at the party just last night.

After a few classes, Nat found herself in the cafeteria sitting next to Russel. Reaching for her hand across the table and gently slipping his into hers, Russel smiled and took a swing from his travel cup.

Alex and her crew had just walked past, with a stunning blonde girl she had not seen with them before.

"Who is that?" Nat asked, pointing in the direction of the blonde who sat opposite of Alex and chuckled sheepishly as they talked about something.

Russel looked to the table before taking his eyes away immediately for fear of being caught staring. "That's Eleanor... a werewolf who just happens to be the only decent one in their circle."

Nat nodded but couldn't help herself from staring at the beautiful girl who had caught sight of her as well. Olivia shot Nat an intimidating look, causing the latter to look back at Russel and away from them immediately. They all burst into laughter within seconds of Nat looking away, causing her to feel uncomfortable and cringe on the inside.

"Ignore them," Russel encouraged her. "They are simply miserable and caught up in this world where they see themselves as superior when they're really not."

Saskia shot up from her seat immediately, causing Nat to shrivel with discomfort within as she wondered if the girl had picked up what Russel just said. Having a fight in school wasn't something she would like. Saskia looked their way for a moment before marching to a table just a few feet from them.

She began dealing with a werewolf who slid his pay into her purse in exchange for a blue colored pill meant to help werewolves boost their speed which wasn't entirely anywhere near those of vampires unless it was a full moon.

Russel called back Nat's attention by tightening his hand around hers. "What do you say about us being official? I mean... being my girlfriend."

Nat blushed wildly and slowly retracted her hand immediately.

"I like you Natalie King," he professed. "Even before the day we met, I could tell you were special. I watched you as a Freshman and I really don't think I can take seeing you with anyone else."

His words continued to melt her heart and eat away at her rigid walls as she reached her hand over the table and connected with his again.

"I will love to be your girlfriend," she whispered in response.

Russel felt himself overwhelmed with happiness so much so that he almost leaned over to kiss her but then paused upon remembering that they were being watched.

"I look forward to our first date," he smiled.

Nat shot him a bewildered look.

"The rave dance and kiss don't count as anything," he replied.

She smiled back at him and they both got to their feet as the lunch break bell rang aloud, indicating that it was time to return to their classes. Alex watched the duo from where she sat with her friends. Her eyes remained fixated solely on Nat and trailed her until she walked right out of the room.

Saskia nudged Alex back into focus and asked, "Where is Hamilton by the way? Nobody has seen him since the incident at the party."

Alex shrugged and got to her feet. "There is something I need to do, so I'm leaving school early today."

Her friends nodded and watched her walk away without any further insight into whatever it was that she was going to do.

CHAPTER FIVE

The sight was nothing short of beautiful; seated in an expensive leather fitted chair flown all the way from Brazil, with a view only fitting for a god-like status as hers, from the tallest building in the state, Brenda Aurelius smiled at herself before taking a look at her watch.

"She should be here already," she sounded in an exhausted tone before getting up from her seat.

Staring at her watch expectantly and intermittently just before beginning to pace, Brenda stared at the portrait on the wall which bore the image of the man considered by many to be the brains behind their company being in almost every country in the world as they had grown more influential with each passing year since his mysterious death.

Brenda felt a thin smile crawl into the corners of her lips while she ran her fingers along the image of her deceased husband. It felt rather fitting for her to continue and even expand on his legacy, seeing she assumed office a week after his demise and even managed to double the company's worldwide girth within the space of few years.

Through the years, nothing much had come to change about the company on the outside; they remained the leading force behind the legal peaceful coexistence between supernatural beings and humans at large. The balance was always something her husband counted as one of utmost importance to their power and influence. She had made certain it remained so, with a few major improvements and tweaks going on behind the scene.

Turning around hurriedly just as the office doors slid open to reveal her secretary, Nora Jones, the bespectacled shape shifter whose role had become irreplaceable over the years as her advisor as well as other things. Brenda walked back to her seat.

"What is it Nora?" Brenda asked with a slight frown.

Nora shifted uncomfortably in her stance and sighed intermittently before looking back towards the door.

Brenda could sense something wasn't right and she was feeling somewhat impatient by the entire ordeal. "Are you going to tell me or am I going to get it from you telepathically!?"

Nora cleared her throat and bowed gently. "My apologies, but I wasn't sure on how to break the news about losing ten shipments of the gene enhancing drugs sent over to the military last month."

Brenda tightened her fists into balls and rammed them hard into the glossy ebony table before her. She maintained a blank expression and nodded gently almost as if she understood what had occurred.

"Who was in charge of the trade?" she simply asked.

Nora began scrolling through the tablet in her hand before looking back up, "Alaric."

Brenda sighed and leaned her head closer to the table. She had felt somewhat troubled when he was tasked to make the delivery but against her burning instincts, decided to allow him to carry on with it.

"And the reason why we lost the packages?" she asked subtly.

Nora replied instantly, "They just were never delivered... they never reached their destination and Alaric hasn't been found since then."

Brenda got to her feet and began chuckling as she stared out the window and looked at the humans roaming the busy streets underneath her, like ants. She always had a fascination about how the ordinary human mind worked and each time she felt she was close to figuring out all they were capable of doing, they always seemed to blindside her on every turn.

"The entire worth of the missing packages would be sixteen million dollars, correct?" she asked from where she stood with her finger drawing an unseen pattern against the massive glass window before her.

Nora shook her head, "Eighteen million dollars to be precise."

Brenda bobbed her head and slowly rolled up her sleeves before revealing a rune extending from the upper part of her arms towards her wrist where it stopped. Slipping her left hand into her pants pocket and taking out a pocketknife, she flicked the blade open and pressed the sharp silver into her wrist, grinning as it made a clean cut and began letting down trickles of blood.

Brenda returned to her table, pulled out one of the drawers and took out a bowl that seemed older than the Roman Empire, then began to mix some items that produced a brightly glowing liquid inside of it. Nora watched on, seemingly fearless and unperturbed by what her boss was doing.

"You might want to take some fresh air for what is about to happen Nora," Brenda warned while she held her bleeding wrist over the bowl.

"I don't need air," Nora replied.

Her response drew a thin smile from Brenda's face, just before she watched the blood brew within the bowl and begin to boil dangerously for a few more seconds until the liquid in the bowl turned colorless. Brenda seemed to take a long pause almost as if she tried to think hard and well about what she intended to do first before slipping her right hand into the colorless liquid and staring blankly at the invisible markings she had made on the glass window earlier.

"Let's see where our little thief is and how we can bring him to justice," she chuckled before sprinkling a handful of the colorless liquid onto the wall.

A series of hissing noises began to escape the glass surface, before the markings slowly gained color and glowed deep red in form of what appeared to be a skull with serpents crawling out through the crevices in it. Nora remained still, feeling her fingers tremble but didn't show just how nervous she was about seeing the serpents come to life from the glass's surface.

Brenda stepped closer to the glass window reaching forward with her hand, she invited the slithery red and black serpents atop her hand while they slowly began to circle her wrist and tighten their grip around her arm without causing her any harm.

"Hear me my children," she whispered. "*Alaric Saltz faracsch illeim srutheda*!"

The snakes slowly lifted their heads, seemed to bob the flattened surface gently and then vanish immediately without further ado. Brenda stared at the markings on the window and watched them disappear slowly, leaving her with the view of the city beneath once again and to her amusement.

"If only things could be done easier," she sighed. "Humans are fickle minded beings and they never see the larger picture until consequences begin to burst forth in their faces."

Nora nodded and looked at the tablet in her hand which had just received a notification.

"She should be here in a few minutes," Nora looked up and said to her boss.

Brenda clapped her hands together excitedly and turned back around with a wild grin. "Perfect! Just perfect!"

Nora seemed confused and could not believe what she had heard. The decision to entertain "Her" when they had something as sensitive as Alaric's situation to handle baffled Nora, but she kept her thoughts to herself, wondering what the lady had in mind exactly.

"You're thinking this isn't such a good idea, aren't you?" Brenda approached her worried looking assistant with a hug.

Nora finally spoke, "She is only sixteen and I don't think she is cut out for any of this just yet."

Brenda waved away the claim and turned back around as the walls began to shudder dangerously, and the ceiling threatened to collapse down hard on them. Yet, Nora remained glued to the spot, smiling at her boss who had the weirdest of expression on her face, granted she was about to do something many if not all would regard to be absolute evil.

Hisses filled the room as though it was occupied by a thousand snakes, and the floor right in the center of the office began to slither irritatingly, prompting Nora to take a step backwards as her boss moved closer to it without a bother.

"Bring the traitor to me, Salzaar!" she commanded.

The hissing stopped and got replaced by a loud sizzling noise like smoke arising from the cracks in the earth place fueled by dangerous gases. The largest snake head Nora had ever seen in her life rose from the center of the room, mighty in its size, and devilishly scary as well while it seemed to have wrapped itself around something.

Brenda circled the snake slowly, clapping her hands together in show of satisfaction and taking in deep breaths. "Don't be greedy now Salazaar... hand the traitor over."

The snake rose up and shifted into a snake like man. It was a J'ra'reth demon. It bobbed its head, hissed and responded, "This one reeks of sins my mistress… he reeks of nothing, but sins and it fills my belly with hunger just tasting him in my grasp."

Nora's face whitened, and her right heel broke just by taking a few steps backwards hurriedly. The J'ra'reth demon didn't seem to have taken note of her presence earlier but it did now and with a sharp swing of its head it looked in her direction and began hurrying towards her at great speed. Nora felt her heart's walls collapse and her lungs suddenly flatten as she struggled for air.

"Nora! Don't move!" Brenda warned her immediately.

The demon serpent hissed with its focus resting solely on Nora. "I've not had a shape shifter in ages! They taste even better than the lowly humans and are great for my skin!"

Brenda snapped her fingers together, causing the serpent to halt but not of its own volition. It struggled greatly against the restraints wrapped around its large body and hissed aloud and angrily in discontent.

"This isn't fair mistress!" it continued to hiss aggressively. "This isn't fair!"

Brenda smiled and walked over to Nora before laying her hand to rest on the visibly shaken lady's shoulder.

"Look at her… just look at how shaky she is," the Salazaar continued. "I bet her fear tastes good and will be even more gratifying than whatever payment you plan on giving me for this current task."

Brenda shook her head and closed her eyes. "You attack only those who I wish for you to attack Salazaar, and this lady right here is never going to be your meal or price, so I command you to remain still."

Salazaar suddenly remained still, granting Nora the first opportunity to see its entire body. Its skin was a mysterious beauty to behold; from the golden traces lining its back to the mix of sliver running along its belly. The black scales were smooth. Its large head was partially human shaped, but it was elongated outward and pointed as a snake. It bore dark shades which shone brightly in the light and bounced off beautifully against the other colors on its body.

The J'ra'reth demon itself was larger than she could imagine, stretching at almost eight feet. It took one more disappointing look at Brenda and a disappointed one at Nora before letting go of a shaken-up Alaric which had been in its grasp all along.

"I had to pull him from the most disgusting place in Brazil," Salazaar explained with a hiss. "He sure reeks of guilt."

Brenda went on her knee, keeping an eye on the demon while it continued to eye the nervous looking Nora. "Are you certain you don't want that fresh air now Nora?"

Nora gave it some good thought but managed to shake her head profusely. "No… I want to be here."

Salazaar spat out and seemed to have laughed hard at her. "This one is strong minded, and I like her even more now."

Brenda ignored them both, getting up to her feet and waving a finger at Alaric who gently rose in the air and travelled across the room before getting pinned against the glass window. Arms spread apart, legs widened and his heart racing wildly while he coughed and gasped for air, Alaric finally dragged himself back into focus.

"Time to wake up," Brenda slapped his cheek gently, prompting him to suck in ample amount of air and gasp upon seeing her face.

Alaric's face whitened, and his lips began to tremble. "It… it… you… you sent a snake after me!"

Salazaar seemed enraged as it slithered angrily over but stopped upon seeing Brenda hold up her hand.

"You call me a snake!?" it fumed.

"Please, I didn't mean to and I can get it back for you if you give me some time," Alaric begged.

Brenda remained still and folded her arms across her chest as she seemed to weigh her options. "We should let someone else decide if I let you live or if you'd become snack to Salazaar."

Salazaar let off a soft hiss. "Yeah… yeah… I get the low delicacy even after doing the biggest job."

Brenda waved at the door, commanding it to open as she ushered in the ebony skinned, slender framed girl with long ebony hair and a school bag slapped on her back into the office. The teenage girl looked around but wore no expression of being confused before halting at the sight of the J'ra'reth demon just a few feet from her.

"Welcome Miss Alexandra," Nora bowed her head respectfully. "It is good to have you join us."

Alex nodded gently but kept her eyes focused on the J'ra'reth demon. "Hello Nora... it is good to see you too, but can you kindly call me Alex like everyone else?"

Nora nodded and stepped aside to grant the girl passage.

"Mom," Alex called out to Brenda. "What is Salazaar doing here?"

"He brought us a rat threatening to crumble our empire," her mother replied with a smile. "I was hoping you could pass the judgment on what happens to our little thief."

Alex sighed and stepped closer to see who the thief was, and her face suddenly fell flat. She recognized the man to be one of their human suppliers.

"Alaric has been loyal for years and you even fought hard to get him out of jail some years ago, didn't you?" Alex took her mother down memory lane.

Brenda shrugged her shoulders and replied, "Which means my debt to him has been paid in full, but here we have him, stealing from me... no, from us."

Alex sighed and nodded her head gently. "Okay mom... but my decision is that you let him go and find other ways to punish him but not by pinning him on the wall while Salazaar salivates about eating him."

Salazaar hissed. "He isn't that much of a prized asset for me to want to salivate over."

"I can hear you," Alaric voiced. "I am human you know and the Oracles... the Oracles that your kinds speak about wouldn't want you harming humans."

Brenda burst into a loud and nauseating laughter before halting immediately.

"The Oracles would definitely have no interest in a low life thieving bastard like you," Brenda said. "Since I promised to allow my dear and compassionate daughter to be the judge to your fate, then I have to comply with what she asks."

Alaric sighed in gratitude and gently began to smile as he felt his arms get freed as well as his legs immediately.

Brenda wrapped her arm around her daughter's neck and began leading her towards the door when she whispered, "Salazaar! Fetch!"

The J'ra'reth demon wasted no time in being obedient, leaping for the man's head and chewing it off immediately. Nora looked away and walked behind her boss while Alex shook her head and sighed in exhaustion.

"You just had to kill him on a technicality, didn't you?" she asked her mother.

Brenda smiled. "You asked that I let him go and not have him pinned on the wall, which was what I did but you never asked for Salazaar not to eat him."

"Can you not act like a lawyer with me right now please?" Alex demanded.

Her mother shook her head and replied, "We are lawyers darling... at least to the world that's what we are and that was what your father wanted us to be, which is why you are going to be a great one once you graduate."

They exited the room and heard nothing but silence coming from inside as they distanced themselves from what was bound to be a messy scene.

"Clean the mess," Brenda ordered.

Nora bowed gently and headed off immediately, while a perplexed looking Alex took a deep stare into her mother's eyes.

"What exactly am I here for?" she asked. "I didn't get anything informative from your message."

"I have an errand for you," her mother responded.

Alex waited impatiently for the elevator doors to slide open as they continued to descend at dangerous speed into the earth and some feet underneath the company. Her mother had never invited her down to the bunker before, so it had to mean something really important is up. Yet, she remained impatient, tapping her finger into the elevator wall and sighing intermittently every chance she got.

"We are here," Brenda voiced before stepping out from the elevator.

Her daughter followed her into what appeared to be an office built inside of the bunker. It was well furnished with state-of-the-art surveillance equipment which she had never seen before. The walls bore paddings to prevent sound from getting out, and the floors shone brilliantly with marble tiles which would be no doubt expensive.

"What is this place?" Alex asked while staring at the big monitors hanging on the walls just a few feet from the single office table and chair in the room.

Brenda circled the table and invited her daughter to have her seat, so they could speak.

"This is the safest place for any of my actions and the one place I can sincerely open up to you without the possibility of being eavesdropped on," Brenda explained. "I have a plan that will…"

Alex shook her head and waved her arms in the air immediately, even before her mother could finish her sentence. "If this is another drug or weapons related dealing, I don't want a part of it. The last shipment operation I oversaw was my last. That filth is beneath me."

Brenda had expected a tough stance from her daughter against any shady deal.

"We have everything we ever need mother," Alex reminded her. "You are a kick ask lawyer to the world and a successful CEO with a hand in over a hundred of companies worldwide."

Brenda soaked in the accolades while she granted her daughter to rain down her moral epiphany as hard as possible.

"Yet, you decide to stand for fraudulent and bad people in court and you always win, isn't it enough to just want to go clean?" Alex concluded. "I mean, I want to be a proud lawyer who fights for the good of the people and not one who simply does it for the riches."

Her mother had about enough and held her hand high to halt her daughter from talking further. She reached into her drawer and took out a remote before pointing it towards the screens behind her daughter causing them all burst to life with images that sprawled across. Alex remained still, staring at her mother before slowly turning around with nothing but a perplexed expression on her face.

"What is this?" she mumbled before stopping in her track. Her eyes widen with disbelief fright and anguish.

The largest screen bore the scariest pictures yet, which were of bloodied human bodies sprawled while creatures called "cleaners," which were quite disgusting beings whose roles were to devour dead bodies, were cleaning up the bodies with a group of armed vampires supervising them.

"Do you have any idea what is going on?" Brenda asked while pointing towards the screen.

Alex felt her heart sink and her throat glued with no response for her mother. Some of the humans weren't entirely dead to have the "Cleaners" clean them up, the vampires ripped their bodies apart with bullets in hopes of making the job easier for the devouring creatures. She stared at their faces and felt herself grow disgusted immediately.

"Those... those are humans," Alex stuttered as she kept pointing in the direction of the deceased bodies.

Her mother simply nodded. "They are human casualties as a result of our own doings in the supernatural world, filled with hunger to overcome each other. Without any legitimate ruling power."

Alex barely heard what her mother had said but she wanted answers as to what exactly was going on and why the vampires were feeding the beasts with human remains that obviously had been battered and left for dead.

"These images and recordings were taken a week ago just south of here, in Beverly," Brenda explained.

Alex turned around immediately with a startled expression. "Beverly!? Isn't that..."

"Gregory Hamilton's turf? Yes darling, it is the area of town belonging to the Hamiltons," her mother answered.

Alex moved closer to the screens and reached for the largest one where the cleaners were consuming the humans whole and without mercy, before drifting to the smaller screens bearing videos of vampires forcefully tying to convert humans.

"You must understand the anatomy on how vampires work, since you've been homeschooled about them and other creatures for years," Brenda stepped closer.

Alex nodded her head with a slight frown. "They are able to successfully mate with their kind to bring forth children or convert humans by biting them and draining them towards the brink of death before letting them live with their venom in their veins until they feed on blood."

Brenda watched on with an impressed look on her face.

"Well, you are correct, but not entirely," her mother noted.

Alex had her gaze on her mother now and didn't plan on looking away. She wanted answers.

"There are some descendants of great vampire bloodlines like the Hamiltons whose venom is too powerful for just any ordinary human to carry within them and so they die," her mother explained. "So, they bite and try to convert as many as possible but with very little success of finding those with the right amount of mental strength to withstand the process."

Alex finally understood why the human carcasses were being discarded. It made her sick to her stomach, but even more disturbing was the fact her family were close friends with the family responsible for such hideous crimes against humanity.

"Why are they trying to turn so many people into vampires?" Alex asked confused. "I mean, don't they have enough pure bloods to continue their legacy without any threats coming their way?"

Brenda simply flipped through the scenes to bring forth an image of a large clinic known to every supernatural being in the country. The large white clinic which embodied equality and peace brought her nostalgic moments as she hurriedly looked away and back at her mother immediately.

"The Hamiltons are smart vampires and very deadly ones with a vicious streak that means they will go at any lengths necessary to get whatever they want," Brenda replied.

"Aren't we just like them, considering how you run things?" Alex shot back.

Brenda shook her head. "They seek to have all the power, and control every creature, which is what owning that clinic would provide them due to something your young mind hasn't comprehended about what it means to own that clinic and the neighborhood zone."

The clinic looked ordinary, asides the fact that supernatural beings couldn't use their abilities when they were inside of it. "The Kings own the clinic, the mayor. Right? Wasn't it passed to his wife?"

"True but the mayor is too busy to run it and the territory is weak, so the clinic is weak. That clinic holds the answers to a lot of questions which the founder took to his grave, but which will become available to whoever comes to possess it," Brenda continued before returning to her desk. "Which is why I need you, darling."

Alex could feel she wasn't about to like whatever requests her mother was going to make. Remaining mute and waving at her mother to get on with it, Alex stared blankly at the woman.

"As you know, Gregory Hamilton controls the vicious cycle of their vampire reign right now and his next of kin is your friend, Marcus Hamilton," Brenda rubbed her hands together slowly. "I want you to bring him to me."

Alex sensed there was more to what her mother had in mind but pushing the woman wasn't going to yield any results. She took another look at the wasted human lives on the monitor screens and could pretty much relate with what it meant to get one's hands pretty dirty in the bid to further a cause but killing humans and discarding them in such manner was just too difficult to stomach.

"Why can't you send Salazaar to get him?" Alex asked without looking back.

Brenda remained silent momentarily before getting up and approaching her daughter. Alex felt her spine trickle with nervousness and her skin crawl as soon as her mother touched her, but it wasn't out of fear but for the fact she just saw another vampire come to the fields with a truck load of dead humans which he offloaded to the "Cleaners" to feed upon.

"I cannot send Salazaar to do this because I don't trust that demon entirely and most importantly because Gregory Hamilton is bad news to mess with and especially not with his family involved," Brenda whispered into her daughter's ears.

"You want to use my friendship with Hamilton to bring down his father," Alex muttered upon figuring out her mother's plan.

Brenda nodded while her daughter slipped out from her reach and began walking back to the elevator. Alex didn't need any more convincing to get the job done; her mother needed her and that was all that mattered.

"I will have him ready to meet with you," Alex promised just before the elevator doors opened and she stepped inside.

Brenda nodded, held her hands behind her back and replied, "I know you will darling. I trust you will."

Alex had no idea where Hamilton was, but she would perform her task regardless. But first, she needed to return to school before any teacher noticed her prolonged absence. She was not an upperclassman and wasn't allowed to be off school grounds without parental written approval.

CHAPTER SIX

Slipping her lips into his, with her eyes closed and her breath slowly being sucked away, Nat giggled excitedly just before pulling away and paused with her eyes fixated on the door.

"What?" Russel asked with a raised brow.

Nat shrugged and replied, "I thought I heard something."

They both waited and listened for the sound again, but nothing came so Russel attempted to continue what they had been doing before they found themselves cut short once again as definite footsteps from more than one person began to trail the hallway. She hurried up to her feet, tucked down her shirt and brushed back her hair in an attempt to look as calm and ordinary as possible, before heading out from the darkroom used by the photography department, and into the hallway.

"Don't come after me," Nat ordered Russel upon looking back at him as he pulled her closer to steal another long kiss.

Nat finally broke loose from him before taking out her lip gloss and applying it on immediately. The footsteps had stopped but she could tell someone, or some people had just walked by, as evident by the sweet scent of vanilla in the air, which she could only guess to be cologne.

"Shit!" she thought to herself, staring at her watch and realizing she was late in submitting an assignment.

She raced down the hall, and past the cafeteria, hoping to use the stairway leading to the Headmaster's office which would make it easier to arrive at her destination sooner. Her legs continued to carry her as fast as they could, but she had gotten into strides too fast and impossible to control when she bumped into someone walking out from a room backwards to her left. "Oh my God! I'm so sorry!" Nat apologized immediately to the girl that had been knocked to the ground.

Olivia appeared in the doorway, frowning and fuming in the face as she neared Nat but stopped on the request of the girl on the floor.

"It was my fault Olivia," the blond-haired girl with rosy pink lips and bright blue eyes said as she stretched her arm out for support from Nat.

Nat reached over to assist her, but Olivia knocked her hand away and chose to assist her friend up instead.

"Stay the hell away from us," Olivia warned.

The blonde-haired girl scolded Olivia immediately, "You don't need to be rude!" She turns her attention back to Nat and stretches out her arm again toward Nat. "I'm Eleanor by the way, but many call me Ella."

Nat stared at the outstretched hand and wondered if she should return the handshake, but Eleanor took her hand into hers and gave it a tight squeeze, doing well to show her strength before bidding the bewildered looking Nat goodbye. Olivia pouted and swore under her breath, but Nat was too taken away by the gorgeous girl she ran into to pay the gruesome one beside her any attention.

Nat felt a hand come to rest on her shoulder, which startled her and sent her shrieking in fright.

"I got you, didn't I?" Russel teased before leaning closer to her and wrapping his arms around her neck.

Breathing heavily and unsure of what response to give him, Nat replied, "Don't do that again please."

Russel nodded, slowly leaned in for another kiss then they walked hand-in-hand, forgetting about the submission she was late for. Walking down the corridor, and just adjacent the cafeteria doors, Nat stopped upon noticing Alex and her group head back up with a shadowy figure donning a rather large hood over their head tailing them.

"Can I catch up with you in a minute?" she asked Russel who looked confused but simply nodded his head.

"Take your time but come back soon as possible or I might have to go home without you," he warned.

It was Friday already, and Nat had managed to forget. They had made plans to head home together and possibly stop at her house first, but she couldn't quite figure out how it would work with her mother. There had only ever been one person to come onto the floor of their house and surprisingly, they felt like strangers and lived in a world far apart currently even while sharing the same space.

"What are you guys up to?" Nat felt curious, sneaking her way up the staircase, looking backwards every chance she got in bid to make sure Russel wasn't following her.

Alex, Olivia and Ella stood before a door, arguing about something she couldn't quite make out, and prompting her to move closer, while crawling along the walls until she saw Ella turn around swiftly and begin to sniff the air. She continued the bizarre act for a few seconds before letting off a thin smile and looking back at her friends.

"I think we have company," Ella whispered to Alex.

Alex remained still, as did Olivia, before the latter shoved her friend out of the way and waved her hand aggressively towards Nat without saying a single word. Nat could tell what was coming for her and in quick flash of action, waved her hand back and dispelled the spell Alex sent her way.

"*Sathia reclusarth Bratheun!*" Alex cried, blinding Nat momentarily and causing her to scream in pain as she fell to her knees and began to breathe heavily.

The spell brought her pain but nothing real harming, while it granted them the opportunity to make their escape.

Nat felt her eyes with both hands and whispered, "*Absencioa!*"

The blindness cleared, and she could see brightly again but they were all gone. Determined to find out what they were up to, she followed the corridor north and ended with a choice between heading to the left wing and the right one. Instinctively, she chose the right wing, marched up the stairs and halted just a few steps in upon hearing the girls bicker angrily about something she couldn't quite figure out.

Saskia seemed the most pissed. "This shit has to stop Hamilton! As much as I hate school, I don't want you messing with how much paper I can make in here! This is my last year to make some real bread here."

Alex remained silent, sighing intermittently and leaning against the wall while the others bickered and complained. They all seemed to be hovering over a large image crouched over and sheltering itself underneath a huge cloak. She recognized the cloak for what it was, which was one that only witches with pure blood could see or use because they were all connected by bloodline one way or another, and such cloaks were made from a witch of pureblood's blood.

"You have to come clean, so we can help you," Olivia mumbled. "I don't even think you are as sick as you're making it seem."

The figure growled, waving its hand underneath the cloak just about enough for Nat to see who was hiding underneath it. She felt her throat clamp shut and her breath almost give her away as she retracted while Olivia looked back and in her direction.

"I... didn't... do it!" Hamilton's weakened voice growled angrily while it he attempted to shove Olivia away from him.

He missed, crashing to the ground and coughing aloud before retching.

Eleanor turned to Alex and asked, "Isn't there anything you can do for him? You're a witch damn it and your mother is someone with knowledge about poisons and stuff."

Alex remained silent. She appeared stymied about what to do as time slowly began to tick against them. Eleanor gave up and flailed her arms in the air before walking to the opposite wall, so she could lean against it while Hamilton continued to suffer in soft growls on the ground.

"That bitch did this!" Olivia fumed. "Wait till I get my hands on her!"

Eleanor smiled to herself, looked in the direction where Nat had been hiding and called on her, "You don't do too well hiding from a werewolf!"

Saskia sniffed hard into the air and looked infuriated for not picking her scent up earlier as she motioned to race over to where Nat was but felt Hamilton's hand around her ankle as he restricted her from doing so.

"Let go of me!" Saskia demanded, kicking her foot out from his grasp and races toward Nat immediately.

She was fast, but Eleanor had no problem being faster than her, as she held the temperamental werecat by her neck and shoved her into the wall. "Easy now and think about whatever you want to do before you do it."

Struggling under Eleanor's grip, Saskia demanded to be set free. "That dork did this to him! He's dying!"

"I'm sorry but I can't let you go till you calm down," Eleanor declined.

Alex looked in Nat's direction, and remained motionless with her leg still against the wall for support while Olivia seemed to be itching to be permitted the opportunity to carry out whatever she wanted to do.

"Let me have her Alex... let me make her talk!" Olivia spoke impatiently.

Saskia grew infuriated and slowly began to transform. Her hands grew furry with black stripped marking no different from that of a tiger, before her face bore fangs and whiskers which elongated from the loser base of her nose.

"Let me go!" she raged, shoving Eleanor into the wall and causing the wall to crack, before gaining temporary freedom as Eleanor's grip loosened around her neck.

Terrified and stricken with wobbly knees, Nat slowly emerged from her hiding place, hand in her waist purse and her legs wide apart as she took the best stance possible for a defense. She wasn't sure if any staff members heard the crash but hoped that at least a teacher in this massive school was close by. Saskia, with deep glowing eyes, purred with a wicked grin as she neared.

"I can smell that shit better now and my guard isn't going to be that easy to break through," she boasted, with her heightened sense granting her the edge into perceiving the contents in Nat's backpack.

Nat steadied her breathing and tried to tell herself she had things under control. Her rapidly beating heart thought otherwise while her chances of outrunning a beast like Saskia were sure to prove her stupid rather than brave. She had to fight, or at least put up one and that was what she planned on doing.

Saskia stretched her limbs and readied herself to attack, before feeling the large hand grab her by the neck from behind and shove her into the wall on the left.

"Leave the witch alone!" Ella growled before grabbing Saskia by her neck and ramming her into the wall again.

Saskia growled and spat in anger, rolling to her side deciding to take a stand against the werewolf. Olivia seemed more concerned about Nat trying to make an escape than about the two who were undoubtedly going to make a mess of things while Hamilton continued to suffer where he crouched on the floor.

Olivia zoomed past the fighting duo who seemed intent on establishing their dominance, while Eleanor had the upper hand already, and ran towards Nat but stopped in her tracks upon seeing someone walk up the stairs and stop just behind Nat.

"I've got your back girl," Sheila whispered, forcing Nat to look around in shock.

Startled by her sight and how she had returned to school without her knowing, Nat's eyes widened, before she watched Sheila deal with the incoming girl who had hoped to play a fast one.

"*Florialis Ascendio!*" Sheila cried with her hand pointed at the floor upon which Olivia stood.

The floor suddenly began to crack and cave in, permitting floral plants to grow aggressively around the girl before wrapping twines of thick vines around her to subdue her, before lifting her high into the air and shoving her against the ceiling. Nat watched in amazement and smiled at Sheila who returned the gesture with a warm smile of her own.

Alex had had enough and yelled, "Enough... all of you!"

Eleanor's knee had been lodged into Saskia's neck, forcing her to struggle for freedom while the werewolf seemed to be having fun with the werecat. Sheila refused to let Olivia down just yet and watched Alex keenly in case the girl tried to play a smart one on her.

Alex approached Nat instead. "You brewed your essence into the wolf's venom, didn't you?"

Sheila looked at Nat and bore a frown immediately, but it slowly turned into smile of admiration.

"How were you able to do that? Cultivating one's essence into potions is dangerous and very difficult," Sheila noted.

Nat nodded. "I've seen my father do it a million times and it makes it easier when you have a vendetta against a blood sucking vampire with no conscience! I also added some other things to make it."

Seemingly intrigued by Nat's prowess with potions, Eleanor slowly retreated her knee from Saskia's throat, granting the werecat the opportunity to get free but also her chance to strike.

"You dog!" Saskia fumed, raising her extended claws in her right hand then motioned to swing down hard.

Alex turned back around and waved her hand in Saskia's direction, making a perfect copy of the same spell Sheila had performed to subdue Olivia but without having to voice the spell.

Obviously impressed, Sheila nodded her head and whispered, "It is as expected of an Aurelius witch."

Nat had heard of it but never seen it before; the ability to copy a spell simply by watching one do it. It often times might not be perfect, but it would come close to the real deal and it was exactly what Alex had managed to do without blinking.

"Are you going to help him, or will you let him die?" Alex asked.

Nat felt torn on what to do but showed no weakness. She felt he had gotten exactly what he deserved, seeing he had tormented her and probably still would have had she not injected him.

"What if I don't?" Nat asked with a raised brow before confidently brushing her hair behind her ear and smiling.

Sheila could sense the air between the two wasn't the friendliest or at least not at that moment, so she slowly stepped backwards.

Alex drew closer to Nat and whispered, "We aren't kids anymore and I am warning you to fix this now so we can all go our separate ways before we all get in trouble."

Nat stepped aside, looked over to where Hamilton was wincing in pain before shaking her head and looking at Alex. "He deserves everything that comes to him."

Perplexed and waving her hands in the air in confusion as to what Nat was talking about, Alex asked, "Deserves what exactly?"

The air between the two steamed fast and Sheila caught the cue to let Olivia down and possibly make her escape. Olivia seemed more grateful than angry upon being released, while the same happened to Saskia who growled and shot Eleanor a rather criticizing gaze.

"For all we know, he could be the one going around attacking people! He could have killed Amos!" Nat shot back at Alex and stood in her face.

Alex could not believe her ears and she turned around briefly. "You haven't changed a bit! You are still the same after all these years, acting like you're the saint while every other person is associated with the devil or that they are pure evil."

Olivia looked bewildered before mumbling at Ella, "They know each other?"

It didn't make sense to her because Alex had never mentioned anything remotely close about any relationship with her or even about them knowing each other before then.

Alex stepped backwards and held out her hand towards Nat, swearing underneath her breath, "If you don't cure him right now, I swear to God…"

Nat readied herself as well, tossing some of her long curls out of her face, then taking her stance. "I will not lose this time!"

An unlikely frame of Saskia raced and stood between them both. "He is dying!"

Her words prompted everyone to look in Hamilton's direction, before they turned around to cast Nat a rather judgmental look. Nat bowed under the castigating pressure that came from the looks and decided to cure him of the poison coursing through his veins.

"Give him some breathing space," Alex demanded of the rest immediately.

Nat knelt by his side, held onto his hand and closed her eyes.

Hamilton's veins became visible from underneath his skin as her potion began dripping from his mouth and nose while Nat continued to hold him tightly.

"Is she purifying him?" Eleanor seemed rather flabbergasted by what she was seeing. "Damn! She's practically carrying out a blood transfusion."

Nat cringed and closed her eyes while the process lasted for a minute. She yanked her arm free and watched Hamilton purge himself of all that disturbed him as he retched and coughed endlessly. Sheila helped Nat up and they both began stepping away from the gang who were even more dangerous with Hamilton now gaining his health back.

"I still don't believe he has nothing to do with Amos Leon's murder," Nat remained astute in her belief, causing Alex to shake her head in dismay and sigh.

Holding her hand up and pointing in the direction of the stairs, Alex commanded the duo, "Looks like you've paid your debt and your presence here isn't going to help anyone anymore."

Sheila nudged at Nat to come with her and they both hurried away immediately, with the latter feeling grateful to have left without further complications.

Upon getting to the bottom of the staircase, Nat stopped and caught her breath. "Thank you… thank you for showing up."

Sheila smiled and patted her on the back immediately. "You and I are linked now… I can read your mind until you learn to block me out."

Nat chuckled, feeling glad about her inability to master the art just yet.

"It is a good thing I'm still lousy at it, yeah?" she chuckled, before she wrapped her arm around the Salem witch's neck and walked away.

CHAPTER SEVEN

Marcus Hamilton knelt and sucked in the disturbing and vile air in his most hated room in the entirety of his father's mansion but knew better than to utter a word out of place. His eyes swept around cautiously, watching out for any sudden movements through the shadows as he wondered why he had been summoned and not only that, but dragged down from school by his father's henchmen.

The golden throne, bearing a lion's head as its arm rest on either side was said to be the first ever fortune their ancestor, "Hamilton The Great" ever possessed, from forcing two Salem witches whom he had captured for fun to forge it for him. Tale will further have it that the mad vampire fed on the witches' blood until their passing, which made him a cursed being bound to pass his madness unto his descendants.

For Marcus Hamilton, the tale was nothing but a tale and while he hated the room he was currently kneeling in, he despised the throne even more because he wasn't sitting on it. Gregory Hamilton walked into the room, clapping his hands together immediately and commanding the drapes shielding the sun-protected windows to slowly part.

"Marcus!" the ageless vampire smiled oddly and settled himself atop his throne with the smile soon vanishing.

Marcus Hamilton kept his face to the ground, knowing it wasn't time to speak until he was demanded to. The act itself only made him furious but the rules were clear and had to be followed.

"You may rise to your feet, boy!" Gregory Hamilton commanded.

Marcus Hamilton did as he was told, slowly standing up but still refusing to look into the deep red-colored eyes of his father.

Gregory continued regardless. "While I was away sorting some business involving some of our enemies, I learnt some pretty disturbing and demeaning news of the events that took place in my absence."

Holding his breath and almost bursting with the urge to cry out and explain his bit of all that had happened, he refrained and swallowed every word, with his hands firmly behind his back.

Gregory continued, "Firstly, I need to show you something."

Marcus watched his father wave at the guards by the door as they ushered in three vampires well-known by Marcus for being his personally assigned guards and protectors.

"What do you say we punish these men for their incompetence?" his father asked with a cynical chuckle.

Marcus remained silent, trying to force out the words he best felt suitable but felt too frightened to do so.

"You are well aware of their sins, aren't you?" Gregory asked his son. "You should be aware, because from what I hear, the entire communities of supernatural beings are aware that my son, my bloodline, and a descendant of the great Hamilton bloodline was defeated by an underage witch."

Marcus replied immediately, "That is far from the truth father!"

The words had aired before he realized it and his stomach walls shrunk immediately while he lowered his head. Gregory looked calm and without an expression, while the terrified vampire guards by his side bore expressions of fear and shock.

"Good for you, son!" Gregory clapped sarcastically. "You can at least stand up to your father! Good for you!"

Marcus motioned to speak but barely parted his lips when a swift moving hand blinded him in outrageous speed and hit into his left jaw, sending him crashing hard into the ground, while it barely looked as if his father had moved from the spot he was in. The only telling fact to his movement was his robe that swung to the dance of the breeze at the edges.

"What was I saying?" he asked and raised his finger. "Ah! Yes, an underage witch from the King coven made a fool of my son."

Bowing his head, Arvelous, the larger of the guards apologized, "We are truly sorry... we weren't sure about following him into the party and that was where it happened."

Marcus coughed and spat out some blood, feeling his orientation and balance continue to fail him as he struggled to get to his feet after three different unsuccessful attempts. Staying down long as he did wasn't something his father was going to tolerate, had he remained there any longer. It was all about dignity and pride for the vampire and Marcus had done just about enough damage to the family name more than once.

"Father," Marcus voiced, unsure of what he had to say, but finding it to be another grave mistake as another blow to his jaw sent him back into the position he had just gotten up from.

Gregory's eyes were full blown red now and claws slowly began to slither out from the slender and aged hands while he sneered and smiled at the guards meant to watch over his son. Arvelous would get dealt with first, because he had spoken without being asked to. He turned around and attempted to make a run for it, but got his right hand chopped off within seconds, then his head came rolling just before his remaining body took a few more steps and came crashing onto the ground.

Wiping his hands clean of blood and tossing the handkerchief away, Gregory walked to the other silent two and held them both by their necks. "You two deserve better deaths and I forgive you."

He snapped his fingers and motioned for Marcus to follow him immediately. Getting to his feet and whimpering in pain, Marcus looked back at the vampires who were now placed before the large windows and stripped of their daylight rings. The automated windows slowly opened, ushering in the golden rays from the beautiful sunlight as it showered its punishment on them.

Screaming in agony while their skins melted away into crisp, and their bones slowly burned into ash, Marcus looked away in pain and winced to keep up with his father. He had just witnessed another execution of their own kind and had he not been the vampire's son, there was every likelihood he would be nothing but charred bone residue like those he had left behind.

"That will be the last time you will make a mockery of the family name ever again!" Gregory warned.

Marcus began to heal as they walked through the large stone door leading underneath their family crypt. Chilling air struck the back of his neck as the growling noise from countless freshly converted vampires locked away in cages filled the air louder the farther they went.

"Oh my God!" Marcus thought to himself.

His father turned around with a raised brow while he stood akimbo. "God cannot help you here son and he sure as hell cannot help us with what the wind is blowing our way."

The crypt, normally empty and large enough to take in up to two hundred vampires was now crowded and filled with cages.

"What do you think son?" Gregory asked proudly.

Marcus remained silent and continued to stare at the newbies, wondering what sort of carnage they were bound to unleash the moment they would be set free for the purpose they were being groomed.

"How is getting close to the Aurelius girl coming along?" Gregory asked.

Marcus finally answered, "As good as it should… I have done as you asked of me."

Gregory smiled and grabbed his son by his shoulder, pulling him closer as they walked towards the inner office where the brain work to their plans were being laid afoot.

"You understand that your role remains the most important aspect to this project, don't you?" Gregory asked his son.

Marcus nodded and sighed. "I will have her in my palms when the time comes."

Gregory nodded and walked over to his planning board and began pouring over what their next move would be. Marcus drew closer to his father.

"Is the Aurelius girl in on our plans yet?" the bold, feminine tone, walking down the staircase just east of where Marcus stood asked.

Marcus's spine felt stiff and his breath heightened, as he cowered in fear just by hearing the woman's voice; the only one who could match and surpass his father in his brutality slowly walked into the room without saying anything else. She walked past him and headed towards the board while they both stared at it in a lengthy manner.

They stood in silence for the next few minutes, seemingly waiting for something but Marcus had no idea what they were doing. They had been gone for months and told him nothing of their plans in entirety just yet.

Gregory looked to his wife and smiled. "Alexia! Were you able to persuade the others?"

Alexia smiled, planted a kiss on her husband's lips and held her cellphone to her ear. "Bring them all in."

Large vampire guards in hoods marched in the numbers of fifteen, one after the other, before lining them up before Gregory and stepping away immediately.

"Shut the doors and leave us," Alexia commanded the guards before turning her attention back to her husband and son.

Marcus remained stiff and nervous as he watched his mother begin to take the hoods off the faces of vampires who he recognized to belong to the ten major groups around the city. The powerful males clearly looked enraged by the act of sacrilege and desecration on their code of conduct and they dd well not to hide their outrage.

Kovac, the two hundred year old vampire with a taste for rage and madness spat at Alexia immediately, "I will drink from your skulls when I get free from these shackles! You hear me! I will drink from your skulls!"

Gregory looked driven by anger, prompting him to veer towards the vampire who had just insulted his wife, but Alexia stopped her husband and demanded that he shouldn't fight for her.

"I will deal with him my own way and in my own time," she promised.

Gregory looked impossible to keep calm and Alexander had seen it time and time again for sure. It was the devil in him who was about to rear its head and Kovac had just overstepped his bound.

"This is against our code," the vampire to Kovac's left said. "You do not kill a member of the council!"

Alexia shook her head, smiled and stood before the vampire as she whispered, "The council has been dead for years... living off past glory and allowing themselves to be ruled by insipid rules whereas we belong at the top as kings."

Kovas chuckled derisively, causing Gregory to become even more unsettled and angry. Marcus watched his father ache to have his way and deal what was required of him as punishment to Kovac, but Alexia remained in his way.

Alexia looked over to Marcus, waved over at her son and brought him face-to-face with Kovac.

"Your fucking wimp has no balls… he got beat by a fucking teenage witch who barely knows her way around the first basic pages of a grimoire!" Kovac continued to urge the need for his own death.

Causing the other vampires to laugh in mockery, Kovac continued to slate the Hamiltons, until he felt his larynx get yanked from his throat, and Marcus Hamilton being the last image he saw before dropping to the ground face flat and bleeding all over the ground.

Marcus turned to his parents and smirked, "He was talking too much."

The message from the Hamiltons was clear as day and the other vampires on the council needed no handbook to understand why they were there. A war was brewing, and they had no choice or say in what would happen in it.

"Anyone else want to spit?" Gregory asked proudly.

Wondering if he had indeed redeemed himself in some way even if it wasn't possible to do that entirely when it had to do with his father, Marcus tailed his parents towards their upper section of the crypt where a makeshift office was, before he was asked to take his seat around the oval shaped table. Gregory sat to his wife's left and they both stared at their son with nothing but mystery in their eyes.

"Do you understand the level of mayhem which is upon us, son?" Gregory asked with his hands on the table.

Alexia remained silent but sighed out loud and slowly rested her back into the chair.

"Vampires all around the world are waning as we speak and it's because there are just too many rules preventing us from being able to live as we are made to," he continued.

Marcus stared at his father and replied, "I thought the treaty was good? Isn't that what keeps the mighty trio of vampires, witches and werewolves in check?"

Alexia burst into an irritating laughter immediately. She saw her son's words as idiotic and wasn't merciful enough not to show him. She bobbed her head gently and wiped a tear drop from the corner of her eye.

"You silly boy," she muttered. "There has never been a treaty, or at least not a real binding one, asides a lame piece of oak signed by our ancestors which is now in that God forsaken clinic."

"Oak?" Marcus asked without realizing it.

His father nodded and sat up slowly. "With it gone and the clinic in our hands, we are bound to make exploits in this world without the possibility of being stopped no matter the cause of events."

Marcus still didn't truly understand what they needed of him. He could sense something coming but all they had done was to lay the groundwork.

"How is your relationship with the Aurelius girl?" his mother asked.

Marcus shrugged and sighed with his hands tucked inside one another. "It's great I guess but we just roll together sometimes and nothing else."

Gregory nodded and smiled. "Her mother just might be the biggest obstacle for me in this war and I need you to be their downfall."

Marcus pointed at himself and raised his brow, as though he couldn't understand what he needed.

Alexia clarified it to her son immediately without holding anything back. "When the time comes son, we will need you to kill that girl... it is the only way to have the upper hand in this fight."

Marcus felt his heart shift from its normal position. His legs stiffened underneath the table and his breath suddenly slowed down as if he was terrified to show them, he wasn't entirely sure about the plan to kill someone close to him. He figured she wasn't part of his clique but even at that, Alex was no ordinary girl and he had seen her do things to those who tried to tyrannize her which was good enough to make his skin crawl.

"She's an Aurelius witch," Marcus whispered as though he was scared to say it out loud.

Gregory let out a damning chuckle then halted abruptly. "We are Hamiltons, descendant of the first order of vampires and the rightful heirs to the throne of supremacy on this earth."

Alexia smiled at her son. "You should be more worried about what would happen to them because we are Hamiltons, than whatever coven their bloodline hails from."

Marcus could see there would be no negotiations on the subject matter. His parents had thought it all out and when their hearts were set on things, there was no going back.

"What about the other vampire council members? What is their role in all of this?" he sought to know.

His mother shook her head and answered, "Time will reveal all of that soon, but first, you must carry out your part for our success hinges on it."

Marcus nodded and agreed. There would be no debating it or even the choice of having one. He slowly got to his feet, bowed his head gently and laid his hands on the table and pledged his unwavering allegiance to the cause.

Gregory looked most pleased and waved towards the door where a pair of twins came walking in with grins on their faces and a rather cold feel to it that always unsettled anyone meeting them for the first time.

"You remember Krul and Kun?" Gregory pointed towards the door.

Marcus's eyes widened upon seeing the twins and his lower jaw dropped heavily too.

"How can I not remember them?" he thought to himself.

The twins often called the "Demon Duo" for their sheer evil and ability to topple peace anywhere they went had not been seen in years since Marcus had joined them in the bloodbath of ten werewolf teens who had crossed their paths. The issue almost resulted in an all-out war had Gregory decided to not kill the werewolves' parents as well and hide all the evidence.

Krul bearing a thin scar running along the left side of his face stepped forward with the bizarre smile he couldn't rid himself of, "Hello Marcus … you haven't aged a bit."

Kun chuckled and laid his hand to rest on his twin's shoulder. "Have you heard the great news Marcus?"

Marcus turned to his parents and asked, "What news are they talking about?"

His heart felt numb and his veins pumped with nothing but absolute worry about what was about to brew. Alexia smiled and slowly got to her feet before rounding the table to stand behind her son. "They are your new school mates… it wasn't easy, but we pulled some major strings to have them join you at Virtus Academy."

Marcus felt his evil side slowly part his lips with a smile as the duo approached to hug him warmly. Virtus Academy wasn't in any way prepared for what was about to hit it, and the Hamiltons knew too well. After all, Gregory Hamilton had created the duo himself in the most disturbing of manners inhumanely possible.

CHAPTER EIGHT

The day has arrived. "The Pairing" as it was being called in Virtus academy, was the most nerve wrecking event the second years found themselves bothered with after a few weeks in school. Nat had heard all about it from Russel, who claimed he felt the universe was trying to torture him when the listings came through. Those with connections and deep pockets were also said to have the higher chances of keeping their friends and families together during the selection process.

Nat tapped her feet into the ground nervously, trying as hard as possible not to show just how riled up her emotions were on the inside. It's been weeks now since her encounter with Hamilton and Alex, and things had gone rather smoothly, which was what scared her the most; the calm before the storm.

Sheila held onto Nat's hand and helped her get back into focus immediately. "It's going to be fine. We will know the results in about thirty minutes."

The class was silent, which indicated that everyone had their minds set on finding out who exactly their pairing mates would be and how their lives for the next year might come to be.

"Who proposed the stupid system anyway?" Nat fumed and fell back into her chair. "I mean, isn't the idea of forcing four kids to become this unit in school the lamest idea ever?"

Sheila didn't seem entirely perturbed, and in fact, she laughed out loud which only made Nat more upset.

"I'm sorry... I just couldn't help myself," Sheila apologized. "The Pairing isn't to force people to be together but to help each individual in the unit find ways to channel their own strengths and better their weaknesses."

Sheila looked away and smiled at herself as though she knew something, she just wasn't telling Nat.

Nat caught on and asked, "What is it?"

"I know the outcome already but I'm sure as hell not telling you anything," she teased. "This should be so much fun."

Nat frowned and stared at the clock on the wall, in front of the class, as it ticked away and continued to make the day feel longer than it was. She looked to her left, where a dull looking Alex seemed rattled by something, while Olivia continued to bicker into her ears.

"Can this day just end?" Nat mumbled.

The closing bell rang aloud almost immediately, prompting the students to race out of the class and head to the board where the list would be posted. The level of excitement in each and every student slowly began to wane when they each caught sight of who they had been paired with for the semester and how largely different some of them were.

"The Pairing is how many legendary supernatural bonds have been formed for ages," Sheila explained. "It is even rumored to be how the Oracles came to be… a group of kids who complemented one another so well in abilities right from their school days that they grew in knowledge, strength and even understanding."

The story was well told, and Nat had heard it before. The oracles, a group consisting of four different bloodlines and supernatural beings, but with a mind that worked as one. They were said to be extremely compatible in such a way their powers knew no limits and their sense of justice just wasn't a joke, but even at that, nobody knew anything else about them other than they existed from a very young age and fought countless battles to bring order to the world.

Sheila clapped her hands excitedly as a group of disgruntled looking kids walked past.

"I got paired with Sean and Vecker the Bailings," one boy mumbled in displeasure.

Alex stood before the board and smiled, before turning back around with Olivia and Eleanor behind her with a new face who Sheila nor Nat had seen with her before.

"This just blows," a girl sighed. "I guess having all the money in the world ensures you get the best of what you want."

Nat didn't really understand what was going on but soon saw it for herself. "Olivia, Alex and Ella are in the same pairing?"

Sheila shrugged and seemed not to expect something else. "Her mother owns half the city and can arguably be called one of the richest women on the planet, so you do the math."

Nat fumed and began scrolling through the list with her finger. She paused upon seeing her pairing sect with Sheila enlisted in it and bringing her a sigh in relief, before the names Leslie Bennett and Arnold Bill."

"Who are they?" Nat turned to Sheila with a frown before she saw a redhead girl with her hands behind her back staring at them just a few feet away with a smile.

Nat was sure she had seen the girl before and not just in their classroom but found it hard to figure out.

"I'm sorry but who are you?" Nat asked politely with a raised brow.

The girl stepped closer, reeking of eucalyptus and donning glasses that helped usher out the blue color of her eyes. "My name is Leslie Bennett and I believe I'm the third member of this Pairing."

Nat continued to stare into her eyes, but suddenly drew backwards upon noticing a spark or two in the deep blue eyes behind the glasses.

"I'm sorry," the girl apologized, taking off her glasses and closing her eyes briefly before opening them again. "I wasn't aware I had them on."

Sheila gasped in excitement and drew closer. "Oh, my fucking... please don't tell me you are..."

She paused and turned to look at the bewildered looking Nat who just didn't seem to know what the girl was or what exactly was going on. She wasn't sure about whatever was getting Sheila excited.

"She's a phoenix... we got a phoenix!" Sheila cried aloud and continued to clap her hands wildly.

Nat suddenly gasped and felt her eyes widen. "That's impossible!"

Leslie snickered and smiled. "Yeah, I get that a lot, but your friend here is right... I am a phoenix and my bloodline might be one of the remaining few."

Nat was impressed and couldn't hide just how she felt. Phoenixes were rare to ever come across and they held unimaginable abilities that made them either loved or easily feared equally by every supernatural creature. How she wasn't known already throughout the school is a mystery.

"What did you do to your eyes?" Nat pointed out the fact the blueness had disappeared from within it an turned an emerald green.

"I can switch eye color and it doesn't really matter," Leslie replied. "I know you two are witches but who or what is our fourth pairing?"

The name wasn't a familiar one and they stood there staring at the name like it would burst forth to life and give them answers.

"How do you know us by the way?" Sheila inquired before looking at Leslie.

Leslie smiled and whispered, "There is the view that Nat here has trouble following her around and after the mind stunt you two played in the classroom the first day, it wasn't hard at all."

Nat smiled and nodded at Sheila. "Well, we are in this together now."

They all agreed with a nod and shook hands warmly.

"I wonder where our fourth member is," Nat looked around and continued to take note of the listing as she searched for Saskia but found no pairing for her.

"How come Saskia isn't on the list?" Nat asked.

Leslie replied immediately, "Werecats don't get along with anyone... it is in their nature and they, and a few other supernatural creatures are exempted from the pairing."

Nat wondered why, and Sheila replied, "Their temper is often times uncontrollable and even worse than that of werewolves."

Nat stared at her friend and shook her head.

"You really need to stop reading my thoughts," Nat mumbled.

Sheila had motioned to speak when they heard a rather loud cry coming from the end of the end of the hall.

Olivia was in rage. She lifted a boy into the air and smiled as she tossed him hard into the ground.

"Do it!" she roared.

The bald head kid simply groaned and rolled on the ground but made no attempt to obey her command. He slowly got to his feet, smiled and shook his head.

"I will not be intimidated by the likes of you," he whispered, rather shyly but just about enough for Olivia to pick up on it.

Alex standing off to the side sighed and shook her head before intervening, "We need to go home Olivia, so let him go."

Olivia shot her a damning look, looked back and hurried towards the boy before lifting him by his shirt and watched him as he continued to smile.

"I will wipe that smug look off your face if you don't show me what I want to see!" she threatened.

Alex seemed tired of the situation and bowed her head in annoyance. She looked to Eleanor whose odd sense of humor meant she somewhat enjoyed watching Olivia bullying the poor looking kid.

"Really?" Alex asked, rubbing her temple as the feeling of migraine slowly began to set in.

Shrugging her shoulders, Eleanor replied, "I'm not getting into any issue with her right now seeing she's only taking out her anger on that poor kid because you wouldn't answer her questions."

Alex had tried to avoid it as best as possible, but the longer time passed, the more persistent Olivia was about knowing. She had never told anyone, and she didn't hope on doing so anytime soon. She motioned towards Olivia to let the boy go but he wasn't doing himself any favors by continuously chuckling and getting her more riled up. Not to mention there were onlookers to give Olivia an audience.

"You vampires are so despicable… always thinking you are better than anyone and should be feared," he mumbled. "We Aradias don't fear any creature… we existed long before you and before time became a concept!"

"This guy has some serious balls, I'll give him that," Alex thought to herself.

Unfortunately, Olivia wasn't in the mood, and the vampire pinned him into the wall with her left hand, while raising her right as she slowly began to bear her claws. Smiling oddly at him with the feeling of satisfaction smeared on her face even while she had not carried out her action, Olivia sniffed hard and sucked in enough air to help her heave out a loud sigh.

"I am so going to enjoy this," she whispered, before planting her lips on the boy's, and blinding his sight momentarily before piercing his chest hard and fast.

His loud growl travelled through the corridors, before the silence as his head dropped and his eyes slowly closed.

Olivia let go of the boy and chuckled, "Aren't you the pathetic kind? All talk and no show."

"You bastard!" the unfamiliar voice came from behind Alex and her crew, but Eleanor didn't seem entirely shocked as she smiled tenderly.

Eleanor turned around and waved at Nat, "I knew that lovely scent was nearby."

Olivia felt enraged that she had not caught their scent, having been distracted by the boy before her. "Well... well... well... if it isn't the new pathetic pairing which by the way seems to be incomplete."

Nat looked towards the boy on the ground and bore a frown. "How am I not surprised to find this group right in the middle of chaos?"

Alex tightened her fist but remained silent, catching Nat's eyes as they stared at one another.

Leslie stepped in between Nat and Alex's line of sight, pointing at Olivia and warning, "Let the boy go!"

Olivia purred, smiling cockily and replied, "I see you might have some spunk in you, unfortunately I don't deal with halfwits. I will let you go this once."

Sheila seemed to smile but none of them saw it, right before she stepped to the side and held out her hand to point it towards the wall opposite of where she stood.

"What are you doing?" Nat seemed confused upon seeing her friend pointing at an empty wall.

Sheila placed a finger to her lips and asked Nat to remain silent. "I need you to trust me."

Olivia bent over the boy she had just impaled and rolled him over to reveal blue colored blood dripping from his chest. The sight of the injured boy angered

Leslie, who rushed over but barely made it close enough as Olivia grabbed her by the throat and shoved her into the opposite wall where she pinned her.

"Alex! Tell her to back off!" Nat ordered.

Alex remained silent, and slowly began to walk away. Nat tightened her fist, slipped her hand into her purse and waited for Alex to stop walking.

"Petty tricks won't help you against me," Alex boasted.

Barely giving Nat the time to think, Alex looked around, lifted a trash bin into the air and shot it right over at Nat with a wave of her hand. Nat waved it away confidently but barely missed Leslie where she remained pinned by her throat to the wall by Olivia.

Olivia stared into the eyes of her captive and then looked at Alex, "What is it going to be Alex? Are you going to tell me, or should I take out pretty girl's eyes?"

Alex fumed and responded, "Stop fooling around and let her go!"

Nat stepped closer, taking out a rather tiny band from her purse and holding it on her palm before casting it into the air and commanding it to fly at maddening speed towards Alex just before she could cast another spell. The band hurriedly wrapped itself around Alex and sent her falling into the ground in a rather loud heap.

"Your parlor tricks blow," Alex mocked while wiggling to get out of the band which slowly tightened around her entire body as it grew in length.

"Tell your minion to let her go or you'll likely suffocate from that binding," Nat warned. "The more you struggle, the more it tightens, so let my friend go!"

Tensions grew but Sheila seemed otherwise comfortable with pointing her hand and holding still in the direction of an empty wall. It baffled Nat but she had Alex to contend with, while Leslie seemed incapable or rather content with not struggling with Olivia.

"I am not an easy prey for you to mess with!" Leslie growled, sounding bolder as if she had ten more people speaking from inside of her.

Olivia raised her right brow, seeming to undermine what the girl had said, before watching Leslie's skin begin to sizzle and get hotter with each passing second. Leslie lifted her hand and tightened it around Olivia's neck, prompting Nat to watch in bewilderment as the girl she was fighting to save finally decided to take charge.

Her body began to glow and scorch, prompting Olivia to hurriedly take her hand off her throat. Leslie was free, but Olivia could barely move as she felt the hand around her throat slowly begin to heat up and cause her serious burns.

"Let go!" she cried. "Let go of me you freak!"

Leslie shoved the vampire away, watching her cry in distress as her body struggled to heal the scarred and burning flesh around her neck.

"You're a phoenix," Eleanor sounded rather pleased with their opponent than sympathetic.

She began to walk closer in bid to study Leslie closely but stopped when the wall behind her seemed to move and Sheila suddenly got agitated.

"Finally!" Sheila smiled and waved her hand in bid to capture whatever had snuck out from the wall but failed.

Whatever it was, it was damn fast, and it raced to assist Alex in getting lose from her binds as it cut through it with ease, before heading for Nat and shoving her backwards. Nat managed to remain on her feet. She felt someone had struck her but whoever it was remained unseen.

"Shit!" she mumbled. "He is a Succubus!"

Nat finally understood why Sheila had been staring at the wall the entire time. The creature had blended itself in and with their ability to remain hidden while also bearing exceptional speed, he was trouble for them without doubt.

Readying herself to confront it, Nat yelled, "Where is it!? Where is it?"

"Behind you," the cold, yet somewhat childish voice replied.

Nat turned around to see Sheila looking frightened with a knife bearing rune marking placed to her throat.

"This blade sucks on magic to work, which means she'll make the perfect prey if she attempts to use her magic in the slightest," the dark sandy haired boy with rather large brows smiled.

Leslie approached but Nat halted her in her tracks and asked her to stop. "Succubus's are dangerous creatures with vile magic."

Alex clapped her hands theatrically before going over to help Olivia to her feet. "I wish I could stay longer for this thrilling episode, but I have to go now."

Nat motioned to move but the strange boy only smiled while the blade pushed closer towards Sheila's neck as though it had a mind of its own. She knew better than to make any sudden move as Alex and her friends make their escape immediately. The rest of the kids cleared out as footsteps came in their direction.

"I really hope we get to meet again," the succubus leaned closely towards Sheila, and planted a kiss on her neck.

Within seconds, he was gone, faster than the wind itself leaving the three girls trying to figure out what exactly had just happened. The boy on the floor slowly groaned and drew their attention, prompting Sheila to race over to where he was. She slowly flipped him over.

"Don't touch him," Nat warned immediately, recognizing just what he was.

Sheila let go immediately and watched the bleeding spots where Olivia had rammed her claws into him begin to sizzle hot and heal back as new.

He opened his eyes, stared up at them and smiled, "Hello Nat, Sheila, and Leslie."

Leslie found herself asking with a puzzled look, "Who is he and what exactly is going on? I have never seen this boy before, so how does he know our names?"

The boy got to his feet, reached his hand into his pocket and slowly slapped on a pair of gloves.

"The name's Arnold Bill," he smiled and reached out his hand to meet with Leslie's.

Nat approached him carefully and exchanged a handshake while making certain that she could see his gloved hand.

"You're a…" she paused.

He interjected immediately with a rather odd smile and responded. "Don't call me a seer… I can only assume the future depending on a host of multiple possible occurrences."

"Shit!" Leslie murmured. "Then why didn't you avoid getting hurt? We heard you scream and came right away."

Arnold motioned to explain but Nat cut him short immediately. "It was precisely so we would come that he let her grab him… their kind never do anything without a reason."

Arnold seemed impressed by Nat and bobbed his head. "You are an observant witch and I'd expect nothing less from the house of King."

Sheila looked gloomy and sighed. She wasn't pleased with almost being nicked by one of Alex's friends. "You realize I almost died because we came to save you, right?"

Arnold looked stricken with lack of understanding on how to respond to the question. "I chose the best possible action that wouldn't lead to either of you getting harmed."

Leslie smiled as did Nat before both girls headed over to meet Sheila.

Nat leaned closer to her friend and whispered, "They aren't really known for their empathy... they don't see world in the same manner as we view it, so you'd have to go easy on him dear."

They turned around and began walking away immediately, but not before Sheila mumbled, "A vegetable would have apologized to say the least."

Arnold looked at her, shot her a smile and tucked his hands back into his pocket. He was dangerously handsome and that bothered as well as thrilled her.

"We are going to be just fine," Nat smiled.

She didn't doubt it in any way.

"Just fine in detention."

They all turned around and frowned seeing Mr. Gideon and Mrs. Quint shocked and angry faces. "What happened here?" No one made motion to answer. Nat was pissed Alex and her friends got away and now they were stuck. After some eyewitness snitched, Alex and Olivia were in detention with them at the end of the day and were both given two more days of detention for starting the fight. Nat seriously feared for the safety of whomever snitched.

CHAPTER NINE

Being in the current situation wasn't one she could have envisioned she would be in, but there was no turning back. The room was packed with students from their level and others from other levels, and as much as the party has been nothing short of wonderful, the current situation still sent shivers down Nat's spine.

The moment the devil's basket had landed at her feet and Eleanor was called out by Saskia who had chosen to host the party provided she would be allowed to bring in her werecat friends, Nat felt sweats of discomfort rolling down her spine. The dare was simple, and Eleanor seemed eager and ready to do it.

"You both have ten seconds!" Saskia cried atop her voice and giggled devilishly.

Upon seeing the werecat giggle, Nat wondered if it was all planned. She wondered if Saskia had planned it intentionally or if it was simply a coincidence. The latter seemed more likely, but there was no turning back now. Alex watched on from the corner of the room where she sat and continued to stare at her watch like she was impatient and needed to leave.

"Don't be shy darling... I don't bite," Eleanor whispered while she drew Nat closer and slipped her hand behind her neck.

Nat smiled from the left-hand corner of her lips and slipped her hand behind Eleanor's head in a firmer grip as she pulled the werewolf closer. The crowd gasped but Nat didn't seem to care. Slipping her lips gently in between the cherry red pair that belonged to Eleanor, the entire room burst into awe with applause and admiration, but Nat had zoned out and didn't seem to hear a single thing.

It was a side to her that she had never portrayed, and she could see the shock in Eleanor's eyes, but the werewolf embraced her courage and diverse sense of interest as well. Their lips tightened around each other's and they shared the warmest and pleasing breath possible right there in the center of the room with about a hundred students present.

Saskia rang the bell aloud, demanding they split, and the girls duly did. Nat smiled, turned around and could feel Eleanor's eyes trailing her the entire time. Eleanor felt there was some amount of adventure to the girl now and it enticed her further. She wanted more but that would have to do. Nat sat back with her friends and continued to smile.

"You want more don't you now!?" Arnold beamed aloud without any tone of discrepancy in his words.

Nat remained silent, felt her lips and looked at the boy. "It felt perfect when I finally learned how to shield Sheila from reading my mind, can you not poop on things by reading me too?"

Leslie burst into a rather mocking laughter while she seemed focused on her cellphone as the events of the night unfolded.

"Aren't you a cutie?" Leslie smiled at her phone and lingered her gaze on a particular image.

Nat snatched the phone and took a good look at the image her friend had been staring at. "I'll be damned."

Arnold drew closer but halted upon noticing Leslie's warning look.

Sheila laughed and spoke, "You know he's Alex's friend, right? He comes for a lot of parties and some of our games."

Leslie simply shrugged and smiled. "Aren't we all friends to someone?"

Nat nodded her head and returned the cellphone to the girl. "Just be careful with that bunch okay? I have my hands full with Alex and her crew watching me all the time like I'm about to mess with them."

"How did you meet him?" Arnold asked.

"Simon comes to my father's martial arts gym a lot on Downing Street and while I was there helping out, we started talking, then he asked if I needed a ride home one night and we've been talking ever since."

Nat got to her feet, straightened her hair and sighed softly.

"Where are you going?" Sheila looked up at her friend and asked.

Nat looked towards the door. "I need some air… when any of you are ready to leave, call my cell."

Arnold motioned to follow her, but Sheila shook her head and warned him against it. He listened, sat back and watched as a familiar senior year girl was being dared to give a junior a lap dance.

Circling the building and staying just at the edge of the forest, Nat sucked in ample amount of air as she heard approaching footsteps. Being afraid wasn't her move anymore or her first move at least, the past few months had brought with it just about enough growth to help her handle her fears. More so, she knew who was approaching or at least she was standing where she was simply because of this person.

"You're becoming a breathtaking witch I must say," the sonorous and ridiculously perfect tone from the daring werewolf spoke.

Nat kept her gaze far ahead and into the darkness, and without turning around, whispered with a smile. "Ella."

Eleanor placed her hands to rest on the young witch's shoulders, prompting her to turn around immediately. Her eyes glowed with excitement, while she continued to bite her lower lip as Nat stared deeply at her.

"You could read my thoughts, couldn't you?" Eleanor asked.

With a shrug, Nat replied, "It was not hard to know what you wanted after that kiss."

They both burst out laughing and then halted with their eyes connecting once again, refusing to break off. Nat reached for Eleanor's hand and took it into hers gently while she caressed the werewolf's skin with her thumb as they shared the silence further.

"What are we doing?" Nat asked in a bold tone. "I mean, what was the kiss like for you?"

Eleanor looked away shyly and smiled at the ground before feeling Nat's hand reach for her chin and help her look back up immediately. Nat seemed pretty certain of what she had in mind but seemed to want to find out about Eleanor's thoughts.

Stuttering and seemingly shy, Eleanor replied softly, "I... honestly... I don't know, honestly but since we met, I..."

The words were becoming too much for Nat to listen to and the fact the gorgeous girl was stuttering wasn't helping matters either. Nat lifted her chin higher, so they could linger their gaze into each other's eyes, before tearing her own lips with a wild smile with her eyes bearing unknown intent.

"How about I help you understand what it was or what it felt like?" Nat asked.

Eleanor barley blinked or managed to part her lips to give a response when Nat leaned closer to her and immediately pulled her head closer as their lips locked and their breaths suddenly ceased. Eleanor felt herself stiffen immediately, and her legs threatened to collapse as Nat suckled on her lower lip and slowly snuck her right hand towards Eleanor's breast.

The firm feeling wrapping itself around Eleanor's breast made her moan softly, causing her to breathe wildly as Nat found her breathing rhythm somewhat distorted too. Sharing their lips with each other, their hands moved wildly around their bodies. Nat slipped her hand underneath Eleanor's top to feel her bare, warm breast in one firm hold, while Eleanor did the same as the girls cared less for whatever was going on around them there and then.

Eleanor paused and drew away, gasping and struggling to breathe as she asked, "What… what are we doing?"

Nat moved closer, slowly planted a kiss on her neck and shortened the remaining gap between their bodies, before sliding her hand down Eleanor's abdomen and headed south.

Eleanor gasped aloud, "Oh! Fuck!"

Nat had connected with her clit and had begun flicking it gently while the werewolf's entire body shuddered and ached for more. Nat reached for Ella's left breast, shoving up her top in the attempt. Finally, with the bare breast and unhindered view of the perfect nipples, Nat immediately took one into her mouth and sucked hard.

The night slowly drifted by without their knowing, and Nat felt herself let loose for the first time in her life. They would continue to enjoy each other's embrace and warm affection until the sound of rustling leaves and snapping twigs would pull them apart. Taking a long pause while they wondered if anyone else was around, Nat looked to her left and there he was; standing and looking pale in the face.

"Are you fucking kidding me!?" a disgusted and betrayed Russel asked.

Eleanor looked to the ground, brushed her hair backwards and thought, "Him!"

Russel didn't look pleased as he turned around and raced off into the forest angrily.

Nat stood there, frozen in a mix of guilt and confusion on whether or not she should run after him. Her and Russel just a few days ago celebrated their one-month anniversary. Her lips still tasted of Eleanor's and her body still trembled in aftereffects of the werewolf's touch.

Nat took in deep breaths and turned to look at Eleanor. "I have to go."

Eleanor reached for Nat's shoulder and managed to grab her shirt just before she went farther away. Prompting the witch to stop while they said nothing to one another, Eleanor tried to conjure her thoughts and words.

"I am truly sorry about you and Russel," she apologized. "If I had known this was going to happen, I would have kept my crush to myself and tried to steer clear of you."

Nat watched the obviously shy girl ramble on about her insecurities which was quite surprising because she was a werewolf and they often were strong willed creatures. Barely listening to all Eleanor apologized about, Nat took a step closer, pulled Eleanor towards her body and locked her lips with her intensely one more time.

With a subtle smile on her face, Nat asked, "Does that taste like regret to you?"

Nat felt her lips with her hands as she walked away, wondering if she had just won something even if it meant she had lost Russel. She then realized that she had rushed too quickly into a relationship with Russel. She wasn't ready. Nat returned to the party where her friends had been waiting for her.

Eleanor snuck into the backseat of the car parked just a few miles from the party spot and smiled uncontrollably before reaching for Alex and wrapping her arms around the girl happily.

"Tonight, was awesome!" Eleanor chuckled.

Alex shot her friend a long stare before turning back around to look at the driver's seat where there was nobody sitting in it or at least that was what it looked like.

"Stop messing around Julian and let's go," Alex said in a rather disgruntled tone.

Julian slowly emerged and took his real form, causing Eleanor to panic and almost run out of breath as she stared at the boy whose face donned the same mischievous smile as always.

"You seriously need to stop doing that, dude!" Eleanor warned him with a frown.

Julian looked away, seemingly disappointed at her ability not to handle his pranks but started the car and drove north as they headed away from the school gate. Throughout the ride, Alex's silence contrasted in comparison with Eleanor's endless giggles and wild smiles as she fondled her phone and took occasional moments to smile and mumble words incoherently to herself.

"Did something happen at the party I should know about?" Alex broke the silence and turned to her friend.

Ella took a long pause, seemed to give it some good thought but shook her head eventually. "It was just normal, asides the crazy games… nothing out of the ordinary."

Alex nodded and seemed to occupy her thoughts with other matters while Eleanor continued to stare at her friend, wondering if she should tell the witch about the fact, she had kissed the other witch earlier and not just any one, but the same girl Alex seemed to be enemies with. It would be a difficult task convincing Alex towards understanding what she felt within herself since the first-time seeing Nat, so she chose to keep it to herself.

"In due time," she thought. "In due time."

The car finally came to a halt around an abandoned warehouse just some miles away from Alex's mother's company headquarters.

"This is the meetup point right?" Julian turned around and asked.

Alex remained mute momentarily, before she nodded her head and slipped a crystal hanging on a neck chain around her neck.

"You guys should stay here while I sort this out," she ordered the duo.

Eleanor seemed uncomfortable with the decision and voiced against it immediately. "I'm coming with you."

Alex turned back immediately and replied, "No you are not! Stay in the car with Julian and you two better behave and stay alert."

Julian licked his lips seductively and slowly, an act that only made Eleanor want out of the car even more.

"I don't want to be in the car with this freak," Eleanor pleaded.

Julian frowned, grew red in the face and clenched his fists into balls as he stared at Eleanor. "Don't call me that."

Alex walked away, hearing the two argue loudly while she shook her head and paused momentarily. The odd wind wasn't the reason for her halt but the fact something else had arrived with it.

Smiling to herself and nodding her head gently, she whispered into the night, "It took you long enough."

She neared the abandoned warehouse and heard nothing emanate from within it, but her guard remained as high as possible as she swept around the old building in subtle gazes. She was sure they were there; there was no doubt about it and especially upon seeing the Mercedes parked just underneath a makeshift shed a short distance from the building itself.

Alex sucked in as much air as possible into her lungs, knowing she would need it for the next few minutes, before pushing open the creaking door to the building letting some light manage to illuminate the path before her. The stale air slapped hard against her face, coupled with what she could make out to be his cologne.

The building itself was barely standing but it had been that way for years and she didn't believe it was about to collapse on her now.

"Just a few minutes," she thought to herself while she waited to hear him move.

Yet, nothing other than endless cobwebs hanging from the ceiling existed.

Alex looked to her left and then her right before sighing aloud and speaking, "Don't even think about it."

The figure sneaking up on her from behind cackled into an unknown laughter that didn't match his voice. Alex turned around hurriedly, staring at the kid with deep red eyes and an odd smile on his face with a scar running down on one side as well. She had never seen him before, but something about him worried her and only heightened her guard.

"How much fun are you?" he asked with a mischievous grin. "Do you play fair or dirty?"

Holding her hands up and balling her fists in readiness to take him on, Alex replied, "Why don't you come closer and find out for yourself?"

She wondered if she should have urged him on, because her gut sensed the creature before her, albeit still unknown, wasn't one to toy with.

Thankfully, the cocky voice from none other than the youngest Hamilton broke through immediately, "Leave the witch alone Krul!"

Krul looked back in disappointment while Hamilton and Kun approached. The trio stood by the door, grinning oddly while Hamilton held his hands by his back and donned a rather long cape.

"I asked you to meet with me here alone," Alex fumed. "You came with people."

Kun stepped closer and waved politely, "We aren't really your average kind of people and you can call me Kun while the scarred one there is my brother and twin, Krul."

Hamilton shook his head and sighed. "You talk righteous for someone who came with two others who are sound asleep after we dosed them in the car."

Kun grinned proudly and indicated he had done it by holding up the empty can of sleeping gas he had used.

Alex looked furious and stepped closer, "If you touched a single hair on their heads, I will…!"

"You'd what?" Hamilton asked boldly. "Murder me? Get me expelled from your crappy school? Or simply stand by and allow your silly girlfriends to mess with me?"

Hamilton was being sarcastic with every word he spoke, he seemed pretty assured none of them could happen.

"I don't know why you asked me here in the dead of the night, but I assure you that I'm not going to be an easy target for you if you've got something planned up," Hamilton whispered.

Kun disappeared into the darkness and jammed his hand into the light switch just a few feet to their right. The entire floor illuminated immediately, causing Alex to squint, before looking around and slowly taking a more composed stance.

"So, why did you ask me to come here?" Hamilton sounded rather impatient.

Krul moved closer, seemingly on edge while he began to toy with Alex's hair.

"Ask him to keep off or I swear to God, I will kill him!" Alex threatened.

Hamilton seemed like he didn't care and Krul didn't stop either, causing Alex to lower her head and disappear her face in between her long hair. Krul had barely touched her hair one more time when she slipped out a silver blade with ancient looking rune marks from underneath her sleeve and slashing across his wrist causing him to scowl in pain as he retreated.

Hamilton's eyes widened immediately. "Oh shit! You shouldn't have done that!"

Kun fell to the ground in agony, holding his wrist as though he had been cut too, while the brothers cried aloud and screamed as the immeasurable pain from the spelled knife spread through their bodies.

"Run Alex!" Hamilton ordered her. "If you want to live, run!"

Instead, Alex took a more composed stance, holding her knife firmly in her hand as it slowly elongated and stopped short of a sword. The rune markings on it glowed brilliantly in golden color, and the blood it had been stained with when it cut Krul suddenly vanished. Hamilton raced towards Krul immediately, shoving him back and hard as he lunged for Alex.

Unfortunately, Kun wasn't staying down either and while he transformed with his fangs growing dangerously from within his jawlines, and his claws dripping from his venom, he raced towards Alex, making sure he wove his way around Hamilton impressively while Krul managed to keep Hamilton occupied by containing him.

Alex had never seen his kind before; from the way he danced across the floor and the way his eyes glowed even more disturbingly.

"Anytime from now," Alex sounded desperate as she whispered.

Kun had managed to reach her and swung hard, barely missing her but not by enough. Just an inch of contact and his claws tore some flesh from her arm. He recoils his advance in hopes of catching her with his leg but was suddenly blocked, as a female vampire with bared fangs grabbed and held onto his leg mid swing and jammed hers into his chest immediately. Kun jumped backwards and acrobatically landed on his hands before slowly reverting to his legs.

"Smart girl, but you're just one more to kill," he mused. "I'm guessing she didn't come in the car with you or we would've pick up her scent."

He was right, and Alex could tell he was kind of smart. Hamilton seemed unable to handle Krul by himself and it bothered Alex because he wasn't one to get beat easily. Kun on the other hand had gotten a taste of blood and by the way he began licking Alex's blood from his claws, he wanted more.

Olivia stared nervously as she kept her back to Alex's. "What sort of fucked up vampire is he? This doesn't look good Alex."

Alex remained silent, just as Kun moved, and they barely saw him do it. Within the split second of his disappearing from the spot they had last seen him, the lights went off, casing Olivia to look around as her eyes shone brightly.

"Even with my eyes, I cannot see him!" Olivia sounded in fright.

Alex took in deep breaths and smiled, causing Olivia to cringe upon seeing her friend being unperturbed. The melee within the room suddenly came to a halt and silence grew before the lights slowly came back on.

Alex relaxed her stance and turned to Olivia with a mischievous smile. "Thanks for having my back, but I made other arrangements as well."

Olivia, looking confused, stared at the three vampires pinned to the wall as they struggled to get lose but unfortunately could not. Krul and Kun seemed the most pissed as their mouths moved looking as if they were swearing but couldn't be heard.

"I will kill you! I will kill you once I get down from here!" Kun yelled.

Alex smiled and looked behind as Nora walked into the room with her hands behind her back and her face beaming with an odd smile. "Thank you for delivering him as promised Alex."

Alex nodded and sighed. "Thanks for saving our asses."

Olivia stood and watched with a dropped jaw as she slowly transformed back into her normal human state. Alex snuck her arm into her friend's and slowly led her out of the warehouse as they heard Nora approach the vehemently angry vampires pinned to the wall.

"The necklace around my neck makes it possible for my mother or Nora to locate me at any time," Alex explained.

Olivia looked back and asked, "What is she going to do with them?"

Alex gave no response and continued to walk towards the car.

Nora clapped her hands together and said to Hamilton, "Your presence is needed by Mrs. Aurelius."

Kun spat down and replied, "You and she can go fuck…

He barely completed his words when the snapping sound of his neck prompted Hamilton to stop struggling as he responded, "Take me to her."

It was the only response his shuddering body could muster.

CHAPTER TEN

*I*t was the first time she had decided to see things for herself from inside the house which she saw as nothing short of perfect. The family treated their daughter like she was a queen and the parents had nothing to do with shady businesses which unfortunately wasn't the same for her family. It had not taken her long to realize that it was probably the reason she would spend most of her day staring at that particular summer house every chance she got.

Yet, she had never thought to go inside or even touch its walls, until that day. The reason was simple; her mother had just managed to orchestrate the largest shipment of rare and dangerous drugs for the supernatural community into the country and she had decided to celebrate it with friends and family like it was a positive achievement.

To make things worse, no less than thirty men had died during the operation, but it didn't seem to matter to her mother and relatives as they jollied happily underneath the full moon, just some distance from their summer house and close enough to chant their treacherous lifestyle that contaminated the peaceful sound of the sea.

Breathing hard while she climbed up the house, using the tall tree by its side as the perfect ladder, she wondered if her tiny frame wouldn't get blown by the evening wind and leave her for dead at the foot of the tree for all to find the following morning. It would be a scandal like no other and one that would shake their world.

Regardless, determined and hoping for a quiet and peaceful night, she reached for the windowpane, dragged herself across and squeezed through the partly opened frame before landing her feet. Breathing aloud and nervously, she turned around in the darkness and leaned against the windowpane while she stared into the distance.

"Peace at last," she thought to herself, almost as if she had won something of high grade.

Laughing gladly and hoping to savor the moment, regardless of how short it might be, she helped herself to a sitting spot on the bed and giggled excitedly at being somehow a part of the "nicer" and "normal" family in difference to the one she was originally a part of. It didn't feel right to be there, but it felt absolutely comfortable.

The view out the window brought the little girl a rather different outlook on life. It gave the impression that life could be calm, without prejudice or dangerous bloody deals and that she could have what other normal girls had. It was wonderful to say the least and she wondered if she could have it forever. She would jump at it if the opportunity had presented itself, but the room door slowly creaked open and everything suddenly felt like it was about going down the hole of turmoil.

Hyperventilating and wondering what to do next, she leapt from the bed and hurried for the window, but she would be seen, and it would mean she had to deal with whoever was coming into the room. Scared stiff and barely able to breathe, she hurried behind a stack of clothes in the bedroom, covering herself as best as she could trying to hold her breath as the footsteps stopped just by the door and the sound of the light switch being flicked startled her.

Everything felt like it would spin out of control.

"What will my mother think?" she thought to herself.

The woman with the perfect image or at least, who proposed having the perfect image to the world would definitely not take lightly her daughter sneaking into other people's homes when they could afford to buy any house they wanted and more, with ease.

"Please cut the lights off.... Please turn the lights off," she whispered to herself, hoping whoever had come in would do as she had said.

Bizarrely, the lights went off, granting the little girl the opportunity to breathe as she peeped through the thin spaces in between the clothes on her head, wondering if the person had gone out of the room and if it would be safe to finally make her appearance again.

"Hello," a soft, innocent and startling voice spoke, just three feet from her.

Her heart skipped a beat and her tongue felt glued to the underside of her mouth immediately. Terrified to speak, she began to blame herself for sneaking into the nice family's home.

Yet, the innocent voice spoke again and even calmer this time, "Don't be afraid… I won't bite or hurt you."

Unsure of what to do, she replied softly, "I'm not a thief."

The girl laughed, reached her hand out and said, "I know you aren't… my cool stuff isn't missing."

The outstretched hand willing to accept her without knowing who she was or what her purpose in the room was, was just another testament to how gracious and loving the family she had admired was. She reached for the tiny framed hand, feeling the softness in it also prompt her to come out from hiding, as they stood face to face but majorly hindered by the darkness.

"Do you care for some pancakes?" the girl asked. "My mom made some and I'll share them with you if you want."

Unsure of what response to give, she remained still and barely said a word. Her heart raced wildly, and her entire world felt odd while the girl continued to get sweet and nice with her.

"I'll get them regardless," the girl said and hopped out of the room.

It was the perfect means to escape and one she would take without thinking twice. Yet, it wouldn't be the last time she would be in that room…

❋ ❋ ❋

After witnessing a rather brutal means of punishment being handed out to a defaulter, she ran as fast as her legs would carry her, with the images of the bloodied man and his family painted perfectly and gruesomely in her mind as she climbed up the window and slipped into the room. This time around, the little girl who owned the room wasn't out, but she didn't care.

All she wanted was a feel of the safety and peace she felt the last time she was there. The beach couldn't do anything about helping her feel safe, neither could the gigantic summer house her mother owned. Instead, the tiny room, part of an even greater house of love was what her heart craved for.

So, when she stood for a minute, face-to-face with the little girl who owned the room, she managed a wave even as her joints felt stiff, and watched the girl grow excited with a smile on her face.

"I knew you'd be back!" she cried excitedly and leapt from her bed to pull the stranger over to come sit and read next to her.

An awkward silence followed, before the marching sound of someone coming up the stairs alerted them both and the little girl raced to the door to lock it from behind.

A man called from the other side of the door, "Honey! Dinner is almost ready, and your mother needs you to wash up and come down."

"I'll be there in a minute dad," she replied, and pressed her back against the door as the footsteps on the other side soon moved farther away. "That's my dad but he is gone now."

They stared at one another, seeming to have a lot to say but without knowing just how to break them out.

The strange girl finally spoke, "You aren't going to rat me out?"

She seemed perplexed and without understanding what the girl was doing or why she had chosen to be nice even when she knew nothing about her.

The girl smiled and replied, "You can stay as long as you want, and I'll get you something to eat but you better not run off like you did the last time."

In that moment, they both shared a soft smile, and it felt perfect in the intruder's little heart. The warmth surrounding the gesture itself was awesome and she wondered if it was safe to embrace it.

"My name is Natalie by the way... Natalie King," the girl stretched out her hand to her visitor but found the girl unwilling to take it. "What's your name?"

Natalie waited but got no response, before nodding her head and sighing.

"What will you like to talk about? Where are you from and where are you parents?" Natalie asked.

The girl shook her head and replied, "That doesn't matter for now... I don't want to talk but can I sit here and just relax?"

Natalie nodded her head. She could sense the girl had things troubling her but had no idea just how to drag it out.

"You're beautiful by the way and I wish to be your friend if you want to be my friend too," Natalie noted before leaving the room.

The trouble minded girl sighed in relief and looked down at her feet. "My world isn't a place you want to get involved in."

She wished things would remain the way they were; she wanted no complications between them and would do everything within her powers to shield her life away from the new girl she admired and hoped deeply within to be friends with.

"My name is Alexandra Aurelius," she whispered upon realizing Natalie was long gone.

It was the first time Alexandra found herself wondering if there could be something good right there for them both.

Surprisingly, five years had gone by since Alexandra first snuck into Natalie's room and things surprisingly had moved on fast and well for the duo. Packing her bags in excitement that morning and hurrying to the car while her mother was busy dealing with some last-minute business as always, Alexandra was eager to get to the summer beach house and hopefully reunite with her friend.

Regardless of the numerous letters exchanged between them both, or the text messages and phone calls they shared through the time they were apart, Alexandra had managed to find a safe haven in being around Natalie and spending hours every chance she got in the girl's room during their summers.

"Can I come visit you in your house?" Natalie had asked more than once, just to show how much their friendship had progressed, but Alexandra met her request with the same response every time.

Shaking her head and answering in the same words, Alexandra would say, "You don't want to get mixed up with my family... yours is perfect and I love being here with you."

She was right as rain and being around the King's house had become so perfect that she had managed to get her mother invited for brunch with them once, even though a host of other families around had been invited as well.

"You're awfully happy to be going to the beach house," her mother had noted that morning.

Alexandra bobbed her head and smiled. They had something planned and little did she know it would come to shape the course of events for years to come.

"I'm just excited to see my friends," she lied.

She couldn't tell her mother she was going on a drag race which she had convinced Natalie to come for with her friends as well.

"It will be fun, I promise," Alexandra had convinced Natalie as best as possible. "Your friends will be there and mine will be there, so we all can have an awesome time."

That was just two hours before the unexpected would come to be. Sitting and smiling as they both cheered on their best friends drag racing wildly in the secluded area of the beach, Alex had spotted the crow, the bringer of bad news, or at least as her mother called it, just before Natalie's best friend's car flipped over after minimal contact from a car behind him the one Alexandra's friend was commandeering.

"Jermaine!" Natalie yelled, racing over as the car flipped and ultimately veered off the road and down the cliff as her best friend lost control of the wheels.

Alexandra stood, petrified and felt her lips mumble the exact words, "I'm sorry... I'm sorry... I'm sorry."

Natalie turned around with teary reddened eyes and yelled, "This is all your fault! It is all your fault!"

The damning words tore through her heart while they watched the car burst into flames and their friendship go with it.

The hurting words and loud cries were the last words her ears rang of before Alex felt a nudge on her shoulder and dragged herself back into focus.

"Alex! Alex!" Olivia nudged her friend hard until she opened her eyes. "Are you okay?"

Alex hurriedly looked around and realized they were still in the car. Gasping for air as she tried to curtail her anxiety, she rammed her hand into the driver seat and screamed, "Stop the car! Stop the car!"

Julian pulled the car to a halt and they watched her race out to puke on the side of the highway as she struggled to keep her breathing steadied. Olivia and Eleanor came rushing over immediately, placing their hands on her back for support.

"Are you okay?" Eleanor asked. "You blacked out and started mumbling words about being sorry over something."

Alex finally gained some control and got to her feet immediately. "It's nothing serious… just the effects of being cut by the vampire's poisonous claw."

Olivia nodded and sighed in relief, while Eleanor stared at her oddly but nodded slowly too.

"I'll be fine once I heal up in the car," Alex managed a weak smile while her face dripped of sweat.

She could feel the vampire's venom coursing through her veins, and it was without doubt the cause of her hallucination as she remembered memories she had desperately tried to lock far away into her subconscious.

"Natalie King," she thought as she entered back into the car with the other girls, and Julian drove off immediately.

"By the way, what the hell happened in that warehouse and how come I don't remember anything?" Eleanor seemed pissed as she folded her arms across her chest.

Alex suddenly remembered her mother had Hamilton now and there was no telling what the woman would do to him.

Feeling a pang of guilt ride her heart, she ordered Julian, "I need you to drop me off somewhere."

CHAPTER ELEVEN

It was meant to be a typical Saturday evening, and not one Nat had looked forward to because it held or at least used to hold positive memories of what her family was like as a complete unit, but not anymore. They had made this Saturday a tradition amongst themselves, to spend the entire day barbecuing and sharing some time together watching movies over the years, but since her father's murder, everything had gone downhill from there.

Hearing a car slowly park into the driveway, and her mother welcoming someone, had prompted Nat to hurry out of her bed and head straight towards the stairs. There, she crouched, eyes glued to the front door and her vision narrowed as she watched her mother hug a well-built man with rather sharp looking shoes before stepping aside to let him in.

"Please don't let this be mom getting herself back into the dating world," she thought to herself.

Nat wasn't sure she could forgive the woman if she indeed got herself involved with another man considering her father's killer was yet to be found and it wasn't anywhere near a year since his passing.

Samantha King looked towards the stairs as their visitor walked through the blind spot connecting the living room to the dining area, and waved over at Nat. Nat was sure the woman had not seen her, but there was no second-guessing how a reputable witch like her mother had sensed her aura.

"Don't be rude and come on down darling," Samantha urged her daughter before disappearing out of sight.

Grumbling and somewhat unsure if she wanted any part of what her mother was cooking up, she felt her neck stiffen and her spine trickled with a feeling of discomfort as she got within a short distance to the dining area.

"Thanks for having me Mrs. King," the voice sounded in appreciation while Samantha King poured him some wine. "I'm really sorry I haven't been around often, as you are well aware that I just got a new job at your daughter's school."

Nat felt her stomach sink, but her legs continued to move independently. She could swear he was the one and without doubt, upon cutting the blinding wall from view, she was standing before none other than the freakishly handsome and young sophomore year history class teacher.

"Natalie, I'm sure you know your teacher Garrett Marshall. He's a very good friend of your father," Samantha smiled and turned around to head over to the kitchen.

Nat had no idea he knew anything, or anyone related to her family. The loss of expression on her face did well to inform Marshall of that as he tilted his head and smiled.

"Hello Natalie," he greeted warmly and waved her over to the seat next to him.

Nat took the seat opposite her teacher instead and never took her eyes off him. He could read the boldness in her stares and the fact she wasn't about to chicken out or grant him the edge in her home.

"What are you doing here?" she asked as politely as she could.

Garrett Marshall stared at his fingers and toyed with them before answering, "Your mom invited me over... I should have come here sooner but I never was able to summon the courage to do so."

It still didn't give any sensible explanation as to what connection he had to her father.

"I'm sorry for your loss though and I wish there was something I could have done but sadly, I was out of town on the day the incident occurred," he continued just as Samantha returned with a pot of specially made lasagna.

Nat paid little to no attention to the meal being laid atop the table or even the fact that she should have helped her mother with the serving. Something about the man before her sent shivers down her spine but she couldn't quite figure it out yet. His charming smile looked too perfect, and his voice continuously seemed to influence her which she could not really explain.

"Thank you," he turned to Nat's mother and said. "It really means a lot to me that you invited me over today."

Samantha chuckled and patted him gently on the shoulder, "You shouldn't be so formal Garrett... you helped my husband over the years and I'm sure he would have loved to have you over any time."

The words piqued Nat's interest and she drew her seat closer with a frown. "How well did you know my father?"

He remained silent momentarily, and slowly set aside his plate so he could speak. "Your father mentored me at the Oak Clinic for two years and I learned a great deal from him."

Nat could and would never have believed it if someone else had told her. She had no recollection of him being there and worst of all, her father never mentioned him. Although in fairness, Nat sparingly visited the Clinic and even when she did, she'd rather stay in the car while her mother went in so she would have no reason to interact with the dangerous creatures her father worked on and with.

"So, you guys were really close, yes?" she pressed further.

Samantha shot her daughter a warning look. "Let the man eat in peace darling."

Garrett Marshall chuckled and shook his head. "It's okay... I'm not really accustomed to hot food... it worries me at times."

Samantha stared at him as though she could feel he was lying, but Nat didn't need to be exceptionally powerful to know he was indeed not telling the truth. Regardless, he had done it for her and that was all that mattered. She felt her level of uncertainty about it begin to drop but not in entirety. His index finger had a ring on it which caught her eye.

"Are you married?" Nat asked intrusively.

He looked to the ring on his finger and smiled. "It is more complicated than I can actually explain. Maybe when I find the right answer, I'd be able to share that with you."

Nat took the explanation and resumed her meal, but while casting a watchful eye on her teacher every chance she got. His eyes swept around the dining table too and would often brush gazes with Nat before hurrying his eyes away and staring back at his meal. It made her laugh and her mother would look at her oddly, but the dinner went relatively well.

Dinner was done and Samantha King upped herself to begin to clear the dishes but stopped upon seeing Garrett Marshall get to his feet. "You were gracious enough to make such beautiful meal… why not allow Nat and I clear the dishes and clean them?"

Samantha paused and looked from her daughter to the young man, thinking on what to do, before nodding and letting go of the dishes.

"Don't worry mom," Nat assured her mother. "We have things covered here."

Samantha sighed in relief and smiled wildly. "I might need to run an errand over at the grocery store for a moment… are you kids sure you got things covered here?"

Nat looked at her teacher and nodded her head, while he confirmed vocally with a resounding "Yes."

Samantha King hurried up the stairs to get her purse and within minutes, headed out the house humming. She left the two of them alone in the house.

A few minutes pass and nothing has been said between them and it felt like one wanted the other to break the ice. Garrett Marshall washed the dishes and rinsed them while Nat dried them off and set them into the dish rack. Like a well-oiled dish washing factory, they simply stuck to their task until Nat decided she was done being silent.

"What was my dad like? I mean, outside these walls and when he is out there helping people in the clinic," she tore through the awkwardness.

He took a moment to think about the question as he paused. "He was awesome… he is most likely the best brain surgeon I have come across in my life and everyone respected him and all he stood for."

Nat listened on but bore no smile on her face just yet.

"He had a vision to build the world around him in such a way that all creatures would find ways to work together without prejudice," he continued.

Nat chuckled and replied, "Isn't that like the Pairing done in school?"

Garrett Marshall shook his head and got through washing the last dish. He handed it to her and felt his thumb brush against hers before hurriedly turning back around.

Running his hand through his wavy hair, he explained, "The Pairing process is meant to help you grow as a unit and enhance your abilities through working together, but what your father wanted was a safe ground like his Oak Clinic spread across the entire world."

Nat had heard the vision before but knew it was too tall an order for her father to want.

"He simply wanted every creature to be unable to harm one another and knowing him, he would have gone to the ends of the earth to find a way to make it work, had he not been..." he paused.

Nat could see him struggling with the final word as he turned around and held his face with both hands.

"They were pretty close," she thought to herself as she realized the familiar sight of pain which was what she felt every single day.

Drawing closer and stopping just as he turned around and bumped into her, they stopped and felt themselves unable to look away, before Nat hurriedly sidestepped and granted him space to move.

"I need some water," he mumbled before opening the fridge door and helping himself to a bottle of water.

Gulping down the entire bottle, he reached for another and did the same before finally calming down as his hands looked as though they were trembling before he tucked them into his pockets and out of sight.

"Your father was a good man and possibly the best one I had ever come across," he finally continued with a subtle sniff.

She nodded graciously. "Thank you... for saying such wonderful things about him."

"It is my pleasure," he replied, before sighing aloud and heading away from the kitchen immediately.

Nat felt her cellphone ring from the back pocket of her jean.

"Tonight... the usual spot... can't wait... xoxo," the words read, with Ella's name being displayed at the top.

"Ella," she thought with a soft smile and slid the cellphone back into her pocket.

Wanting some more information about her father, she approached the nervous looking teacher who was pacing around the room before seeing her.

"Are you okay?" she asked with a bothered look.

He motioned to speak but stopped immediately, sweating profusely and unable to steady himself into a static state for too long.

"I'm really sorry," he apologized. "Often times I'm more composed than this but for a moment there, I lost it and I still cannot believe I wasn't around to save him."

Nat shrugged and replied, "Nobody could have known this would happen and I'm sure you really cared about him as well."

He reached for his left pants pocket and took out a card, handing it over to Nat as he said, "If you need anything at all, kindly call me."

Nat stared at the card ad nodded her head.

"I should take my leave now," he muttered and began walking to the door.

He stopped, turned back around and walked back towards her with his hands wide apart from his body, before slowly wrapping them around her.

"I'm really sorry about your father," he whispered. "He would have been proud of what a beautiful, independent and strong lady you're growing to be."

Nat felt her heart flushed with blood as he let go of her but left his scent lingering all over her. She walked him to the door and watched him head to his car.

"Help me thank your mother for me and I hope we can do this some other time," were his last words before driving off.

Nat smiled and whispered, "I hope so too."

In contrast to what she had thought and expected of him, he seemed sweet and emotional, which had gotten her comfortable being able to converse with him. Her cellphone buzzed again with messages from none other than Eleanor urging her to remember their date.

"I will be there Ella," she typed back, biting her lower lip and wondering what the night would hold for she and the werewolf.

It had been weeks since their first kiss and since Russel found them making out and flipped. Things had been getting better for her in every department and she began punching in a cellphone number before placing the call to her right ear as she leaned against the front door.

"Hey girl," the feminine voice on the other line said upon the lines connecting.

Nat toyed with her hair and replied, "I'm good... are we still on as planned tonight?"

"You mean the plan where you keep lying to your mother and getting me involved that you're sleeping at my house only for you to be steaming up things with the werewolf chick?" the other caller asked extensively and laughed aloud. "Of course, I got you girl... go have your fun!"

Nat chuckled and smiled, "Thanks Sheila."

Stepping out of the cab and waiting for the driver to zoom off, Nat turned around and stared into the alley which was meant to be their meeting spot. It was empty and unusually so, since Eleanor had always arrived earlier than her the past three times, they had chosen to meet there before heading for a hotel to spend most of the night into the morning.

Baffled Nat dialed the werewolf's cell before putting her cellphone to her ear. She got no response, so she tucked the phone away.

"Where are you Ella?" she asked herself, feeling cold and somewhat nervous while she looked around.

Five minutes passed by, but felt like five hours, prompting Nat to finally decide on taking things a notch further. Taking out an old looking map from her purse with ancient language scribbled across it, she tossed it into the air and watched it stand still, before she gently snuck out the ribbon Eleanor had given her on their last steamy meeting as a parting and remembrance gift until they would be together again.

"This should do for a locator spell," she smiled, while holding the hair ribbon in between her hands as she closed her eyes to begin the spell.

A tender, yet frightening hand came to rest on her shoulder, which caused her to frantically jump in fear and almost knock the figure behind her to the ground.

"Easy now my beautiful witch," a smiling and quite pleased looking Eleanor said with her arms wide apart.

Nat sighed in relief. "You almost scared me to death, and I was this close to blowing you to pieces."

They shared a loud laugh, followed by Nat leaning closer to kiss Eleanor while they shared the wonderful taste of their lips for the next few seconds.

"I'm so sorry I was late," Eleanor apologized. "I had to get ready for something first."

She held up the bag containing the items needed for the night. Nat smiled, received them and slowly walked towards the east wall to begin preparations.

"I was thinking a lot about you today on my way here," Eleanor whispered with her arms circling Nat's waist and settling in front of her pants zip. "How much I love you and how amazing you and I have been these past weeks."

Nat gulped down some air in difficulty but gave no reply. She stepped backwards, waved her hands at the bag and began to levitate the chains and their pins in the air, before ramming the hooks into the wall and ascertaining they stayed there with a slight tug.

"Your magic is getting pretty strong," Eleanor noted.

Nat turned around and placed her hands on the gorgeous werewolf's shoulders. "I've improved tremendously and can handle myself better than you can imagine right now."

They smiled, hugged warmly and found a sitting spot just beneath the hooks in the upper part of the wall.

Nat stared into the distance and sighed. Her mind was riddled with thoughts upon recalling the fact Eleanor just mentioned that she loved her. She had wondered what sort of feeling Ella had, because she just couldn't explain if she had such feelings. It had indeed been an awesome couple of weeks for them and the sneaking around had been fun, not to talk of making out in the oddest of places, which often than not, were instigated by Nat.

Eleanor brought the distracted looking Nat back into focus by slipping her hands under her shirt and reaching for her breasts in a firm cup. "What's going through your mind my love?"

"Nothing of importance… just the full moon and all," Nat lied through her teeth coupled with the fakest smile she could summon.

She shifted back around some and slipped Eleanor's legs apart without really breaking gaze with the girl. Eleanor smiled, succumbing to her demand as she had become accustomed to. Watching Nat take charge in such moments not only got her aroused but riled her inner beast up and she loved that greatly.

"How do we spend the time before the full moon?" Nat giggled and leaned closer to kiss her deeply. "I missed you and I missed being able to lavish these." Nat's hands slide under Ella's top,

Eleanor purred and pulled her closer, with their arms wrapped around each other, and their breaths entangling at maddening speed. Nat unzipped her dress from behind and slipped her left hand up the werewolf's thigh to find her dripping wet. It brought a tender smile to her face as she parted the drenched thong aside and felt herself gain full access to the freshly shaven region.

"Oh!" Eleanor cried upon feeling the thumb toying with her clit.

She shrugged and tilted her head backwards, prompting Nat to head straight down her neck and in between her chest with wet kisses threatening to melt away her skin. The witch slipped her hand towards the right breast, shoving aside the clothing covering it clamping her hand firmly around the breast before reaching for the nipple with her tongue in tender flicks.

Eleanor bobbed her head aggressively and could barely control how she felt with Nat's finger still toying with her bundle of nerves and her lips clamping hard around her nipple. Her senses dimmed and her awareness of her surrounding slowly began to fade, while Nat paid no attention to Eleanor's glowing amber eyes.

"Fuck!" she growled rather than moaned, prompting Nat to momentarily look up as she felt Eleanor's chest begin to get covered by hair slowly.

"Oh my God!" Nat cried upon realizing what situation they were in.

She crawled backwards with both hands and hurriedly looked to the moon to find it becoming brighter and fuller, which wasn't what they had expected so soon. She took a hurried look at her watch immediately and it was exactly eight o'clock.

"Shit!" she cried and got to her feet.

Confused and sweating profusely but with the determination to protect herself, she held her hands out and pointed them at Eleanor who had begun to growl and twist on the floor in a contorting and quite disturbing manner.

"Run Natalie!" Eleanor cried with the remaining piece of humanity left in her. "Run!"

Nat wasn't sure running was the best idea. Getting into a sprint race with a transforming werewolf on the night of a full moon would be nothing short of suicidal.

"We can still get you chained up," Nat replied before racing towards one of the chains and managing to hook it firmly around her left leg.

Eleanor grew in size tremendously, her bare breasts in view and her clothes slowly tearing off as she swung hard for Nat and missed by inches while the witch struggled to get the second restriction onto her other free leg.

"How could we have miscalculated?" Nat thought to herself in anger and worry.

She managed to get the second restraint onto the other leg, but still had the hands to contend with, which quite frankly would rip her to shreds should she step any closer.

Holding her hands out and pleading with the fully transformed werewolf that bore no remembrance of Ella now, Nat spoke, "Don't make me do this... Ella, I know you're in there, so please help me keep the beast under control."

The beast suddenly seemed to obey her, which led Nat to breathe in relief and attempt to get the chains around its front leg, before the sudden swing of its paw slaps her hard against the wall to its right. Now trapped in the dead end of the ally, and unsure of how to maneuver her way past the dangerous wolf, Nat slowly got to her feet and frowned.

The urge to fight back definitely grew within her, but they were both going to get hurt. All she needed was to get the restraints around its legs and they will be fine, but that seemed even more dangerous than taking food from a white shark's mouth.

Sobbing softly while she healed her somewhat sore shoulder, Nat pleaded again, "I don't want to hurt you... please!"

There seemed to be nothing left of the sweet girl she had just shared a breathtaking kiss with or warm intimacy with a few minutes ago. She was alone with the beast now, and with the painful realization that she had to fight to save herself. Swirling her fingers in the air quickly, she conjured a rather strong shield which took the heavy blow the beast intended to strike at her skull. The magic from the protective shield blasted it backwards and hard into the wall but that only enraged it and caused it to come for Nat harder and faster and with renewed interest and strength to harm her.

Nat strengthened the shield and took a strong stance with her left hand ready to cast a defensive but also an attacking spell back against the beast as it raised it dangerous claws ad swung them down hard towards her. She closed her eyes, waited for the perfect moment to make her move, but heard something else which wasn't from her.

It was a loud bang, followed by red streak which had forced the wolf into the wall and caused it to remain on the floor for a few seconds before getting up angrily and lunging for the frame that had just blasted it into the wall.

"Don't mess with me!" the girl said, waving her hands faster than the beast could swing its own, and rammed it harder into the wall, causing it to fracture its skull and pass out immediately.

Hearing her own heart pump hard, and her face drenched in sweat, Nat slowly got to her feet and moved closer to Eleanor, where her transformed state remained unconscious.

"Are you crazy!?" the girl who had dealt the beast the final blow screamed. "Do you have any idea what could have happened to you or even her if things had gotten worse!?"

Nat clenched her fists and closed her eyes before shooting back immediately. "What are you doing here Alexandra?"

Alex stepped into the light with her eyes beaming with anger and her breath unsteady as she looked at Eleanor and then slowly moved her gaze back to Nat. "Apparently saving your ass again from an absolutely stupid move."

Nat fumed and turned to look at her. "I had everything under control and didn't need your help! How the hell did you even know we were here and how is this any of your business!?"

Alex chuckled derisively, almost as if she could not believe what she was hearing.

"You're a fucking idiot," she sighed. "You ask me what I'm doing here while you're sneaking around with my friend? You must be out of your damn mind."

Eleanor growled softly as her fractured skull began to heal, causing the two girls to look at her. Nat leaned closer carefully, sighed and waved her hands as she commanded the remaining restraints to confine her front legs immediately. She turned around immediately before picking up her purse and walking away without a single word to Alex.

Alex grabbed her arm and pulled her back, until Nat shoved her hard into the wall, causing Alex to fall to her knees and groan.

"Don't fuck with me!" Nat warned her.

Alex coughed, sighed and whispered, "Stop messing with her when you know you don't love her. She obviously is already in love with you."

Alex got to her feet and readied herself to fight, while Nat wasn't taking a backseat either. The backdoor to the night club close to the alley creaked open as a man stepped out to have a smoke before heading back in immediately upon noticing them.

"Stay out of my way," Nat warned once again without looking back.

Nat had come to realize Ella's feelings too, but she was in no mood to have something more serious than a fling or being friends-with-benefits with Eleanor. She could feel Alex's eyes glued to her back though and she knew their rivalry wasn't about to end there without a doubt. For Nat, it felt odd that someone she once used to share so much with was nothing but a pain in her ass she wishes she could rid herself of.

Two hours later, Alex stepped off the elevator to her dorm room floor. She walked to her dorm hallway drenched. The hall only had five rooms, and they were meant for those who had extra money and connections to get them nicer accommodations. She didn't expect anyone to be on the floor but as she passed a corridor to get to the hallway where her room was located, she heard a voice.

"Didn't have a spell to keep the rain off you? I'm surprised you let your leather get wet," Nat's tone is full of amusement as she chuckled at the sight of Alex. Her night with Ella was ruined so she decided to turn in for the evening. She went back to the dorm knowing she couldn't go home after she told her mom she would be at Sheila's house and couldn't go to Sheila's house without having to explain what happen with her and Ella. She stood at the floor's soda machine and glanced at Alex again before turning around to make a selection.

Nat was truly shocked Alex let herself get wet while wearing her favorite leather jacket. It was her favorite jacket as a child, too big for her back then but her father had given it to her after she kept sneaking it on. One of the rare stories Alex finally shared with Nat. Alex would fight anyone who touched that jacket, except Nat, she always let her wear it or the both of them huddled under it at the beach at night making up stories or watching a movie on their tablets.

"Don't start with me tonight," Alex smacked the soda machine with one hand, leaned against it as she rubbed her forehead. Nat stared at her but didn't say anything right away. She just scoffed and grabbed two drinks.

"Whatever, I don't want my food to burn…"

"Lasagna is easier to burn then most think. Yeah, yeah, I remember," Alex sounds bored and exasperated as she cut off Nat.

"What?"

"I can smell it from here chef, and I remember being a frequent guinea pig."

"First of all, you've never complained about trying my food. And second of all I haven't wanted to be a chef in years." Nat walked down the hall pass Alex room and to hers on the left side of the hall not noticing the heavy sigh from Alex or how she waited for Nat to close her door before going to her own.

CHAPTER TWELVE

Nat voiced in dismay upon hearing the news about the school's security doing a sweep of the school including the dorms. "They cannot be serious about this." It seemed to be the only thing swirling around campus other than the fact they were going to be due for the first round of the semester exams in a week from then.

Storming out of the classroom as soon as the bell rang aloud, with her friends behind her barely saying anything, Nat headed for the exit door. She barely made it anywhere near there when she saw Alex and her group walking over from the opposite direction. Keeping out of each other's way had been the rule since the alley incident. It only fueled the bad blood that was already between them. Nat wasn't chickening out regardless.

"How come you don't feel in the slightest way worried about this?" Nat asked just as Alex walked past.

Olivia motioned to respond with tightened fist when Alex stopped her. Through the rising tension Eleanor waved softly, blushing and waiting for a response from Nat who seemed too engrossed in her anger and desire to get an explanation from Alex to even look her way.

"I really don't know what you're talking about," Alex smiled, rather annoyingly, knowing it'd piss off Nat.

Nat chuckled derisively with her hands placed on her waist. "The school is going to do a sweep. I'm surprised you all who are involved in so much bad stuff aren't concerned. We all have to suffer for the rest of the week on lock down because of idiots like you and those you hang around."

Alex barely moved, obviously provoked but for some odd reason, still maintained her composure as Nat seemed to be looking for a proper response.

"I understand your need to play righteous asshole every chance you get, not to mention the fact you have everyone believing you're the queen of goodness, but I'm not the cause of anything." Alex looked into her eyes with a scowl. "Just get out of my way and we will be fine."

Nat didn't move and it bothered Alex. Over the past few months, something had definitely changed about the shy girl she saw in the first few weeks of resumption. She wondered if the change had come from the moment she injected Hamilton with the potion almost killing him. It took some balls to do something so dangerous.

Nat spoke one last time, "Get Hamilton under control and nowhere near me, and tell Saskia to get her drugs out of here before the upcoming dance is cancelled."

Her tone sounded like she had just laid down a valid threat. Nat motioned for her friends to come along, leaving Alex mortified and unsure of what response to give as Nat walked away majestically.

Olivia fumed and leaned closer, "You should have let me slap the taste out of her mouth or something!"

Alex shook her head, turned to her friend and replied, "She will definitely hurt you."

Olivia seemed stunned by Alex's discouraging words.

"I don't understand," she replied.

Alex sighed and lowered hear head. "Something is different about her now. I can tell… it is something you feel as a witch and I can sense it in that Salem girl too."

Olivia wondered if Alex was being overly dramatic or not. Alex knew how strong she was, she could easily take on Nat and was about to voice so, but a smiling and chuckling Eleanor caught their attention and caused them to turn to her.

"What has gotten you in such a happy mood?" Olivia asked with a raised brow.

Eleanor shook her headed continued to smile wildly.

Julian, previously morphed into the wall slowly manifested into his physical from, startling the already edgy Olivia who cursed and swore at him angrily. "If you keep doing that, I will kill you one day, you freak!"

Julian ignored her and walked around to stand before Eleanor so he could stare into her eyes. "She's happy about Natalie of course, since they both have been sharing some breathtaking naked nights."

Eleanor's eyes glowed in anger, prompting her to take a fast hit at Julian which sent him into the locker to their left. He groaned, got to his feet and chuckled devilishly as he approached Eleanor for some payback but found Alex ordering them both to stop.

Alex turned to Eleanor and asked, "What do you know about her that I don't?"

Eleanor shook her head aggressively and tightened her fists. "I don't have an issue with Natalie. She's your problem so find a way to get information on her without going through me." She tried to walk away.

Olivia blocked the werewolf's path immediately and smiled before toying with Ella's blonde hair. "You'll do whatever Alex wants. Is this because you two are banging? You know she's just using..."

She paused and took another look at Alex who warned her to stop.

"Don't fucking talk to me like I'm naïve!" Eleanor shot right back. "I like her, but I know we're just... I can see things clearer, so don't fucking touch me again or I will break your fingers."

They stopped bickering for a moment as a group of students walked by.

Eleanor sighed and remained silent for a few more seconds, "All I can tell you is that she is way different from before... Just a couple of weeks ago, she dealt with Arman the werecat after finding out he had been tailing her movements on Saskia's request."

"What do you mean dealt with Arman?" Julian asked.

They all knew Arman. On the scale of madness, he wasn't far from Saskia herself.

"She broke every limb in his body before he could even come close," Eleanor replied. "I could hear every snap as it happened and even, I was terrified."

Alex smiled tenderly and felt somewhat relieved that she was right after all. She had sensed it and she wasn't wrong; something had definitely changed about Nat.

Arnold shook his head for the umpteenth time before rejecting their request again. "I can assure you there is no chance in hell that I will dance."

Nat chuckled and slid across the bleacher with a bottle of whisky in one hand while she took gentle sips from it before offering Leslie the bottle. Leslie turned it down and waved her head.

"I'm meeting someone later on and I don't think being drunk or stinking of whisky will help my chances," she smiled.

The others suddenly looked interested and drew closer to her immediately.

"Someone has a boyfriend," Arnold snickered.

Leslie smiled and shrugged. "Things have progressed a lot."

Nat and Sheila dance together and around Arnold, still trying to motivate him to dance with them. They had decided to sneak out to the football field and were on the bleachers enjoying a night of no homework. Leslie pushed pause on Sheila's phone which was playing the music they were dancing to.

"Hey, I was just about to get up and dance." Arnold complained.

"Yeah right," Sheila scoffed.

"Guys, shut up." They all looked at Leslie.

Nat could sense something was troubling the girl and she was about to ask why Leslie had asked them to shut up when she heard a scream. They all heard the scream and it was not far away from them.

"Someone is in trouble!" Nat pointed out immediately.

She leapt down from the bleachers to the steps without thinking things through as the feminine voice continued to tear through the air mixed with pleas and sobs.

Sheila called after Nat, "Wait! We need a plan!"

Nat replied over her shoulder, "Arnold, I need you to cover me… Leslie, get ready for any surprises, and Sheila, you are my eyes behind!"

Just like that, they had a plan, one Sheila didn't like. They weren't sure about what they were heading towards. Nat traced the sound on the opposite side to the football field.

"Isn't this place meant to be out of bounds?" Arnold asked in a worried tone as they got deeper into the woods.

Nat ignored him and continued to race fast as her legs will carry her. "The screams are coming from here, so at this moment, no it isn't."

Arnold agreed halfheartedly and they continued on their rescue mission before stopping at a small building. The sight of the large door with broken locks which was an obvious sign that someone had forced their way through, gave them pause. Nat took a knee and examined the padlock, stared at it before waving her hand over it to watch it glow red.

"This was locked with magic and whoever broke it definitely isn't a novice," Nat turned to Sheila seeking confirmation.

Sheila could see it for herself too and it seemed to sink her stomach immediately. They headed through the door and found themselves in nothing but a dark room with their labored breathing being the only thing they could hear. Nat snapped her fingers together, causing the lights to slowly burst to life in old lanterns hanging on the walls which lead down what appeared to be a tunnel.

Arnold didn't look so pleased with the rescue mission his friends had taken up. This bunker or whatever it is, felt dangerous to him. Since their pairing, he had found himself growing towards accepting their crazy acts and becoming a part of it, but this was not one he could easily accept.

"You're with me," Nat whispered. "You will be fine."

Arnold waved his hands in the air aggressively. "I don't do well in tight spaces and definitely not in a tunnel leading us towards what we don't know."

Sheila nudged him ahead. "Stop being a cry baby and just move... if shit hits the fan, you can just play dead, you know, like a possum."

The trio laughed and caused Arnold to grind his teeth together in anger. Leslie began glowing the further they went into the tunnel, with nothing but damp walls on either side.

"Please don't hurt me!" the voice cried one more time causing them to hurry ahead until they all halted into a hurried stop.

Nat had her finger to her lips while they watched three hooded figures chanting while one had a girl from their class on his shoulder. She had passed out but they refused to move from where they were. Nat wondered what they were planning on doing but it suddenly hit her and made her more nervous than she was before spotting them.

"They know we're here," she whispered to her friends.

There was no need hiding any longer, so she stepped out of the shadows with her friends.

Pointing at the tallest one holding the girl, Nat commanded him in a rather bold tone. "Let the girl go!"

He simply stared right back at her through his hood and with a covering just about his entire face excluding his nose, before gently laying the girl to the ground. The three hooded figures slowly approached, raking out sabers from their waists.

"Here they come!" Arnold yelled in fright.

Nat spearheaded the group, flanked by Leslie and Sheila, while Arnold stood at the base of their formation.

"We can take them," Nat sounded confident, but something within her wasn't entirely sure of what they were taking on which meant they didn't even know their weaknesses.

The first of the three also the tallest lunged at her immediately, striking his saber down hard towards her face, but Nat held her hand high, commanding the blade to halt just a few inches from her head. Shoving him backwards with her left hand in a manner that sent him hurling across the room and into the opposite wall, she spun to get out the way of another attack.

He roared with anger, got to his feet and began to race around her in speedy circles. Nat couldn't see him easily; however, she wasn't about to give in to fear. She clenched her fists together while her mind worked out the next best thing to do. Sheila on the other hand had commanded fire but it was not enough, as she managed to set her attacker ablaze, while Arnold lunged at him and tackled him to the ground.

Arnold knelt atop of him and giggled. "How about I take something dearest to you?"

Laying his hand to rest on the boy's forehead, Arnold yelled and felt his entire body feel like it had been set on fire as he hurriedly crawled away from the hooded figure who now got back to his feet. He approached Arnold in confidence, holing up his saber high enough to make a good impact once he brought it down.

"Oh no you don't!" Nat waved her left hand towards him, shooting out blue streaks of lightning which struck Arnold's attacker hard in the chest and sent him screaming through the air before hitting the floor hard.

Nat heaved a sigh of relief before turning on the leader while Leslie and Sheila had made good work of the second attacker. The only one standing seemed rather confident as he battled the girls at once without flinching. For each jolt of lightning sent his way by Nat, he managed to reflect it off of his saber, while doing well to avoid Sheila's magic and Leslie's burning flames.

Nat could feel their loss coming sooner than later and without a moment's notice, grabbed unto Leslie, and tossed her in the air, commanding the phoenix's light with her magic to shine brightly and momentarily blind the hooded figure who had to cover his eyes with his saber, which left himself open for an attack from Nat and Sheila.

"We got you now bitch!" Nat cried, clapping her hands together causing a whirlwind to lift him up in the air and toss him dangerously against the ceiling and down to the ground.

Leslie safely returned to the ground and they rushed over to help Arnold up. He seemed absolutely frightened stiff and could barely breathe while he mumbled, "We need to leave here! We need to leave!"

Nat agreed with him just as their attackers groaned and seemed to be coming awake. Sheila commanded the kidnapped girl over with her magic and shielded all of them in a cloud of smoke while they made their escape.

"Help her to her feet!" Nat commanded Leslie and Arnold.

The five students began running back in the direction whence they had come earlier, while their pursuers slowly regained consciousness. Nat wondered if the tallest one she had just fought was Hamilton, but the fact he had not moved swiftly like a vampire and the use of sabers made her think otherwise.

Nat nodded. "Let's just get out of here and get someone to come and arrest those guys."

Arnold couldn't agree more; he alone knew what he had seen inside of the figure he touched earlier, and he wasn't sure he had come across anything like it in his entire life. It made his stomach churn with fear and his heart race terribly while he thought of the best way to tell the others that they might be in more danger.

Nat slammed the door shut behind them and bolted the locks back into place with magic once they got to the school building.

"What are you kids doing?" the familiar voice of Mr. Sadon asked from where he stood at the top of the stairs.

Nat pointed behind her and managed to answer, "Bad people… send someone."

The words seemed rather oddly composed but upon watching her collapse to the ground, they notice she was bleeding from a gash they had not noticed on her back.

"Natalie!" Leslie cried in a worrying tone, while the others gathered around her.

Mr. Sadon raced down the stairs. "Allow her some air… Allow her some air!"

The girls slowly retreated, watching the scared teacher lift Nat in his arms and hurry her up the stairs immediately.

Sheila turned to Arnold immediately and asked, "What did you see in those tunnels?"

Arnold stared back at her blankly and replied, "That can wait. We need to see how Nat is doing and get this girl up to the med wing."

Parting her eyelids slowly upon feeling the burst of sunlight blind her momentarily before she looked away, Nat sucked in air deeply and exhaled before feeling her hand tighten against someone else's. She looked towards the side of the bed where the bowed head and napping frame sat.

"Mom?" she asked in shock, barely able to recall the incidents that followed from the moment she cast the lock spell on the door.

The white colored room with a strong smell of ammonia meant she was in the school clinic. She had been there once; after Arnold's attack and Leslie was paranoid that he might have been infected. It had turned out that his healing was only part of his abilities to absorb other's strength when they attacked him, and he was fine.

Slowly, her mom woke up. "Natalie, I'm so happy to see you awake. You scared me nearly to death." Her mom smiled and sat up to place a kiss on her daughter's forehead.

"The three hooded..." she spoke weakly and found her throat feeling tight. Her mom grabbed a cup of water next to the bed and helped Nat drink. Mr. Sadon appeared and walked closer.

He shook his head. "They were gone by the time some other teachers and I went back."

Disappointed and wishing they could have caught them, Nat looked away.

Mrs. King tugged at her hand and gained her attention again. "Don't beat yourself up... you were brave and had you kids not been there, who knows what could have happened to that girl."

Nat gave off a small smile and absorbed the strength her mother tried to give her.

"Your friends should be here in a minute... we had to ask them to leave and take some rest after they refused to leave your side for hours," Mr. Sadon chuckled. "The cut on your back had some poison in it from the blade that struck you, but it has been dealt with now and you'd be out of here in a few hours."

The news was a relief, but Nat still looked gloomy.

"Your father would be proud of you," her mother said. "I know I am. I need to have a few words with Mr. Parker about the serious lack of security recently then we can have lunch before I leave." Her mom got up and left. As the door was closing behind her, it suddenly opened wider as her friends burst in.

Nat had never been happier to see Leslie, Sheila and Arnold, while three more girls with one being the girl they rescued tagged along.

"That's our star!" Arnold teased, prompting Nat to shoot him a grin.

Leslie set herself beside Nat on the bed and took her hand into hers excitedly. "Here… I brought you something to help heal the pain."

Nat received a tiny vial with some droplets of liquid inside of it. "Is this what I think it is?"

Sheila nodded. "Phoenix tears… it heals any wound and can stop any pain one is feeling."

Thankful and equally grateful, Nat hugged Leslie before watching the girl they rescued slowly approach her.

"My name is Susan and I just want to say thanks for saving me," the girl with thick reddish-brown curly hair smiled. "I would really love to be your friend, if you wouldn't mind."

Nat looked to Arnold who was grinning wildly. "That will be cool, seeing we've been looking for a replacement to Arnold here for a while."

The grin on Arnold's face disappeared immediately, while they all burst into cheerful laughter. However, Arnold wasn't looking gloomy because of the joke being made at his expense, but for what remained trapped in his mind.

CHAPTER THIRTEEN

Alexia Hamilton wasn't ever one to panic but something about the situation sent shivers down her spine. For the umpteenth time, she took a glance at her watch, and managed to weave her way through the darkness but obviously not fast enough as whatever was moving through the cold and chilling air managed to keep up without lose sight of her.

The fort was still miles ahead and having chosen to handle business for her husband personally, she was in no man's land now. Yet, the situation seemed to bring more smiles to her face than worry, and an even more disturbing grin on her lips as she feared not for herself, but for those who lurked in the darkness, waiting for the perfect moment to strike.

"Amateurs," she smiled to herself after sniffing the air and catching their scents.

Her feet quickened momentarily until she reached the abandoned clothing factory just on Wareline Pines and majestically walked through the front door before fondling the wall to her right for the light switch. The air stank desperately of neglect mixed with rotten flesh which she could assume was from dead hobos known to live in the area.

Stretching her arms and flexing her muscles before hearing the footsteps hurry into the room, slowly scattering themselves in the best possible directions and vintage spots to make their moves. Alexia steadied her breathing and sniffed the air loudly, taking in their count and noting exactly what they were.

Without turning around, she clapped her hands together and chuckled, "Well done... well done."

Silence aired just after the echoing sounds from her words and her hands clapping aloud.

"An alliance between werewolves, werecats, and witches all against a lowly vampire as myself," she giggled irritatingly before turning it into an evil cackle.

It was rather rare, and many would laugh at seeing such a combination come to work together.

A large sized man donning a rather dirty gray coat and muddy boots stepped forward with his hand pointing her way. "Alexia Hamilton… you're coming with us for stealing the sacred scroll belonging to Oak Clinic which was directly handed down by the Order!"

Alexia barely flinched as she held out the scroll in her hand and stared at it still neatly tucked in its casing. "You might want to address me properly Egor… also, you might want to get on a knee and address me as the Queen I am."

The large man laughed and shook his head fervently. "I pay no respect to thieves and especially not one like you who would stoop so low to desecrate on the peace between beings like ourselves."

She finally turned to look at him. "The time is ticking to kneel Egor… the time is ticking for you all to kneel, but I'll take his first."

"Hand over the scroll!" Egor yelled at her with an outstretched arm.

Alexia shook her head and sighed. "I still want you to kneel before me."

Her cold, calm and rather composed voice didn't seem to reflect the fact she was outnumbered in any way. Egor burst into a hysterical laughter, just before Alexia tossed the scroll his way and the lights went off immediately and came back on in the space of a second.

"Fuck!" Egor cried from where he knelt, with his right leg chopped off. "You bitch! You fucking bitch!"

Holding the dismembered leg of the werewolf in her hand while staring at it, Alexia asked, "How pitiful it must be for the Oak Clinic to have someone of your nimbleness guarding such an important place… Maxwell King must be rolling in his grave out of hurt right about now."

Egor rolled around on the ground cursing and yelling in pain, while Alexia tossed away his severed leg and waited for the others to make their move. She made the count of five, excluding Ego who obviously was of no use in the fight and of them all, she could hear their heartbeats ramping hard in fright, except for one.

"Who are you?" she thought, staring at the cloaked figure that had barely moved an inch the entire time through.

The werecats readied themselves while the sole standing werewolf turned immediately. The mood was getting rather more exciting than dangerous for Alexia. She smiled eerily in face of death, with the feeling that she would be the one to introduce them to the underworld as soon as possible.

"Don't be shy," she waved them over. "Let's dance."

Alexia smiled as the first wave of attack came from the two werecats who were more than willing to engage her while the sole witch present bided his time perfectly. Like a game of chess, he had chosen to let the pawns go first and that suited Alexia who barely moved a muscle before the werecats got to where she stood.

Ducking swiftly, and ramming her feet into their chests, before spinning high up in the air acrobatically and managing to land just a few feet behind them. Their orientation was slower than she had anticipated, and their combination as a duo also seemed pretty odd for those being chosen to guard the Oak Clinic.

Holding two werecats' hearts in her hand, bloodied and smirking, Alexia sighed. "Guarding the Oak Clinic must be some sort of joke these days, if these amateurs are what's good enough to come after me."

She smirked and tossed the hearts towards the cloaked creature whom she guessed already to be a witch. The hearts rolled and seemed like they would take forever to stop by the cloaked figure's feet. Not before Egor made a rather speedy recovery and got to his feet. Shocked, but not granted enough opportunity to grasp an understanding of what had happened with Egor, Alexia felt herself take the first few steps backwards to avoid the deadly punches from the two attacking her.

Doing well to swerve and dodge some more, with no room to get on the offensive, she decided on using the one advantage she had over them; her speed.

"How is it possible Egor?" she asked with her feet moving along the walls at maddening pace that left Egor and his partner too confused on how to grab hold of her.

Egor grumbled, looked at his healed leg and replied, "Wouldn't you like to know?"

Alexia paused momentarily, hanging on the south wall watching Egor and his partner search for her. Werewolves had perfect vision in the dark, but their large frame meant their speed wouldn't be anywhere near those of vampires, unless it was full moon, and thankfully for Alexia the moon was absent in the skies outside.

"How about I teach you just how dangerous the dark can be?" Alexia asked calmly, before disappearing from Egor's sight.

He turned around frantically to find her but anytime he was close to doing so, he felt a limb get torn off his body.

Egor yelled in pain.

His partner had not spoken or made a sound for a while until the lights came on and the trail of blood leading from Egor's decapitated arms led towards the corner of the room where a dismembered werewolf body lay, with its head severed and tossed far away from the rest of the chopped limbs.

Alexia sat on a bench, in the store, crossed her legs and yawned as though everything had been a game. Alexia wasn't fooling around but she still wasn't done; there was one left after all.

They aren't really guarding the Oak Clinic, are they? Alexia thought trying to make a connection. "Knowing Egor and his easily persuadable zeal for some extra cash, I'll say you hired him to lead this team of bozos." She stared at the cloaked figure.

It was in that moment that the cloak moved and slowly brought to light the masked face underneath it. The slender frame belonged to a woman, and her tight fitted leather strap showed just how classy whoever the wearer was, but also the fact that she wanted her identity kept secret as much as possible.

"I never play fairly with men, but seeing you've got the goods like me, how about things get really serious?" Alexia laid the scroll down to rest by her feet and teased the cloaked lady.

The air within the large room felt like it stood still and watched for who would make the first move. Their focus took into account every single movement and sound within the store but never left each other as the tension grew and their fingers flexed the muscles within them. Alexia was born ready and even while she couldn't gauge her opponent's abilities just yet, she could tell the battle would be one to her liking.

So, the vampire moved first, shifting her left leg outwards to take a better stance, before slowly bearing her claws and smiling. "How about I make this fun?"

The cloaked figure tossed off her covering and spread her arms apart, smiling and finally speaking, "That scroll is mine, one way or another and it can either be with your lifeless body or with your chopped off arm."

Alexia nodded and moved, but it barely seemed as if she had done so. She landed behind her target, reached for the head and could swear she was moments away from grabbing hold of it when something pierced hard into her chest and caused her to cry in pain. The figure she had assumed was before her had someway found its way around her.

"Interesting," Alexia chuckled before yanking herself out from the blade and staggering forward.

The witch snapped her fingers and commanded the floors to slowly begin to turn into hot steamy lava all around Alexia. Alexia looked pleased rather than shook which would have been accustomed to such a situation. Her claws grew longer, and her feet moved even faster, striking hard this time with precision that sent her swiping her claws at the witch causing her to bleed.

"You will pay," the witch cried. "You will pay dearly!"

She commanded the lava on the molten floor to move around while it chased the fleet footed Alexia. Alexia danced around the walls, dodging endless lightning sent her way, while the witch controlled the elements just well enough.

"What kind of witch is she?" Alexia thought to herself, finding it almost impossible to get free of the elements chasing her around the room.

A whirlwind slowly rose upon with witch's command, attempting to slow down the extremely fast vampire's movement and it managed to blow her hard into the opposite direction and into a wall. In a loud growl and eyes burning red with anger, Alexia stood and watched her dislocated arm heal immediately.

"It has been a while since I last faced someone this formidable," she chuckled. "Unfortunately for you, I'm a Hamilton and we don't go down easy."

The witch calmed the floors back into their normal state and smiled. "I was hoping you would say that."

She tore off the roof of the house and laid them bare to the elements as best as possible.

"You're a commander of the elements, aren't you?" Alexia asked. "You're a tricky one, but your kind always makes one stupid mistake."

"What is that?" the witch asked.

Alexia readied herself while the witch prepared a storm to blow her away. The brewing storm had nearly completed when Alexia moved from where she stood, tearing through the air in supersonic speed to find herself inches before the witch who didn't seem to understand how she had gotten even faster all of a sudden.

Alexia let off a wry smile before swinging her claws hard against the witch's throat sending her head rolling down as the storm brewing simmered into ordinary air.

"Your mistake was assuming I'm slow enough to be stopped without some real magic," she smiled.

The entire time through, she had baited them all; stepping up her speed only when the time demanded it.

Gently leaning closer to pick up the fallen head, she whispered to it, "I am Alexia Hamilton… thank you for the entertainment… I never really get any these days."

Alexia rounded up the bodies immediately before searching them one at a time but found nothing other than a stack of cash tucked inside Egor's shirt. Taking out a lighter from her pocket and flicking it on, she set the bodies on fire then laid it to rest on Egor's body before walking out of the building as the smell of burning flesh soon filled the air.

Barely a mile out from the building, Alexia's cellphone rang and she gently placed it to her ear.

"Is the task done?" the bold and vibrant tone of her husband asked.

Looking back at the dead bodies burning in crisp, she replied, "Yes and as we expected, Brenda showed her hand."

A long pause soon followed before he replied, "She will get what's coming to her… the plan is almost perfect." Alexia Hamilton nodded her head and slipped the cellphone back into her pocket. It felt like a perfect day for her, but she remained somewhat disappointed about the number that was sent to come after her.

CHAPTER FOURTEEN

Alex slowly woke up from her spot on the sofa. She took a moment to remember her surroundings. It was a fraternity house, there had been a big party she and her friends attended. Alex groaned as she moved her stiff body before noticing someone was standing next to the couch.

She was for sure startled, however did her best not to show it. Alex speaks in a low groggy tone, "Look what the cat dragged in."

Nat folded her arms across her chest and said nothing as she continued to stare down at the girl she once referred to as her best friend. Nat had gotten a call from Leslie to come give her a ride because she didn't have a car and Simon was too hungover to drive. And once she saw Alex she couldn't help but walk over to her to give her a piece of her mind.

"I sincerely hope this isn't heaven, because if it is, I'll take hell," Alex continued.

Nat responded immediately, "You keep hanging out with these delinquents you roam around with and heaven might come to you sooner than later."

Alex's jaw dropped immediately, and her breath became heavy as she tightened her fists into the bed.

"I seem to recall your friend in here having the time of her life as well." Alex fumed. Someone sleeping on the floor moved in, so Alex tried waving Nat off.

"Don't you see how crazy this is? I mean, look at you and what roaming with Hamilton and Saskia the most psycho senior and junior in school brings you?" she asked. "I know you, or at least I used to know you!"

Alex got to her feet and chuckled rather annoyingly in Nat's face. "You never knew me... you never knew half the shit I had to go through while you played princess with your perfect little family."

Nat decided she had had just about enough and began to walk away.

Alex continued and screamed, "How about you step down from that mighty righteous horse you're riding? You can keep on living like the world is white and black, even while those like your dead daddy and my family see the gray side to it!"

Alex felt her throat clamp shut immediately, realizing she might have gone a tad too far, but it was out there and there was no taking it back. Momentarily, Nat seemed too horrified to turn around as she stood and said nothing.

"Oh no, you didn't!" Nat yelled, turning around immediately looking furious.

Alex remained silent and gave no apology, which she could tell Nat wanted from her.

"You take that back!" Nat warned.

Alex scoffed and shook her head as Nat slowly approached her with a storm brewing in her eyes.

Nat had heard enough to flip her switches, causing the air around her to grow static momentarily, before the storm kicked in. Her hair floated in the air behind her, and her jaws cringed as she stared hard and dangerously at Alex. Alex made light work of the situation, by smiling and chuckling.

"Oh! The sweet little princess is getting mad at me for telling her the fucking truth," Alex goaded the already enraged girl. "What are you going to do? Give me your best shot!"

Nat didn't give it another thought, before lifting the table just a foot away from Alex and ramming her hard into the wall with it. Alex yelled in pain and felt the table threaten to crush her ribcage as it pinned her dangerously against the wall.

"Take it back!" Nat ordered her. "Take those words about my father back!"

Alex paused and moaned softly in pain while the chairs in the room slowly began to levitate on Nat's side of the room as Alex struggled to get herself free. Nat's eyes slowly fueled blood shot red and her pulses began to race while her emotions clearly had begun to get the better of her. Alex finally managed to set her right hand free and unpinned, before waving at a candle stick which had fallen off a table Nat had behind her and swinging it hard ramming it into Nat's head.

"You wanna play rough!?" Alex asked, watching the girl get distracted enough to weaken the grip of the furniture pinning her into the wall. "Let's play!"

Nat rubbed some feel into her temple and managed to regain her balance while the furniture around her returned to the ground immediately. Alex wasn't done, and with her feet not firmly planted into the ground, she swung a set of vases towards Alex, catching her in the face and causing her to stagger backwards while she barely had the opportunity to keep her feet firmly planted in the ground.

Doing just about enough to dodge incoming shards of glass, Nat wore the thickest frown across her forehead and held her hand towards Alex. "This ends now!"

Raging in thoughts, the entire room began to shudder dangerously as the floorboards around Nat began to uproot themselves and float around her, before hurrying fast towards Alex, who managed to dodge and block a good measure of them with a large table. Yet, a thin broken piece managed to slice her face, causing her to make a loud shriek as she felt the impact.

Nat managed a chuckle and a satisfied look on her face, but Alex wasn't taking her actions lying down. They didn't care if anyone was in the building. Alex snapped her fingers and seemingly every piece of wood in the room began baring shape of what appeared to be arrows. Nat felt her breath cease momentarily but her instincts kicked in upon sighting a large keg not far away from her.

She ripped the top off and commanded the liquid within to spread into a rather large film of protection before her as she watched the sharpened wooden sticks get stopped by the leather-like film of alcohol, but one managed to tear through the protective layer and rip into Nat's left shoulder. Roaring in pain, Nat waved the large film of water over at Alex and began to wrap it around her like an unbreakable ball.

"You aren't getting a hold of me that easy, you hypocritical ass!" Alex yelled.

Tearing through the hydro film by commanding the particles apart, she lunged for Nat and missed by an inch. Nat knew she was lucky to dodge the attack. Alex readied her fists high in the air, surrounding each of them with a buzzing blue flame of magic, prompting Nat to improvise immediately.

Managing to shove Alex back, Nat took a moment to breathe before closing her eyes and opening them with a damning smile on her lips.

"What are you going to do? Kill me with your smile?" Alex mocked.

Nat had other ideas and with her left-hand waving towards the electrical circuit in the corner of the room, sparks burst into existence, causing a rather wild skull shaped flame that came roaring towards Alex.

"I don't mind sending you to hell, since that's exactly where you belong!" Nat shot back.

Alex watched the flame near her with her heart almost stopping, but quickly managed to move the sofa over to her, shielding herself from the inferno heading her way. Yet, the fire seemed too tough to be withstood as it brazed the objects in its path and raced along the walls in dangerously consuming manner.

Alex's eyes widened, her lips curled in a painful and frightful twitch, while her nostrils flared just as the fire burned through the sofa, the last line of defense and almost caught her foot before a gust of wind startled both girls.

The roofing collapsed in between them, and a groggy looking Nat managed to drag herself back to her feet but felt something snap just within her thigh. Alex spat out some blood with her back to the ground and her breathing becoming labored as she stared at the damage they had done to the frat house.

"I've had enough of your nonsense!" Nat yelled from where she continued to struggle to get to her feet.

Too weak to speak back, Alex cackled devilishly and collapsed her head backwards as she passed out. Nat held out the middle finger on her right hand and fell onto her stomach as her world slowly darkened and her consciousness withered away.

Waking up to her joints feeling stiff and the sight of an angry looking Mr. Alan Parker wasn't the prettiest sight to awaken to, but even more troubling was the sight of an elderly lady, elegantly dressed lady with two suited men behind her. Alex coughed and looked to her right, where Nat lay.

"You caused this!" an angry Nat hissed at Alex.

Samantha King soon arrived, looking nervous and going completely white in the face upon seeing and learning of the damage her daughter had caused.

"Hello Samantha," Brenda called out to the mayor with a wave.

Alex and Nat watched their mothers converse intensely, nodding their heads and both looking at their daughters with the staunchest of gazes. They weren't happy and oddly so, the two families would have to find a way to get their children towards coming to a common ground.

Muttering with a weakened voice, Nat felt her eyes close as the words came out, "Stay the hell away from me."

Alex sighed and closed her eyes, while the nurses hurled them away on their stretchers.

"Time to reconstruct everything now!" Mr. Parker announced, urging everyone to clear off asides Samantha King and Brenda Aurelius.

The three stood and stared at one another momentarily before turning around and independently began to set things back into place accordingly.

Brenda shot Samantha a smile and whispered to herself, "This almost feels like old times."

Samantha King had heard but only showed so with a thin smile as the trio sorted the full damages. The task itself was nothing Samantha could not handle alone, but she could very well guess Mr. Parker had decided to stick around and assist. Brenda was there, and there was always more than what meets the eye with Brenda.

Brenda let off a soft cough and looked at Samantha again with a wry smile. "You are as majestic as ever Samantha... the years haven't done you badly at all."

Samantha remained silent, weaving her hand in gestures as objects began flying across the room and settling where they naturally ought to be. Brenda seemed to take some joy in the fact her daughter was powerful enough to cause such level of damage. Yet, something about it also made her wonder about the other party in the fight.

For such level of destruction apparent to them, two powerful witches had to be involved in making it happen without fail.

Brenda reached for the back of her neck and rubbed it tenderly, connecting her fingers with the thin scar running along her spine and towards her back with some memories of the fateful incident that was coursing through her mind again. She could not believe it had been years and even more, she could not believe the different paths their worlds had taken through those years.

The room finally took shape and the trio paused to marvel at their work momentarily. Samantha took less time than the other two before turning around and heading for the door immediately.

Mr. Parker cleared his throat and watched Samantha King halt in her tracks just by the door. "Are you leaving us so soon Mrs. King?"

Samantha shrugged, turned around slowly and replied with a blank expression on her face. "I have some important things to deal with."

It was unlikely she was telling the truth and the man could feel it. The tension in the room had grown from the moment they both stepped in there and he had racked his mind and brain hard on how to go about it ever since. Brenda was no easy feat to deal with and her demeanor was one that could easily topple anyone and cause them to take her as being naturally condescending.

"Shouldn't we first tend to the crisis we have on our hands in here?" he asked politely with a thin smile.

Brenda rubbed her hands together and spoke, "Kids will always be kids… I remember having many squabbles during my days in school as well, but I turned out fine when maturity kicked in."

Mr. Parker shook his head gently and sighed. Being calm and soft with them just wasn't going to work and he wondered how he had not seen it earlier. The women continued to avoid each other's gaze as they stood in proximity.

"Let me rephrase my words," Mr. Parker spoke in a rather stern and quick tone. "You two have kids who are willing to tear down our school if left unchecked… I want it sorted immediately or I will expel them."

His message was clearer this time; they weren't going home or anywhere they planned on eloping to while they left the school to deal with two witches with nasty streaks running around the school.

Mr. Parker walked forward with some spring in his steps as he smiled tenderly, "Shall we?"

Samantha rushed out the door immediately, while Brenda followed behind without a single word and the disturbing blank expression on her face as well. The day was about to be a long one for both parties.

CHAPTER FIFTEEN

The silence that followed was the most disturbing aspect of the entire ordeal for the duo. Endless sparks flew when their eyes connected and each time, they broke it off within seconds in hopes the school wasn't going to get set ablaze. An hour had passed and there didn't seem to be any resolution put into place to help quench the witches' spat and the tense air between them.

Nat moved her shoulders gently and hoped to see if she was fully healed from their battle, while Alex remained static, with her back to the bed as her eyes rolled in their sockets as she stared at the ceiling. She wanted out badly, but there wasn't any getting past the spells put in place by the Headmaster's assistant. It was obvious the intent behind the spell was to keep them within regardless of how difficult the air or atmosphere might be for the duo.

Nat sat up in her bed and looked outside the window with a yearning for her freedom. She missed her friends and wondered how Leslie was and if she was going to forgive her for being a horrible friend. She also misses not having to share a space with her arch enemy who was now just some feet away from her. She wished she could be far away and if nothing else, for the silence to come to an end.

It was messing with both of their heads and they could tell. The room was specially constructed to deal with pupils who have gone on a rather damning act as the ones they performed in the clinic, and even worse, meant to deal them some psychological blow while they stared with whoever they had gotten into a spat with. The "Silent Room," it was called and it indeed, was living up to its reputation.

Alex finally slowly sat up and looked at Nat without having any intent to pull her gaze away. The past hour suddenly felt like half a day had dragged by, and her pulse raced wildly with discontent as she tried to figure out what exactly drove the girl's motives and need for acting righteous.

Alex parted her lips to speak but halted, while Nat broke through in words immediately, "You should be proud of yourself now."

They weren't the choice of words which anyone in their position was expected to spill but Alex didn't seem entirely surprised as she continued to lock Nat in stern gaze.

"I promise you I will not be less merciful when next you talk smack about any of my parents," Nat threatened.

Alex smiled at the ballsy girl and nodded her head gently. It felt perfect just watching her fume with rage by doing nothing whilst still managing to enrage her some more.

"You can keep whatever grudge you have inside until we step outside of this damn room," Alex replied casually. "It is no use spitting so many threats in a room where you cannot perform magic."

Alex looked at the ceiling with strange runes and markings inscribed into it, before casting her gaze towards the front door where a white substance ran along the floor of the door and outside of the room.

"You should be familiar with what this room is made of," Alex continued.

Nat frowned and looked away immediately, trying to tune her mind and hearing off from whatever Alex was about to spill. She could take some good guess on what it was, and she didn't want to hear it.

"It is said that it is one place with the ability to negate magic and other supernatural abilities, like the Oak Clinic " Alex narrated further without caring for how it would annoy Nat. "From the wood that line the walls, to the essence placed at the core of the room, which I was made to believe was Mr. King's essence."

Alex had nudged hard against Nat's hot button, her father, again and she could feel Nat ready to implode. Nat flipped around, tightened her fists into angry balls as she lunged forward and hoped to strike Alex hard in the face even if it would get her into trouble. Alex remained still and made no notion to move as she watched Nat freeze just few inches away from her.

It felt comical enough to provoke a smile from her lips as she waved her fingers lightly and felt Nat's breath warm her hand. "I forgot to tell you there is one more twist to the effects this room has on you."

"What?" Nat asked with a hushed tone while she grabbed at air and tried to break through whatever restraints was keeping her from clawing Alex's face off.

Alex slipped out from the bed she had been sleeping in and walked around some bit in circles before stopping a few feet from Nat and sighing aloud. "You cannot touch any other person placed in this room with you."

It was the perfect setup put into place to both torment those who had issues to iron out, while also taunting them with the fact that they would be that close, alone with no adult supervising them, and yet, remain unable to inflict any of their personal desires on the other party. Nat felt her muscles relax immediately, as she closed her eyes and wished everything would return to normal.

"It is pretty neat isn't it?" Alex smiled and continued. "It is my first time in here but when you have someone like Olivia as a friend, you're bound to know the inner workings of such disciplinary rooms well enough."

Nat turned around and walked away immediately. She headed for the window and leaned her head against the wall just to the left of it, breathing heavily as her mind raced with numerous thoughts she just could not place into a collective ball. Hell was real and she realized that she might just be living in it already.

Alex didn't seem entirely bothered though and Nat could guess why; she drew enough strength from seeing Nat suffering mentally and battling with her anger and was feeding on it to amuse herself until they were released from the room. It was a method that worked nicely and had she figured it out earlier, she might have chosen to adopt it.

"What happened to you?" Nat asked her words bouncing off the wall upon which her head was placed.

Alex stepped closer but remained without an answer as it seemed the ambiguous question wasn't one she could genuinely answer.

"You and I…" Nat paused and ran her fingers through her hair immediately. "You and I used to be friends."

Alex nodded her head as if she was attesting to the notion but hurriedly shook her head again.

"You and I were never anything," she whispered.

Nat felt her jaw drop and her eyes widen as she stared at her feet not wanting to shed any tears. She wasn't expecting such words and even while Alex never minced her words and would come off as rude, she had genuinely assumed they were friends years ago. It felt like eons now. Nat had not really given it any thought until they resumed school together again, but it was something that stuck inside the depths of her heart every time she had an encounter with Alex.

Alex turned her head and looked at Nat. "We were close, but I guess I could never be friends with you considering we don't run on the same moral compass."

The words were true and without any blemish or doubt; their moral compasses swung in utterly different directions and Nat wasn't going to deny it as she bobbed her head gently.

"You chose your path and stuck with unfair reasons to hate me, while I was and I still am the bad girl in your world or how you perceive it," Alex noted. "We were never friends... I have real friends now and you don't count as any of them."

Alex turned around and began walking back to the bed she had gotten up from. Nat walked over to her bed for the first time and sat on it with her hands locked together as she stared blankly and in a less moody expression at Alex.

"I wish we never crossed path back then," Nat whispered in a bold tone as she stared at a rather blank faced Alex.

Alex nodded and they both fell silent immediately. The oddity in the room suddenly seemed to simmer away, almost as if both had come to peace with their dislike for one another and that they were willing to go through life like that. Nat wondered if others who had been confined in the room found positive resolve with their spat partners or if they were too far gone and broken like they were to even find or make peace with one another.

The door slowly moved, in loud grinding noises like a stone was being dragged along the floor, before the three adults standing outside in the hallway came to view. Mr. Parker flanked by the two women didn't look pleased, but neither were the ladies by his side. They remained silent for the next few seconds, staring blankly at the two girls before Samantha King waved her hand at the entrance and lowered the barrier so she could step in.

Brenda followed her immediately, while Mr. Parker the school Director remained outside. Nat wondered what her mother was about to say, as she tried hard and did her best not to look in Alex's direction in fears she might get provoked once again.

"Go and get your things," Samantha King whispered. "We are going home."

Nat knew the tone; it meant she was in serious trouble. However, she could not understand what her mother intended or how she was going to go about it.

Brenda wrapped her arms around her daughter's neck and smiled as she whispered into the girl's ear, "Nora is waiting in the car outside and we should not keep her waiting."

Alex nodded, stole a slight glance at Nat with the intent to goad her, but fell short of doing so as she noticed Samantha King's eyes tailing her mother with the same expression, she held on her face for Nat.

"That's weird," she thought to herself before exiting the room.

Mr. Parker waited for them all to leave before placing the spell back on the room and heading off in the opposite direction.

"King and Aurelius," he mumbled. "Two families I have never been able to get a handle of."

Sighing aloud, he wondered what it was going to take to break the two girls completely.

Nat shook her head fervently for the umpteenth time, hoping it would somehow alter the decision her mother had made in lieu with Alex's mother, on their behalf. She had done well to pressure her mom on what they discussed while they were with Mr. Sadon for hours, but the woman had maintained her resolve and chosen to speak only when they got home.

Seated exactly where her mother had instructed her to, and with her arms folded across her chest with the same look of disbelief on her face, Nat shook her head vigorously once again while hoping she had heard wrong.

"You cannot be serious," she sounded rudely and attempted to get to her feet.

"Sit your ass down before you make me do something I will regret later!" Samantha boldly instructed her daughter with an outstretched hand.

Nat obeyed immediately, frowning deeply and mumbling words incoherently at her mother in spite.

"You should have done better by thinking of the consequences if you didn't want to get punished," Samantha mumbled while she paced across the floor with her hands on her hips.

Nat fell silent and stared at the large portrait of the man she loved more than life, on the opposite wall from where she sat. She wished he was alive ad there with them. She knew he would understand or at least, handle things differently even if he would scold her. The image on the wall saddened her heart and brought her lips to subtle trembles as she fought hard to hold back her tears.

"She teased me about dad you know?" Nat whispered without looking in her mother's direction.

Samantha had caught on and she paused before looking in the direction her daughter stared.

"She feels I'm naive about how the world is and I don't see things for how they truly are," Nat bowed her head and sighed deeply. "I wish he was here."

Samantha neared her daughter but did it cautiously as she slid into the empty seat by her side. They remained silent for the next few seconds, sharing in each other's loud breathing before Samantha decided she needed to speak.

"Have you been facing all of this at school on a regular basis?" she asked her daughter.

Nat refused to give an answer; it wasn't worth it having her mother fight her battles for her and it wasn't going to bring forth any respect for her from her classmates if her mother went raging in to fight her daughter's battles.

"I understand if you don't want to speak to me," Samantha nodded. "I wish you could though, and I sincerely wish your father was alive, but life can be cruel, and it definitely can topple our beliefs and personal judgments."

Nat sighed and leaned into the chair without looking at her mother still.

"Your father was the best man I have ever come across, and if Alexandra says differently or tries to make you believe he didn't live the best life, you shouldn't listen to her," Samantha reached for her daughter's hand but failed.

Nat shot her mother a scornful gaze. "Does this mean I don't have to work out things with her, or that I'm not grounded?"

Samantha got to her feet, began walking towards the kitchen door and waved her hand in the air. "You're still grounded honey, and you have to find common ground with Alex or I'm allowing Mr. Parker to deal with you two as he pleases."

Nat grumbled and cursed underneath her breath as she waited for her mother to disappear before venting out her rage. Swinging her arms in the air in rage, two flower vases shattered into zillion pieces as they collided with the wall before her. She tossed the couch pillows into the air and stormed off to her room as the thought of having to work things out with Alex infuriated her beyond words.

"I will kill that girl if I have to," she said to herself before slamming the door shut and loud enough for her mother to understand her discontent.

Samantha King heard her daughter's tantrum and felt her anger from the kitchen where she served herself a chilled glass of red wine.

"I did worse," she whispered with a mischievous smile on her lips as she sipped from her glass some more.

Alex could not understand why they had teleported home while Nora drove home without picking them up as her mom had insinuated earlier while they were with Nat and her mother.

Brenda walked ahead, fast and swiftly as her heels knocked onto the ground and her hair swung along her back, resting gently on her perfectly carved ass as she stopped before a marble door and placed her hand on it. The door swung open, granting them both access into the personal elevator.

Brenda waited for the elevator doors to close before turning to her daughter. "So, that was pretty much exciting."

Alex felt her lower jaw almost drop; it wasn't what she was expecting to hear from her mother.

"Your fight with Nat," her mother continued. "I sensed her aura in that room more than I did yours."

Alex finally understood; the hint of sarcasm in the first sentence slowly became apparent. Her mother wasn't nearly as impressed with her as much as she was about Nat. The woman had a thing for carnage and appreciating it regardless of how distasteful the act of destruction might be, she always seemed to know how to make it seem ordinary.

"I did not want to hurt her," Alex spoke in her own defense immediately. "She got angry after I teased her about her father."

Brenda nodded and snapped her fingers together, waiting for the elevator to halt suddenly before staring at her daughter long and hard in the face. "You've never been good at lying to me, so don't start now."

Alex looked away.

"Asides the obvious fact that girl generated enough power to blow that room apart, almost killing you in it, which quite honestly, you did fight back mildly and not enough of what I'd expect of my own daughter…" she paused to look at Alex briefly before continuing. "What did you notice about her?"

"What did I notice about what, mother?" Alex looked up confused.

Brenda nodded her head and waited for a response from the obviously befuddled looking girl. Alex was short on words and could barely manage a response as she stumbled in thoughts while trying to conjure a reasonable one.

Brenda sighed at her daughter's failure to take note of the obvious and important things. She snapped her fingers aloud once again, feeling the earth underneath them move and sink downward some more as the elevator moved at great speed until it finally came to a halt. They both stepped off immediately, walking right towards the archive room where Brenda kept her most important files.

"You understand why I don't have magic guarding any of these items right?" she asked her daughter.

"Warding items with magic only pique the interest of others and brings more trouble," she replied.

It was one of the major lessons her mother had taught her from a rather young age. Alex watched her open the next door with a large key she produced from her pocket and shove open the steel gate in between the hallway and the room, filled with scrolls.

"It is here somewhere," Brenda mumbled while searching through the stacks of scrolls lined along the shelves on the wall.

Alex watched her mother struggle through finding what she intended to find, as she wondered if the woman was in any way bothered about being called down to her school on disciplinary issues. It seemed more likely that she was far more annoyed about feeling Nat's essence within the damaged clinic than Alex's but in the moment, she was up to something else and her daughter could only watch.

"Here it is," Brenda voiced aloud and smiled as she waved her daughter over.

The thick scroll, dusty and old, bore the large perfectly scribbled words *"The Kings"* across the top of its page, with writings in different inks running along the page and towards the back.

"Is that a compilation of information on Nat's family?" Alex asked in a surprised tone.

Her mother ignored her question and walked over to a large marble table in the center of the room to place the scroll down underneath the bright light. Alex maneuvered her way over to her mother, shoving aside cobwebs and holding her breath intermittently to avoid breathing in so much dust.

"I always wondered what that sniveling woman brought to the table and thanks to you, I just might have found it," Brenda giggled mischievously.

Alex stood with her hands on her waist, while sweeping her gaze from her mother to the scroll in her hands and then back at the woman. "Mom, what exactly is that?"

Brenda leaned closer to the scroll and began to read the words on it in subtle mumbles until she was satisfied enough. She sucked in ample air, expelled aloud and fell back into the chair as she waved Alex over to the seat opposite her. Alex did as she had been commanded, feeling her mind race with thoughts bordering along the line of discomfort and worry.

"I'm pretty sure you're familiar with the workings of the room you were locked in earlier, are you not?" her mother asked.

"Yes mother, I am," Alex replied. "It is similar with what the Oak Clinic is made from, of."

Her mother nodded excitedly and clapped her hands aloud.

"Perfect my dear child! Perfect!" she smiled. "Did you see the way Samantha cast aside the spell binding the room?"

Alex did not notice so she shook her head.

"Oh, sorry, you were on the inside, but the gimmicks with that room is that it should never allow magic reside inside of it, much like the clinic," the woman explained in an excited and less moody tone. "But, guess what?"

Alex shrugged and remained lost.

"Samantha King not only canceled the magic holding the door in place, but also everything within the room the moment she stepped in," Brenda finally laid down the juicy news.

It sounded totally unbelievable and beyond everything they had been told or even briefed over the years on how the Oak Clinic worked.

"So, I had my powers restored in that room? How come I didn't feel anything?" Alex asked in confusion.

"I'm guessing the magic suppressed it so hard it came back slowly, and you never truly felt it, but I did and it is the most remarkable discovery still," Brenda gushed hard.

Alex leaned in with her elbows on the table and smiled mischievously.

"It means the Kings have the greatest ability very few and rare witches have," her mother sighed. "They can negate any mystical power and also reinstate them without fuss."

Alex gasped and her eyes widened. "Do you think Nat knows this?"

Brenda rubbed her chin gently before waving the idea away immediately. "She is still too young and still untapped into her abilities to know something that grand."

Satisfied with her discovery, she held the scroll before her and used a black ink begin to scribble her new findings on the page. Watching the words get completed, she folded it neatly back in place and returned it from the spot she had retrieved it from earlier.

"I have a job for you again," Brenda said to her daughter as she dashed for the door.

Alex followed her mother hurriedly. "Does this mean I don't get punished for today?"

Brenda remained silent…

Alex waited on a response from her mother with her hands behind her back. The air felt good and jolly and it seemed perfect for her to not get reprimanded from what she had done earlier. Yet, Brenda's blank expression held some measure of doubt as she seemed to be drifting in thoughts elsewhere.

"Mom," Alex called out again and in a sterner tone.

Brenda snapped out from whatever thoughts riddled her mind as she stared with widened eyes at her daughter, "Yes?"

Alex cleared her throat, took a different stance and crossed her arms over her chest. "Am I still getting punished for the incident at school?"

Brenda smiled, bobbed her head and replied in a gentle tone, "What do you think missy?"

Alex wondered if it was a trick question and delayed her response, she toyed with her fingers nervously and wished her mother would put her out of her misery already. The cunning woman exited the room and waved on to her daughter to follow immediately.

"You have some serious work to do for me darling," Brenda muttered before cackling out loud in an evil manner.

Alex worried for Nat and her mother immediately. She didn't need to be briefed on her next duty or who the subjects were going to be; her mother had found herself a new fascination in the Kings and it was never a good sign.

CHAPTER SIXTEEN

A week passed since the infamous incident that threatened to level the entire frat house and everyone seemed to have forgotten about it. Words still floated about the measure of power Nat held within her, as many veered on her side as regards just to what sort of witch she was, but Alex felt her stance in school slowly slide down the ladder of ridicule as few believed she wasn't capable of toppling Nat.

Yet, the atmosphere had never seemed or looked more peaceful, with everyone hyped about the afternoon as they trooped into the volleyball court one at a time with jerseys supporting their classes and favorite teams that were about to play. Teachers lined the large sized hall and remained as vigilant as ever, in bid to prevent the sort of attack that almost left them to deal with a student's death.

Mr. Sadon had ordered the highest form of security they could have, and even brought in magical elves specialized in binding spells for protection to help ward off intruders from the school. Yet, in the shadows lurked the feeling that something was waiting for the perfect moment to pounce. It was without doubt a feeling many students kept close to their hearts as they wandered around the school grounds.

The large school clock struck aloud and indicated noon had dawned upon them. Numerous feet slapped onto the ground as they hurried along the school corridors and towards the sports venue.

"What if they win?" Leslie looked at the boy licking an ice cream cone to her left.

Hurriedly looking at her, he replied, "What if who wins?"

Sheila grunted and shook her head seriously in disbelief. They had been on the subject matter about who could win the first game between teams consisting of sophomores, and those filled with juniors, while Arnold obviously decided to pay better attention to his ice cream than their conversation.

"Are they always like this?" Leslie asked Sheila in a whisper.

Sheila shrugged and took another look at the annoying fourth member of their group. He seemed to care less about everything and harbored little to no interest in what others had to say or what they were interested in voicing about either.

"The only thing I know for sure is they lack empathy and they have a way of ruining games for you before they even begin!" Sheila fumed.

Leslie seemed lost on what the witch was talking about and looked at Arnold for some explanation or at least a tip. Arnold smirked his lips and licked his fingertips before looking at Leslie and casting a smile across his face as though he had no idea what she was speaking about.

"Don't be a douche Arnold," she pleaded in the best way she could. "What game did you ruin?"

He pointed in the direction of the court and whispered, "The one in which Alex and Nat are about to play as teammates."

Leslie gasped and felt her ears ring with disbelief. News on the sophomore teams had been kept a secret for reasons best known to coaches John and Zack.

"How can you possibly know that?" Leslie yanked at Arnold's arm while Sheila looked around the arena in anticipation. "It has not even started yet. More so, placing those two on the same team is a recipe for losing."

Arnold shrugged and sighed. "I need more ice cream and to answer your question, they are going to…"

Leslie waited for the words to come through, but Arnold only continued to gurgle and hold his throat in discomfort as his eyes bulged and network of veins stretched along the side of his neck and head.

"Are you okay?" Leslie asked, drawing closer and noting he was in serious discomfort.

He shook his head fervently, pointed in Sheila's direction and grumbled incoherently as he seemed to struggle with whatever was going on with him.

Leslie looked in Sheila's direction, sighting the witch with her fist clenched and pointed in Arnold's direction. "He is not going to spoil this game for me any more than he already did."

Leslie smiled softly. "You can't hold his breath forever."

"I only plan to do it for the next hour until the game is finished," she replied. "I can release him on one condition alone though, and it is with his word that he will not speak of the game or say anything in relation to its outcome."

Arnold bobbed his head immediately and gasped as his windpipe felt a rush of air running through it again. Reddened in his face and with curled lips, he cursed at Sheila before he walked away and got himself a seat on the third row so he could see the game properly.

"Try not to be so aggressive," Leslie whispered to Sheila, before taking a seat by Arnold's side, while Sheila continued to look around the hall like she had misplaced something. She then got up to join her friends.

Out of nowhere Leslie sighed out. "You have got to be kidding me."

Sheila turned towards her and asked, "What?"

Leslie remained silent with her arms folded across her chest. Her breath became heavy and she moved in her sit, displaying a rather uncomfortable aura around her. Simon had just walked in with a laughing Olivia on his back.

"You're definitely not okay," Sheila sounded in a worried tone before leaning closer to Leslie.

Leslie waved the words away. "I will be fine… I only wish the game would start already."

Her nerves were at the point where she could feel herself wanting to scream or doing something crazy. What troubled her dearly was fast approaching and there was no telling how she was going to handle the situation.

"We are here for Nat," she whispered underneath her breath. "We are here for Nat… we are here for Nat."

The seats in the hall filled faster than expected, with students seemingly eager to have a taste of what the games had for them. Leslie felt 'his' aura slip into the seat behind her, but she stiffened her neck and refused to utter a word or give in to the urge to turn around. In all fairness, him being behind her wasn't the reason she felt enraged, but for the fact about who he was with.

"Leslie?" the masculine voice of Simon called out from behind in a rather surprised tone than a direct one.

Leslie remained with her gaze solely on the court while Sheila turned around immediately. Arnold smiled as he seemed to enjoy the uncomfortable situation.

"Hello weirdo," the annoying tone of Olivia who was sitting by Simon made Sheila's inside crawl as she turned around immediately even though she thought of blasting that vampire with a fire ball.

Leslie was determined to give Simon the silent treatment after seeing him and Olivia dancing closely at a bar where he invited her to meet him at. Simon tried to get her attention again. Arnold turned around and told Simon to back off and resume his begging another time which caused the two girls to chuckle.

"The game is about to begin," Sheila stated, choosing to pay no attention to the fact that Olivia was seated directly behind her and stared at the court in hopes of seeing Nat. The week had been the hardest for them all; from the constant monitoring, to Nat and Alex spending hours after school to clean up classrooms and restrooms without being able to use their magic, had barely left them time to function as a group.

"Come on baby!" Olivia yelled in excitement from behind as Alex stepped onto the court.

Leslie strained her eyes towards the court and whispered, "What are those things around their wrists?"

"Restrictors," Simon replied behind them.

Leslie felt her neck stiffen as she tried hard and well against her desire to turn back and engage him in a conversation.

"They prevent the players from using their powers within the first three rounds, but they get taken off for the last two rounds which are the most crucial," he explained.

Leslie shook her head and bowed slowly as she looked at her feet and ignored the starting whistle which brought along raucous cheers from the students.

"Are you going to ignore me all through the game, Leslie?" the boy asked, with his hand reaching for her shoulder as he leaned closer.

Olivia yanked at him and pulled him backwards. "What are you doing?"

He shrugged, unsure of how to answer the question as he slowly returned to an upright position in his seat and heard half of the hall cheer aloud. Leslie jumped to her feet and seemed to be overcompensating as she cheered on Nat who had just scored a point for her side

Olivia looked to Eleanor who had been awfully silent the entire time. "Why did Alex ask us to take these seats?"

Eleanor replied without breaking her gaze from the court, "It helps build the impression that we are getting along."

It was the biggest hoax and Olivia hated it. She would rather be elsewhere than watching the game near those losers and even more, she hated the fact something was going on between Simon, her cousin and the pesky phoenix that was sitting right in front of him.

"I know it isn't easy for you, but you could please try and do this for Alex," Eleanor pleaded. "We don't have a choice, so play nice and go easy."

Olivia nodded her head and closed her eyes while she counted from ten downwards. Feeling less tensed, she parted her eyelids, took a relaxed position and clapped aloud in support of Alex's team cheering her on. It felt rather odd to watch the two girls play on the same side though and what appeared even odder was the fact Alex was doing it with a smile on her face as she laid a pass for Nat to make a perfect strike.

Arnold leaned forward and looked to his right so he could take a look at the temperamental vampire behind them. With a content smile drawing from the edges of his lips, he sat back and hoped to enjoy the game.

Bearing frowns across their faces and with their eyes trying hard not to look in each other's direction, Alex and Nat wished Mr. Parker would speak faster and let them leave without further ado. Yet, the man seemed content by simply staring at them and allowing them to stew in how their actions had affected the course of the game earlier.

Getting up from his seat and walking towards the cabinet with thick looking files tucked into them nicely, he yanked one out and flipped through the pages gracefully before heading back to his seat and slapping the file on the table before him.

"Looks like the magical universe always finds a way to balance past events with current ones," he tittered, before leaning back into his chair and staring at the two girls.

Alex flinched, but felt her wrist stiffen as she rubbed her hand against the restrictor still fastened around her right wrist.

"What puzzles me the most is the fact that both your mothers never got along and now it seems to be extending to the both of you as well," he continued.

Alex looked less shocked in contrast to Nat whose widened eyes was enough to tell of her ignorance.

"What are you talking about?" she leaned closer to the table and placed her right hand with the blinking restrictor on it.

Alan Parker smiled and leaned closer as well, turning the file around so they could look at younger images of their mothers pinned into the files bearing what appeared to be some disciplinary records.

"What I'm saying is, if they both could make up and sort whatever differences they had, then you two can do the same or even better," he replied before getting to his feet and walking to the door. "Your arrogance and desire not to work with each other was the downfall of your team today."

Alex sighed and got to her feet. She was glad she could finally head home, even if she didn't feel like it and would rather have remained in school with her friends.

"See you tomorrow, girls," he smiled while they walked out the door.

Nat paused and held out her wrist with the restrictor around it. "I assumed we were getting this off after the game?"

Mr. Parker nodded his head but shrugged with a mix of confusing actions.

"I assumed so too, but I think we'll leave them on you two for a while," he rubbed his chin softly and replied. "It is a small price to pay considering you literarily almost tore each other to shreds on the court today."

"I cannot catch a break!" Nat mumbled while Alex seemed unperturbed to be without her powers as she dragged her feet away.

CHAPTER SEVENTEEN

Silence was scarce, but it still seemed like that alone was what enveloped them on that particular last period for the day. Students stared at their watches blankly, hoping for time to take a rather giant leap and bring the rather boring class to an end as soon as possible. Yet, it trickled away slowly and continued to haunt them as many decided to grant their eyes some rest while the teacher scribbled blandly on the board.

"What use is Astronomy again?" Arnold leaned closer to Leslie and asked.

The witch remained mute, stewing as she had been doing for the past few hours as she toyed with her cellphone underneath the table.

"Are you even listening to me?" Arnold asked before shaking his head and looking away from the obviously distracted witch.

Sheila leaned closer to the Arnold and whispered, "She's still messed up over Simon. It would be best to give her space."

Arnold wore an immediate frown, as he casted Leslie another look before turning back his attention to Sheila. "The guy at the game?"

Sheila tapped her nose in confirmation before sitting upright as the teacher took a moment from scribbling on the board. Arnold focused his gaze on the board.

"I need four volunteers," the stout looking man with rather oddly shaped Van Dyke spoke aloud. "Are there any brave students willing to step forward and attempt to carry out the art of divination as I have explained today?"

Nat held her hand up slowly, while the classroom stared at her as Alex did the same.

"This should be interesting," Sheila mumbled.

Leslie looked up slowly and wore a frown immediately as she briefly looked to the far corner to her left where Olivia's steadfast gaze seemed to have been glued to her skull for the past few minutes.

"Bitch!" Leslie thought to herself before watching Alex and Nat get up from their seats and begin to walk to the front of the class.

Arnold whispered to Sheila, "Don't they need magic to be able to do anything?"

Sheila shrugged.

"Why are you beating yourself up over Simon?" Arnold asked bluntly. "Is it because you feel he chose Olivia over you and that has somehow damaged your self-esteem?"

Sheila nudged the outspoken boy hard and caused him to wince in pain immediately.

"Hey! What did I do?" he asked, frowning.

Leslie fumed and got to her feet, shoving past her desk and left the class. Arnold laughed aloud while Sheila wished she could smack his head off.

"Do you know anything?" Sheila turned to Arnold and asked.

Arnold shrugged and replied, "Maybe I do, and maybe I don't."

Sheila sighed and stared at him with a frown. "Are you going to stop being a douche toward your friend and tell me what you know or what?"

Arnold smiled and simply replied, "Fine, fine, he's Olivia's cousin. He's really into Leslie and once she gets back to her dorm room, she'll find him waiting with flowers."

Sheila wondered how they had gotten paired with someone like Arnold. His level of insensitivity was beyond understanding. "You need to apologize and tell her what you know. Text her now."

Mr. Banks broke their conversation by calling out a boy just a few seats away from Arnold to the front of the class to complete the numbers he needed up front.

"I need each of you to man a crystal ball of your choosing, so we can begin immediately!" The excited teacher cried at the top of his voice.

Alex picked the biggest ball in the locker that was provided to them to pick from, while Nat opted for something smaller. Alex and Nat barely broke their gaze from one another. Seemingly trapped in a world of their own, Nat wondered if the true reason behind Alex choosing to volunteer for the experiment was the same as hers. The yearn to feel alive again by being temporarily granted her magic had made her raise her hand, considering she imagined the teacher could easily take it off for them to use the crystals.

Sighing exhaustively, he rubbed his palms together and chuckled excitedly, "Now, let's begin!"

At the end of the lesson Mr. Blinks announced that they all would have a final project to present before the term was over and it was a team assignment. It would count for seventy percent of their final grade. He went down his list calling out pairs, Nina and Gale, Hector and Iris, Arnold and Olivia.

"What?" Olivia yells out and Arnold just grinned, he must have foreseen who he was going to be placed with. The teacher continued unperturbed then announced the most shocking pair of all, Natalie and Alexandra.

"The selections are final, so I suggest you all get along for the sake of your grade or not move on to the next level."

Nat passed out.

※ ※ ※

Sucking in a dose of berry tainted air into her lungs, she laid down as she tried to gather her surroundings. Her back felt cushioned against the softest object she had ever come across yet. Eyelids parted permitting the ray of light bursting into her eyes. Nat squinted and rubbed her eyes clean with the back of her hand, before remaining still and choosing not to move for the next few seconds while she tried hard to figure out where exactly she was.

The beautiful looking room bore all sorts of art works from paintings to sculptures on the wall with a glass ceiling that magically reflected and refracted the wonderful rays of the golden sun without allowing the scorching effect of the sun rays to come through. She marveled at the sight and wondered how she had gotten there, when all she remembered was being in class.

"You're awake!" the tender masculine voice spoke in surprise. "That was quite some nap you had there."

Nat stared at Garrett Marshall strangely and pondered to herself on what exactly was going on.

"I had passed your classroom and heard a commotion, so I went inside and saw you had fainted. I offered to bring you to the nurse but thought you might want some alone time," he explained with a glass of bluish liquid in his hand which he offered to her.

Staring at the glass and looking at him intermittently, she asked, "What's that, and, where am I?"

"This is my personal lodgings at the school," he replied.

"It is just a normal room like every other one, but spiced up with magic," Mr. Marshall stated with the glass of blush liquid still outstretched to Nat. "Drink up and you will feel better, I assure you."

Nat remained still and silent, hoping for an answer to her first question before even considering the possibility of downing something she was not familiar with.

"It is phoenix brew and a rare magical drink used to replenish one's strength," he explained. "Since you've been without your magic for a while, I thought it best to provide you with a boost."

Nat lifted her wrist immediately to see the restrictor had been taken off. Her heart leapt with joy even while her body still felt numb and ordinary. "How come I still don't feel a thing?"

The teacher gave no response. Crossing his legs over one another, and with his eyes barely looking away from Nat, he watched her gulp down some bit of the brew before downing the entire glass upon realizing it didn't taste badly.

"You will not guess where I learnt how to make that potion from," he gushed and shook his head as the wildest smile crept into his cheeks.

Nat took down the glass from her lips and whispered in a guess, "My father?"

Mr. Marshall nodded his head in testament slowly.

"How was he?" Nat asked in a calm and rather relaxed tone.

Mr. Marshall adjusted in his seat and leaned his elbows into his knees as he drew his face closer to Nat.

"How was my father?" she asked again and explicitly. "What was he like when you were his assistant?"

Mr. Marshall ran his fingers through his hair and allowed himself a trip down memory lane.

"Your father was the kindest man I have ever come across," he replied in shaky tone. "I'm not sure I can be half the man he was or even grow to be as daring as he was during his lifetime."

Nat smiled and felt her interest piqued as she adjusted in her seat.

"How did you guys meet?" she pressed further.

Mr. Marshall smiled and broke into subtle laughter as he shook his head and replied, "No… no… no, you don't want to know."

Nat wasn't backing off obviously and she pressed for an answer with her raised brows and her eyes fixated on the teacher who seemed to be the closest person to her father whom she had come across, asides her mother.

"Okay, I'll tell you," he replied, before getting up from his seat and clapping his hands together aloud.

The reflective ceiling slowly disappeared and became replaced by a more traditional one, but the walls remained as beautiful as they had been with art works lined all around them. It grew in size though, springing forth a resting area which housed a large sized mattress and a couch with a large screen television that was hanging on the west wall, not far off from the exit door.

"What I want to show you should remain our little secret," he warned.

Nat nodded her head. Her teacher soon returned with a thick brown file bounded by a ribbon made from leather. Slapping the book with both hands, he made certain to rid it off dust before settling on the big couch in the living room.

"I started keeping this journal from the first day I met your father," he narrated with shaky tone. "In fact, he had given it to me after the most infamous raid on the dark witches' coven in our history."

Nat felt her heart leap in unsteady beats as she reached for the journal and flipped open the first page which bore a rather old and torn looking article on a newspaper publishing with the words *"Dr. King Leads Assault on Deadly Coven to Rescue Trapped Children"* boldly printed at the top and was filled images of children being led out from what appeared to be a crypt of some sorts.

"How come I have never heard of this?" she looked up to the man and asked.

He shrugged, smiled and flipped to the next page, "Your father always wanted a private life, and this was his last raid and assault on the cult that stole children and used them for their evil purposes."

Nat had never felt prouder of her father. She glued her eyes on each page as though she never wanted to stop seeing the man's picture. He was without doubt younger and with a certain gravitas about him as well. He posed for pictures with the then mayor and the four children he had saved from the witches' lair.

"What happened to the kids?" Nat asked, running her fingers along the page while trying to understand what those little kids must have felt and gone through.

They were no more than ten years of age and each looked malnourished, tired and definitely scared stiff even while taking those pictures; three girls and a single boy. Garrett Marshall got to his feet and began walking away from the couch while Nat absentmindedly regaled herself with more newspaper articles slapped on the pages of the journal.

Suddenly, she halted on a particular page bearing the image of the little boy she had seen earlier and her father standing before the Oak Clinic on the date it was launched. The boy had grown and obviously was a teenager with his curly hair flowing down his shoulders and his previously sullen face now donning the biggest smile yet.

"Still wondering what became of the little boy saved from that coven?" Mr. Marshall asked with his hands spread apart from his body, and his shirt partly opened.

Nat felt herself swallow hard immediately, while she struggled to look away from the journal in her hand. Maybe it was the truth behind having to look up at the man that worried her, or the fact that she could be in presence of a being who had gone through so much turmoil in life.

"Your father is the reason my life is worthwhile," Mr. Marshall spoke in trembling tone before wiping some tear drops from the corners of his eyes.

Nat finally understood why the man was keen on being there for her. Asides his naturally soothing persona, he had gone through enough despair to want to assist others in quenching theirs. She finally looked up and sighted the scars he was showing her.

The sight was heart breaking but equally joyous for her in a mix of bittersweet knowledge. Her father was no ordinary man who ran a clinic for supernatural creatures, but a helper through and through and a warrior whose tales he had managed to keep a secret because he didn't care for personal accolades or spoils.

"Can I...?" Nat asked with an outstretched hand as she laid the journal to rest on the couch.

Mr. Marshall closed his eyes and nodded as she approached. She helped herself to feeling the first scar that ran along his belly and up his chest, before stopping to run her fingers over a shorter but equally thicker one to the left-hand side of his rib.

"Sorry to ask, but why are the scars still there?" Nat asked, while trying not to sound insensitive.

He simply replied, "Because your father asked that they should be left to heal naturally."

Nat slowly retracted her hand and wore a rather befuddled expression on her face. It made no sense to allow anyone get subjected to such level of pain or even harbor that number of disfiguring scars on their skin when magic could easily have made everything perfect.

"Yes, it sounds confusing does it not?" he chuckled and began buttoning his shirt back. "It was the best decision I would have made if I had the understanding your father had back then."

Nat wore a frown to show her lack of understanding in anything he was talking about.

"Most of my magical nerve endings had been severed after my body was subjected to endless cutting and healings, which would have made it nearly impossible, but there was another reason he asked me to keep them," he explained.

He led Nat back to the couch where they sat and stared at each other.

"Your father believed these scars have too many tales about my life to tell and erasing them wouldn't be worth it, especially when I look back some day and recognize how far I have come," he added.

It made more sense to her and sounded a whole lot like her father too; the man whose foresight was far greater than anyone's she had come across in her life. Nat approached Mr. Marshall and gently laid her hand to rest on his chest, prompting him to leave the last three buttons on his shirt undone as he stared blankly at her.

Slowly gliding her hand over the opened part of his shirt, she whispered, "Does it still hurt?" Nat asked while doing her best not to look into the man's eyes.

He bobbed his head gently and whispered in soft tone, "Yes, it does, but not the physical scars."

Nat slipped her hand over the done buttons and could barely have guessed what was coming next when he scooped her into his arms immediately. Her heart halted, and her nerves seemed to relax immediately and oddly so, as he brought her face within reach of his, before locking her in a rather stern and seductive look until Nat found her soul melting away into his right there and then.

She motioned to speak but he wouldn't allow it as he placed a finger to her lips.

"Mr. Marshall ..." Nat whispered before feeling the familiar finger landing on her lips again.

"You can call me Garrett," he urged, smiling wildly while his eyes burned brightly too.

Nat nodded her head gently, felt his face draw closer as she closed her eyes and parted her lips gently... his warmth felt consuming and even more was his body being pressed against hers. Something was brewing right then, and she wondered what might come of it if she allowed it to blossom.

Her lips waited still, parted and willing, while her heart resumed pumping blood in copious amounts through the entirety of her body.

CHAPTER EIGHTEEN

Samantha King came into the living room and removed her heels before she walked over to hug Alex who sat with her daughter on the sofa. "Alexandra, so good to see you again."

"Good to see you too Mrs. King."

"How's the project coming along girls?"

"Good mom, can we get back to it?" Nat didn't want to make Alex too uncomfortable and have her make some excuse to leave. This project was too important, and they hadn't worked much on it. They kept getting into arguments about their topic and had trouble focusing at school where their friends would also clash. A week had passed since the project was assigned. Earlier today in class Mr. Banks asked everyone for a progress report for extra credit points and while many had little progress, they at least thought about what their topic would be. Alex and Nat however had nothing to report and were punished by not being able to turn in their homework for a grade. Nat suggested they get away from school and their friends and come to her house to work.

"Sure, but Alexandra…."

"Please, it's Alex." Alex cuts in.

"Sorry, Alex, it's been so long. What are you doing this Saturday evening?"

"Nothing," "Mom, no." Alex and Nat spoke at the same time which made Alex turn to Nat in confusion. Mrs. King just smiled.

"Great, you can be Natalie's date to the mayor's annual fundraiser. Which is myself and I can't have my daughter go to another party with important figures dateless. It just wouldn't look right. Please, do it for me, all those times I welcomed you into my home. You're like a second daughter to me."

Nat rolled her eyes so hard at the obvious guilt trip her mom was playing that they get stuck for a second.

Alex was visibly nervous but smiled awkwardly anyway. "Sure, why not."

"Great, I'll go order some pizzas for you two and leave you be. I have a phone conference in a few minutes. I'm suddenly a mediator for the Scorpion gang and the Vok'rati warlock clan."

"You didn't have to do that. I will tell her no when you leave." Nat closed the book on her lap.

"She always made me feel welcomed and allowed me to run around her house and go everywhere with you guys even on expensive trips without wanting anything in return. Not many would do that. Anyway, my mom was going to the party and might have made me go anyway. We'll just tell anyone who ask us questions we're there as friends so that way you won't have to touch me in anyway." Alex marked some notes from her computer screen down onto the white board in front of them.

An hour later and they still hadn't picked a topic, though they did narrow it down to their top three.

"Our best bet is working with the meteorites as you suggested earlier and see if we can put them back up in space and collide with a star, do a report on the meteorites, and results of impact." Alex took one of the two meteorites and started packing her things. "Let's do the meteorites first, I take one and you do the other then we can meet again when it's done."

"Alright, see you Saturday, I'll send you the picture of my outfit." Nat started cleaning up.

An hour later Alex found herself at the courthouse waiting for her mother. Flexing her nerves around her fingers as she watched the ball of fire disappear and reappear on her palm as she smiled to herself, the past three days had been better than she could have imagined it would. Having gone for a while living like a common human with no magical abilities seemed to make the rush of having her magic return even greater than she had expected it would.

"Miss Alexandra," Nora called from the end of the hall as she waved her hand.

Alex put out the flame in her hand immediately and hurried towards her mother's personal assistant. "You and my mom do understand I have better things to do than to be in a courthouse full of corrupt people."

Nora smiled and wrapped her arms around Alex warmly.

"I relayed your feelings to your mother, but she felt you needed to see this for yourself," Nora replied. "More so, since you're planning on becoming a kick ass lawyer, you might want be at these court hearings once in a while."

Alex scoffed and knew too well why her mother wanted her there; it was to show off on just how good she was at handling and winning cases. Her reputation as one of the best lawyers in the world only continued to grow and the woman always went for the hardest cases with the most enticing monetary offer if she was to stand for anyone, regardless of whether they were guilty or not.

Nora led the way and was about pushing open the court room door when Alex held her hand and stopped her. "Which of the world's scumbag is my mother representing today?"

Nora smiled and took a second to maul through her mind for an answer. "Vladimir Kchikoff… I believe you must have heard of him."

Alex shook her head but wasn't in any way disappointed or let down upon hearing the name and knowing of the crimes the man himself had committed.

"You're speaking of the human hunter who not only eats them, but also uses their organs and entrails for dark magic? Do I know of him?" Alex sounded certain even while she asked sarcastically.

Nora laughed shortly and stopped immediately as a group of lawyers walked past them.

"Just be on your best for the both of us when you step in there will you? Please?" Nora pleaded with a warm smile.

Alex understood the consequence of shaming or even belittling her mother's reputation in public. All hell would break lose, and hail and brimstone will fall upon anyone who dares do such a thing even if they were family or close companions.

"Sure Nora," Alex assured her. "We both wouldn't want the courtroom burning down, now would we?"

Nora laughed aloud and opened the door for Alex to venture inside, while she followed behind. The room was filled as expected, with many more interested in seeing how the well-respected and formidable Brenda Aurelius was going to convince the jury to set a confirmed and rather convicted killer in the frame of the Russian maniac free.

Alex could feel sweat trickling down her neck as she made her way to the reserved seats in front of the court and not far off from the judge. Eyes trialed her as she strolled past with Nora while the duo pretended as though they could not tell how much their presence had attracted endless murmurings and castigating looks.

"Is that her daughter?" one lady asked the man to her left.

He bobbed his head and frowned at Alex. "That's the viper's daughter."

Alex stopped in her tracks, wore a frown and clenched her fists as she felt Nora stand in between her and the man whose voice had obviously infuriated her. Nora waved her hand slightly and tried to usher Alex forward, but the girl wasn't in the mood to act passive when she had been labeled or her mother had been tagged with such despicable name.

"A viper?" Alex mumbled and made eye contact with the man who hurriedly looked away.

Nora smiled in the corner of her lips and whispered, "That's what they call her, and she has quite grown fond of it if I must tell you."

Alex had never heard her mom being regarded as such but in relation with how the woman acted, she very well conceded in belief that it just might be a soothing name.

"The trail is about to start, and we shouldn't be lingering around," Nora encouraged Alex as they left the man who was already cowering in his boots.

Two huge looking policemen escorted a chained prisoner into the courtroom and to loud whispers and endless mumblings that tore through the air immediately. Having heard of the maniac's exploits all around the world but never seeing any image of him or having knowledge of what he looks like, Alex was more than baffled to reconcile the figure being led into the courtroom before her to the one people quaked in their boots about.

Thin and short to say the least, he didn't seem imposing enough to be able to abduct teenagers or even adults, talk less of committing such heinous crimes against over six hundred people over the span of fifteen years. His calm demeanor and lack of presence made the man the least person anyone would expect to be a killer.

"How is mom going to win this sort of case when the entire world has heard of him to be a killer?" Alex asked before planting herself into a seat behind her mother's

Nora shrugged before leaning closer to Alex and whispering, "This case is far more complicated than you can come to imagine."

Alex felt a rush of anxiety riddle her entire system as her mother walked in majestically; donning her trademark body fitted black suit and high heeled shoe which did more to announce her presence in the court room from its knocks against the ground than anything else. Brenda walked past her daughter and Nora without so much as a smile in their direction; it was time for work and she had her best game face on.

"She is going to win, isn't she?" Alex asked.

Nora nodded her head affirmatively as they both watched the court proceed within a few minutes.

"Your Honor," Brenda Aurelius got to her feet to state her case with her arms tucked behind her back and her lips wearing a wicked smile as she approached the jury box.

Alex slipped her hands in between her thighs, nervously shaking in her boots as she wondered how her mother was about going through her client's defense.

"My client has been labeled with ridiculous charges for which he pleads not guilty, unless there be any willing testifier or witness who can actually prove for a certainty that he is the Maniac they claim he is," she spoke calmly. "They have been able to provide no evidence at best and nothing incriminating other than the words of a drunk prostitute who claims she had been lured to his house some months ago and made the discovery of human remains."

Vladimir smiled and rested his elbows on the table before him while he obviously seemed satisfied by his defense's proclamation of his innocence.

The judge nodded, and spoke immediately, "In lieu of the charges levied against Mr. Vladimir, what evidence does the prosecuting team have in place to make their case?"

The opposing lawyer got to his feet and unbuttoned his suit as he approached the judge's stand. He seemed rather nervous and could barely contain his emotions as he mumbled angrily at Brenda while both slugged things out at the judge's desk.

"What is going on?" Alex leaned towards Nora to inquire.

With a rather odd smile growing on her face, Nora replied, "Just watch."

Alex turned her attention back to the judge who shook his head and ordered both lawyers away from him immediately.

Ramming his gavel down hard and startling everyone in the court room, he sighed and declared his verdict, "Upon learning of the prosecuting team's inability to provide a credible witness or any source of proof to back their claim against Mr. Vladimir, I have no other option but to call this trial a mistrial and apologize to Mr. Vladimir and his family on behalf of the court for whatever discomfort this might have brought them."

Different from the expected cheers of joy that came with someone being discharged and acquitted of any wrong doing, the room fell into a graveyard-esque mood. Alex could hear her own breath, while she noted the cocky smile on her mother's face too.

"We won," Brenda smiled at her client and whispered.

Mr. Vladimir slowly got to his feet, clapped tenderly and smiled at the judge who couldn't bear to look in his direction.

"You will get the remaining five million dollars as discussed sometime today," he whispered to Brenda as she drew closer. "You truly are as they say you are."

Alex couldn't quite grasp how such a trial could be so brief and come to an end without any tussle. It did not seem right and by the looks of disappointment and anger on the prosecuting team's faces, she could tell she wasn't the only one feeling that way.

Brenda finally acknowledged her daughter with a stiff smile. "Cases are better won when you don't need to say too much or go back and forth."

Alex could tell the woman was trying to teach her a lesson of some sorts, but she wanted answers to what exactly had happened to the prosecuting team's chances of winning. The woman had knocked them down hard and well without giving them any chance to jab back or even weigh any punches. Nora nudged Alex and motioned for them to leave, since most of the audience in the courtroom had walked out angrily.

Normally, loud protests would have been the case, but nobody wanted the sting from taunting or attacking the woman who continued to show why they had nicknamed her the "Viper."

"What the fuck just happened in there?" Alex asked in a disbelieving tone.

"Your mother won as she always does," Nora replied proudly.

Alex walked past the now empty seats previously packed with those wishing for a fair trial or at least a scintillating one, but whose hopes and expectations had been dashed by her mother.

"Congratulations mother," Alex managed to smile and attempted a subtle hug with the woman but stopped upon seeing her hand held high and preventing her from coming close.

"You have no idea how badly I'm losing right now," Brenda whispered in a discontented tone as she walked past.

Alex shared a brief gaze with Nora who shrugged and followed her boss hurriedly.

"Has he arrived?" Brenda asked as they exited the court.

"I managed to track him down and bring him in earlier this morning," Nora replied.

Alex, lost and unsure of what was going on with her mother, tugged at Nora's suit and raised her left brow. "Who is she talking about and what is going on?"

Nora remained without a response as the trio got into the awaiting limousine.

"How is the assignment I gave you with the King girl coming up?" Brenda asked.

Alex looked to the floor and felt the car move as she replied. "It's slow but there is progress."

There was no need to tell her how disappointed her mother was with the response. She wasn't in the mood for failure or incomplete tasks.

"The time to get results is upon us Alex," her mother mumbled while she looked out the window. "Gregory and his nut wife are moving fast, and I am barely ready to topple him as I plan."

Alex felt her thoughts drift towards the one person whom her mother needed to make her plan in that regards come to fruition and it left her weakened within immediately.

Within minutes they arrived at their destination. Alex still didn't know where or why but she followed her mother and Ms. Nora.

"What is the meaning of this?" a disgruntled looking Hamilton asked while flailing his arms in the air as Brenda approached with the two ladies behind her. "I have been waiting for the past three hours and you come in when you please?"

Brenda ignored him, snapped her fingers and the walls around them slowly began to melt away and get replaced by what looked like paddings made from a rather strange material.

"You needn't whine Marcus." Brenda warned. "At least, you shouldn't in my presence if your tongue is of value to you."

Alex looked at the obviously enraged vampire who seemed to be reconsidering his actions as they waited for whatever Brenda was doing to get completed. The room, previously walled with thick glass, was now nothing but padded wall with a large sized window to the right which stared into the ocean.

Alex recognized it for what it was; an illusion created towards the minds of the dwellers within it from being read or even tracked by anyone outside.

"We had an agreement, but I haven't heard or gotten anything of note from you since we last spoke," Brenda circled the nervous looking Hamilton with a wicked sneer on her lips.

Hamilton choked down hard on a bolus of saliva, before sneaking his hands into his pocket. "I have been busy, but even at that... I... I did deliver you the information about the scroll."

Brenda stopped in her tracks, standing behind the nervous looking boy and signaled at Nora with a slight wave as the lady exited the room through the walls without fuss.

Brenda continued, "Your information was indeed useful, but there was no toppling that woman when my minions tried obtaining the scroll from her."

Alex stepped closer to speak but her mother cut her short immediately.

"Ms. Aurelius…" Hamilton held his nerves while doing just about enough not to stutter. "The scroll is with my father now and it is going to get even more difficult to pull off what you're thinking and get it from him."

Brenda nodded her head in affirmation of the kind of mess things were dallying in. She rubbed her chin and continued to circle the boy, only to break her steps with brief pauses and continue until Alex could no longer take her mother's odd actions.

"He has done well enough and they will kill him if they found out he is helping us!" the little Aurelius voiced her opinion.

Brenda waved her hand and rammed Alex into the wall behind her, pinning her there and preventing her daughter from speaking with a mesh of the padding stretching from the wall and covering her mouth immediately.

"The information was correct, but I still do not have the scroll, do I?" Brenda cackled and stopped. "Which brings me to why I had you brought here."

Peeping through the corner of his eyes, he watched Alex continue to struggle against her mother's restraints, causing him to gulp down some more bolus of discomfort, and clench his fist in fright of whatever she might intend doing to him.

"I need you to draw me a map of the fortress Gregory hides away in and also provide the exact location if you will," Brenda finally stood face to face with the boy, smiling and running her slender fingers down the side of his face.

Hamilton felt the first trickle of sweat roll down his face, before subsequent ones began to race down the back of his neck as the witch continued to do everything in her power to make him falter.

"The fortress is impenetrable and even if I drew you a map, how will you get past the countless numbers of vampires fully trained to rip even the most formidable witches to shreds?" He asked, hoping to deter her.

Nora arrived immediately, announcing her return with a subtle cough and bowing tenderly as Brenda came to receive what she had in her hands. The object, wrapped in black clothing, looked no less than a jewelry box as Brenda unmasked it and gently laid it to rest at Hamilton's feet, smiling awkwardly and watching the boy fret as he struggled to move his feet.

"I believe I might have started our conversation giving you the thought that you might have a choice," Brenda chuckled. "Forgive me, but I have to rephrase and say, I want you to bring your father down for me this coming week and do it by whichever way I so choose."

Hamilton looked towards Alex and hoped the girl would do something to assist.

Brenda slid open the box and revealed a thin silver blade, shining brightly even in the absence of ample light, as she picked it up and gently held it before his face.

"What... what... what is that?" he stammered while trying to look away from the blade.

Brenda inhaled deeply and exhaled slowly as she replied, "A little something I whipped from the venom of the one person who can actually bring your father to his knees."

Hamilton's eyes widened and his jaw dropped as he wondered how she came to figure it out. He shrugged and tried to move his feet but whatever held him in place wasn't budging and it was becoming apparent that Brenda had purposely brought him to that room to restrain him.

"All you need to do is make sure this blade scratches your father," Brenda whispered. "A painless and absolutely undetectable scratch and I will handle the rest."

The sound of tasking him to murder his own father with his mother's venom laced knife sounded preposterous

Alex finally broke through by biting at the restraint against her mouth. "Taking over everything from his parents is one thing but asking him to kill his own father is completely insane!"

Brenda roared in anger and jammed Alex further into the wall. "Shut it! I want to hear nothing from you, considering the fact that you are yet to fulfill the task I have bestowed upon you!"

Hamilton felt his stomach sink and his heart fail to function momentarily. His nerves felt like they were shutting down and he could swear the witch was in no mood to play around.

"He will not do it!" Alex yelled back at her mother with enough aggression in her voice to show she wasn't in support of the plan.

Brenda shifted her gaze from her daughter to Hamilton whose silence meant he was desperately thinking of a solution to the current conundrum. Nora remained static as ever, refusing to show any emotion or even give her token of thought into the occurrence. It wasn't her place to utter a word and it wasn't her place to meddle in such businesses especially when she wasn't granted the fluency to speak.

"If you so strongly feel he shouldn't carry it out, then, how about a little convincing?" Brenda laughed and lessened her grip on her daughter before racing towards Hamilton.

Firstly, snapping waving her hand in the air and commanding Alex into a deep slumber, Hamilton watched on in loss as Brenda hummed and giggled excitedly. Next, she conjured a wild and rapidly growing fire in form of a ring around Alex, Brenda smiled at Hamilton and without words, gave the boy a conundrum he needed to solve. The test was simple; agree to carrying out the deed, or watch Alex burn into crisp and have the guilt etched into his heart. Hamilton could also guess there was the possibility he was going to be next once Alex was dispatched without mercy by the fire created by her own mother.

"Are you nuts!?" Hamilton asked.

Brenda shrugged and turned to Nora. "What a coincidence… someone else asked me the exact question today after I asked her to choose her freedom or get eaten by sharks in the pacific in hopes she wouldn't testify against a client of mine."

It finally dawned on Alex; her mother had meddled with justice once again and not for the first time, neither was it going to be for the last.

"Let her go!" Hamilton yelled.

Alex had begun to cough from the fumes that were seeping into her nose while her mother seemed to care less about her daughter's suffering and pending death if she didn't put out the fire.

"You know the magic word Marcus! All you need to do is say it and she will be set free!" Brenda cackled.

Hamilton couldn't believe his ears nor his eyes. He had always assumed his mother was the toughest and possibly the most heartless woman he had come across, but obviously she was nowhere near the witch standing before him, giggling and looking unperturbed about roasting her daughter all for personal gain and power.

Defeated and drained of strength to ignore what the woman wants, Hamilton yelled, "Yes!"

Brenda leaned closer and confirmed with a subtle tone, "What did you say?"

Hamilton yelled at the top his voice as the fire neared Alex's head, "Yes! I will do whatever you want!"

Brenda chuckled, stared at Brenda and winked from the corner of her left eye before quenching the fire growing wildly around her unconscious daughter. Alex slowly broke into consciousness, staring oddly at Hamilton who looked like he had just seen a ghost.

"What… what just happened? What did I miss?" a confused sounding and looking Alex asked.

Hamilton wished he could spill and explain the entire blackmail in detail, but any strength he had within him was to fuel his rage and hate against Brenda Aurelius and nothing else.

Brenda immediately waved away her daughter's question with a soft chuckle. "You didn't miss much honey. Hamilton here simply needed a little persuasion to agree to my cause."

Alex swept her gaze away from her mother to the bothered looking vampire, who did well to look away immediately in fears he might show exactly how angry he was.

"Prepare our little partner for his deed, Nora!" Brenda commanded as she transformed the room back into its usual structure. "By the end of the week, I should have that darn scroll and Gregory's head on a pike where I want it to be."

Hamilton stared blankly at Alex upon watching the girl's mother leave the room. He wondered if the witch had any idea or experience on how terrible her mother's urge and hunger for power was. He also wondered if Alex knew she was willing to sacrifice her own daughter in the feat to gain what she wanted.

"We need to talk," Hamilton voiced through his mind, hoping Alex would pick up the thoughts.

She nodded as she gently fell to her feet from the wall where she had been pinned and sighed exhaustively as Nora whisked Hamilton away immediately.

CHAPTER NINETEEN

Smiling wildly upon getting through with their Chemistry test, Nat led her friends out of the classroom. Her joyous mood felt contagious and Sheila was smiling from ear to ear and hummed and added some spring to her steps as she walked behind Nat.

"I need to catch up with you guys later. I have to see Mr. Marshall about an assignment." Nat spoke up, changing the plans they initially had to go down to the baseball field and watch the team practice. It was Arnold's idea and the girls agreed but not before teasing him about going just because Olivia was on the team. They're worried about him being too friendly with her but didn't want to cause too many problems and have him fail Astronomy. She walked off.

"Hold up guys, I need to use the restroom." Leslie stopped at the restroom and went inside.

After a few minutes Sheila got worried and went in to check on Leslie. "Leslie, you alright?" Sheila called out not knowing which stall she was in.

"Shhhhhhh!" the voice whispered.

Sheila stepped backwards, leaned against the wall by the sinks and looked from one stall to another, wondering which one harbored the phoenix she was searching for.

"Leslie?" she called out in a pretty tiny voice, before watching the stall opposite of her slowly open.

Leslie waved her over immediately, placing a finger to her lips as she beckoned on the witch to come over immediately.

"What are you doing?" Sheila asked, tiptoeing towards the girl and the stall.

Leslie pointed at the wall dividing the ladies from the men's and motioned with her hand as she indicated something was going on in the other room.

"I saw Hamilton and Alex go in there a minute ago but didn't want to tell Arnold," Leslie whispered.

Unable to hide her shock and surprise, Sheila nudged Leslie out of the way and peeled her ear to the wall in hopes of picking up sounds. "What do you suppose they are doing in there?"

Leslie shrugged and shook her head. The thick wall prevented anything from travelling through and regardless of how silent they tried to be, they couldn't hear a single word or sound coming from the other side of the wall.

"Can't you do something?" Leslie whispered.

Sheila shrugged and looked lost. "Like what? Blast the wall away so we can see them?"

Leslie frowned and did not seem to appreciate the sarcasm in her friend's tone at all.

"You're a witch," Leslie reminded her. "Do something witchy to help us listen or even see what they are doing."

Sheila casted her friend a rather glum glare and hissed before walking away from the wall and heading out of the stall. Leslie couldn't believe her eyes; Sheila was usually eager to take on a challenge or do something risky.

"You can gawk all you want, but I don't think there is anything interesting enough for me to blow up the bathroom wall and get myself into trouble for," Sheila noted.

Leslie stomped her feet and began to glow wildly as her anger surfaced in flames.

"Okay, I might have an idea," Sheila said, trying to calm her down. "It might not last past a minute, but it will work!"

Leslie managed a thin smile in the corner of her lips as she asked in reply, "Really?"

Sheila nodded and wished the girl would cool off immediately. Leslie cooled off, burning out the flames within seconds.

"We might only be able to listen to whatever they are saying for a minute and nothing more," Sheila warned in a bid to prevent any other tantrums.

It was more than enough for Leslie who waited for Sheila to begin the processes impatiently. Sheila stepped closer to the wall, placed her left hand on it and rolled her eyes backwards in her skull while she mumbled silently. Leslie looked around for some observable or noticeable change, but nothing could be seen as she wondered if her friend knew what she was doing.

The spell took no less than a minute before Alex's voice came blaring aloud in an angry tone from the other side.

"Cool!" Leslie whispered and stood still hoping to make no noise while they listened on the duo.

Alex lowered her tone and whispered, "You agreed to it, which means you have to either make it happen or you are paying with your own life."

Hamilton took his time before responding, "I am only doing this because of you, you set me up… do you think I want to kill him or even be a part of it?"

Taken aback by what they had heard, Sheila gasped, and Leslie clamped her hands over her mouth in shock.

Alex continued, "He is no mean feat to take down, and even worse, she isn't going to make it easy for you if you fail."

Hamilton sighed aloud and in an exhausted manner, before ramming his fist into a stall door, causing Sheila to leap backwards, with a frightened looking Leslie doing the same.

"Shit!" Leslie whispered.

Sheila looked lost as she paced around the room immediately in confusion.

"They are going to kill someone!" Leslie sounded in a frightful tone.

Sheila remained silent, battling with what response to give and what action to take. She wished Nat was around to give her insight, but the young witch was off enjoying some loving somewhere else.

"What if they are the ones responsible for the …" Leslie was about completing her sentence when Sheila placed a finger to her lips and asked the girl to stop talking.

The restroom door opened, and a rather disturbed looking Alex stepped in. Completely caught off guard to see the two girls in there, she paused, shot them blank expressions and proceeded to do her business while the two girls remained oddly silent. Alex got out within seconds, washed her hands and exited the room immediately.

Sheila turned to look at Leslie immediately and whispered, "We need to tell Nat immediately!"

Leslie seconded her reasoning and immediately asked, "You think she's still in Mr. Marshall's office?"

Sheila scrambled through her thoughts for the best possible answer but found none other than the need to tell the truth lingering in there.

"She's definitely still there probably on her second orgasm by now," Sheila let out immediately.

Leslie's stunned expression was duly expected. Her dropped jaw and widened eyes depicted just how unbelievable the news was for her and it was partly why Nat had chosen to keep things on a low for the time being and had only told Sheila.

"She must be crazy," Leslie mumbled in disbelief. "You realize he's our teacher, right?"

Sheila nodded but offered no counter thoughts or words.

"How did this even start and why is she taking such a risk?" Leslie ranted on.

Sheila dropped her shoulders and simply replied, "You will have to take that up with her."

Leslie stormed towards the door and replied in a disgruntled tone, "I sure as hell will!"

Nat bit on his soft lower lip and kissed him all over again, before slowly unlocking hers lips from his and leaned backwards against the wall behind her. Her eyes glowed and her lips widened into a rather warm smile while he continued to stare right back into her eyes.

"It's been weeks and you still won't come visit me at my house away from here," he complained for the umpteenth time.

Nat brushed her face to the side and hoped she could avoid the discussion. He had invited her from their second meeting and while everything about him felt intoxicating, she wasn't sure about visiting his home outside school grounds.

"You know I live alone," he reminded her "which means you and I can have all the time in the world without being sneaky about it."

Nat loved the sound of the freedom, yet she didn't agree. To distract him she lunged forward ripping off his shirt, not worrying about his office door getting knocked on. They had been more than lucky for some time now and the luck could soon run out, which bothered her some.

"I have some great stuff from when I worked with your dad and some magical artifacts, I'd like to show you if you promise to come over," he tried enticing her some more.

Curious to learn more about her father and obviously falling for the dashing young teacher, she bobbed her head and felt herself agree to pay him a visit at his house.

"You can send me your address," she giggled.

Garrett smiled and tucked his hands into his pocket before he leaned closer and kissed her neck gently before he ran his lips down her neck just between her partly unbuttoned shirt. Mr. Marshall didn't seem to have the intent to stop. He snuck his hand toward her thigh and pushed up her skirt immediately.

"You're the most beautiful girl I have ever come across," he whispered softly.

Nat looked away shyly, then reached for his chest and twirled the hair on it with her finger. "Am I the only girl you would say that to, or are there many?"

Garrett paused and smiled, planted a kiss on her cheek before rolling on his side. He held her in place, with her head rested perfectly on his chest.

"I have never really been able to connect with any woman," he whispered. "As difficult as it might sound, I have dedicated most of my life to my career."

Nat snuggled up to him some more, enjoying the warmth his body brought, and some degree of security she felt with it. Everything about him seemed to bring her peace, and the way he spoke of her father in good words only continued to flatter her heart and make her desire him more. She began to unbutton his pants when he stopped her and slowly got to his feet and looked at the door, prompting Nat to do the same but with a more worried expression on her face then he did.

"We have guests," he whispered.

Nat wasn't sure what he meant, but the taps on the door which came in successive manner did well to explain. She rolled on her side, stared blankly at the door and turned back to him.

Nat cursed underneath her breath, whisked away the bed she had conjured into the room and began to get herself dressed. He sorted everything in the office back into place before helping Nat assume a less accusatory appearance.

With a heavy heart unwilling to leave him, Nat hurried to the door, straightened her dress some more and yanked at the door.

Leslie parted her lips with hand in midair ready to hammer onto the door again as she whispered, "Nat."

Nat stepped out of the office immediately, closing the door behind her. She shot them a rather accusatory and discomforting gaze, but Leslie was in no mood to even notice as she yanked at Nat's arm and led her away from the office as far as possible.

"We have a serious problem and need to talk!" Leslie broke out, her tone filled with worry.

Nat exchanged a brief glance at Sheila to Leslie and back again for some answer.

The latter just shrugged and sighed. "She is right, there is a serious problem."

CHAPTER TWENTY

Leslie walked into an empty classroom, unsure of where to begin and remained calm about the fact that her friend has been keeping secrets from her. Nat's curiosity reached the roof as she tried hard and well to figure out what the urgent meeting was about. Her attempt to ask on two different occasions had been met with a rather glum look from Leslie.

"Are you going to tell me what is going on or do I have to get bored to death watching you pace back and forth?" Nat finally broke her silence.

Leslie finally halted as her action coincided with Arnold hurrying into the classroom and looking as annoyed as Leslie that he was left behind and had to struggle to find them. He held out his cellphone for the three to see.

"Did you guys know someone died a few weeks ago?" he asked, holding his phone out for them to see the image of the boy.

Nat received the cellphone and took a closer look into it, trying to figure out if she knew him or if she had met him before.

"I saw a vision from a janitor as I passed him by. He died mysteriously but nobody knows what the circumstances were and to top it off they're keeping it from us," he explained further.

Sheila handled the cellphone and gave it a close look but could not come to any recollection of ever meeting or even knowing the dead boy.

Leslie blared aloud and in frightening tone immediately, "Those two are responsible!"

"Which two?" Nat asked with a frown.

Sheila slapped her face with her hand as she shook her head in disbelief how Leslie had handled the information they gathered earlier.

Arnold, whose interest had been piqued as well, drew closer. "Who and who are responsible?"

Leslie locked Nat in a rather deep gaze with her face lined with a frown and her lips curled while the boy and girl waited impatiently in suspense for an answer.

"Alex and Hamilton," Leslie finally let the words she had been craving to spill out.

Nat froze, while Arnold seemed to accept the response immediately.

"Some balls those two have!' he fumed and kicked his foot into the table closest to him. "It is one thing doing as you please outside of school, but killing a student? That is insane!"

Sheila noted Nat's silence and stared at her friend for some response. Nat continued to stew in her own thoughts, totally blocking the trio around her out until she felt someone nudge her in the shoulder, dragging her out from her own mind.

"What is going on with you?" Sheila asked.

Nat wasn't sure on how to answer. Firstly, the fact the boy died weeks ago, and they were just finding out about it seemed weird, but even more was the possibility of Alex directly being involved with the killing. She could boast about knowing the witch and what she was capable of; even while Hamilton was a beast in his own light, she wasn't sure Alex could intentionally set out to kill a someone.

"Alex might be crazy and annoying, but I don't think she could've done this," Nat replied.

Arnold shook his head and looked away, while Leslie's jaw dropped immediately, depicting just how shocked she was by the statement.

Nat shrugged and shook her head. "Look I know Alex and 'murderer' is a different level for us to put her on."

Leslie snorted mockingly and burst into a rather hysterical laughter. She slapped her hand on her forehead then threw her hands in the air.

"Is there something you'd like to share?" Nat asked. "Something I am missing?"

Leslie finally stopped laughing and turned around to look at Nat.

"Alex is responsible, and I know for certain because we overhead her and Hamilton scheming another murder plan," she explained in a cold and icy tone.

Nat's veins grew icy cold with chills, and the hairs on the back of her neck stood immediately. She looked to Sheila for confirmation, while Arnold wouldn't tear his gaze from Leslie. The phoenix seemed to have a rather annoying smirk on her face which he couldn't quite figure out.

"No!" Nat felt the word escape her lips without realizing it.

Her dismay fueled her eyes as it reddened immediately while Sheila nodded gently to indicate just how well Leslie was speaking the truth. Arnold fell into a seat closest to him. Just when things between the two groups were getting quiet and some peace built, there's going to be another storm, Arnold could just tell.

"If I may also ask, since when did Alex become someone you vouch for?" Leslie pushed on.

"You heard her agree to murder someone?" Nat asked to be certain.

Leslie shook her head and stormed off to find herself a seat away from Nat.

Sheila took over the reign immediately. "We overheard her and Hamilton planning someone's death and from what I could tell, it is a really big deal."

"Wow!" Nat exclaimed with her fingers pressed against her temple.

The thought of it alone baffled and troubled her. There was no telling what Hamilton could do or how he got to make Alex choose to be his sidekick on this.

"We need to find out more," she stated. "Whatever Hamilton has on her has to be huge."

Leslie got to her feet, rammed her hands into the table and burnt it to a crisp in a burst of fire as she frowned at Nat. "Are you fucking messing with us? You're the same one who was convinced she was responsible for the first death that happened at the beginning of term, and now the person who also tried to kill you at the frat house is so innocent."

Nat knew no sensible answer to give her, so she remained silent.

"At first, I assumed you were simply off your game blinded by some hormonal storm when I learned you're shacking up with Mr. Marshall, but hearing you say this makes me wonder if you haven't lost it completely!" Leslie went all out.

Arnold ignored the other aspect to the rant when he muttered in shock, "You're sleeping with Mr. Marshall?"

Nat got to her feet, held out her hands and shook her head vigorously. "I am not sleeping with anyone, it hasn't happened, yet I mean, and whoever I chose to have an emotional interest in shouldn't be causing you this much rage, this is why I didn't want to say anything."

Leslie scoffed Nat's words away immediately. "I'm supposed to be your friend, not someone you keep secrets from and not someone whose word you cannot trust. We've stood by you and haven't questioned you."

"When you two finally decide to stop fighting, I'd like to point out that we need to make a report about Alex and Hamilton," Sheila noted. "Whatever blood they plan on spilling this time will be on our hands if we don't act."

"I say we tell a teacher and get this issue sorted before things get really worse," Sheila suggested.

Leslie nodded her head and agreed, while Arnold seemed totally indifferent.

"Who do we tell?" Nat asked.

Leslie locked her in gaze, almost certain of who Nat might have in mind but deeply wishing Nat wouldn't say the name. She switched her gaze towards Sheila, who seemed to be waiting for someone to at least make a suggestion.

"What if they don't take us seriously?" Nat asked while looking at Leslie. "What if they believe this is just me trying to get back at Alex?"

The notion was pretty much plausible, and it would have brought an enormous amount of concern for them. They didn't need Nat on constant watch again.

"If my hunch is right, you're pushing towards us telling him, correct?" Leslie asked in a less hostile tone, but with some degree of judgment still laced in her words.

"As much as it might not be what you want to hear, she is right you know?" Sheila told Leslie.

Leslie sighed and remained mute, rubbing her chin gently as she tried to spring up a better idea in her mind. Nat stared at the phoenix and wondered what was up with her.

"Why don't you like him?" Nat asked. "I have never seen you act this way about anyone."

Leslie shrugged, sniffed some bit and rested into her chair. "I don't know if you know, but we phoenix have what you might call a sixth sense and everything about him just sets my alarms off not to mention if you two get caught your reputation will be fucked and with all of your other troubles, you will get suspended, and he will go to jail."

"If you feel that he will handle this right, then you should give it a go," Leslie finally caved.

Nat's eyes widened in great relief, while Sheila managed a smile as the three girls warmed up to each other with a small hug.

"I better not be right about him," Leslie warned before heading out of the room.

Arnold waited for the tapping sounds from Leslie's feet against the floor to disappear into the distance before turning to Nat. "She could be right, you know?"

Nat nodded her head and replied, "Trust me, I believe I know some bit about this man, I mean my dad trusted him."

"He has had a really rough past, but to the best of my knowledge, he is clean," she added. "We all have past experiences, but we shouldn't be judged by them and I trust him to keep us a secret."

It wasn't an entirely compelling point, but Sheila and Arnold agreed to go with it and hopefully end the air of discomfort they'd all been rolling in for some hours now.

"So, how and when are you going to tell him?" Sheila sounded impatient.

Nat bit her lower lip and replied, "This weekend, when I visit him for the first time at his house."

Sheila gasped then winked with a smile at the other witch.

"Take your mind out of the gutter!" Nat chuckled, before leading Sheila out of the room.

Nervous and drenched in sweat he moved through the darkness, paused intermittently as he could feel the blade poking against his thigh in the protective wrapping Brenda had presented it to him in.

"One cut from it will destroy you, but not instantly," Brenda had warned. "It will give me ample time to find you and make you wish it killed you instantly."

Hamilton closed his eyes and pinned his ears towards the voices coming from the inner sanctum where his father and a group of hired mercenaries were. The man had spent the past few days in there, meeting with people, sketching out plans and erasing them with his wife solely by his side and the guards at the door at all times.

"I am going to die for this," Hamilton thought to himself before approaching the two guards standing by the door.

"I'm sorry, but nobody is allowed past this point without prior notice," the guards informed Hamilton immediately and blocked his path with their spears.

Baffled and befuddled at the same time, he stared at both men, obviously humans and strong breeds at that without doubt, considering his parents decided to keep them as their personal guards. He stared into their eyes, smiling cockily and holding his hands behind his back as he remained silent and hoped they will reconsider.

"Sir, you cannot go in there," the second guard reiterated the first's earlier words.

Hamilton nodded, pretended to take the note and head back, but swiftly turned back around while he slipped his hand behind the taller one's head and stared right into his eyes, "You will let me pass!"

He stepped backwards immediately, waiting for the effect of what he had just done to manifest, but instead, the men burst into laughter after a prolonged and confused moment of silence. Their laughter enraged Hamilton, who could see his folks deeply engrossed in their discussion with a hooded figure around the round marble table.

"Like we said before and we will say again, there is no chance in hell that we will let you past without proper invitation," the man he had tried to compel spoke rather boldly. "For your own information, your mind mojo doesn't work on us."

They were both hired mercenaries and not some ordinary flock of humans whose willpower were taken away through mind manipulations.

"You leave me no choice then," Hamilton looked to his feet and sighed.

Looking back up with extended fangs and reddened irises, he bore his claws and slashed at the closest one of the two, which was the shorter man, but found himself missing as the man swiftly dodged and readied his spear to attack. His partner laughed, tore off his shirt to reveal tattoos which Hamilton couldn't quite figure out, before lunging at Hamilton with the intent to maim rather than mess around.

His moves were swift, but not fast enough for a vampire, as Hamilton made good work of his attacks and finally grab hold of him by his throat with his fingers slowly digging into the flesh as he bore his fangs out some more.

"Let me pass or your friend here dies," he warned.

Chuckling and tightening his fist around his spear some more, the second guard replied, "Do as you please with him but I assure you of nothing but painful death afterwards."

Hamilton felt irritated by the duo already and slowly reached to dig his fangs into his captive's neck when he paused upon hearing a loud roar.

"Let the guard go, Marcus!" his mother commanded. Hamilton tossed the guard to the ground, sighed and stepped towards the door but saw his path blocked again by the second guard.

"Let him in Omar!" Alexia commanded.

Omar spat at the ground and stood aside, eyeing Hamilton as the vampire walked past.

"What brings you here son?" his father asked, looking away from his guest momentarily.

Hamilton stiffened in words, while he stared at the hooded figure oddly.

"Can we sort whatever you need to talk about after my meeting?" his father asked.

Hamilton motioned to speak but halted, feeling somewhat overwhelmed as he continued to stare at the hooded figure whose face remained unseen and inaccessible to him. His mother got up from her seat, leaned closer to him and placed her hand on his back before leading him away towards the door.

"Whatever you need to discuss with your father can wait," she whispered. "This meeting might be the turning point we need to put that bitch, Brenda, in her place," his mother sounded pretty excited.

Hamilton looked over his shoulder once again and asked, "Who is that by the way?"

Alexia looked in the odd figure's direction and smiled. "One of Brenda's most trusted men now defected to our side."

Hamilton stiffened immediately, refusing to go any further while his mother noticed it.

"Is she assuming I cannot get the job done?" he thought to himself.

"Is something wrong?" Alexia asked with a frown as she tried to get a good understanding of her son's expression.

His heart began to pound, and his neck filled with sweat washing down his back. His knees weakened and his inside felt hot with worry as he slowly turned around, while still unsure of what to do or how to go about all he had been asked for.

"Mom, we need to get that man out of here right away!" Hamilton warned.

Alexia could barely make sense of her son's paranoia when Hamilton whizzed away from her side and yanked the figure meeting with his father by the throat.

"Have you gone mad, boy!?" Gregory raged and roared aloud as he got to his feet.

Hamilton ignored his father, while he pinned the defector into the far corner of the wall farthest from his father's complete view.

"You!" the voice raged from underneath the hood. "Do you think..."

Hamilton permitted him no more words as he held out the uprooted vocal cord, he had just deprived the fellow of. Tossing it to the ground and sneaking the sword he wore around his thighs into the man's hood, he tossed him to the ground and fumed red in his face.

"I recognize him as one of Brenda's and trust me, he hasn't defected one bit," Hamilton explained, while sounding as convincing as he could be.

Gregory upped himself from his seat and slowly began to approach his son with the obvious intent to gather better information.

"We vetted him ourselves and he came out clean," Gregory spoke in softened tone. "You better have a solid explanation for your feat of madness, boy!"

Hamilton leaned on the lifeless body, searching the hood carefully and as if he knew nothing about what he was trying to find, before pulling out the silver blade he had previously hidden in the man's body.

"I might have just saved your life, father," he said, holding out the blade to his father, who slowly neared and received it into his hands.

Ensuring the silver portion didn't make contact with his skin, Gregory examined the knife carefully, marveling at the structure and the markings on it. There was something else to the blade that immediately caught his attention and senses.

"That devilish woman and her antics," he growled before holding the blade towards his wife for her to access it. "Be careful not to touch the silver, but I want you to examine that blade and tell me what it reeks of."

Alexia accepted the deadly knife into her hands, almost allowing the silver to graze her skin but luckily doing well enough to avert it.

"No!" she gasped and stared at her husband with shaky voice and shuddering hands.

Gregory nodded his head and looked at their son.

"This isn't possible," she sounded in disbelief before gently placing the knife close to her nose to perceive it. "That bitch took my venom? How?"

Gregory kicked against the dead body until it smashed into the wall opposite them.

"It doesn't matter how or when," he mumbled with clenched fists. "We are done waiting for that woman to nick out throats in our own home."

Hamilton nodded while he wore the deepest frown indicating how ready he was.

"We strike in a few weeks," Gregory Hamilton whispered. "We officially declare war on Brenda Aurelius and her entire household!"

Alexia smirked and wore an evil grin on her lips immediately. She seemed to like the sound of chaos when it came and this time around, she had personal scores to settle as well.

Alexia placed her hand on her son's back and led him to the door in slow walks. "How did you figure out the snitch?"

Hamilton held his breath, trying to prevent himself from stuttering or sounding rather unsure. His nerves stiffened and his heartbeat slowed its pace while he feared his mother could hear it ram hard against his chest if he was nervous.

"She approached me, looking for a way to bring father down," he replied, hoping some honesty would make him sound less nervous.

Alexia nodded her head and sighed.

"I wasn't going to do it and I hate that woman even more now," he continued.

Alexia let off a tight-lipped smile and nodded her head. "I trust you son... we trust you."

She led him past the door, urging him to leave while the two guards by the door stared at Hamilton awkwardly as he walked away with a grin. Alexia took a moment to reflect, standing akimbo in between the door frame and just a few feet from the guards.

"You were meant to frisk him before letting him in," she whispered in disappointed tone.

Omar turned around, but it was a little too late for him to see anything as blood gushed from his eyes as he heard his partner shriek in pain. Omar placed both hands on his sockets with the missing eye balls and cried in pain, but his voice too would soon be taken from him. Alexia wasn't going to let them go scot free for almost getting her husband killed.

"We need to get that hag!" she said to her husband as she wiped her bloodied hand off with a napkin.

Gregory gave no response as they both walked off immediately.

"Are we really waiting that long to get her?" Alexia asked.

Gregory shook his head, "We attack in two weeks... I'm not sure I trust Marcus either... I could smell that silver on my son a mile away."

Alexia smirked in an evil manner and nodded her head; she too had perceived the silver blade on her son but wondered if he had had a change in heart.

CHAPTER TWENTY-ONE

Nat laid out all the ingredients she had picked up on the table for Alex. "Mandrake, snake eyes, sage, nails of a banshee, hair from a fae and lastly the leaves of the Fureloth plant."

Alex started to make the potion. Nat hopped on the table to sit and watched her. Nat still had not talked to Alex about what her friends told her they overheard. She was too nervous.

"What is it for exactly?" Nat asked as she watched on hoping it's not for something horrible.

"You don't want to know." Alex added in the nails and the potion began to smoke a silvery blue hue.

"Right, of course I wouldn't want to know if I'm being an accomplice to some dark shit. I thought you didn't like shady business?" Her tone was laced in sarcasm trying to get information without actually asking.

"The world isn't black and white Nat. It's gray. I cannot afford to be weak. There are humans and non-humans who would kill me just because I'm Brenda Aurelius daughter. They don't give a damn if I'm a teenager, a girl, or more importantly not my mother." Alex looked back down at the cauldron and continued with the potion.

"You've never been weak." Nat caught tiny movement of Alex's lips as if she was trying to not smile. Nat hoped whatever the strong potion was meant for was to keep Alex safe, then she wouldn't feel guilty in having helped. Ever since her father was murdered Nat knew the world was unfair.

"I haven't seen Hamilton at school, did he finally drop out?" Nat asked while she tried to peak at the book Alex reads from.

"He's a senior and you're not. Of course, you wouldn't see him. He's also been staying away from you since you poisoned him." Alex started to speak in Latin over the potion.

"True, I was just hoping we were rid of the psycho."

"You're doing it again. Judging others when you don't know them. I can't excuse everything he's ever done but he's loyal, capable of love, courageous, and has problems like the rest of us." Alex started to put the liquid in vials. "He's a vampire, not a cute little rabbit."

"I know what he is...,"

"Then don't judge him for being what he is or for being raised a certain way." Alex once again interrupted Nat mid-sentence. Nat frowned and didn't say anything else. She understood somewhat what Alex was saying, however she still struggled with it.

"When you dated Russel, he didn't feed in front of you? He's a vampire too and has to drink blood to survive. Ever ask him where he got his supply, or were you too happy to be ignorant?"

Nat hopped off the table. "I'm going to go before we get into an argument. I have plans tonight anyway too."

"Stay safe and call me tomorrow, I'm done with my part of the project, so we need to go over what we've done and plan our attack for the rest of it." Nat put her jacket on and left.

A few hours after leaving Alex, Nat found herself at Garrett Marshall's off campus house. Breathing nervously with her finger pressing against the doorbell, she heard the loud ring echo as she stared at the lovely looking house. It looked old and big.

"He must be wealthy," she thought to herself as the door slowly creaked open.

Standing in a sweater vest and shorts, Garrett smiled at Nat and stood aside to allow her inside. "I wasn't sure you were going to show."

Nat felt the words to be nothing but humble ones, considering the air smelled lovely by whatever he was making in the kitchen. His large living room bore more artwork and a really comforting allure to it as he led her to the couch.

"I might need an hour or less before things finally get sorted in the kitchen," he assured her. "Can I get you anything?"

Nat paused, stared blankly at him and then smiled. "Water will do nicely, and quite frankly, you didn't need to go through all the stress of cooking."

He clamped his hands over his ears, indicating he couldn't or didn't want to listen to anything she was saying as he hurried out of sight immediately.

"Silly man," she thought, while understanding that he was going out of his way to be as romantic as possible with her.

He soon returned with a glass of water, before disappearing towards the kitchen again while she regaled herself with some choices of movies on the large sized television screen. She got to her feet and began walking around the living room, marveling at the beautiful art works on the walls, before running her finger along a sculptor bearing resemblance to a stone man.

A sound behind her, just a short distance from the television alerted her senses as she watched what looked like a trap door in the wall open up.

"Oooh!" she exclaimed excitedly. "A secret room?"

She went and peered into the kitchen, to see Garrett too engrossed in whatever dish he was making, determining he wasn't going to be catching her snooping. Nat slipped out of sight toward the hidden door. Nervous and fearful of whatever could be inside, she stepped inside slowly and heard the stone door slowly close behind her before the lights come on immediately.

The tiny room barely big enough to fit in five people properly looked like a work shed with a large drawer slammed into the wall. A large table with writing materials stood before a single leather chair as well, while the ceiling bore paintings of a young boy, she could recognize to be the teacher.

"What are you hiding in here?" she asked in a whispered as she approached the drawer.

Reaching for the topmost drawer and yanking at it, she felt it refuse to budge even while there weren't any lock holes embedded in any part of the locker's body.

"It must be protected by magic," she thought to herself.

Staking a few steps backwards and pointing her finger in the direction of the locker, Nat whisked her hand in the air and felt something snap inside the drawer. Excited, yet careful, she raced towards it and slowly yanked open the topmost drawer and began to run her hand inside of it in search of whatever was being hidden in there.

Feeling somewhat odd by the fact her hand couldn't quite connect with anything, she peered her gaze into it and frowned. "What was he keeping it locked for then?"

She leaned backwards and opened the next drawer to find nothing as well, before frustratingly yanking out the third and stopping in her tracks immediately. It wasn't holding many items, but she recognized two of the items in there and was sure of it because of an etching with a name she was familiar with on the backside of one of them.

"Is this...?" she motioned to complete her sentence when she heard Mr. Marshall call out for her from the kitchen.

She picked up the two items, snuck them into the pockets of her jeans and hurried out the room immediately. Watching the door lock behind her, she hurried to her seat and feigned ignorance as he walked into view with a puzzled expression on his face and his dirtied apron around his waist.

"I've been calling out for you," he stated.

Nat feigned ignorance as best as she could when she replied, "I... sorry... do you need me for anything?"

He gave no immediate response but slowly looked in the direction of the wall where the trap door was meant to be. Nat made certain not to alert him by not following his line of sight, but instead gluing her gaze on the television. The air within the room grew rather awkward too fast and too soon, and Nat struggled with whether she should inform the man of her findings.

"Is something wrong?" he asked with a smile before slipping into the chair by her side.

Nat shook her head fervently, trying to dissuade the notion.

"Hmmm," he mumbled. "Is this about the girl?"

Nat stared at him but without looking surprised, so she wouldn't give him the opportunity to shut down the conversation he was leading to.

"It is about the little girl in the frame over there isn't it?" he asked and sighed.

Nat remained silent still and watched the man get to his feet and rush to the fireplace to retrieve an album which he opened before her and flipped through the two pages only bearing images in them. Nat felt her interest piqued as she stared at the two photographs in the entire album. It had one showing Mr. Marshall and another showing a little girl no more than ten years of age.

"Who is that?" she asked with a raised brow.

He motioned to speak but closed the album first before looking into her eyes. "I know we haven't spoken about everything we ought to and whatever I'm about to say to you might come as a shock, but I don't want you to freak out."

Nat feared the worst was coming. Her heart had begun beating rapidly while her mind scared the organ within her ribcage by pulling up several disturbing thoughts.

"I used to be married, but not anymore," he confessed.

Her nervousness took a downward pace slightly, while her interest in finding out more about his marriage increased.

"It is a part to my life which I don't really fancy speaking about," he continued.

"What happened to the marriage?" Nat asked, regardless of how he sounded and seemed to feel about speaking of the dissolved union.

He got to his feet, walked to the window and stared outside of it with his hands behind his back.

"She passed away," he spoke softly without looking at her. "She was human, and she died giving birth to that seven year old child you see in the picture."

Nat's heart felt weighed with pity for the man. His eyes grew sullen immediately, and his shoulder slumped as he tried to avert his gaze from her. She reached over for him, pulled at his arm until his body leaned against hers and she held him tight while her mind raced with endless questions.

It wasn't strange for magical creatures to have secret hideouts or rooms in their houses, but his was strange and didn't seem to bear any form of magical artifacts in hiding. There were also issues of the items she had found, which steamed her thoughts.

"Can I ask you a question?" she asked, still undecided on whether it should be about the things she found in the hidden room or not.

He leaned closer into her body and wrapped his arms around her waist as he encouraged her to go on with a nod.

"Where is she?" Nat expelled without giving it much thought. "Where is your little girl?"

His response was slower than she had expected. It took him too much time and it was beginning to feel like he was trying to think of an answer or didn't necessarily have the answer to her question at heart right there and then.

"I don't want to talk about it right now," he whispered.

Nat agreed to respect his right to privacy and watched him ease out of her embrace to take off his apron.

"Did you come here to interrogate me or what?" he asked, wearing a frown and squeezing the apron in his hand before tossing it into the couch.

Nat held out her hands and apologized immediately. "I am truly sorry… I was just feeling concerned for you and…"

She paused, and tried to reach for him, but he turned around and walked to the kitchen immediately. He was obviously angry, and he wasn't acting like his usual self, which made her worried. Loud noises indicating items were being scattered and smashed against the wall caught her attention as she raced to the kitchen and halted by the door.

Dinner content within a pot were scattered all over the wall and his hands shuddered from a long gash extending towards his wrist.

"Oh my God!" Nat sounded worried as she approached the bleeding man.

He flinched and stared at her blankly, almost as though he was pleading for her help. She led him to the kitchen stool and sat him on it, before getting a bowl of clean water to wash the wound with. He barely flinched or acted like he was hurt, as his eyes remained glued on Nat and his lips seemed to curl with an odd smile.

"What is going on with you?" she asked in exhaustion. "Why are you this way today?"

Garrett sighed, looked at the wound on his hand and looked back at her without an answer. She cleaned the wound as best as she could and applied some pressure on it with a clean towel in hopes the bleeding will stop.

"Look at you, forgetting you're a witch," he chuckled.

Nat shook her head and realized he was indeed right. Her worries for him mixed with the endless unaired questions in her mind had somehow blocked her from focusing on what she ought to do or what could be done.

"I'm sorry," she apologized as she held her hand over his wound and looked in his eyes.

"It shouldn't be hard," he assured her. "Do it just as I showed you with the rabbit with the broken leg last week."

Nat had not really been paying attention to him on that day. In fact, she never really paid attention to him when he taught her how to perform better with her magic, but instead, always occupied herself with the sight of his cute bum or the perfectly shaped lips which she always yearned to take into hers.

"I still don't know what got you to get this way, but please do not scare me like this ever again," she pleaded.

Holding her hand still above his wound, she closed her eyes and felt some warmth emanate from the injury as the torn flesh began to slowly heal back into place, while the bleeding stopped immediately. The process took longer than she had expected and showed just how much she needed to train and get better at her magic, but she successfully managed to seal the gash.

"Since our plan for dinner has been scattered all around the house, I guess we will be eating out now, yes?" she asked with a raised brow.

He smiled and bobbed his head endlessly. The duo turned to the scattered and rough looking kitchen to begin cleaning and arranging everything back into place immediately. Garrett smiled to himself briefly, while Nat noticed the bizarre expression on his face, she made no mention of it. The man wasn't acting in any way like the one she knew, and she wished she could find out why.

Firstly, she needed to leave…

"How about we order some pizza and see a movie?" he asked gleefully.

Nat agreed without any delay. She wore the best smile she could summon, while her heart continued to pose questions to her without any answers.

"I am sorry I freaked out on you earlier or that you saw that side to me," he apologized.

She waved it off with a less than genuine smile.

"You must understand there are certain episodes to my life that just comes with immense hurt and I still don't know how to navigate them when they come up," he explained with the cellphone in his hand while he placed their order.

Nat nodded again, while wishing time could do her a favor and race by fast so she could head back home.

/

Samantha King glanced at her watch for the umpteenth time before racing to the front door upon hearing the doorbell ring. With a frown and a raging heart with lots of questions for the little girl, she pulled open and stood in the doorway with widened eyes.

"Hello, Mrs. King!" Sheila greeted with a warm smile before turning to Nat. "It was great studying with you today and I hope we are still on for next week?"

Nat replied briefly and with warm hug, "Sure!"

"Good evening, Sheila," Mrs. King replied, waving the girl off as she raced to her car and sped off immediately. "Drive safely!" she added, a bit too late too.

Nat walked past her mother with a mischievous grin and set her bag on the couch before sitting down. Samantha approached immediately, wearing a curious expression on her face, and a really ponderous gaze being attached on her daughter as she approached.

"What kept you so long? We were scheduled for nine and it's ten," she decided to reprimand the girl.

Nat had readied herself, as she turned to look at her mother with forgiveness seeking eyes. "I was having some difficulties with an assignment and Sheila decided to put me through."

Seeing Sheila had dropped her off made it seem entirely plausible and the woman decided to believe her daughter immediately without further questions.

"You have to promise to call me whenever you're running late okay? I don't like being worried," she noted before turning around and heading for the stairs.

Nat hurriedly snuck her hands into her bag and took out the items she had retrieved from Garrett's house. "I was hoping you might recognize these."

Her mother turned around and approached slowly, before quickening her pace upon catching glimpse of the objects in her daughter's hand.

"Oh, sweetheart!" she exclaimed as she collapsed into the couch and stared at Nat nervously. "Where in the heavens did you find this?"

The truth wasn't an option and spilling just about any lie to the question wasn't going to be easy.

"I bought it from an anonymous person online," she replied.

Samantha stared at the items and whispered underneath her breath, "I remember your father calling me to complain about someone stealing this watch at the clinic while he was working, but this is also his wallet, which means the same person took it."

She flipped over the watch to reveal the engraving with her initials, "S.K" boldly written on it.

"It was a gift for our tenth anniversary, and it cost me an arm and a leg if I can remember," she spoke in fondness.

Nat watched her mother cuddle the items as she walked away, reminiscing and allowing the euphoria of the time she spent with her husband to flood back. She wished she could tell the woman about the items' true source, but it would hail fire and brimstones, and there still wasn't an explanation as to how it might have gotten into her teacher/boyfriend's hand.

"This is too weird," she mumbled to herself while she punched Sheila's number into her cellphone and lifted it to her ear.

"What did she say?" Sheila asked immediately, barely allowing the phone ring before doing so.

Nat fell silent, allowing her friend to crave a desired response, while she used the moment to think through everything her boyfriend had told her. She felt he wasn't being entirely truthful, and it was bound to hurt her, seeing she had gotten into a fight with Leslie while she defended his honor.

"They do belong to your father, don't they?" Sheila sounded conclusive.

Nat bobbed her head and lowered her face into her hand with tears rolling down her cheek. "It was stolen from my dad's clinic."

Sheila went numb immediately, simply breathing into the mouthpiece showing her shock, just as Nat was struggling with hers.

"He isn't truly who he is claiming to be, is he?" Nat asked.

Sheila replied immediately. "Meet me at school tomorrow after Geometry class."

Nat ended the call immediately, feeling her face begin to drown in tears, as she struggled with what to think and what not to assume of her boyfriend.

CHAPTER TWENTY-TWO

Bidding her time perfectly for the hallway to clear before venting her rage, Nat turned to Sheila in disgust and asked, "What the hell is she doing here?" Leslie had not expected a rather warm welcome, owing to their previous fight and the sensitivity attached to issues.

"Relax," Sheila attempted to calm her down. "You might want to listen to what she has to say."

Nat shrugged, feeling embarrassed and somewhat betrayed by Sheila's action. Leslie waved them over into the empty Geometry classroom behind them and slowly closed the door while she peeped down the corridors and hoped they weren't being watched.

"What does she know that I need to hear?" Nat asked impatiently.

Leslie pointed at a laptop placed atop the table and nudged her head towards it. Nat looked at Sheila, who motioned for her to do the same. Dragging her feet and mumbling in displeasure about Leslie being brought into the fold about her worries about her lover, she arrived before the screen and paused reluctantly as Sheila joined her.

"Click on any button to wake the screen," Leslie instructed.

Sheila leaned towards the laptop and brought the screen to life, with an image so damning that Nat felt her stomach burn and her knees collapse immediately. She reached for Sheila immediately, finding support by gripping hold of her friend's shoulder tightly.

"No!" she shrieked.

Leslie replied subtly, "Yes."

Nat turned to her with blood fueled eyes before Sheila cut her steps short immediately.

"You fabricated this!" Nat yelled. "You wanted to get back at me so badly didn't you? You are a piece of work!"

Leslie shook her head, paced back and forth in the room some bit, and turned to look at Nat but couldn't quite summon her words correctly.

"You are an ungrateful idiot!" she finally shrieked. "To think I stayed awake all night and missed classes just for you!"

Sheila seconded Leslie's words. "She is pretty good with the internet and finding things you and I will only ever dream of! I asked her to do you a favor last night and she came through!"

Nat looked at the screen once again, reading the allegations being levied against the man her heart had been beating for in the last few months, and tried hard not to believe a single word spread on the article page which was listed under a Federal Government classified section.

"Nothing about what is in there is entirely certain, but I felt we needed to dig into this guy and find out more," Sheila tried to calm the enraged witch down by placing a hand on her back.

Leslie drew closer too. "I know I came off as rude and judgmental earlier and I should never have made my approach in the manner I did, but it is because I care about you and I never want to see you get hurt."

Nat stretched her right hand out, urging Leslie to come lock her fingers with hers, as they stood before the damning information on the laptop screen with thudding hearts and absolute loss on what to do next.

"What if we report to Mr. Parker?" Leslie asked.

Nat shook her head. "This guy is really good and might weasel his way out from the human allegations with a bizarre story."

She turned to Leslie, with tears rolling down her cheeks and settling on top her lips and tried to smile.

"I am sorry," Nat whispered. "I should have at least listened to you. Apparently, you were right."

Leslie warmed her friend with a tight hug immediately.

"I am also sorry. I didn't want this," Nat dug her face into Leslie's shoulder before easing herself away from the embrace.

Sheila's eyes widened and she barely motioned to act when Nat poked her in the forehead and send her slumping to the ground.

Catching her halfway, Nat whispered, "I know you girls love me and this might get messy, but I have to confront him before we report anything to anyone… I love him and there just might be a perfect explanation to all of these."

"What on earth are you doing!?" Leslie thought to herself, struggling to move feeling her nerves which stiffened the longer she tried to do so.

Taking one more look at the laptop screen and the pages of information opened across its pages, Nat raced out of the room immediately.

"Natalie!" Leslie cried to herself inwardly. "Please, don't go!"

Her words arrived in her head too late and even at that, remained without access to the outside world. Nat barred the doors from the outside and disappeared out of sight immediately. Fretting and without an option, Leslie thought of what to do. Her mind felt blank and her thoughts continued in one path; towards Arnold.

"If you can sense me, please Arnold!" she pleaded with her eyes which were refusing to blink. "Come help us!"

There wasn't any certainty about it working, but it was worth a shot…

Catching her gaze for the third time within the space of fifteen minutes, he felt convinced about trouble coming his way. She made no move but glared uncontrollably while he felt forced to look at his smoothie and sip hurriedly from it with the straw.

"I might always attract trouble, but this is way past my desire," he whispered to himself turning his back to her and hoping that would bring the lingering to an end.

Unfortunately, she arrived in the seat adjacent his, and in his assumed line of sight, with her golden locks of hair flowing down her shoulders beautifully. Arnold nearly choked on an excessive gulp before attempting to look away once again.

"Had I known what you were the first time we met, I might have spared you immediately," she purred.

She reached a hand over toward his smoothie and yanked it gently from his hand before taking a sip using the same straw he had previously been drinking with. He wondered if her plan was to make him uncomfortable. He could not predict his own dilemma and even worse, without any external influence coming into play to disrupt it.

"Really, is that supposed to impress me Olivia? I really don't want trouble," he spoke sincerely. "I just want to have my drink, head back to the dorms and forget this weird encounter ever happened."

She stopped sipping momentarily to lock him in a gaze and produce a weird smile on her face. He could finally tell she was taunting him but for reasons he could not understand as he tried hard not to make anything of it. His life was a curse and he wished it was different; had it been others, he could very well tell what the girl before him was trying to do or the possibilities of what she wanted with him but with Olivia, he was stumped. They managed to work on their project together without her attacking him again and he tried to make things easy but her trying to talk to him outside the project was freaking him out.

"I have to go," he mumbled, picked up his bag and raced past her like a nervous ticking time bomb unsure of when it would go off. Oddly, she wasn't the reason he had gotten up that fast and he had hoped to stay longer to see where things were going with the vampire and if he could figure out her game. Something else had been lingering in his ears and had caused his heart serious discomfort. It felt like an ear worm he could not kick to the curb and a heart ache constantly nagging at him.

Olivia watched him exit the room and smirked to herself while she held his remaining drink in her hand. "I'm gonna get that boy."

"Well, that boy can tell the future and he is going to get you into trouble," Alex walked over from the table Olivia left her at, grumbled and sighed.

She turned and looked at the witch without a care in her eyes. "He did not seem like he knew about his future with me."

Alex sighed, tugged at her friend and bellowed, "That's because his kind never see their own future, Olivia!"

Olivia grumbled and got to her feet immediately. The young ladies walked out the door while Alex felt badly nervous the entire time through. The feeling had been lingering on for days now, but if felt worse at that moment in time.

CHAPTER TWENTY-THREE

She scoffed derisively and managed to turn her face away from him as her heart continued to race and ache. His words had barely come out straight while he tried to defend himself.

"I should have listened to my friends and not trusted you!" she screamed. "How much of everything was true!?"

Garrett Marshall froze, stared at Nat without a word to defend himself while the girl paced around his office and kicked against the chairs in her path.

"I am sorry…. I never meant for you to find those items, but I could not return them either," he apologized. "I was going to on the day your father was killed, but it would have meant that I was selfish and… and…"

Nat looked up and met her reddened and teary eyes with his. He had not denied the accusation about the kidnapped girl he was claiming to be his daughter and one birthed to him by his ex-wife, whom wasn't real and never existed.

"What were you doing with my father's watch and his wallet?" she asked.

Garrett Marshall hurried to the door and locked it behind him as he faced Nat. "I have a problem, okay? I gamble and I ended up losing more than I could afford, and one day, I was looking for something easy to sell…"

Nat's heart broke immediately, and her knees felt defunct as she struggled to have a grasp on where the conversation was headed.

"I nicked the wallet and wristwatch on my way out to this gamer's house, who I knew had won big the night before," he continued, "I swear to you that I don't steal and in fact, he had won my money just the night before and I thought of taking some of it back."

Nat's lungs followed in the crumbling effect, while she struggled to breathe or even in any way, get a grasp on reality in that moment. She slumped into a chair that was willing to receive her while her lover paced around the room in guilt.

"I don't know what happened… I swear it to you, but… but the person must have come for me and attacked your father instead," he tried to puzzle the deeds and events together but could not.

She could not believe her ears, while her heart felt duped, as did her body, which she had given to the man and was now feeling like it was all for nothing.

"You gamble, you steal, kidnap a little girl which you somehow managed to hide and keep away from the whole world," she narrated as she got to her feet. "And in some way, you managed to get my father killed too!"

Her head began to spin, and her throat clogged up with pain as she began to hyperventilate and struggle to cry at the same time. Nat knew her father's death wasn't in anyway just a coincidence or that the man was a victim of a random thug related event. He had been killed because of the one man he trusted and helped through life.

"Natalie!" he called to her in pleading tone. "I love you… I swear I do, and I have done many bad things in my past, but that is all in the past, please!"

She scoffed, wiped off tears now smearing the entirety of her face, before racing for the door. He stopped her in her tracks and yanked at her arm, before tossing her back towards his desk.

"I know you're pissed, but you need to calm down," he ordered.

"No! Not anymore! I will not listen to words from you anymore and what I need right now is to tell my mother that the same teacher and man we trusted is nothing but a thief, liar and an instigator of an innocent man's death!" she bit back hard and yelled.

Nat ventured forward once again, but he shoved her backwards even harder. "You cannot tell anyone about this and I can take care of your friends' memories about all of this, but your mother cannot know."

Nat stared at him and wished her looks could kill, before waving her hand at him and hoping to ram him into the wall so she could gain passage to the door. He remained unmoved and seemed to smirk at her childish attempt to use magic on him.

"I'm sorry Nat," he whispered while he drew nearer. "If you cannot forgive me and keep this between us, then I don't think you heading out that door will be possible."

Nat parted her lips to suck in some much needed air, but it wouldn't be enough to help her get away from the evil coming, as her attempt to duck to the side was well calculated and met with firm grasp by two large hands pinning her by her shoulder and shoving her towards the wall.

"Let me go!" she managed to yell and get out some words, but with each passing second, her throat felt tightened and even more difficult to permit any word out. "Let... me..."

The evil grin on his face did well to show just how he was on the inside. The devil within him had finally unearthed itself to the surface, and Nat had only been able to see it with the man's hands around her neck while he threatened to choke the life out of her.

"You shouldn't have gone into that room," he whispered. "You should not have found anything," he sounded as though he was pained but his grip only tightened.

Nat waved her hand towards the door, but her magic seemed to be waning fast and without any focus, she could not command the locks to come undone. She felt helpless, again, and in a time, she needed every part of her to come to life. She could tell from the evil grin slowly creeping from the corners of his lips that he was sure he was going to win.

She was only a minute away from giving up and feeling her breath totally ease away, while he led her towards the ground slowly, never letting go of his death grip on her neck.

"I loved you Nat," he spoke in past tense, further entertaining the fact she would soon be dead.

Nat felt her vision dim immediately, and her body slowly begin to relax as they embraced the possibility of death. Air ceased from getting into her lungs successfully, and his deeply brown and betraying eyes were the last imprint she had in her memory as she slowly passed out and taunted death to come take her away.

"Nat!" the soft but certain voice from her father seemed to ring in her head. "You aren't weak, Nat!"

It was the exact words he had used when she was six and had gotten bullied on the playground. Images from memories of that day flooded her mind as he pointed at her chest and told her there was power residing inside of her.

"You are a King and we Kings never stay down!" he challenged her. "He is no match for you! They are no match for you, so get up, Nat!"

Nat felt the surge of electricity stream down her spine and slowly warm her belly as she jerked back into life in a loud gasp. Her body glowed as his hands began to burn from where he had them tightened against her neck. His widened eyes suggested just how well he was surprised, but there was little to nothing he could do as the burst of light only grew wilder and brighter.

"Turn it off Nat!" he pleaded as it swarmed him and slowly began to burn off his clothes.

Nat slowly sat up, as the light got to its peak and burst into a loud explosion, sending the teacher far into the opposite wall, and the windows shattered into pieces and the walls shuddered dangerously with cracks running along them while the ceiling bulged a little.

"Oh my God! What did you do?" the embattled looking Leslie gasped as a blast sent the front door unhinging and permitting the trio entrance immediately.

Nat whispered to herself in response, "What have I done!?"

Garrett Marshall's body laid motionless a few feet from them, eyes opened and blank of life, while his body looked badly burnt as Arnold approached to affirm if he was still alive. He turned around and shook his head gently.

"He was going to kill me... he... he... he was going to kill me!" a traumatized sounding Nat tried to explain to her friends who surprisingly bore no judgmental expression on their faces.

"We need to sort this now and fast!" Arnold warned.

Leslie crouched on her knees and stared into Nat's face as she held the girl's head in place. "Whatever you are trying to blame yourself for, it isn't worth it, I assure you."

Sheila joined in immediately, "You did not do this on purpose and I'm sure you had every right to kill that lying bastard."

Leslie slowly reached for Nat's neck, revealing scratches and red ligature marks inflicted on her by his fingers, then Sheila healed her up nicely. The physical wounds were gone, but the mental ones remained as she toiled in the betrayal that the man had inflicted profoundly on her. She was sure he would have ended her life had the outburst of magic within her not come to her help.

"I don't mean to interfere with any emotional debacle you are going through, but we have less than ten minutes before someone walks through that door and finds his dead body with us," Arnold whispered with his hands pointing at the dead body.

Sheila got to her feet immediately and wrapped the body with a sheet she conjured, while Leslie helped the traumatized looking Nat to her feet and warmed her up by wrapping her arms around her.

"You will feel better," the phoenix whispered into her ears, as she tightened her arms around Nat and began to glow.

Nat felt some if not most of her worries slowly begin to burn away as though they never existed. Memories of the events still lingered in her mind, but she no longer felt the drowning guilt that came with killing the man who attempted to kill her. Sheila and Arnold dragged the body towards the center of the room immediately.

"Nat, I know this isn't a good time, but I need your help," Sheila pleaded. "We need to do a reform spell."

She agreed and rubbed her hands together, while Leslie ad Arnold stepped back some bit.

"I saw what you did there, you shouldn't mess with people's emotions," Arnold whispered to Leslie. "Yet, people see my kind as insensitive and heartless when there is your kind walking around with the righteous badge."

She struck him hard with her hand behind his head, while they watched the two girls perform the reform spell on the dead teacher's body. They transformed him into the form of a dead cat, slowly placed him into a large bag, and Sheila headed right out the door with him.

"Arnold, I need you to come with me and Nat, cleanse any trace of us from the room," Sheila commanded.

Arnold grumbled before racing out the room immediately. Nat nodded, felt her heart weigh heavily as she held her hands apart and closed her eyes, picturing just how the entire office was right before her magic outburst. The room slowly began rearranging itself, with the shattered windows getting reconstructed immediately as well.

The room looked set within minutes and Nat exited it with the door slammed shut behind her as she tugged on Leslie's arm. "I need a favor from you, and I need you to keep it between us."

Leslie could smell something disturbing coming, but she and Nat had been on opposite ends for some days now and getting back on track seemed to be the sensible thing to do.

"What do you need?" Leslie sounded willing.

Nat looked around, before yanking out a mini laptop she had nicked from the dead man's desk and handed it over to her. "He used to gamble a lot and I need you to help me find out the names of his gambling buddy or anything related with gambling which might be on this computer."

Leslie stared at the laptop nervously but took it immediately with a grin as they forged ahead.

"Nobody can know about this, Leslie," Nat reminded her.

Leslie bobbed her head and smiled. "I'm good with computers and even better with secrets."

Nat hurried away, to meet with her other friends soon and hopefully find ways to dispel the incident from their minds.

Nat mumbled to herself in promise as they walked down the corridor with students breezing past them. "I will get better… I will never be caught off guard like that again."

It was something her father had always wanted for her; the ability to stand up on her own magically and not be second choice or play second fiddle to anyone. Being in that room with her life dangling by a thread had opened her eyes for her need to train to get better. More so, she couldn't continue to rely on freezing or allowing her emotions to get the better of her during battles for her life.

At the end of the week, Nat found herself at the closest coffee shop arguing once again with Alex. Nat groaned and slammed her hand down on the table and leaned in closer to Alex. "Come on, don't play games with me, I'm trying to help. I saw you and Devon arguing in the parking lot yesterday. And for the last few days you've been acting strange."

"Stalking me now?" Alex replied while staring at the book in her hand.

"What? No! We're in a lot of the same classes, remember? I don't know why I'm even bothering with you." Nat flopped back against her chair. She had no plans on approaching Alex about Devon as she was too consumed with her own problems until she came into the coffee shop and saw Alex sitting by the corner alone and felt her feet move before her mind could catch up.

"I don't know either. It's my business. Stay out of it. I can take care of him."

She just slipped up and the way her body tensed up was obvious. Nat leaned back in and lowered her voice not wanting to bring attention to them.

"I seem to recall taking care of him last time by kicking him in the balls when he kissed you." They both smile for a second at the childhood memory then sobered up.

Alex sighs heavily. "My mom is working with his father on some million-dollar deal and wants me to influence Devon into pushing his father to agree to the deal. Same power dealing crap. Devon is all too eager to make our parents and his dick happy by dating me."

"She's pimping you out. She can't do that. What the hell, Alex!" Nat angrily whispered. Alex finally gave her full eye contact and raised a brow. Nat then realized she was being too passionate about this and cleared her throat.

"Look, no matter where we stand, this is wrong."

"Yeah well as I said, I got this. It's only until mother gets what she wants then I can figure a way to dump his ass without causing my mother to lose the relationship with those evil rich bastards."

Nat almost choked on her frappe as an idea came to her mind and she tried to speak with her mouth full.

"I got it. We will pretend to date. It's perfect. Devon knows we were close friends and he already doesn't like me. He has too much pride and ego to go after someone already taken, sloppy goods and all so if we can convince...."

"Hold up, that's stupid. We hate each other, everyone knows it. We'll never fool anyone. I can't stand being around you." Alex cut off Nat.

"I hate you as well, but you did save my life that one time..."

"Two times."

"Whatever, two times and as you like to say my self-righteous self owes you. Or I must just be a masochist...."

"Well that might be interesting enough for me to say yes." Alex cut her off again.

"Screw you, I'm being serious, this can work. And it'll help get the school off our asses about all the fighting we've gotten into."

"Fine, this is a little less painful than the idea of having Devon's sweaty body on top of me. But then again I could be the one on top." Alex leaned back and folded her arms together while looking up as if she thought of the hardest math problem ever invented. Nat started to get annoyed again and offended.

Nat pushed her chair back away from the table and got up to leave but stopped when Alex grabbed her arm and pulled her into her lap.

"Alright, if we do this no one can know. I don't need anyone in my business nor my mother finding out and punishing me. We do this for at least a month to make it believable then I break up with you." Alex held Nat in a tight grip as Nat tried to stand up being very uncomfortable with her current position and the fact, they were in public. She stopped trying to get up at the words 'break up'.

"I'm doing you the favor; I should break up with you."

"Remember I saved your life twice honey." Alex gave her arrogant smile that usually set Nat off but in her current predicament Nat found it slightly charming.

"Let me go."

"Why? You'll have to get used to PDA if we're going to convince everyone. But fine, we'll mutually go our separate ways with no dramatic break up, but the how we got together I say one day when we came to blows then we had some hot angry sex and it kept happening before we decided to just give it a go. Sounds the closest to reality."

"I'm not a prude or anything, you can ask Ella, but what a mighty big ego you have." Nat huffed and slid back to her own seat to finish her drink wishing she never came over to talk to Alex. Now she'll have to lie to her friends.

"It is pretty big." Alex winked at Nat. "Maybe if I can find a potion for eliminating nausea, I'll show you my most famous magic trick that has all the ladies coming to the yard."

"Oh God, you are still such a dork." Nat laughed picturing a younger Alex in her room dancing to that song in her pjs. She didn't even care about the underlined insult thrown at her. She shifted in her seat trying not to think about what kind of magic Alex knows.

"We have our basics down, so I guess I'll see you at school tomorrow."

"No, you won't. I have to miss school. Some important business to deal with. I ordered someone delivered untouched and they weren't." Alex wrote down her cell phone number and passed it to Nat. "That's my number, put it in your phone and text me when you get home. I'm supposed to meet Devon to give him something for his father, a manipulation attempt by mother of course. You will accompany me so he can start seeing us together." Alex left Nat puzzled that she had told her the truth about where she was going to be the next day. Nat was also scared that she was making a bad decision. Alex wasn't the girl she used to know, she was her mother's daughter and trained to be a person Nat didn't know if she can ever again be friends with.

"She saved your life. You're just being a decent person." Nat tried to convince herself of her decision before she got up and left too.

* * *

Alex shook her head for the umpteenth time, while she felt her ears might actually begin to bleed if her friend didn't stop speaking about Arnold who she oddly tried to seduce in the cafeteria earlier.

"So, you're saying it will not work?" Olivia asked.

Alex stopped in her track and caused Olivia to do the same. "That's not what I'm saying, but you cannot badger a guy into liking you or forgiving you for kicking his ass in front of everyone in the first month of school."

Olivia looked lost and unsure of how that was meant to work for her. Since working on their final project together Olivia has found Arnold's uncut attitude and straight forwardness attractive. Alex brushed it off and stared at her watch, seemingly worried as their friends were running rather late.

"For someone who drives fast as Julian does, shouldn't he be here already?" she asked impatiently while Olivia barely seemed to be listening or interested in anything she had to say.

Alex shook her head, stared at her watch again, as the cold air snuck into her lungs.

Frustrated and wishing Olivia would say something, she turned to her left and her gaze met with Olivia's body lying on the floor motionless.

"Hello Alex," the scrummy voice she was sure she had heard before called to her.

Alex parted her hands and readied herself for whatever he was bringing, but he remained in the dark, choosing not to reveal himself.

"Kun!" she whispered, hearing her heart begin to beat rapidly and violently.

"Watch your back, Alex!" he giggled. "I could easily snap your neck as I did your friend's, but I want the moment when I end your life to be perfect and fulfilling," his voice echoed some more.

She could sense the vicious vampire moving at a pretty disturbing pace that made it impossible to pinpoint where he was. Soon, he was gone, confining her to fright and paranoia. Olivia slowly gasped and came back to life, before getting to her feet and looking at Alex weirdly.

"What happened?" she asked.

Alex wasn't sure about how to explain it to her. Kun wasn't any ordinary vampire they could deal with on their own.

"Kun happened. We need to leave now. No telling if he'll come back with his twin." Alex sounded worried, before dragging Olivia away. Finally, Julian and Ella pulled up.

"What took so long?" she growled out.

"Woah relax, we stopped to get some blood just in case Liv needs a boost." Julian said as he bit into a burger with no shame.

"Kun made an appearance and threaten Alex." Olivia glared at the two new arrivals.

"Let's just go. We are wasting time." Alex got in the car and they all followed suit with apologies. Alex had been working too hard to make sure this night would go right. Tonight, she would gain her own first stretch of territory. The only way to get herself more protection and to slowly get from underneath her mother was to get her own individual power.

They arrived at the Scorpion casino owned by the Scorpion gang, only a ten minute drive from Oak Clinic. Alex' goal was to take over the whole neighborhood the Oak Clinic is located in. Everyone was fighting for the territories and some bold ones wanted the clinic. Alex was going to bring down the Scorpion gang, they controlled five blocks in the neighborhood and the casino brought them lots of wealth.

Alex had a meeting with Kim Jin the leader. She went in flanked by Olivia and Ella while Julian went to take over the security room.

"Thank you for meeting with me," she takes a seat opposite Kim who sits at his desk.

"When you sent me those files from the major's computer revealing the FBI agent who has been intercepting my shipments, I was pleased to meet with you. I'm surprised you didn't give the information to your mother."

"She didn't ask," Alex shrugged and smiled mischievously then lifted her bare leg and placed it over the other watching Kim's eyes linger on her short dress. "And I felt you would show more appreciation for the information. I didn't give you all the information I have though, so much more. Your middle man who took the files ended up being very useful to me in other ways. Where is he?"

Kim stared her in the eyes, his expression blank as if he was trying to quickly solve something in his mind. "He's been missing for two days. I'm starting to think you might have known that." He leans forward and lays his arms on the desk.

Alex smiled and tilted her head. "Maybe I do. I felt so honored you would meet me tonight, tonight of all nights when you're supposed to get such a big shipment. What did Roland say it was going to be? Guns, twenty young girls, weed and cocaine all with a street value of twenty million. Right?"

Kim jumped out of his chair, looking furious "If you touched my shipment, you will die right here. This was all a trick by your bitch of a mother." He turns to one of his guards "Call the boat now!"

Alex stood up and his guards made a move to pull out their guns, but Olivia and Eleanor were too quick and disarmed them. "My mother has nothing to do with this. You have what I want, simple as that."

"I will kill you all, you can't touch me. You won't get out alive." Just as he was getting around his desk, the door opened to reveal Simon, which shocked Kim. "Julian has everything taken care of and we've cleared our way out of here."

Alex smiled and nodded at Simon before turning her attention to Kim. "You were foolish to think I was no threat to you; my people have infiltrated this place for over a week. Slowly I learned everything there is to know about this building and your security detail and put my crew in here since the doors opened for the day slowly poisoning and taking out your security without you knowing to make it all so easier to take over once I had arrived." Alex laughed mockingly and it infuriated Kim Jin who rushed her but got stopped by Simon who grabbed the human up by the throat and slowly crushed the life from him.

"Spread the word, anyone left better get out of the city and never return or they come here before sunrise and bow before me. Or else they die." Alex spoke to one of the guards then killed the other. It makes her sick to do so but these people were evil. She was going to have to start doing things she didn't like if she wanted to have the power to clean things up.

"Come on let's go have some fun, I'm feeling lucky." Alex led her friends out the door to go gamble.

CHAPTER TWENTY-FOUR

Geometry was one of two classes she didn't have with her friends. She hated math. Nat has been having a bad day and Leslie still hadn't found out the information she needed to find who killed her father. She was finally so close to finding out. That along with the stress of her proposal to Alex for them to pretend to date. Today Alex said she would be at school and so far, no Alex. Nat took out her cell phone and texted Alex for the fifth time trying to see where she was. They were supposed to walk to the building together from the dorms.

"Texting me?" Nat jumped at the voice beside her ear then turned to see a smiling Alex,

"Where have you been?" Nat growled out.

"I'm sorry honey, here." Alex brought her hands from behind her back, placed a coffee cup on Nat's desk then handed her an orchid in her other hand. Nat smiled. Alex remembered her favorite flower. Nat noticed that Alex didn't tell her where she had been. Alex made the guy sitting next to Nat give up his seat then she pulled it up against Nat's chair and kissed her cheek which started a storm of chatter.

"I still want to know where you were." Nat poked Alex's side ignoring their classmates gawking at them or huddle together talking.

Mrs. Talia turns around "Everyone quiet! I want everyone to group up and solve the problems on the board. Everyone will have to come to the board and solve a problem."

"Saskia held me up, nothing for you to worry about." Alex pulled Nat's notebook closer to her and wrote the problems down.

Nat rolled her eyes and dropped the conversation until the end of class. She barely had a B at mid-point of the term. She needed to stay focused as the end of term was only a couple of months away. As time went by, Nat remembered how annoying Alex was and how much she wanted to punch her every minute that went by. Alex grabbed Nat's bag before she could get up and walk out.

"Skip Chem with me." Alex tried to take hold of Nat's hand, but she pulled it back then held out her hand.

"Can I have my backpack back?" Nat leaned more on one side jutting out her hip, and stared Alex down. Alex frowned then rudely dropped it at Nat's feet instead of handing it back to her. Nat's anger was ignited, and she opened her mouth to curse Alex out but Olivia rushed in front of them.

"What the hell is everyone talking about? You kissed this loser? Are you feeling ok?" Olivia grabbed Alex by the shoulders acting as if she actually believed Alex was ill. Nat wanted to blast Olivia across the hall. Alex beat her to it and raised her hand before balling it into a fist sending Olivia up in the air with her throat visibly constricted. Everyone around was shocked. No one had ever seen Alex attack her best friend.

"I don't remember having to explain myself to you or anyone else in this school." Alex glanced around at the crowd. Some ran off while others stuck around trying to look busy. "Nat and I are dating now and if you disrespect her again you won't have any fangs to feed with." Alex let Olivia go and she fell hard on her feet.

"Come on Nat." Alex grabbed Nat's bag again and shove it into her chest. This time Nat didn't go off. They have to keep up appearances but once they got alone she was going to slap sense into Alex.

"Why are we skipping school?" Alex ignored her and kept walking to the parking lot. "You're going to keep ignoring me? I guess we'll take my car since you're used to being driven. Do you even have a license?"

Nat continued to talk and follow next to Alex before she noticed Alex walk in a different direction, so she increased her steps to follow. "Where are you going?"

"Will you shut up?!" Alex finally spoke.

"You are so damn rude! We could not last a whole school day pretending to like each other because of you." Nat yells out.

Alex waves her hand and sends Nat flying into a car before getting into her face. "We don't like each other, remember? I said this wouldn't work when you suggested this crazy idea. I tried to be nice then you as always have to go against me for no reason. Something so simple as me carrying your bag then I defend you against Olivia and you continue to bitch. I wasn't going to stay in there any longer and have to pretend not to hate your guts." Alex let Nat go then walked off again to her car, a Bugatti Chiron.

"Excuse me Queen of tantrums. You got all upset just because I wanted to hold my own backpack! You're ridiculous and overly sensitive. I didn't know I was signing on for a needy girlfriend. Should I buy you flowers?" Nat stopped talking at the sight of Alex car. "Damn, this is a nice car. You going to open my door?" Nat asked with her arms folded and grins at Alex taking enjoyment in pushing Alex over the edge.

"What, you lost your independent attitude already? Make up your mind. And I didn't say you were getting in my car." Alex got in the car and Nat opened her own door and hopped in. Alex made her sneak out of school, there was no way she was going back all alone.

"Just drive." Nat turned the radio on and went through Alex's playlist then started to sing once she found a song she liked.

It's only been ten days since the day Nat had asked Leslie for help. That's what it had taken for Leslie to spit out the name "Bally Rider", a thug and well-known gambler with a knack for cheating on the same street where her father's body had been found. Nat held the note in her hand with her eyes boiling with rage, and her insides churning with discomfort as she sat in darkness and waited for the killer to return home.

The entire room smelled funny and wasn't kempt, but it wasn't her concern. The interesting find, which was in her hand after her rigorous searching of the room made her want to confront him even more. She needed answers and not just the name and information Leslie had pulled off the internet.

Nat sighed and bowed her head, with a sharp pain prodding inside her skull. The pain had been there off and on since Garret Marshall's death and it refused to go away. It almost caused her to pass out while she asked around the bar a few blocks from where she was, for information on Bally Rider, choosing to bribe the bartender before he would spill all about the man being a loser with some illegal dealings.

"He always comes home every night," his neighbor had said, which was the premise for why Nat was in his living room, sitting comfortably on his couch waiting for him to return so she can get answers.

She twitched upon hearing keys dangling as someone stood before the front door. The door lock came undone and the somewhat average sized figure stepped into the room before switching on the lights. The look of surprise on his face was well noted as he caught sight of the hooded figure seated on his couch doing just about enough to keep her face hidden from him.

Disguising her voice best as possible, Nat asked, "Are you Bally Rider?"

His response indicated his rage. "Who the fuck are you and why the hell are you in my house!?"

She slowly got to her feet and kept a safe enough distance from the man who tossed down the bag he had in his hand.

"How the hell did you get into my house?" he repeated.

He rushed towards her as he yanked out a knife from his pocket, but soon halted as Nat held out her hand and made every muscle in his body freeze against his control.

"I don't want to hurt you, all I want are answers to some questions," she whispered.

He chuckled, spat to the floor and replied in a stern and confident voice. "I am not telling you shit! Whoever you are, whatever the fuck you want with me, I don't care and I'm not talking!"

His stubbornness was well founded from her research about him, as was his violent streak and aggression, which was the cause for him not having a wife anymore.

"Very well," Nat sighed. "The hard way it's going to be."

She stepped closer and watched the man sweat profusely, before placing a finger to his forehead and whispering an incantation he could not fathom. His body slowly began to burn but without any flame in sight, as he shrieked and roared in pain with some curse words escaping his lips as fumed at Nat.

"I'm going to kill you!" he cried. "I am going to fucking kill you!"

Nat cared less for his threat, choosing to watch him burn and suffer as penance for what he did to her father.

"Why did you do it?" she asked.

"Why did I do what, you fucking lunatic?!" he cried in pain as the burning sensation engulfed his body. "Make it stop! Make it stop you bitch!"

Nat refused his request, hoping to break the man best as possible and have him complying to her questions easily.

"You killed Maxwell King, didn't you?" she asked.

He paused momentarily but continued to groan in pain before holding his breath and exhaling aloud as he tried to deal with the pain.

"I am not telling you a damn thing!" he remained as stiff as possible, choosing to continue to wallow in the immense pain, taking deep breaths.

Nat grew frustrated, neared him and kicked him hard in the face, but only provoked a derisive chuckle from the man.

"You have no idea what I am going to do to you if you don't kill me," he whispered while enduring his pain.

Nat nodded her head and paused momentarily, before gently placing her hand on his head and closing her eyes.

"What are you doing?" he asked in fright. "Don't... please don't... what are you... ?"

He halted, gasped and screamed louder than he had before. Hundreds of invisible pins poked and prodded every inch of his body while the burning sensation didn't look like it would stop either. Bally Rider was in hell inside his own home and he had no idea who was dealing him such torment.

"Okay! Okay, I killed the surgeon, but only because he fucking stole from me," he finally broke down and replied. "The son-of-a-bitch broke into my house and stole my cash!"

Nat knew for certain that her father had not done anything of such but wondered what conviction he must have had to make him think so.

"How do you know this?" she asked.

He sobbed, sniffed and replied, "The fucking ID card you've got in your hand, you bastard!"

Nat gasped and stepped backwards immediately. She had assumed he retrieved the card from her father when he killed the man, but that wasn't the story.

"I walked into my house and found that on the floor not far from my safe which had been emptied," he continued.

Nat's heart felt broken some more as she stared at the man and wondered on what to do. He growled endlessly in pain, while she battled her own suffering as well. Drained of what to do, she slowly walked past him, heard the man curse at her but cared less for anything he said as he wailed in pain. With a heavy soul, Nat exited the room immediately and headed back home.

"I am going to find you!" he cried. "I am going to fucking find you and kill you!"

The spell she had cast on him would wear off after another few minutes of pain and Nat was sure he had not seen her face to identify her, but one thing she didn't fathom was how vindictive the man she had just tortured was when it came to getting back at those who hurt him.

"What next?" she asked herself as she dragged her feet to the car.

Her father was murdered because of Garrett Marshall's greed. The story will haunt her for the rest of her life. She wished she could explain it all to her mother, but that could not happen. She had blood on her hands already and things were more complicated than she could imagine.

TWO WEEKS LATER

The cafeteria was loud and bustled with students. Most of the whole school had gotten over the shock of Alex and Nat dating. Not everyone believed the relationship was genuine such as Ella who thought there were ulterior motives or Alex has something over Nat, forcing her into a relationship as some cruel amusement.

"Arnold come on, let your girl drive your bike." Nat took Olivia's side in the debate that had started before they even arrived in the cafeteria. For a guy who was quiet natured and avoided danger and violence, Arnold owned a pretty cool motorcycle.

"She'll just crash it or use it to run someone over." Arnold tried to defend himself. His words caused Olivia to put on her best shocked and offended face which was very comical. Nat chuckled and kept quiet as the couple's debate got more intense.

Ella leans over and grabbed some of Nat's fries. "Hey, you're not sharing any of your stuff." Nat smacked Ella's hand.

"Girl, you know I'm always down for sharing my stuff." Ella winked and flirtatiously smirked at Nat. Nat felt Alex shift next to her, so she quickly turned her head away from Ella. The damn werewolf knew how to mess with her.

"Babe, did you do the homework for next period?" Nat leaned into Alex in an attempt to get her attention.

"No, and I thought I said don't call me that, honey." Alex doesn't turn her head and resumed texting on her cellphone.

Nat grabbed the phone out of Alex hand and slipped it into her bra. "Can you be normal and talk to your friends, or you know, eat?"

Alex rolled her eyes and glanced at her barely eaten food before she took two bites out of her chicken salad wrap. "Satisfied? Now give me back my phone."

"Nope, I'm not." Nat smiled as Alex temple vein visibly throbbed. Nat leaned in and gave Alex a kiss on the cheek to soothe her from not getting her way.

"Come on love, for me? Eat please." Nat pouted and once Alex sighed and placed a kiss on her lips, she smiled knowing she had won. Alex started to eat.

Leslie had gotten up without Nat noticing and came back with two slices of cake. She handed one to Ella.

"Why didn't you tell me you were getting some? Is there anymore?" Nat asked Leslie.

"Sorry, no I grabbed the last two and no you can't have any." Leslie smirked and took a big bite of the cake. Nat had chosen to get dessert after she ate since her tray was full.

"Here, Nat." Ella held out her fork with a piece of cake on it. Nat happily opened her mouth and took a bite. They exchanged turns until the cake was finished. Unknown to Nat, Alex was steaming at the exchange.

Nat felt a hand caress her thigh and glanced over at Alex. They usually do not go beyond needed touching. Nonetheless she smiled and leaned into Alex.

"What?" Nat questioned Alex in a low tone having decided to play along.

"Nothing, you're just sexy." Alex sultry tone made Nat blush. Alex leaned in and kissed Nat. Her lips opened and Nat felt Alex tongue seeking entrance so caught up in the moment Nat allowed the kiss to deepen.

Nat tried to move back out of the kiss, but Alex grabbed her ass, pushed her tighter against her and recaptured Nat's lips. A groan sounds out.

"Damn you two, get a room." Olivia's laughter cut through the fog in Nat's head. Nat tried to gently push away from Alex, but Alex challenged and prevented her. Her hand began to slide up Nat's shirt. Nat grew angry and shoved Alex back. Ella got up and left. Nat stood up as well and stormed out the room.

"Stop walking away!" Alex yelled out to Nat as she tried to catch up to her without running. Nat continued to storm off.

"I said stop." Alex caught up to Nat and pinned her against a locker before she was shoved away. Alex didn't give up and stepped back into Nat's space.

"Oh, come on, don't act as if you're so innocent. I've seen you kiss both Russel and Ella out in the open."

Nat pokes Alex in the chest angrily "First of all, I never kissed them like that…."

"Not my fault they can't kiss ri…" Alex interrupted.

"…in the cafeteria, in front of everyone to put on a show. You were being an asshole as usual. The kiss was fine until you decided to rub it in Ella's face we're together and go overboard and disrespect me in front of everyone." Nat tried to walk away again but Alex rushed and grabbed her from behind.

"Are you upset at my actions or upset Ella's feelings are hurt?" Alex tone was low and sounded accusing and enraged. The softness and sweet smell of her body in comparison to her dangerous yet low tone sends sparks down Nat's spine. She turns around in Alex arms and didn't push away sensing that Alex might have acted out of jealousy. Her anger reduced to annoyance.

"She has a right to be hurt, it wasn't that long ago she and I was…"

"She was practically fucking you with her eyes while you're right next to me, then fed you some of her cake. It's disrespectful, you belong to me, it doesn't matter if she's not convinced, we're together." Alex had removed her arms and was starting to yell.

Nat smiles at the outburst. "First off, I don't belong to anyone, and she's your friend so you best start acting like it. You don't have to be threatened by anyone, I'm loyal and won't eat anyone else's cake but yours. Happy?" Alex looks like she's about to argue so Nat grabbed her shirt and pulled her closer for a kiss and it deepened quickly. They only break apart after someone whistled. It was their first kiss that was not for show and they stood still not sure of what to do or say. Thankfully the bell rang to signal that their lunch period was over. To keep up appearances, Alex still walked Nat to her class.

After school, Nat sat on one of the outside walls as she watched some of the football players joke around and toss a football.

"Alex is the jealous type you know." Devon came up from behind her making her tense up and startled. He sits next to her.

Nat took the lollipop out of her mouth "Why are you anywhere near me? You don't need to tell me anything about my girlfriend."

Devon looked appalled by her reaction to him, then chuckled "I was looking for Alex and I saw you so I figured you would know best where she is, since she is your girlfriend. See, I'm having this party tonight and Alex is going to be my date. I wanted to make sure the dress I sent her fitted right, that ass has to be properly displayed."

Luckily the lollipop was still in her mouth or she would have bit through her tongue with how hard she bit down in anger. Nat blast Devon off the wall causing some of the jocks to laugh. Johnny and Scott from the football team jog over. "You ok Nat? This guy bothering you?"

"Yes, he is, can you help him find his way?" She smiled and waved at the guys who were taking great enjoyment out of Devon's struggle in their hold as they drag him away.

"Hey, you didn't have to wait for me. It's too cold out here," Alex sat next to her facing her side. There was beautiful snow covering everything and yet she felt hot, burning hot. Nat turned her head and glares at Alex. "Why can't you go to the bar with us tonight again?"

Alex took a few seconds and raised her brow, "I told you, I'm busy. Who made you upset?" She wrapped her arms around Nat the best she could with their coats on. "I'll beat them up." She was trying to make Nat smile, but it did not work.

"Well you'll have to beat up Devon because he says my girlfriend is his date at one of his stupid parties tonight."

"What? Why was he here?" Nat couldn't believe that was the response she got.

"How does that matter? He was here to see if the dress he sent you…how did he say it…mhmm…displayed your ass." Nat yanked around and got down. She didn't want to hear anything else Alex has to say.

"Why am I always having to chase after you? You don't understand, the party is something I'm forced to go to. After the power move, I made a few weeks ago my mother has been more of a demon than usual. I have to go and it's not a romantic date, there will be the next generation of important families there." Alex moved in front of Nat and walks backwards knowing not to touch Nat when she was steaming.

"What are we doing then if you are still going to hang around Devon and do what your mother says?" Nat stopped walking then got closer to Alex so no one else could overhear them "Whatever, I know this isn't real, but I thought this whole time we were starting to be friends again. I see I was wrong, once again disappointed." Nat side stepped Alex and left

"Are you sure?" Leslie asked with a frown, while the others except Arnold had the same look of bewilderment on them.

Nat nodded her head and held up the cellphone for them both to see the name of the caller from whom she had gotten no less than eight missed calls already.

"Something odd must be happening," Sheila noted.

Nat nodded her head and sighed, before taking her last sip from her third martini and sighing out loud. She was trying to think if getting up for two more shots was worth it. Having spent the past weeks training even harder as a means to block out thoughts of Bally Rider and what he did to her father, as well as the terrible incident that involved Garrett Marshall whom the school still believed went on some form of leave to sort personal issues.

"Nat," Arnold called to her suddenly while he shoved away his glass of wine.

It was the first time he would speak since their arrival at the bar and his tone seemed rather bothersome too as he locked her in gaze. Nat answered with a raised brow, while she awaited the strange boy to speak whatever he had in his head.

"You seem tensed Nat… are you still fighting with Alex?" he asked. "Or is there something else you aren't telling us?"

Sheila swept her gaze towards Arnold immediately and wore a frown. "We should be asking that question, considering the nonsense you've been on lately."

Arnold looked at her with loss in his eyes and a level of uncertainty they all could read. Deciphering him wasn't always an easy task.

"The Olivia thing?" Nat asked the other ladies to be sure.

Leslie nodded her head and laughed hard. He had mentioned the fact that he and Olivia had spent the night together and none of them believed him. The reasons were obvious; Olivia was a ballbuster and an ass, and the fact he always had something up his sleeve, it might have been a joke.

"I wasn't joking about Olivia and I and as much as there are still too many variables concerning those placing a bomb underneath Nat's car as we speak, I am telling the truth," he sounded stern.

Nat's heart flushed with fright immediately and Sheila could read it pretty much. "What?"

Sheila cast aside her drink and asked Nat, "What did you do?"

A loud bang erupted, sending people into frenzy and causing pandemonium as people raced away from the car which had just exploded a block away from the bar and people inside started to move around and some under tables.

Arnold donned a smile on his face.

"What is going on?" Sheila looked around in fright as the streets outside shuddered with chaos.

Arnold replied. "Hell is about to reign on us for the next few weeks."

Leslie punched him in the arm immediately, causing Arnold to groan in pain, while Nat could barely breathe or get over the fact that someone just tried to kill her.

"The day just keeps getting interesting," Arnold smirked before looking towards the door expectantly.

They watched the bar door swing open and a bewildered, if not frightened looking Alex stepped into the room, looking around and halting her gaze on Nat the moment she caught sight of the girl. She marched over, paid little to no attention to the others, before yanking at Nat's arm and forcing her to exit the building with her. Olivia waited at the door and nodded over at Arnold with a smile on her face.

Leslie turned to Arnold and asked, "What the hell is going on and what's that about?"

Arnold shrugged, took a sip calmly from his glass and whispered, "All I know is a terrible omen has been following us around for some days now."

Simon came over. "Hey, come on guys we need to get out of here. Alex told me to make sure you guys get back safely."

Outside, Alex rushed Nat into her car and sped off, only slowing down as police and firetrucks passed them by, then she picked up speed again. "Don't worry you're fine." Alex tried to comfort Nat while she herself was shook and furious.

"Where's Devon?" Nat ask confused why Alex was even there. She was thankful and happy. Alex burst out laughing.

"Really? Some idiot tries to take your life, sure he couldn't even put it on right, and it went off killing him or her instead but…you are the weirdest person I know. You're a dog with a bone just like Olivia. I thought about what you said earlier, and I decided a way to respectfully not attend and spend time with my girlfriend and her loser friends." Alex turned to her and smiled which made Nat smile in return.

Alex had barely gotten them far away from the bomb scene when her phone rang and caused her to stop to have a look at who was calling.

With a saddened frown, she placed the phone to her ear and whispered, "Hello?"

"Everything is falling in place as planned... get your mom ready," the male voice whispered from its end. "It might be sooner than we think."

Alex bobbed her head and brought the call to an end immediately. It was exactly what she had been waiting for all along. The end was nearing, and as much as it terrified her, she knew within her soul just how much it was needed, if things were to go accordingly to plans.

"Call your friends and let them know we're having a sleep over. We need to figure out what's going on and I promised my friends a night of drinking, so I still owe them. My dorm, Julian is going to sneak in all the good stuff."

"I think I need to call my mom first and let her know not to freak out when she gets the news. My car is under her information."

For the rest of the ride no more words were shared between the two.

CHAPTER TWENTY-FIVE

A week had passed since the bombing and the occurrence barely scratched the top ten of the oddity going on around the school. Most notable were the official new love birds whose news travelled around the school like wildfire.

"Olivia and Arnold the seer are shacking up!" the words read on the school blog, causing a stir of endless gossip as very few found it plausible.

As odd and as baffling as the information was, Nat couldn't be happier as it managed to deviate attention from her own odd relationship as well.

Alex stepped out from the classroom opposite them and walked over to her locker with her.

"Hey," Alex greeted Sheila. Out of their group circle Sheila and Ella were the least accepting about her relationship with Nat. Their month deadline ended that week but neither brought it up.

Sheila stared blankly at the witch who had given them problems since the first day of school and chose to detach herself from the new couple to avoid any awkward conversations. Just yesterday Sheila had to listen to Nat rant for hours then cry about how Alex had used stolen information from her mom's home office when she was over during their first project session to take down the Scorpion gang and cause all those deaths. Yet, somehow before 3am, Alex had sweet talked her way back into Nat's heart and she was telling Sheila they were going to work things out and Sheila couldn't convince her otherwise. She was tired of the two's drama and needed a break from the crazy couple. Eleanor coincidentally stepped in the hall as well, doing just about enough to ease back and go undetected as her face turned red with jealousy and anger.

"Where are we on the information you promised to get about those you claim you saw around my car the day of the bombing?" Nat whispered.

Alex held out her cellphone and showed her the pictures of the three culprits she assumed were responsible, and right in the middle was Bally Rider. "I already found out about where they live and who they are."

Nat knew just how bad an idea it would be to face the men herself. Her mother was furious and, had gone on a manhunt, using all her sources to get the police to speed up their work. So far, a lot of evidence was destroyed by the explosion, but they are going through surveillance.

"I know one of the guy's house too, but we need solid proof to lead the police there and make an arrest."

Alex stopped walking just as they arrived at the edge of the stairs. Wearing a condemning gaze on her face, she sighed and shook her head.

"Really? You want to deal with the man who murdered your father in cold blood by getting the cops to do it for you?" she asked.

Nat nodded her head. "Yes. I cannot take justice into my hands and become what he is."

Alex broke out a burst of mocking laughter and almost fell to her knees. Nat didn't appreciate her action as it drew attention to them.

"If someone murdered my father the way the guy did yours, I would rip his nuts off and feed it to him," Alex explained. "More so, half the cops in this city are dirty and I know this for certain because my mother owns many of their asses. I just acquired one of my own."

Nat felt like she was being called naïve and didn't like it, but there was an element of truth in Alex's words.

"I don't care," she remained astute. "We need evidence to tie him down to the crime and call in the proper authorities... my mom is the mayor and she will make sure justice is served."

Alex could not believe her ears, but she wasn't going to protest. Compromises and not judging each other's choices were part of the deal for their newly found friendship.

"Meet me tonight at the Park," Alex said before making her way over to Eleanor whom she could sense had been stewing and tailing them for the past few minutes.

Nat watched Alex walk away, trying to think why Alex wanted her to meet there.

* * *

Alex wore a frown upon seeing the hooded figure gallop towards her. She didn't need a soothsayer to tell her who the figure was, but she might have asked one if available, why Nat had on such a disguise when she was a full-blooded witch capable of covering her tracks.

"Really? Is this necessary?" Alex asked with an exhaustive sigh.

Nat brushed the criticism aside and walked over to her friend. "His house is over there by the one with the blue picket fence."

Alex looked over to the house whose lights were off and no car in the driveway.

"I still don't see any reason in this good girl nonsense," she mumbled. "He is human, which means handling him should come as easy as pie to you."

Nat ignored her, crossed to the other side of the street and held her hood high enough to prevent her face from being made in case there were people watching".

Grumbling still, Alex paused and scowled as Nat handed her a pair of gloves.

"Hey! Keep your judgmental tone to yourself!" Nat warned. "We are doing this my way, alright? I didn't even want to be here. He's human which means we have to be extra careful, if we expose ourselves, we'll be in big trouble which I doubt our parents can save us from."

Alex agreed, slapped on the gloves and hurried to the door which they bypassed with ease. The room was no different as the last time she had been in until Alex conjured up a dozen little balls of light.

"Looks like your bomber is a stalker too," Alex noted several pictures of Nat on a wall, before hurrying towards the wardrobes in the bedroom while Nat decided to peruse the contents in the living room first.

"Just be careful," Nat warned, watching her new ally walk away briskly.

The search took fold and within seconds, she found a magnum, tucked into the hinges of a loveseat fully loaded. The safety remained on, but the choice of hiding spot for such a weapon baffled her as she struggled to contain her anger and hate towards Bally Rider.

"I found something," Alex called out, prompting Nat to place the gun back into the hinge where she had found it.

Alex appeared, holding what looked like a hunting knife, but with markings and runes all over it.

"Are you sure this person knows nothing about magic?" Alex asked.

Nat looked unsure and her uncertainty placed them at a disadvantage as they heard the front door shut close and heavy footsteps slowly begin to march their way into the room. Alex placed her finger to her lips and demanded that Nat remained calm while they found themselves a good exit spot from the house if it was at all possible.

"He might not know we are here, so keep quiet," Alex whispered.

The footsteps suddenly stopped, and the loud cocky tone came through, "I can smell your cheap perfume and I'm so winning some money tonight for betting you will be back."

Alex looked pretty much composed, while Nat felt distressed about falling right into the killer's plan.

"Can we be ourselves now?" Alex asked with a grin.

Nat gave it some thought and shook her head. "No... we talk our way out and threaten him with the cops."

It sounded lame to her, talk less of Alex whose contorted expression did well to indicate it.

Slowly making their appearance from the bedroom, Nat led, while Alex followed. "Here we are you bastard!"

She pulled down her hood and revealed herself to the two men of different height and body mass standing before them, armed with nothing but their balled knuckles.

"It is a shame I'd have to leave you on the same spot as your father, but I promise you we will have a nice time first," Bally Rider smirked and winked at Nat.

"You have no idea what you are up against," Nat boasted but her words barely broke a line of worry on the man's forehead.

He looked at his companion, signaled to him and within seconds, they both pounced towards the girls. The one focused on Alex avoided the blade in her hand and shoved her into the bedroom doorframe. Bally Rider remained focused on

Nat and she remembered the fun and raced from the hall further into the living room.

He knocked her into a lamp, smirked and pointed at the ceiling "After our last encounter, I got myself some really good insurance."

Nat knew magic was her only hope, so she waved her hand towards him, but nothing happened; the spell etched into the ceiling negated any magic within the entire space it covered, and it meant she was on her own. Alex was dealing with the other guy. Suddenly a scream filled the air; Nat's heart dropped in her stomach as she tried to evade Bally Rider and think how to save herself and Alex.

Unfortunately, he moved too fast for her, catching her by her arm and overpowering her as he shoved her into the large couch and pinned her down with his knees. "If your father didn't want to die, then he should not have stolen from me!"

Nat spat in his face in response to his insinuation about her father. "You bastard! He never stole from you! Someone else did and if you had half a brain you would have tried to find out!"

The man didn't care, and he began unzipping his pants, causing Nat to hyperventilate at the thought of what he would do to her before eventually killing her. She struggled against him, got her right hand free, while she struggled to find the gun she had found earlier.

Bally finally unzipped and was in his briefs, while he snuck a hand up her shirt and marveled at the pain and paranoia spreading across her face.

"You will enjoy this," he grunted, pinning her neck down with his other hand, while trying to undress her lower half to have his way.

Nat could see her own end flash before her very eyes, while there remained no certainty about whatever was going on with Alex. The loud screams and bangs from things clattering into the wall had ended some seconds ago.

"Fight back!" she heard the voice in her head yell to her. "Fight back damn it!"

Clawing him hard in his eyes to cause him some serious pain and distract him, she felt his knees ease off while he screamed and rubbed some feel into the right eye she had jammed into. It gave her time to pull herself further against the chair with both hands, before he dragged at her feet and back fully to the ground. Nat struggled some more, feeling powerless and wishing luck would be on her side.

"You nasty little bitch!" he raged, spreading her legs apart fuming with his blood shot eye.

Nat turned onto her back, holding the magnum to his face. He slowly retreated to his feet.

"Have you ever shot a gun before, girl?" he asked.

She pulled the safety off and tightened her hands around the handle, with her finger itching to squeeze the trigger.

"Easy now," he pleaded with one hand held high, and the other sneaking towards his back.

He motioned to pull out something from behind him, prompting Nat to shoot him in the kneecap first.

"Shit!" he cried in pain. "You little piece of shit!"

She capped him in the other knee, causing him to squirm terribly in pain, while he cursed and swore at her with saliva bursting forth from his lips in the process.

"I am going to kill you," he promised her. "No... no... I will fuck your brains out before putting my cock in your mouth and then, I'll kill you!"

Nat pinned him to the ground with her leg to his chest and leaned.

"How about I put this in your mouth," she whispered to him, before placing the nozzle of the gun at his mouth and shot before shooting him again in between his eyes.

With one gentle squeeze, a loud bang filled the air, with a moment of silence interrupted only by gentle claps from Alex who seemed to have been watching the entire event unfold.

"Look who has the balls to cross the line when she needs to," she sounded with a note of mockery in her words.

Nat slowly stepped away from the dead body and felt herself grow some sense of relief about Bally Rider leaving the world. Her father's killer had been dealt with. She had killed someone else now. How was she going to get out of this?

"I know what you're thinking, and I know a way," Alex urged her to hand over the gun then they raced out of the house together immediately.

Upon making their exit, Nat stared at Alex, as the latter opened her thoughts to the former to read through and act accordingly.

"Fire will do nicely," Nat agreed, taking a few steps backwards, while Nat did the same.

The witches turned their back on the house, the moment it went ablaze in steamy hot fire which would rapidly burn the to the ground in less than ten minutes.

"We make a mean team," Alex chuckled.

Nat nodded. "I don't take joy from other people's pain though."

The words enraged Alex without doubt, but she remained mute; she might not understand Nat's need to be upset over killing someone who tried killing her but she's remembering that same pure light once drew her in like a moth to a flame.

CHAPTER TWENTY-SIX

Two weeks after Alex and Nat took care of Bally Rider, their fake relationship ended in an explosion but both heated girls decided to be friends. Both of their circle of friends continued to get closer as well. It was the seventh day in December, Nat's birthday. She still had two more final exams to do before the break but tonight she didn't care, she just wanted to party with her friends.

"Happy sixteenth birthday Nat." Simon comes up behind Nat and picked her up before he spun her into a bear hug. She laughed and tried to get out of his grasp before hugging him back. She then hugged Leslie who arrived with him.

"Thanks guys, I won't ask why you both were late." She winked then ran over to the bucket of ice where the beers were being kept and grabbed two for them. "Everyone else is here already." The guests included more than her close friends and some of the school's most popular students. There's no way to have a party with no one finding out about it and she wasn't going to complain. The Richard triplets put a silencer barrier around the party space at Nat's request that was backed up with blackmail since she had proof the triplets were responsible for Saskia getting kicked out of school for a large drug possession. They were bringing weed to a party and someone was coming into the swim team locker room and they shoved the packet into a duffle bag, and it turned out to be Saskia's bag.

The party was held outdoors so Nat could enjoy the beauty of wintry snow, but they had many magical fire balloons floating around and open tents to provide warm shelter which the invisible silencer barrier didn't provide. The falling snow rolled off the barrier.

"I know you went behind my back and made the triplets put protection spells into the barrier," Nat throws her arm around Alex's shoulder who had just walked over face stuck into her phone. Alex looked up and smiled.

"With you around trouble is not far away. You can't blame me. I made sure you had a great DJ and dancing snowmen, appreciate the skills."

Nat rolled her eyes then kissed Alex's cheek distracting her enough to yank her cell phone out of her hand. Alex tried to take it back, so Nat tucked it inside her bra. "No, you will drink, dance, and have fun. Where's the party crasher, anyway, shouldn't she have your face in her?" The words were out before Nat realizes what she said.

Alex raised her brow and smirked at Nat. "My girlfriend is not a crasher, she's my plus one and she'll have more than my face in…" Nat rushed and closed Alex mouth with her hands then went to dance with Jason her online school mate. Nat started taking two law school courses online and Jason was her study buddy and her professor's TA.

Two songs in and Sheila and Olivia came over to drag Nat away from Jason so she could help them win the werewolf polo game.

"I turn my head and you both start gambling at my party?" Nat folded her arms over each other, playfully scolding her friends. Ever since Sheila started working at Alex' casino to get enough dirt on Alex to break her and Nat up, she found out that she was great at numbers and making money so much that she stayed even after Nat talked sense into her about her undercover work.

"Look there's five hundred on the line and we're down a rider. Gale's non-driving ass broke her leg and everyone else is too much of a pussy to step up." Olivia tried to persuade Nat.

"Actually, you're down a rider and a wolf, so I'll take my money now." Jace thrust his hand out with a smug grin on his face that made both girls groan and look around to see the two werewolves had fought and one was in indeed down.

Nat starts to look concerned at people getting injured at her party. "Guys, I think we should just end the game."

"No, we shouldn't, come on we'll team up." Ella came over and Nat found it almost impossible not to stare at her chest with the tight dress she was wearing which put her breast on display.

"You're a great rider, never fell off me before so it's an easy win." Ella smiled seductively and took off her leather jacket, the one all members of Alex' gang had, before shifting in front of everyone. As a large wolf she trots closer to Nat and licks her hand.

"Great, it's settled!" Sheila fist pumped the air and Olivia began to announce the final match and take final bets. Nat hopped up on Ella and grabbed her mallet.

"Wait, since we're outdoors shouldn't it be four instead of just the three of us?" Nat realizes the numbers were off then noticed she had no idea where the goals were. "Where's the goal?"

"Stop being so logical Natalie. That tree there with the hole and that tree over there, the one you want. The first team to four points wins. The money pot is at fifteen hundred now so don't lose."

"It's Nat!!!!" Nat tried to remind Olivia as someone whistled and Ella took off too fast for her. She squealed and grabbed hold of Ella tightly. Nat recovered in seconds and received a pass then worked on staying on top of Ella as she neared the goal and Jace rammed his werewolf into them. Ella stayed upright and Nat hit the ball with her mallet, and it went in.

The ball shot out back to the middle of the makeshift field and they all ran back toward it and everything moved quickly. Each team made a point back to back until there was one point left to win. Jace had the ball and his arrogant ass was not passing it to his open teammate and then he fouled Nina who was on Nat's team, but this wasn't a game with real rules, so the game continued even though Nina went down hard.

Nat rushed and swiped Jace's mallet with her own as she turned Ella sharply into him making his werewolf slow down to limit the impact, giving Nat enough space to steal the ball and race the opposite way to their tree goal. Ella snapped at Thomas opposing team member nearing them and tripped him up bringing his rider down with him before Jace caught up and hit Nat's wrist which caused her to scream and drop her mallet.

Ella continued to race after Jace. Nat tried to focus on anything but the pain and used her magic to bring the mallet back to her. "Ella fall back, hit his left leg," Ella slowed down then rams forward. Jace went flying off. Nat got the ball and passed it to her open teammate before racing down to the goal to get open. The ball was passed back to her, but it hit too hard and Nat had to pivot Ella then race to the ball. She couldn't hit the ball properly, so she slid up to Ella's neck then reached out all the way to smack the ball into their tree goal before the other player has a chance to steal it, just inches away. Nat lost her leg grip and fell down rolling into the hard and cold dirt.

Everyone cheered and screamed. Nat groaned as she stood, her back and butt bruised. Ella had shifted back to her human form and helped Nat up concerned and not bothered by anyone seeing her naked. Olivia and Sheila raced each other toward Nat but Alex beat everyone and shoved Ella to the ground.

"What the hell is wrong with you? You could have gotten her killed?" Alex was so furious even Nat could feel her magic sparking off her. Her friends stopped running toward her and hurried the other way not wanting to get near Alex and get in trouble too.

"Woah stop Alex. I'm fine and no one made me do anything." Nat got in between Alex and Ella and Alex moved forward while behind her Jace was up in the air body twisting.

"Alexandra Aurelius, if you don't cut the bullshit out right now and end up ruining my party, I will show you what being close to death really is." Nat poked Alex in the chest with each word making Alex grit her teeth and glance away. Jace landed back down and Ella huffed before walking away to get dressed.

"Here, put this on and get Leslie to warm you up." Alex took off her leather and put it around Nat before walking off to grab a drink.

Nat rolled her eyes but complied anyway. Everyone went back to partying. Nat found Ella and celebrate their win with a few shots being shoved at them one after the other by Julian. She grabbed Ella's hand five shots in and rushes to dance with the snowmen. They were bumping and grinding, getting lost in the music and each other when suddenly Ella stopped and says she'll be back. Confused but drunk enough to not care Nat walked over to Simon and Leslie to talk with them.

"Isn't that Alexandra's jacket?" Rachel, Alex' girlfriend came over and asked Nat. She doesn't look too pleased.

"Yeah, it is, so?" Nat slurred and Simon laughed before grabbing her cup and finishing it for her. "HEY!"

"She doesn't want anyone wearing it. Where is she?"

"Are you accusing me of stealing it? Maybe she just doesn't want you wearing it. Don't want it to smell like skank." Nat was being a jerk, but she never liked Rachel. The witch was known for being a slut and a cheater.

Rachel looked as if she was going to attack Nat. "I see what she's talking about. You really are a snobby bitch. You're just jealous of our relationship. She told me how you two were faking the whole time, she could never trust you to really date you. You would let Alexandra burn at the stake. One day she'll stop playing with her life and stay away from you before you become her downfall."

She turned and walked away leaving Nat stuck and her friends trying to convince her Rachel was wrong about her and try to find out if the relationship was a fake like Rachel exclaimed. Nat couldn't take all the questions and walked away. She was shocked that Alex told Rachel the truth about their previous dating when she was so strict about Nat never telling anyone.

She slowly sobered up and walked toward her own tent so she could have privacy, but Olivia ran to her stopping her progress. "Go get your girlfriends in check, I can't stop them. Those two are so territorial and boneheaded, they should be men." Olivia sighed loudly then walked away pointing in the direction Nat should go.

"I'm not sober enough for this." Nat groaned out to herself.

Before she even got inside the tent Olivia pointed out, she heard the voices of Alex and Ella yelling. Nat pulled the flap aside, "You're just pissed she still gets all hot for me and you never made her so excited and hungry for you." Ella is an inch from Alex face.

Alex shoved Ella then punched her down before Nat could get in between them. "You must have forgotten who you are speaking to! You were and always will just be a warm body to use." Alex pinned Ella with magic as Ella growled and tried to get up.

"Both of you are going to give me a migraine. What the hell is wrong with you two? Alex, let her up now." Nat shoves Alex away from Ella. "Look, I don't understand why you care about Ella since our relationship was all pretend, that's what you told Rachel, right? And you Ella, I don't know how many times I've said to check yourself. I love you as a friend and that's all. I'm sorry I could not love you more but if you both keep up this macho nonsense, I'm not going to be either of your friend."

Nat yelled at them both and instead of listening they start to argue about who started the fight and Alex tried to make up a reason why she told Rachel.

"She was getting too jealous and suspicious of us hanging out too much, so I had to reassure her there was nothing between us…"

Ella over talks Alex "I knew there was nothing between you two and she had something over you. What did you do, blackmail her?" Ella growled at Alex and approached her.

Nat slapped Ella then pointed at her. "Stay."

Alex chuckled making Nat swiftly turn and give her the glare of death. Alex stopped. "You two are friends and need to start acting like it. Are you both really fighting over a girl? I am awesome, I know. I could start a few wars." Both scoffed and smiled at Nat trailing off. "Anyway, like I said you two are friends and would die for each other. Alex, Ella has always been at your side and has scars to prove it. Ella, Alex has always been a great friend to you and helped you get independence from your pack. You two are family. She's not your alpha or master…"

"Actually, I am in charge…" Nat elbowed Alex hard for interrupting and continues talking. "She's your sister and you both better apologize to each other and shake hands before I make you hug and kiss it out. NOW!"

They look at each other worried Nat would make them hug and kiss and quickly start apologizing and it turned sincere the more they listed off things they were sorry about then shook hands before they look at Nat.

"You two can go now. Oh, and Alex, your girlfriend is looking for you." Alex left and Ella made way to do so as well but Nat stopped her.

"If you challenge Alex again, I won't stop her from punishing you however she sees fit. You two might be friends but you are her Lieutenant or whatever and she has the right to kick your ass for such disrespect," Nat ignored Ella's look of shock then walked off to enjoy the party before everyone started to leave.

Simon and Leslie were running in the woods away from the party, hiding behind trees playfully trying to avoid each other. Simon caught her and kissed her deeply. He guided her to a secret underground entrance to get back to her dorm room quicker. Once inside, Simon attacked her lips again. Leslie hushed Simon whose hand was tucked into hers and waved her hands to create a ring of fire above them so they could see each other.

"Are you scared? We can go back outside and walk." he spoke in a concerned tone as they walked deeper through the tunnel.

Leslie shrugged, smiled and whispered, "No, and it's worth the risk, considering you're leaving me for two weeks to go to Paris."

Simon shook his head, lifted the daring phoenix from her waist and helped her wrap her legs around his waist, before pinning her against the wall and slowly began to unbutton her top. Sneaking his cold hand over her warm breast, Leslie let out a soft purr, before she dragged his head closer and kissed him passionately.

Consumed by her desires, and barely allowing the boy any breath, she felt him stiffen, just before he slowly peeled his lips from hers and wore a look of fright on his face.

"Leslie," he whispered, with his breath going cold, and his face turning white as something hurried through the darkness, rattling the walls softly then suddenly ceasing. He stopped caressing her and put her down. "Do you hear that?"

She pinned her ears towards the silence, but nothing stood out beside the walls shaking a few seconds ago as if a train was going above them. Discarding his concerned expression, she wrapped her arms around his neck once again, and resumed their passionate kiss, before slipping her hand down his pants and feeling his already hardened erection.

"Somebody is feeling somewhat..." she paused, feeling something hurry past them in maddening speed that they could only feel the breeze it left behind smashing their faces.

Simon turned around immediately. "I felt it this time... there is something in the shadows."

Leslie's heart began to race but she kept a calm expression, as she tried to ease Simon's worries. He nudged her hand away respectfully, before waking farther away from her and past the ring of fire she had put in place.

"Stay back, while I check it out," he warned her.

Conjuring a fire with a wave of his hand, and sending it forth to illuminate his path, Simon kept his eyes glued ahead, but nothing seemed to be around.

"It is nothing!" Leslie called out to him in hopes that he would return.

Determined to check properly before returning to her, he held out his hand upon hearing something coming his way. It traveled fast and barely registered in the light when the fire went off and a cold chill engulfed Simon's spine and caused him to stiffen immediately. Leslie engulfed herself in fire and raced towards Simon who couldn't move his limbs.

He was in trouble, and she could see it, but she didn't have the kind of magic to expel toward him and didn't know where the attacker was.

"Leslie!" he whispered with his breath seeming to fail him. "Please… find me!"

His last words rang a thread of terror in her mind before a monstrous entity dragged Simon north into the tunnel, causing Leslie to chase after it immediately, before heading west, back towards the grounds where Nat had saved a student's life weeks ago.

Falling to the ground in a loud clatter, before hurrying back to her feet and racing through the darkness, Leslie screamed as loud as she could, "Simon! Simon!"

The pace at which he was being dragged away intensified, causing her to stutter in her steps, and fall to the ground a few times as her energy to stay engulfed drained her.

"Simon!" she cried once again, before finally hitting a dead end, with brick lined across and nothing else in sight.

She stepped backwards, clenched her fists to punch the wall down but it wouldn't budge, as it remained firm and unyielding.

Her heart sunk as she fell to her knees and sobbed fire out completely. "What have I done? What have I done?"

She would had insisted they go back to the dorms instead of one of the tents. She cursed the decision she forced him into making and sniffed with copious amounts of tears rolling down her cheeks. Then she took out her cellphone to send messages to those she could rely on.

Leslie stood up and raced back to the party not waiting on them to see her messages.

The evil lurking in the school had reared its ugly head once again and this time, she saw where it headed.

CHAPTER TWENTY-SEVEN

Pandemonium broke through the school like wild fire, forcing students to be placed under restrictions while the teachers and entire school authorities tried to get a grasp on what had befallen Simon, the outsider whom had been taken right within their school.

Mr. Sadon and Headmaster Parker stared down at Leslie for the umpteenth time, refusing to blink as Mr. Sadon asked, "What direction was he taken again?"

Leslie looked bland in expression; grief stricken. Mr. Sadon had led the search with other teachers and guards the moment Leslie and her friends sounded the alarm. The men had no luck breaking through to her. He sighed in exhaustion, broke away and raced out of sight to gather a plan. Leslie barely moved, allowing her hair fall down her face as she wondered if Arnold's words about some bad omen befalling them were finally coming to light.

Loud footsteps hurried in her direction as a slender hand slowly raised her face so she could see Sheila before hugging her tightly.

"Everything is going to be ok." Sheila tried to comfort Leslie while the others stood around.

Nat popped into view as well, looking distorted and barely able to keep her emotions in check as she attempted to speak on numerous occasions but just could not.

"What happened? Did they say they found anything?" Nat asked, trying to get an update as she passes a bag of pastries and a coffee mug to Leslie. No one had gotten any sleep, only passing out off and on as they waited for news from the search party.

Leslie shook her head, clamped her lips shut as she felt her tear ducts empty themselves, unable to water her worries any longer. The night had been the longest of her life and one she still could not believe to have happen.

"Leslie, talk to us." Nat called to her friend, assuming a seat by her side so she could feel somewhat comfortable.

"This is messed up!" Olivia punched a hole in a wall and began to pace. This was her cousin who was missing and there are no leads. Arnold hugged her before rubbing his face.

"How do we know she's not responsible?" Olivia spoke out pointing at Leslie.

"What? Why would I, I loved him! Where were you? You weren't at the party when I got back!" Leslie stood up fuming.

"Stop it! You both are just upset. Olivia that wasn't fair, you don't have to be such a bitch all the time."

"She could not have done it because she was with me," Arnold spoke up. "Quite frankly, we weren't anywhere near what is coming, and I warned us at the café, didn't I?"

Nat shrugged off his words of doom and approached Olivia. "I still don't trust you or even understand why all of a sudden you developed a thing for him."

Arnold seemed offended and his frown did enough to show it. His attempt to speak for himself only got halted by Olivia who held up her hand to silence him.

"Why does it bother you?" Olivia asked. "Does it have anything to do with you not being able to understand or conceive the fact that others can have something good for them and not just hop from student to student then screw your teacher?"

The blow was low, and Nat was prepared to respond with her left hand brewing some magic in it before something restrained her.

"If you all are going to keep on crying and arguing fine, but you might want to do it after we find the bastard who took Simon," Alex pulled Nat away from Olivia, causing the air to both get more tense and somewhat mellow at the same time.

She approached Leslie, and looked into the girl's eyes, before shaking her head.

"This is our business and we will handle it as we choose, I wouldn't want to break anyone's morals," Leslie stood her ground and eyed Nat in hopes that her friend would stand by her.

Arnold gasped, wore a frown and mumbled, "Are you guys serious right now?"

"Yes!" Julian rubbed his hands together.

"Yes, I'm very serious. You all tried it your way with the teachers and they came back with nothing. Now I'm going to find Simon." Alex waved on her friends.

"Maybe you guys should sit this out instead," Nat suggested.

Alex shook her head with amusement and clapped to further lengthen the level of sarcasm she hoped to portray. "You are a piece of work, aren't you? You are always full of this hypocritical bullshit. I thought you had changed and grown some balls."

Nat shrugged her words off. "Are you done?" She asked then smiled.

"You should sit this out because we're going to get Simon." She looked at Alex with a smug smile and looked around at everyone. "You all are like animals snapping at each other the moment something gets shaken. Come on, we're all a team, if we're going to get Simon we have to work together."

Alex looked mad for a few seconds before sighing loudly. "You had to waste all this time to pick on me just to end up saying let's work together, when you could have saved a whole lot of our energy not playing games?"

Olivia stepped forward; hands locked with Arnold who donned the most serious expression yet.

"Tell them Arnie," Olivia looked somber.

Leslie beckoned on Arnold with a worried expression on her face. "Tell us what? Is there something you know that you aren't telling us?"

Ella looked in their direction, while Alex's attention was solely onto the duo as well.

"You know how my ability revolves around a million and one possibilities when it comes to predicting the course of events for others?" he asked.

Leslie nodded, while Nat groaned and drew closer.

"Well..." he paused and looked absolutely drained of blood in the face. "Blood is about to get spilled if we go in pursuit of Simon."

Their faces dampened immediately, and an eerie silence soon greeted the air.

"I don't care," Leslie replied. "I don't care, if there is any possibility in which we can beat your prophesy, I will take it."

Olivia stared into Arnold's face blankly, unsure of why he didn't tell them the entire truth but remained mute herself.

"I stand with Leslie," Alex stepped forward. "I am not saying it will be easy, but someone we all care about has been taken and we have a chance to get him back."

"What's a hunting party without a wolf?" A jubilant and quite dashing looking Eleanor glowed from her eyes, eager for a fight.

Arnold seemed reluctant to pledge his allegiance as the others just did. He stiffened and refused to go with Olivia when she stepped forward.

"Arnold!" She called to him, but he shook his head and looked away. "Well, I'm never one to run from a fight, so, count me in."

Arnold turned his back on all of them and began to walk away to the dismay of Olivia especially.

"Really!?" she yelled in disgust. "You're going to turn your back on your friends when they need you the most!?"

Arnold halted momentarily, lowered his head and replied, "I'm only turning my back on my friends because I don't want to have to watch them die."

"Them?" Nat turned to Olivia and asked.

Arnold said nothing more and simply walked away, leaving the girls and Arthur staring at him with a mix of anger and befuddlement.

"Lead the way, Leslie," Nat commanded.

They sneak out of the building and maneuver with difficulty behind the backs of the security guards and ran once they had a clear path to the woods. Once the buildings began to get harder to see they all slowed down so some could catch their breath. They continued to the tunnel entrance and they walked and walked seemingly forever before they get to the dead end.

Here," she finally stopped, before the large brick wall, far away from where the teachers and other school employees were searching for the missing boy. "Whatever took him went through here and no matter how hard I tried to blast it open with magic, it wouldn't budge."

Nat stepped forward and felt the wall with her hand. "That's because the wall is protected by an anti-magic barrier of some kind."

"Is the school even aware of such a thing within their grounds?" Eleanor asked in a surprised tone.

Alex shook her head, shoved her way through until she was beside Nat. "The school cannot know, because whoever had this installed is skilled in covering her tracks more than anyone else."

The level of specificity in her words baffled everyone and they all cast their gaze on Alex for answers.

"My mother had this wall installed," Alex explained in what was a jaw dropping moment for everyone.

She pointed at the top right corner, where a little etching of her family insignia was barely visible unless you knew where to look. She was telling the absolute truth, and in the process, opened another debacle about what exactly was going on.

CHAPTER TWENTY-EIGHT

Nat felt the silence linger long enough as she motioned to touch Alex but halted when Alex suddenly ran her hands along the brick lines in the wall, pushing hard against bricks simultaneously while the others watched in awe.

"If I know my mother well enough..." Alex grunted as she tried to work whatever puzzle her mother had made the lock into. "She wouldn't rely on magic for things she feels are vulnerable."

She finally shoved a large piece of brick inward and hard, before slowly stepping away as the others did following her lead. They waited, and they stared at the wall waiting for something worthwhile to happen. A loud and disturbing grumbling shook the earth beneath them, causing them to brace themselves, before a loud hissing noise and clank followed.

Anxious and frightened at the same time, they watched the wall remain still, causing an impatient looking Julian to approach it as his hand leaned against the wall as he said, "Is that all?"

The wall caved inwards immediately, causing him to fall, while the others barely permitted themselves the chance to laugh.

"I am scared," Leslie confessed, reaching for Sheila's arm and gripping it tightly.

Nat felt her senses heighten immediately as they walked through the rather dark path, which burst to light the farther they went, until another dead end was reached.

"Can you sense it?" Nat grabbed hold of Alex's hand while Sheila stood by her side. "Something isn't right about this place."

Alex couldn't agree more, but there was no going back as their foreheads got drenched in sweat, and their hearts pumped blood copiously through their entire body in fright. The door behind them shut finally, and like a relay of pulleys at work, the large dark stone wall before them slowly began to give way.

"Here we go," Alex whispered to herself.

Nat took the first step forward, watching the entire surroundings light up immediately in white fluorescent as it became apparent, they were in some kind of laboratory.

Thunderous claps soon aired and caused the kids to turn around slowly as a lady donning a perfectly tailored dark suit and black high heels with a devilish smirk on her face, appeared from the shadows.

Parting her hands to the side and nodding her head gently, Brenda Aurelius yelled, "Welcome Alex! Thank you for bringing exactly what I need to me!"

Everyone turned to Alex, scared and unsure if they should feel betrayed as the young witch looked befuddled herself.

Brenda Aurelius walked down the metal stairs just above a section where a stout lady with a scar on her face, glasses and a lab coat raced around endlessly, engrossed in her work, ignoring Brenda. While they were on the verge of shitting their pants.

"What is all of this, mother?" Alex stepped forward and asked.

Brenda Aurelius approached them and stopped before Nat with her gaze peering into the girl's eyes. "The future my darling Alexandra! This is the future!"

She walked away briskly, waved over the woman in lab coat who came running over.

Brenda pointed in Nat's direction, smiled and whispered into the lady's ear. "One of the Kings... you know what to do with her."

The lady hurried over, took Nat's hand and attempted to yank her along, but Nat gained control of her hand before voicing, "What on earth is going on? What do you need me for and what is this place?"

"Where's Simon?!" Olivia voiced out.

The lady looked over to Brenda, who gave her permission to speak.

In a squeaky excited tone, she replied, "My name is Amy and this section of the school which has been abandoned for years is the Orb, where really cool experiments go on."

Amy giggled excitedly, attempted to pull Nat once again but instead met Ella who shoved her back.

"You don't understand," Amy rushed out. "Your blood is the last ingredient for my next project after the beta testing of the…"

Brenda yelled, "That's enough Amy! Get the girl and do what you need!"

Alex stepped forward, shaking her head, "What do you want to do with her?"

Brenda helped herself into a seat with her legs crossed.

"The same thing I needed her mother for, you dummy," her mother replied. "Their blood is key to owning the Clinic and being able to use it at full capacity!"

Leslie's jaw dropped. "You two were in on this the whole time?"

Brenda chuckled aloud, causing the others to turn on Alex immediately. Nat remained silent, choosing to believe in Alex even while everything seemed otherwise.

"We trusted you!" Leslie ranted on.

Amy ignored the girl throwing a tantrum to try and grabbed hold of Nat one more time while the other were distracted, but the girl wasn't having any of her nonsense.

"Don't touch me!" Nat yelled, blasting the scientist hard into the wall to her right. She was not done.

Feeling her insides filled with rage, she motioned towards Brenda immediately, prompting Alex to chase after her in bid to stop her.

"Nat, don't!" Alex cried in warning.

Nat held her hand out, fumed and began to breathe unsteadily. "Where is he? Where is Simon!?"

Brenda chuckled and waved off her actions.

"I must admit the little show you put on there was rather entertaining, but what are you going to do with me?" Brenda asked as she got to her feet.

Alex stood before Nat and urged her to calm down. "You are angry, and I get it, but trust me, you cannot…"

A bright red streak of light flashed and struck Alex immediately, causing her to slump to the ground while she struggled to breathe properly. Nora appeared from the shadows, smiling and bobbing her head towards Brenda.

"I told you she was going to be a pain in my ass," Brenda sighed. "First, she had to collude with that vampire cretin of a boy and now she wouldn't even see the vision in what I am doing here."

Nat hurried to Alex's rescue, but stopped upon seeing Nora raise her hand in her direction. "I wouldn't do that if I were you."

Brenda sighed, yawned and looked to Amy with a frown before muttering, "Take care of things here for a few minutes, Nora."

Brenda vanished immediately, while Amy groaned as he slowly woke up. She got to her feet immediately and dusted herself before marching over to Nat like nothing had happened to her.

"I am so going to enjoy cutting you open!" she chuckled derisively in a manner that frightened the teenagers.

Nat shook her head, "Hell will freeze over before that happens!"

Amy stepped backwards, snuck her hands into her pockets and waited for Nat to get on with business. Sheila continued to look glum, almost as if she was trapped in her own mind the entire time through. Alex motioned to move, but Nora subdued her once again, grinning wildly and almost as though she no longer bore the same care, she had for Alex anymore.

"Why?" Alex managed to grumble. Nora pinned her foot into the girl's shoulder and replied, "You kids wouldn't understand what this revived laboratory is capable of, or what dreams it holds."

Alex turned her head uncomfortably while flashes of light burst alive between Nat and Amy. The laboratory looked old, but the equipment within it was new and reeked of her mother's money.

"This is what you two have been hiding from me while you kept me distracted with the Hamilton thing isn't it?" Alex growled, while Nora continued to pin her down with her foot.

"Your mother decided you didn't need to know and like always, I followed her command," Nora spoke bluntly and without a hint of emotion.

A loud burst of flame and bang emanated between Nat, which had caused Amy to jump backwards. Nat held her right hand out, fixated her gaze on the lab scientist whose immense magical ability had been nothing but amazing, and carefully approached.

"We should help her," Leslie whispered to Sheila who still had not said a thing.

Olivia sighed, closed her eyes and parted them open. Her fangs slowly emanated, and her claws grew from her fingertips as she winked at Leslie and raced ahead. Nora caught sight of her immediately and sent a blast of fire in her direction, but the vampire was rather fast and did well to maneuver.

"I will not be that easy!" Olivia yelled, circling Nora and catching her with a punch into her gut through her blind spot.

Alex rolled on her stomach, slowly got to her feet and nodded at her vampire friend.

Julian giggled excitedly, smiled at Leslie and Sheila and whispered, "I guess it's time for some fun for me too."

He vanished immediately, racing past Nat and knocking down Amy as she tried to get to her feet.

Nora pulled herself from the floor and wore a frown at Olivia. "Amy! Get serious and stop fooling around!"

Amy suddenly paused, slowly turned around and her eyes turned blood red, just like Olivia's.

"Hello Natalie," she whispered before her bruises began to heal as she approached Nat.

"What in the heavens are you?" Nat asked.

Sheila replied, "Forbidden creature... she is a forbidden creature and it is what they are creating in this laboratory... it must be what they hope to turn Simon into! A mutant!"

Everyone turned their attention to Sheila, who had her eyes solely fixated on Amy.

"It is good to have you on board," Nat whispered to Sheila who stood by her side and wore a faint smile. "Let's kick this bitch's ass."

Nat took a step forward, hoping to catch Amy unaware, but the little devil seemed to disappear out of sight immediately. It left both girls stunned, while Alex and Olivia battled with Nora at the same time.

"Where did she go?" Nat sounded confused.

"Over here!" Amy screamed, before planting her claws into Nat's shoulder from behind causing her to growl in pain.

Sheila shot a gust of wind at Amy but missed.

"She is as fast as a vampire," Sheila noted, sounding rather surprised.

Nat barely had time to think, as Arthur appeared and rammed Amy into Nat. She grabbed hold of Amy's hand as tight as she could, stared into the little devil's eyes and smirked in the process. Causing a rather tender flame to grow around her arm, she linked it into Amy's, and sent the lady into flames immediately. Amy began shrieking in pain.

"I guess fire does work on her too," Nat smiled.

Still not done, Nat stepped forward, raced towards the burning lady, and swung her leg in the air, just about high enough to connect with the screaming and shrieking Amy, to knock her out cold. Her body burnt faster with each passing second, before completely turning to crisp and ashes.

"You're really bad ass," Sheila complimented Nat while Leslie nodded in agreement then went to search for Simon.

Nat smiled, waved it away and replied, "I have been training."

"Nat! Alex is in trouble!' a frightened sounding and looking Ella screamed.

Nat looked towards Alex and Olivia; both had their necks being grasped in a death grip by Nora who had suddenly transformed into a large sized werewolf with some deformity in her appearance. Nat needed no further invitation as she raced over, sliding on the ground while conjuring large sized tree vines to sprout from the tiled surface and twirl rapidly around Nora's huge legs attempting to lift her up.

"Now!" Nat yelled, while Sheila tormented the werewolf with a burst of fire then a dark purple sonic wave that unsettled her enough to trip over and fall on her back.

Nat helped Alex to her feet, shared a brief gaze with the girl and read her thoughts immediately. Swirling their hands in the air, they began wrapping Nora up as fast as they could in magically entwined tree vines, until no region of her body could be seen. Olivia, Leslie and Sheila watched in awe of the two witches working together and in a formidable manner.

"We did it!" Nat and Alex yelled in chorus and excitement, hugging one another and briefly breaking apart in the process.

The others raced over to join them before Ella spoke, "We still need to find Simon in this laboratory."

Leslie stepped backwards, closed her eyes and held out her hands as tiny spark of glowing balls began to emanate from her body, and spread across the entire room. Olivia gasped in awe, while Sheila looked at Leslie proudly. "If he's alive one of the balls should bring us to him."

Alex turned to Nat and yanked at her arm gently. "I swear it to you; I didn't know anything about this place."

Nat stared into her eyes and could very well see she was telling nothing but the truth. She nodded and took her hand. She needed her strength right now as they began to search the room for their friend.

"I found something!" Olivia called out, prompting everyone to race towards her.

In her hand was an article, dusty and old, in black and white prints.

"It says this facility was part of the school project put in place in an attempt to build more stable and rounded magical creatures," she read.

Nat took over the paper from her and perused the content slowly to her dismay and angst. "They were experimenting on different creatures and humans in order to make super creatures with more than one unnatural ability."

Sheila gasped aloud immediately.

Nat bobbed her head without looking in her friend's direction. "Yes, and it says the program was shut down and the lab sealed once they found out what Amy was secretly doing, but..."

"Nat?" Sheila's voice came out croaky in tone as she called out to Nat. They all turned around to the sight of Nora with her fist jammed into Sheila's chest, while she wore a damning smile on her face that unsettled the girls, as well as Arthur.

"Now that you know, I believe making you one of the collections wouldn't be a bad idea," Nora giggled into Sheila's ear.

She yanked out her hand, causing Sheila to pause and gurgle in pain momentarily, before sidestepping and stumbling her way towards Nat whose nerves felt frozen as she watched her friend collapse to the floor blood flowing out of her mouth.

"Sheila!" Nat yelled, hurrying to the bleeding witch's side, while everyone else hurriedly stood before the girls in hopes of shielding them from Nora.

"Why are you doing this, Nora?" Alex asked, in hopes of finding some reasoning.

Nora shrugged her shoulders, smiled and replied, "Like I said, you children cannot possibly understand what..."

She stopped talking mid-words and stared blankly at them.

"Guys!" Julian's voice came crawling out from Nora's body. "I don't know how long I can take charge of her body for, but we need to do something now!"

Nat placed her hand over the deep wound in Sheila side, and whispered, "Hold on please! I will heal you! I promise you!"

Sheila gurgled some more blood, causing everyone to take their attention away from Julian and Nora.

Alex knelt beside Nat and placed her hand over the injury as well, "We can do it together."

Both combined their powers and tried to heal the deep wound but to no avail as something seemed to be restricting it from closing.

"There is venom mixed with magical poison in that wound," Julian informed them. "Whatever this woman is, I haven't seen anything like it before!"

"How do we heal her!?" an enraged Nat got to her feet and began to storm towards Julian in Nora's body, but Leslie stopped her.

Julian remained silent momentarily, before a wicked laughter broke through and the cold recognizable voice of Nora replied, "It cannot be done!"

Julian's screams could be heard shrieking through the air, before his body rolled out from Nora's and fell to the ground. Wincing in pain and groaning, he attempted to crawl over to meet with Alex and Olivia, but Nora stopped him with her leg to his neck and her left hand slowly bearing claws.

"Not on my watch, you abominable bitch!" Ella's voice broke through, as the blonde girl came running pass Leslie and Olivia.

Nora turned, hoping to make her move in time before Eleanor came closer, but the werewolf was abnormally fast and already behind her before she could make a full turn. Swinging her hand hard at Nora and watching her duck just about enough to prevent the heavy blow from reaching her, she was immediately blindsided to the vampire behind her, waiting for the perfect opportunity to strike.

In swift counter move to follow Eleanor's, Olivia slashed her claws right at Nora's throat, causing the lady to yell in pain but not loud or even lengthy enough, as Eleanor rammed her hand into her chest and yanked out the slowly beating heart that soon lost its tempo. Nora looked empty in her face and her eyes lost its spark as her body fell to the ground in unison with the heart in Eleanor's hand.

"Hey, I could have eaten that." Olivia joked and high fived Eleanor, before the werewolf raced over to Nat whose face dripped with tears. "She is not healing."

Eleanor looked at the wound and shook her head, "This is bad, I doubt vampire blood will help."

The words coincided with the cackling laughter from Brenda who appeared in the room immediately. "Yes, it is... for all of you."

Nat got to her feet, while Alex and the others hurriedly formed a protective ring around Sheila whose consciousness was slowly beginning to wane.

"You meddling kids!" Brenda raged upon seeing Nora lying in a pool of her own blood not far from her heart, and her scientist empty of breath as well.

Alex stepped forward and pleaded, "Mom! Please, let our friend go! She's hurt badly and we need to get her some help!"

Brenda remained silent, almost as if she was considering it, but Nat was on guard, as was Julian who was still recovering from his episode with Nora.

"If only you hadn't tried to betray me with that vampire boy or killed the one person whose loyalty to me over the years eclipses yours," Brenda whispered in scornful tone. "More so, I cannot let her leave."

"Why not, you psychotic bastard!?" Nat asked in an angry tone.

Brenda turned and stared at them all with a damning gaze and stare in her eyes.

"A Salem witch holds uncountable abilities that can assist what I am trying to build here," she replied.

Nat could tell there was no reasoning with the woman, and she looked to Alex for some indication to what their next move was. She grabbed for her phone to call her mother. They needed back up, but she saw that her phone was too far damaged to make a call.

Leslie stepped forward with her head lowered to the ground, "My kind shouldn't indulge in fatal violence, but we protect our own and your actions have done nothing but put mine in danger and kill one!"

Brenda wore a frown, unsure of what she had before her, as the young girl slowly began to glow hot and it hit her.

"That's our cue," Alex whispered to Nat and they agreed with a nod.

Leslie charged ahead, with Alex and Nat flanking her on either side.

"We need to help them, but you have to stay with Sheila and protect her," Olivia commanded Julian who was more than willing to not get involved in the fight yet.

Leslie attacked first, sending a rather large ball of fire to consume Brenda, which she attempted to dispel but found impossible to do so.

"This isn't some ordinary magic, you crazy woman!" Leslie reminded her.

Brenda swung the fire aimed at her towards the wall, where it melted the bricks away immediately.

"You meddlesome phoenixes and your stupid abilities," Brenda muttered while she did her best to evade and cast aside the unquenchable fire being sent her way again.

Nat winked at Alex, held out her hand, towards the floor where Brenda had landed upon dodging one of Leslie's attack, and began melting the floor beneath the witch until she sunk inside of it.

"Do it now!" Nat yelled at Alex who had arrived before her distracted mother.

Alex placed her hand to her mother's head, instantly numbing her of her abilities by blocking every nerve ending through which her magic flowed, permitting Nat the ability to begin sealing the woman in molten rock made from the floor upon which Leslie's flame had melted.

"Look who has grown and is showing such promise magically," Brenda mocked Nat before Nat slowly covered her entire face with the molten rock and formed balls of molten rock around the woman's hand so she wouldn't be able to perform magic.

"We need to get Sheila out of here now," Nat turned around immediately, while Alex followed her.

Sheila had begun wheezing and unable to keep her eyes fully opened as Julian and Nat lifted her from the ground and began slowly carrying her towards the door. Sheila's magic was doing all it could with Alex and Nat's magic to keep her alive, but it was useless. Eleanor led the way with Alex while they began searching for a way to open the large stone door but to no avail.

"Why isn't it opening?" an impatient sounding Leslie asked.

Alex answered nervously immediately. "I don't know!"

The response coincided with a rather loud laughter, followed by shards of rocks flying in every direction as the students turned around to see a levitating and oddly smiling Brenda Aurelius staring down at them.

"Let me kindly return the favor," she giggled.

Nat moved first, but found darkness engulf her immediately, even before she could lift a finger. The others found the same fate and came to truly understand what a being as powerful as Brenda could do. Alex succumbed last, just after her mother had made certain to allow her to catch a glimpse of her friends going on their knees immediately.

CHAPTER TWENTY-NINE

Groans filled the room, but not as loud as the sound of water droplets in a continuous manner that unsettled Nat back into consciousness. Barely able to move, while her eyelids slowly parted to permit the first ray of fluorescent light in, she felt her heart slowly thud, and her joints feel absent, as the loud rattling sounds from chains jolted her back into proper consciousness.

The others had slowly began waking up as well, in loud groans and ample silence following upon realizing where they were and what they were surrounded by. Nat had never seen anything so cynical in her life while she slowly crawled to the edge of the cage Brenda had locked her in, just like her friends.

"Oh my God!" Nat whispered.

Men and women as well as children locked up in huge cylindrical tubes in an inactive state surrounded by bluish liquid made her insides churn and her eyes hurt just staring at them. The cylindrical tubes spanned for yards into darkness in what looked like an underground cave with a well-equipped room than the one they had been in. "How big is this fucking place?" Nat is starting to think they are below the whole school property.

"Oh, you're all awake!" Brenda giggled before she walked over to stand before their hanging cages.

She looked from Nat to Alex, starting from her extreme left to right, while the students glared at her with nothing but hate and contempt.

"What have you done to Sheila and Simon?" Leslie asked with a growl.

Brenda raised her left brow, waved at Leslie ad forced her to kneel immediately. "Calm down firefly, I have special plans for that amazing gift of yours, and Simon is dead so you can stop fretting over him."

Nat noted the woman was doing well to avoid answering the whole question. It made her uncomfortable and to make things worse, the cages they were locked in weren't ordinary ones made from steel; they were well reinforced with anti-magic spells to neutralize whatever abilities they had while they were within it. Leslie's umpteenth attempt to enable her abilities ending in failure further provided proof to Nat and the others immediately.

"What did you do to Sheila?" Alex asked in an annoyed tone.

Brenda looked at her daughter and replied, "I saved the show until you guys came back to consciousness."

Nat reached for the bars of her cage and yanked her hands as it burned her badly.

"Oh, I added a little bit of something to keep you all on good behavior," Brenda said over her shoulder. "I don't care for rattling and deafening screams while I work."

She waved over a table to the center of the room, sheathed with a teal cloth and an arm sticking out from underneath it.

"The two people you need are dead, so what are you doing!?" Olivia voiced.

Brenda ignored her, swept aside the large sheet covering Sheila, and began walking around the surgical table until she was standing directly before the girl's head. Nat watched on in horror, as Sheila tried to plead for mercy but could barely get a word out. They all watched in pain as Brenda whisked a large bowl underneath Sheila and slowly began to make cuts into her body for the blood to drain right into the large bowl that was waiting to receive it as if the huge hole in her chest wasn't enough.

"Your kind is considered to be way more powerful than even us Aurelius," she whispered into the groaning and gurgling Sheila's ear. "Never in my life did I assume I will have a Salem witch to work with."

Nat wrapped her hands around the burning cage and yelled in anger, without caring for the burn marks on her hands. "Let her go! Let her go!"

Brenda snapped her finger in Nat's direction, forcing her to stagger backwards and fall to the floor of the cage, squirming and groaning in immense pain as she struggled to breathe.

"You're next, King," Brenda smiled. "I have to save the best for last, don't I?"

Alex stared blankly at her mother before falling to her feet wondering if the figure was the same one, she knew on the outside world. She wondered how the woman figured out her betrayal plan with Hamilton or even sense it, but Nora's dead figure a few feet from her cage gave her a hint that she might have been tailed by her mother's assistant for a very long time.

"You're killing her, you spawn of hell!" Eleanor voiced surprisingly, causing Brenda to let go of Nat and grant her some much-needed air into her lungs. Eleanor was always the most obedient out of her daughter's friends.

Brenda turned her focus to the dying witch on the table, smiling and rubbing her hands together gleefully, while the hateful and cursing gazes of the others behind her meant nothing.

"If we don't do something, she is going to die within a minute or two," Olivia whispered to Alex. "Your mother is keeping her alive somehow, but it'll be over once she's drained of her blood."

Alex looked lost, broken and dejected while she continued to struggle with understanding why her mother had harbored such dreams.

"I cannot believe you'd do all of this just for the Clinic," Alex whispered in dismay.

Her eyes grew soggy, and her lips trembled, as the strong hearted girl broke down into tears for the first time Nat could ever recall. Alex wept profusely, while her mother didn't seem to care a single bit. She wanted their blood for her experiments and that was all that mattered, even if it meant killing every single one of her daughter's friends.

"We are going to die here," Julian sighed and sat down with a frown.

Olivia shot him an angry look, "You sound so much like Arnold right now."

"At least he's here and didn't chicken out like your guy," Eleanor shot back.

Olivia looked red in her face, unsure of what response to give as she pondered on why he would have left his friends and even her, his love.

"Like I said, we are all going to die here," Julian said again with his head bowed, and his eyes closed.

Some part of Nat and Alex believed him. The others did too, and Brenda was sure without doubt that they all weren't going to live.

All wearing anguish on their faces, with the taint of sadness at the edge of their tongues they watched Brenda heave the lifeless frame of what used to be their friend, to the ground like a carcass of meat about to be diced and sold on the market. Her emotions were lacking as she rolled Sheila's body away and began walking over to Julian's cage with a grin.

"Whatever it is that you are, I'm sure I'll find a good use for you," she smiled.

Nat sobbed softly, unsure of how her tears might help Sheila, as she stared at Brenda wishing for help. Brenda shot her a wink, slipped her hands into the pockets of her suit pants and took out a key opening it then yanking the boy out whose yells and curses filled the air.

"Mom!" Alex yelled. "Please, stop this madness! I am begging you, please!"

Brenda slammed the boy into the table and fastened him down immediately with belts. Julian looked frightened, with widened eyes as he watched her whisk another large bowl underneath the table, with which she would collect his blood as she had done with Sheila's.

"You should feel proud about yourself," she encouraged him. "Once this is done, and my army is well fueled to break those sniveling Hamiltons, then everything will fall in place perfectly."

The earth beneath them shuddered immediately, causing Julian's table to topple to the side, as the stone door blew apart and sent debris flying everywhere.

"What the..." Brenda muttered, coughing and waving her arms to clear the dust slowly escaping into her lungs.

Huge looking figures masked by the smoke stood firm within the new opening, before they began marching in one at a time, halting just a few feet from the entrance.

"Hello Brenda!" the cocky, cynical and terrifying voice of none other than Gregory Hamilton called out.

Brenda looked shocked and hurriedly cleared the dust that was hindering her line of sight from the room.

Alexia stepped forward and stood by her husband with a smile on her face. "I'm guessing you never thought things would even out this way."

Brenda gritted her teeth in anger, clenched her fists and bade her time to make her move.

"How on earth did you find this place?" she inquired before looking at her own daughter, who looked equally as surprised as her mother was.

"Don't look at the little rabbit," Gregory instructed Brenda. "You should imagine the look on my face when this odd kid came knocking on my door assuring, he could hand you over to me on a platter of gold."

Alexia added. "The juicy note was when he told us what we might or might not find in here depending on how soon we acted and came with him."

A lanky framed boy slowly walked from the back of the large bodies and stepped forward with a sadden expression on his face.

Olivia gasped. "Arnold!"

Nat looked up, as did the others, with joyous hearts.

Brenda looked to the ground, paced back and forth in a unilateral manner, before stopping. "Even if you managed to find this place, you still don't know what you're in for."

Gregory nodded his head and smiled, waved at the men behind him to step forward, as Brenda realized they were all members belonging to the other vampire clans. Gregory controlled them now and it meant he had autonomous power over almost every vampire for thousands of miles.

"With them, you are easy prey to me," he teased her.

"Unfortunately, I will be the last thing you see before I pluck out your eyes," Alexia added.

Brenda remained without a word, holding her hands behind her back while she mauled through her thoughts.

Gregory stepped forward and sighed. "I must say it was a nice touch and a rather bold move trying to use our son against us… you played on the gullibility of a child with ambition and honestly, we couldn't be prouder of Marcus for deciding to go along with your plan."

Hamilton stepped forward upon his father's request, donning the same brown leathered coat with his parents, and looking ready to fight.

"His death will serve for a cause well plotted then," Brenda casually spoke before stepping backwards and disappearing into the shadows.

Everyone gasped, as they looked around for the witch but couldn't find her.

"The boy already plotted your possible actions, you sneaky witch!" Alexia yelled, waving on her men who began to draw runes around the building immediately. "She does not leave this building until I have her guts in my hand!"

Nat caught Arnold's gaze in her direction as he hurriedly looked away again. She could tell he was hurting, from his eyes glued on Sheila's motionless body. Brenda's loud growl as she materialized back into the room drew Nat's attention as it did the others as well. Arnold's true ability was in flow and he seemed rather determined not to allow the woman any upper hand against those he brought in as reinforcements.

"Like I said, you are mine bitch!" Alexia raced forward but halted as Brenda got into sight and parted her arms.

"Not on my ground and definitely not when my rules apply!" Brenda yelled.

The cylinders began to crack open, and the bodies within slowly fell to the ground as the first breath of air seeped into their lungs. They growled and yelled in pain momentarily, but all stopped in unison as they got to their feet and slowly marched behind Brenda.

Alexia burst into hysterical laughter immediately. "Are we meant to be afraid of your minions?"

Gregory sensed something discomforting about the creatures in human flesh behind the witch.

"Brenda, what have you done?" Gregory asked with a frown.

Brenda looked back at the nude figures awaiting her command and turned to look at Gregory. "The same thing you would have done if you were granted the chance."

"The Oracles will not be happy about this though," Gregory warned as if his own actions weren't cause for punishment.

Brenda ignored his words, and held her hands out from her body, while the figures behind her waited to move.

"Rain hell on them, my children!" she sneered.

The creatures sped ahead, transforming into a blend of different magical creatures combined into one body. Alexia readied herself, claws drawn and an evil grin on her face as she tackled the figure ahead of the pack. It was a mix of vampire and what looked like a poorly made werecat, but not for long; its head rolled on the ground and landed before Brenda within seconds with Alexia standing on the remaining part of its body.

Brenda's fears that they had not perfected the creatures came to life immediately, but they weren't going to go down that easy. First blood was drawn and with that, Gregory sent his vampires into the battle ground. Loud clashes ensued, followed by eerie sound of flesh being ripped to shreds in uncanny and inhumane manners.

Arnold found himself an opening through the battle, while Hamilton battled along his parents fiercely. Brenda refrained from getting involved in the fight yet.

"Arnold!" Nat sounded happy to see him as he rammed at the lock on the cage with a stone.

"We don't have much time. You guys need to help Hamilton," he instructed Nat before breaking her free from her cage.

Brenda realized the girls were getting freed and began racing towards them, but Alexia blocked her path immediately. "You and I have a score to settle."

Brenda conjured a burst of flame towards Alexia, which the skilled vampire duly dodged as she danced her way towards Brenda. Brenda commanded three of her minions towards the incoming vampire, but they could barely hold her, as she made quick work of them in seconds.

"That won't stop me," she taunted, before something she didn't see rammed its large fist into her face then yanked her back aggressively.

A giant looking figure held Alexia in its hand and stared at her while Brenda smirked and walked away. It flung Alexia south, and into the wall, but barely gave her the chance to get to her feet when it raced over surprisingly fast, and kicked her in the gut, forcing her to spit out blood.

"Hell, to the no!" Nat yelled, commanding some of the debris around to float before her as Brenda approached.

Brenda looked towards the shards of broken glass around the cylinders and commanded them on her side. Nat looked back at Arnold who struggled with helping the others out and needed proper covering through the entire ordeal. She made her first attack, tossing a large piece of wall at Brenda and watched the woman disintegrate it into little bits, but not fast enough, as the younger witch commanded some nasty looking vines to sprout from the soil and wrap wildly around Brenda's face.

Brenda sounded surprised as she had been taken aback by the girl's swift movements and quick counterattacks.

Arnold seized the opportunity to set the others free while Brenda cast the poisonous plant off her face.

"You came back!" Olivia sounded delighted, before planting a kiss on Arnold's lips.

Julian shrieked at them both. "Keep things in your pants while we deal with the devil in Prada!"

Brenda watched her daughter stand by Nat, looking formidably and enraged as the other six came over and stared at her.

'Half a dozen, all for me?" she chuckled. "How frightening."

Nat moved, while Alex followed her like their minds were in sync. Leslie burst into flames immediately, sheltering every inch of her body with the beautiful golden glow that was deceiving with its looks and capable of melting even the toughest of metal.

Olivia, Ella, and Julian motioned to assist in the fight, but Arnold held them back. "They can handle her, but this battle isn't as one sided as you might believe, and Hamilton needs help."

Julian stared at Arnold with some degree of disbelief in his own eyes; he never would have thought he would be taking orders from Arnold.

"What about you?" Olivia asked. "What side are you on in all of this? What part are you playing?"

Arnold paused and looked to the battle ground, where limbs were being dismembered at ferocious speed by Gregory's men. "The path my kind always plays in battles."

Arnold raced out of the battle ground immediately, leaving Julian with an expression indicating he was as confused as Olivia was about the creature. Olivia ducked instinctively upon seeing a creature resembling a troll, but with wings lunging at her. She bore out her claws, smiled and danced her way to the left, before striking it hard behind the neck and sending it to the ground.

Eleanor had gotten on the battlefield fully transformed as her frame doubled in size into a wolf looking formidable as she tore one of Hamilton's attackers to shred.

"Thanks!" Hamilton smiled at her.

Ella nodded and stood on Gregory's side, waiting for the next batch of Brenda's creatures.

"A werewolf on our side?" Gregory smiled and winked at her, before tossing off his coat and holding his hand out in command for his men to stop.

No less than twelve of Brenda's creatures approached at a maddening speed, but Gregory looked unperturbed, as he nodded gently towards his wife, who returned the gesture and in the blink of an eye, they disappeared from sight. The room suddenly fell silent, and Brenda noticed while she battled Nat and her friends but could not do well enough to turn her gaze away.

The creatures paused, almost as if they were being held in place by something invisible. The moment Gregory and Alexia appeared back in front of their crew, Brenda's creatures fell to the ground in a loud and sudden heap. Spotless, and without a scratch on him, Gregory smiled, with his hand tucked into his wife's.

"That is how you put on a show, Marcus," Gregory winked at his son whose face looked swollen with guilt. "You should be proud you dared to plan a mutiny behind me, for you truly show ambition."

Gregory slipped his hand into the breast region of his suit jacket and slowly took out the same blade Hamilton had brought as proof of Brenda's plan to kill him, before holding it out while his wife wore a slight frown of confusion and gazed into her husband's eyes.

"What are you doing? We have this place at the palm of our hands and…" Alexia voiced her concern before stopping.

Gregory gently laid his hand to rest on his wife's shoulder and whispered, "He is a Hamilton too and my rightful heir, but his loyalty swayed one time and I need proof that he indeed is back on our side."

Marcus received the blade from his father cautiously, while still unsure of what his ordeal was meant to be. The last batch of Brenda's beasts slowly awakened as they prepared to make one last and damning attack on Gregory and his cohort of vampires.

"Deal carnage like never before and show to me that you are worthy of the throne," Gregory instructed his son.

Alexia felt her stomach stiffen at the sight of no less than twenty beasts awakening from their chambers. Her son was to take on them alone and it didn't seem to bother her husband in the slightest.

Alexia motioned to speak but Gregory yelled at her, "He fights alone! Should anyone dare defy me, they will be dealt with accordingly!"

Hamilton bore the blade in his hand and wrapped his fist around the handle. He could feel his fear begin to rise, as his guts threatened to leave him.

"Oh great!" he felt the words escape his lips as the creatures began racing towards him.

Gregory smiled, and Alexia looked away, showing emotion which wasn't very much known to her. Their son could meet his end, and there was nothing anyone could do about it, or at least until Gregory stated otherwise.

Nat circled Brenda while the woman tried to pin her down with a spell, just before Alex kicked her mother in the back and led her towards Leslie who embraced the woman briefly, enough to burn her.

"I'm done being nice to you kids!" Brenda yelled, letting out an outburst of power that sent the girls hard into the floor. "Do not underestimate me!"

She looked to her left arm, still burning from Leslie's flames, and unable to get healed no matter how much she tried. The girls struggled to get to their feet, but she wasn't granting them enough time, as she moved swiftly, beginning with Nat, lifting her up until she was high enough from the ground to let her fall to her death.

Nat screamed for help and found her fall get broken by the large hairy back of Ella.

"Ella!" Nat whispered.

Eleanor struggled to her feet. The impact caused enough additional damage to shift her back to her human state. She helped Nat to her feet and they both turned on Brenda, while Alex slowly limped over, bleeding from the side of her head, while Leslie had passed out cold.

"Your numbers don't matter," Brenda boasted. "You think not having control of my left-hand changes anything?"

Ella shared a brief gaze with Nat who motioned for her to proceed. The werewolf still moved faster than anyone ever imagined, complementing Nat's attack, as Nat cast numerous spells at Brenda which the witch canceled out perfectly. Alex joined in on the assault, forming a triangle against her, while Eleanor sought the best opening to strike.

In one dangerous attack, she nicked Brenda in the back, causing her to groan and fall on her knees, before slowly healing herself from the werewolf's attack.

"I will kill you all!" Brenda raged, with her eyes rolling back in their sockets, and her lips mumbling incoherently.

Alex yanked at Nat and Eleanor, "This is bad! We need to make a run for it now!"

The three girls raced backwards, hoping to find some cover, as a ball of bright red lights grew around Brenda and suddenly burst out towards them. It was too fast and an attack they couldn't run from, causing them to turn their faces away, but they felt nothing happen to them. Alex was sure it was just inches from them, and Nat had felt some part of it burn away her shoe, but other than that, they were fine.

"Leslie!" Nat yelled upon realizing that the phoenix had taken the entire blast inside of her.

Leslie wore a thin smile and crumbled to her knees immediately, prompting her friends to scramble over to her side. "I guess Arnold was right when he said we will die in here."

Nat rubbed her forehead gently as she grew cold and slowly took her last breath.

"Well, that was a waste," Brenda sighed.

"Unfortunately, that line wouldn't be used on you," Alexia stood in between the girls and Brenda. "You cannot keep avoiding me witch!"

Brenda cackled aloud in an evil manner. "Who has been avoiding you?"

Brenda lifted her left arm and motioned to cast a spell before realizing she was left incapacitated.

"Shit!" she mumbled.

The girls watched on as the two grownups clashed heavily, sending debris everywhere at the clashing of magic and pure speed and brute strength at their best. Alexia was no easy feat and Brenda wasn't about to go down easily either, as the women battled for supremacy, leaving the battle floor torn as Hamilton struggled with the hoard of creatures attacking him.

"Help me with her body!" Nat urged Alex, while they dragged Leslie's corpse to the side and out of harm's way.

Nat's heart sunk and her eyes swelled with tears. She clenched her hands into fist and slowly got to her feet. "We need to end this battle now!"

Hamilton had fallen on his back, while a large sized human with tentacles emanating from every part of his body pinned the boy down. Nat raced towards him with a fury of fire and brimstone hailing down on the creatures in her path. She rammed some into the wall and detached their spines from their backs, before helping Hamilton to his feet.

"Oh, you shouldn't have done that," Hamilton stared at her in fright as they both looked towards his father.

Gregory raged and yelled. "You silly little girl! Interfering in what doesn't concern you!"

Nat readied herself to face him, while Alex joined her side. Eleanor and Olivia battled the vampires coming at them, as Hamilton made good work of the remaining beasts left to finish off.

"This might turn out bad," Alex whispered.

Nat snuck her hand into Alex's to combine their powers and replied, "Bad for him you mean?"

Gregory came at them head on, managing to dodge the girl's attacks as they worked in uniform without necessarily seeing where he was. His speed was a problem, but their strength as a link, channeling each other wasn't one he had anticipated to be that formidable. Alex managed to blast him in the chest and send him backwards, while Nat restrained his hand with a gust of wind which turned out to be specially brewed magical twines that appeared from thin air.

Gregory struggled to get his hand free but couldn't, as Nat and Alex approach him.

"Kill them! Kill them all!" Gregory ordered his men who lunged towards Alex and Nat.

Hamilton interjected, causing them to stop in their tracks. "How about I respectfully propose something else to you?"

The men remained silent while the embattled look on Gregory's face did well to indicate he was unsettled.

"I want to propose a new era," Hamilton explained. "One in which you don't have to be forced into these kinds of senseless battles at the risk of your own lives and that of your kin."

"Will that restraint hold?" Alex whispered to Nat while Hamilton took his time towards convincing the men to follow him.

"It is my first time conjuring it," Nat replied.

Gregory yanked at the magic thread and growled aloud, as his wife was too engrossed in bringing Brenda to her knees to realize her husband was in trouble.

"What do you say to a new era of vampires where we all rule our territories and clans without interference?" Hamilton asked.

"You traitors!" Gregory yelled. "I will have your intestines!"

Hamilton ignored his father, while the men slowly walked over one after the other to his side of the room. They were tired of the needless bloodshed and battle for power. They were all sick of Gregory's short reign by the look of things, and Hamilton had timed his move well.

"Hamilton! Watch out!" Nat yelled at him.

He turned around swiftly, just in time as Gregory had broken from his restraints and lunged towards his son with his claws fully out. Hamilton ducked, rammed the blade in his hand still dripping of blood from the beasts he had slain, and the toxic venom Brenda had laced it with earlier, into his father's chest then ripped out his heart all in a moment that startled everyone.

Alexia felt something implode in her chest, almost as if a part of her had died and then, she knew what had happened.

"Marcus!" she yelled from where she had Brenda in a choke hold, while they both bled profusely.

Brenda took advantage of the opening, jammed her palm into Alexia's chest, and watched the vampire widen her eyes as she slowly looked down at the hand perfectly lodged into her heart. Slowly falling to the ground, she cursed Brenda one last time.

"Bitch!" Brenda sighed and dragged herself to her feet and she limped.

Hamilton gathered his newly acquired men, while Alex, Nat and the others readied themselves unsteady on their feet, some not on their feet.

"Surrender now Brenda!" Hamilton urged her. "You have nothing else on your side!"

Brenda smiled and whispered, "That actually isn't true… my one successful creation is yet to reveal itself."

She waved her hand and the earth beneath them began to tremble and gave rise to a transparent cylinder with a huge frame inside of it in chains.

"Behold, what has been roaming free in your school for the past few weeks and the one who took your friend Simon," she smiled.

The creature smashed its way out of the glass as Brenda took away its restraints. It stood tall, formidable and without a hint of emotion or humanity in its eyes. His claws looked no different from a mix of vampire and werewolf, but Eleanor sensed there was more.

"Kill!" Brenda commanded and within a twinkle of an eye, it moved, not to be seen by anyone.

The first hint of its action was the dropping of three dead bodies from Hamilton's crew, followed by a loud growl as it levitated in the air with wings and came swooping down dangerously.

"Meet your ends!" Brenda yelled in a happy tone.

"Oh my God!" Alex marveled at the disturbing creature.

Nat and Alex attempted to cast it off, but their magic was weakened and powerless against it as it swept down hard towards them. Nat's heart readied itself to give way, while Hamilton wasn't anywhere near enough to cause harm to the creature.

"Enough!" a thunderous tone yelled, accompanied by seven men in white cloaks as they walked into the room.

Mr. Sadon accompanied them with Arnold who had changed into a white robe with strange markings on his head. Brenda spotted them and made her attempt to leave but halted when one of the cloaked figures held out his hand and froze her. The creature altered its attention and flew towards them but burst into flames within some feet of the cloaked and hooded figures.

"Brenda Aurelius!" the one in front of the line slowly let down his hood. "You have not only broken the code and rules by which the magical community lives and abides, but you have successfully created abominations!"

The others revealed their faces one at a time, showing three women and four men in count. All of them bore lengthy white hair.

"Lies!" Brenda yelled. "What proof do you have!?" Other than the dead bodies and surviving teenagers, it would be their word against hers.

Arnold walked forward and raised his head as he spoke, "I am Khalil Caster, heir to the Order of Light, and an assigned figure to the Virtus school under command from the High Order! We answer to no one but the Oracles!"

Olivia gasped and watched the others drop their jaws as well.

"I am living proof, as are the others in this room, to your treachery and unlawful actions that contradicts the code and defies our laws as magical creatures!" he continued.

Nat had never assumed she would come to see the Order of Light, talk less of being in close presence of them.

"You shall come with us for prosecution for your many crimes," the seven spoke in unison, before Brenda vanished into thin air immediately.

Arnold walked over to them and held Olivia in his arms. "I couldn't tell any of you."

Julian asked, "What happens now that everything is over?"

Arnold sighed and looked over to where Sheila and Leslie's bodies were. "Now the Order deals with Brenda accordingly, you all return to your lives in school and in the outside world."

Nat gasped and hoped to speak before everything went blank and darkness engulfed their senses… one thing was certain, and it was the fact that she sensed relief and peace; they all did.

EPILOGUE

The world felt silent, and, came with some indwelling sense of peace she had not felt for a while. Nat wanted some more of it as she refused to open her eyes or take in the reality that life wasn't as perfect as it felt inside her head. Images of the entire events that had passed coursed through her mind, asides the end to it all; it remained blurry and almost as if it never happened.

"Natalie... Natalie!" a voice called out, prompting her to slowly open her eyes against her wish.

It was that of the woman who bore the same gorgeous looking eyes as hers, with her hand laced into hers and her face close enough that they could feel each other's breath.

"Mom!" Nat whispered faintly.

Samantha King smiled and planted a kiss on her daughter's forehead before slowly stepping aside so she could see the entirety of the room. Nat gasped and felt a bead of warm tear roll down the side of her cheek.

"They are all doing fine thanks to your heroics," her mother whispered. "If the Order doesn't find Brenda I will and will kill her myself."

Nat shook her head slowly and replied, "I am alive because of them."

Alex coughed aloud from the bed next to Nat's before slowly opening her eyes and smiling weakly.

"What happened in there?" Alex asked. "I know I saw my mom getting away, but nothing else makes sense".

Samantha shrugged and replied, "When we came in, we found all you kids passed out on the ground."

Nat looked around to her left, and sighted Leslie's body and Olivia seated by Arnold whose broken hand was in a cast.

"Leslie?" Nat asked in a choked whisper.

Nurse Bethany walked into the room and replied, "Did she die? Yes, she did, but phoenixes never really stay dead, and their best form is reborn after their first death."

Leslie began to move and then sat up. She looked even more beautiful and glowed wonderfully in her bed. Hamilton walked into the room with two large sized men by his side. He waved at her and walked over to meet with Alex who coughed and struggled to sit up slowly.

"You girls really held your own out there," he bowed gently. "I never would have taken my father's post without you and for that, I am eternally grateful."

"I am just glad my mother is taken care of," Alex sighed. "What do you suppose will be done with her?"

Everyone turned to look at Arnold who tried to evade their gaze immediately.

Olivia nudged him and whispered, "There is no hiding it now, they all know and saw what happened in there."

Arnold sighed. "The Order of Light has a way of dealing with individuals like your mother... she will be taken care of accordingly to her crimes."

It left a hole in Alex's heart to witness her mother's defeat, but it also brought her some breath of relief.

"It means her company and everything else is yours to control, you know?" Hamilton reminded her. "What are you going to do with it?"

Alex gave the idea some thought and imagined just how corrupt everything about the company stood for was; from the list of dangerous clients her mother stood for, to the illegal means and businesses which she ran as well.

"You have to finish school first," Samantha King replied just as Leslie's parents came back into the room.

"And I will but I still have to get some things in order."

Hamilton smiled from the corner of his mouth and turned around as he bade Mrs. King and the others farewell. Alex closed her eyes, as she felt Nat's hand slowly reach for hers.

"You can come run things with me you know?" Alex whispered. "As a friend and a good moral compass."

Nat laughed hard and felt her sides hurt.

"I am being serious," Alex continued.

Nat shook her head, closed her eyes and sighed aloud. "I know you are." She was about to speak again when Rachel, Alex' girlfriend rushed in and to Alex side.

Olivia looked away from Nat and Alex who slowly returned to sleep and back to Arnold. "How come you never told anyone about you being, you know?"

Arnold shrugged, put on a rather drab expression face and replied, "About me being what?"

She burst into laughter immediately, as did he, then they shared a passionate kiss. Everyone had played their roles well, and their world felt safe once again.

It was Christmas day and Alex was at home all alone. Weeks had passed by in a blur filed with funerals, classes, and disruptions in the city's top families. Olivia's parents loyal allies of Brenda Aurelius disowned their daughter, so Olivia moved in with Alex while Ella struggled with her pack. Everyone had holiday plans with love ones except Alex who was in the midst of packing. As she packed two suitcases and her briefcase, she saw the gift box Nat had given her after Sheila's funeral as an early Christmas gift. She had never opened it. Alex walked over and ripped open the wrapping revealing a jewelry box. She opened it and couldn't help but gawk at the beautiful ring inside. She then rushed to open the card.

I thought you should have your own, I mean every great leader has a ring for people to kiss right? All Al Pacino like. I just wanted something that said I love you unconditionally. You've always been a loyal friend and I should start doing the same. When I did what I did to solve my father's murder you didn't blink or judge me. I'll start giving you the same.

Merry Christmas!

Natalie

P.S I'm keeping your jacket since you forgot to get it back.

Alex stared at the card again then read it over two more times. Alex could only repeat the word love in her head before she rushed out of the house. She pulled up in her car outside Nat's house and got out, but still staying in the driveway. Mrs. King is still not a big fan of Alex so Alex calls Nat and tells her to come out.

"Thanks for the ring I, loved it."

"I got a good discount on it," Nat shrugged then laughed and gave Alex a hug.

"So, does this mean I'm on best friend level again?" Nat asked as she bumped Alex with her shoulder and walked pass her to her car to pet it. "Come inside, you shouldn't be alone on Christmas."

"Here open your gift." Alex handed her a small box with a ribbon and Nat grabbed it excitedly then looked confused at the set of car keys inside. "Athena is all yours."

"WHAT! NO WAY! You can't just give me your car." Nat tried to hand the keys back, but Alex held her hands up shaking her head.

"I only bought the car because I knew you loved cars. Just like I tried to impress you and dragged you to the street race so you could see all the cool cars. I don't even like driving and didn't buy it really for myself."

Nat's mouth hung open at the vulnerability Alex was showing and some shock at her own self for not feeling any pain or rage at the mention of the day Jermaine died racing.

She looked down and sighed before looking up at Alex. "I'm sorry I blamed you all that time."

"I'll forgive you if you take my gift. I'll continue to take care of the insurance and all since I know your mom hovers over your bank account." Alex' confidence started to rear its ugly head.

Nat slowly started to smile then squealed before racing to the car to kiss it.

"You can also drive me to the airport." Nat turned around confused.

"What, why? You can stay with us." Nat walked back to Alex.

Alex smiled "I don't think my girlfriend would like that but I'm going to meet with our international locations to reassure them that I will continue to lead the company to prosperous years. I've been trained to lead this company since I could crawl. Now mother is gone there will be a lot of unrest. I must get ahead of it and start weeding out who I can trust and not trust. While I'm in school one of my father's old friends and national board member is going to step up as CEO protecting my assets. To the legal world I am still a child and cannot legally run my business or even take care of myself. He's going to be my legal guarding as well."

"I can't just leave though; my mom will kill me. We're supposed to start making gingerbread houses with my cousins and the police chief is stopping by later." Nat whined.

"Oh, come on Nat, I thought you gave up being a good girl." Alex grins and holds open the car door for her. Nat looked back at her house then back at Alex and groaned in defeat knowing she was going to go even though she'd have to deal with the wrath of her mother, aunts, and uncles scolding her when she gets back. She got in the driver's seat and drove off fast down the long driveway and down the road. Nat didn't know how long the peace would last or what was going to happen to her and her friends, but she knew that no matter what happened, they were always going to be there for each other.

Jamila A. Stone